LET THE BELLS RING

Seventeen-year-old Hannah Ashe and her mother Esme are lucky to escape when their Merseyside home is destroyed in a bombing raid. Forced to move in with Esme's difficult sister-in-law, Hannah thrives in her new job repairing fighter planes. Her workmate Gina Goodwin becomes a firm friend, and Hannah enjoys spending time with Gina's family, especially her handsome brother Eric, but she's a little afraid of Gina's father who acts strangely when she mentions Esme's name. When Hannah asks questions, Esme forbids her daughter to visit the Goodwins again, but Hannah refuses to obey...

LET THE BELLS RING

LET THE BELLS RING

by

Anne Baker

Magna Large Print Books
Long Preston, North Yorkshire,
BD23 4ND, England.

British Library Cataloguing in Publication Data.

Baker, Anne
Let the bells ring.

A catalogue record of this book is
available from the British Library

ISBN 0-7505-2519-3

First published in Great Britain 2005 by Headline Book Publishing

Published in Large Print 2006 by arrangement with
Headline Book Publishing Ltd.

Magna Large Print is an imprint of Library Magna Books Ltd.

Printed and bound in Great Britain by
T.J. (International) Ltd., Cornwall, PL28 8RW

BOOK ONE

CHAPTER ONE

3 March 1941

Esme Ashe lay quivering and panic-stricken on the mattress in her Morrison shelter. It was the fourth air raid of the night.

Beside her, her daughter, Hannah, whispered, 'That last bomb was close.' Esme gathered Hannah into her arms; her daughter's body felt rigid with terror. To know she was frightened too made Esme feel worse.

She ached with love for her daughter, who would be celebrating her eighteenth birthday in two days' time. She'd brought her up alone and they'd been all in all to each other. She wanted to keep her safe, protect her from danger and make sure Hannah had a better life than she'd had herself, but Hitler's bombs were making that an impossible dream.

It was the fourth consecutive night on which they'd had air raids on Merseyside, but tonight there were more of them and the bombs were falling much closer. Esme felt worn out, and even Hannah had lost her smile and zest for life. With her slender frame and long straight blonde hair, she looked very much as Esme had at her age, but Hannah's eyes were bigger and a brighter blue, and her features were neater. She was prettier than Esme had been.

So far, their house, in one of the streets running down to the river near Seacombe, had not been damaged, but all around them the chaos was mounting. Although Seacombe was on the Wirral bank of the Mersey, it was separated by only a mile or so of water from the main Liverpool docks, and it received a share of the bombs aimed at them. Esme was filled with dread that it must be only a matter of time before their turn came.

Tonight, the heavy bombers were coming over in wave after wave. She could hear their drone overhead again, and froze as she heard the 'crump, crump' sound of bombs exploding. Birkenhead must have caught that lot. Her stomach felt wobbly.

Suddenly, the house shook as a bomb dropped nearby. The explosion was like a thunderclap. As the glass in the bay window blasted in, Esme ducked under their eiderdown and felt Hannah do the same. She'd had her Morrison shelter, which looked like a strong metal table on metal struts, set up in her front room. It was the size of a double bed and took up so much space it was only a yard or so from the window. The glass was crisscrossed with sticky paper to prevent splintering, but whole panes of it crashed down on the roof of their shelter and the tinkling seemed to go on for ever.

'We're really getting it tonight.' Hannah struggled out of her mother's arms.

Esme groaned. She could smell the soot that had been blasted down from the chimney. 'It'll have made a dreadful mess!'

Several of their windows had shattered in a raid

just before Christmas, so they both knew the work involved in cleaning up afterwards. Esme was proud of the home she'd made for them both. She'd rented this little house since Hannah was four and old enough to start school. Who knew, if these air raids continued, whether they'd even have a home?

'What's that noise?' Esme jerked her head up. 'It's not the roar of flames?' She was terrified of incendiary bombs.

'No, Mum.' Hannah sounded calmer than Esme was herself. 'All I can hear is the siren of an ambulance.'

'It's not a fire engine?'

'No.'

'I can hear shouting.'

'Probably just the civil defence workers calling to each other.'

Esme felt quite agitated. 'I can feel the house vibrating.'

'That's the ack-ack guns opening up.' There was a gunsite nearby.

'If the house goes on fire,' she'd told Hannah several times, 'we've got to get out, no matter what.'

Yesterday, she'd watched fires burning all day long on the Liverpool waterfront – too many and too large to be got under control.

Esme could hear bombs continuing to rain down, and tried to guess, from the intensity of the explosions, how near or far away they were falling. Suddenly, an almighty crash made her snatch Hannah back into her arms. The blast was ear-splitting and her head sang.

The floor beneath their shelter seemed to move, and great lumps of plaster and brick came thudding down on the top, followed by what sounded like a shower of gravel.

Hannah let out a squeal of terror and Esme was expecting the worst. She held her breath as thick clouds of choking dust and grit came inside and got into her mouth and her nose. Hannah's fingers were biting into the flesh of her mother's arm as they clung together waiting for what surely must be their end as the house collapsed on top of them.

'Are you all right, Mum?' Hannah whispered after what seemed an age. Bits were still coming down but they couldn't hear the outside noises as clearly now.

'I think so. Are you?'

'Yes. I'm going to try and get out.' Esme felt Hannah climb over her. 'I can't, Mum!' There was momentary panic in her voice. Then more calmly she said, 'The whole ceiling must have come down, perhaps the roof as well. What are we going to do?'

After a lot of feeling around, Esme found the torch they kept here. It shone dimly through clouds of dust. Hannah was right; their way out was blocked by piles of rubble. 'There's a huge lump of masonry right here against us.'

'I'll try and push it out of the way.'

'No!' Esme dragged her back under the shelter roof as more pieces hurtled down on them. 'You'll get hurt. Goodness knows what you'll dislodge. Don't try that again.'

'I can't budge it anyway.'

'Not much we can do then,' Esme said, feeling utterly helpless. Her stomach was more than wobbly; she felt she could throw up.

'We'll have to wait and hope somebody comes to dig us out.' Hannah's voice was matter of fact.

'But who?'

'All the neighbours know we have this shelter. They'll tell the ARP warden.' Esme was amazed her daughter could remain so cool. Hannah had grown up without her realising it.

'We've still got the flask of tea,' she went on. They always brought one with them. Usually they drank it before they went to sleep, but after several sleepless nights, they'd come here at nine o'clock last night and had gone to sleep straight away.

'We've never needed it more.' Hannah found it at the bottom of their mattress and poured out two cups.

It was lukewarm and gritty, but Esme savoured it as it washed the dust from her mouth.

'Better if we don't drink it all now,' she said. 'It could be a long time before we get rescued.'

She felt for her handbag, which she always brought with her, as well as a bag containing her valuables. She insisted Hannah bring hers too. Esme understood only too well the problems it would cause if ration books and clothing coupons were lost. Equally important were her insurance policies, their birth certificates and her identity card. She'd brought her jewellery too, although it didn't amount to much – a ring set with a nice garnet and a string of pearls, though she knew these were artificial. She had to show Hannah that she valued the photograph in a silver frame of the young man in his Great War uniform of an army captain, so that came too.

She found a handkerchief and blew her nose. 'That's better, I can breathe now. You have a blow.' She passed the hanky over.

'Thanks, Mum.'

Esme couldn't calm her fears. The cacophony continued outside. Nothing could shut out the noise of the exploding bombs.

'I wonder how long we'll have to wait.'

'Turn your pillow over to get rid of the grit,' Hannah advised, 'then try to go to sleep.' She was trying to settle herself.

'Hannah! We've narrowly missed death! If we'd stayed in our beds...' Esme shuddered, only too well aware they might yet succumb if nobody dug them out. 'How can you possibly feel like sleep now? Ugh, this awful stuff is in my hair and my ears.' She patted the heavy pink hairnet she wore in bed to keep the waves of her perm in place. 'It's got everywhere.'

'If we go to sleep the time will pass more quickly,' Hannah said, shining the torch on her watch. 'It's nearly three o'clock; there's nothing else we can do.'

Esme lay back and pretended to try, but she had too much on her mind for sleep. Where were they going to live if this house was badly damaged and not habitable? There were too many families in the same boat, hundreds of them, and they'd all be seeking other houses to rent.

The only family she had was her sister-in-law. Philomena had been trying to persuade her to give up her little house and live with her again. She'd suffered from rheumatoid arthritis for years and was now a semi-invalid needing help about the house. She said she was getting worse but she was a bit inclined to cry wolf. She had a woman who came in six mornings a week. Brenda was reliable and had been working for her for years, so Esme thought her sister-in-law could manage. Philomena said she needed somebody in the house with her at night.

Esme knew she owed Philomena a great deal. She'd been her brother, Fred's, wife and they'd come to her aid when trouble had almost overwhelmed her. Fred had been the vicar of St Augustine's church in Rock Ferry for more than twenty years.

They had taken Esme in when she was expecting Hannah and given them both a home when she'd had no other. They'd given her financial and moral support until Hannah was old enough to go to school and even then they'd paid her school fees at the convent. Esme had then been able to find a job and get back on her feet; she'd had several office jobs over the years and was currently working as a clerk in the local Food Office. She'd been content to provide for herself and her daughter, but the war was playing havoc with everybody's life.

Last December, poor Fred had been killed, along with twenty-four others, when the public air-raid shelter in Delta Street had received a direct hit. He'd been doing his duty as an air-raid warden, helping to dig out the women and children who'd been injured, when more of the structure had collapsed and buried him and two other rescue workers.

Philomena had had to move out of St Augustine's vicarage, of course, but she had been brought up in the house next door. Since the death of her parents, she'd owned Highfield House and had been very glad she hadn't rented it out to somebody else.

Since then, Esme had gone to Philomena's house every Sunday, which was Brenda's day off, to cook dinner for her. It was like going back to her previous life, but now there was no Fred to provide sympathy when Philomena reminded her of the dreadful secret they must keep from Hannah, come what may.

Esme shook herself awake – was that somebody shouting? Yes, she heard her name.

'Mrs Ashe, are you hurt? Mrs Ashe, can you hear me?' The voice sounded a long way away.

Hope flared within her. 'Yes,' she called. 'Yes, we're here. We're unhurt but we can't get out.'

The man on the other side hadn't heard her. 'Mrs Ashe, can you hear me? Is there anyone there?'

She dug Hannah in the ribs, but it wasn't needed: she was already yelling her reply. Esme joined in, screaming at the top of her voice.

'All right, we're digging down. It'll take a little time but we're doing our best.'

'How long?' Hannah yelled.

'An hour or more. Are you in the shelter? Can you both move?'

'Yes.'

'OK, love, hold on.'

Hannah put her head back on the pillow with a sigh of relief. 'I told you they'd come and dig us out.'

'That's a load off my mind.'

Hannah was pouring out the last of the tea. 'This will buck us up.'

Esme drank it gratefully though it was cold now. Her mouth seemed dry and full of dust again.

Hannah shone the torch on her watch. 'Quarter to five – not bad. We should be out in time for breakfast.'

Esme had to chuckle; she felt a little better. 'I'm afraid our kitchen won't be fit to cook our eggs and bacon in.'

'Did we have eggs and bacon?'

'No, it was going to be toast and marmalade as usual.'

It was seven thirty when Esme emerged into the morning light clutching her handbag and valuables.

'I had a suitcase packed,' she told the men who hauled her out. 'It was standing by our shelter. Can you get it?'

'No sign of anything like that,' she was assured. 'Are you sure it wasn't inside with you?'

'No.' Esme felt shattered. 'There was no room for it inside.' Every night she'd taken it out, every morning she'd put it in again. It was months since she'd packed it with basic essentials in case this happened – nighties, a change of undies and some warm woollies.

'Must have been flattened or blown to bits.'

When she turned to look at her house she was shocked. It was in the middle of a terrace, and some of the roof was gone, with the part still attached to the neighbouring roof moving in the slight breeze. She felt dazed, in a stupor.

Hannah was covered with dust and grime, her bright blonde hair a greyish colour. She didn't seem clear-headed either. She'd pulled the eiderdown they'd been using up after her.

'It might be all we have tonight' she said, as she stood blinking in the fresh air. 'Mum, you look awful. I've never seen you in such a mess. Take your hairnet off.' She did it for her, trying to shake some of the dust out of her hair.

'I feel awful, but at least we're decently covered.' Esme dusted herself down. She had insisted that when the air-raid siren wailed they pulled on warm clothing, and in the winter months they'd needed it. She'd equipped them both with a siren suit, a one-piece garment of trousers, jacket and hood, which was considered the ideal garment to wear in air raids. They were all the rage.

'I can see my wardrobe.' Hannah let out a gleeful yelp. It had lost most of its mirror but was in one piece, lying on its back, where their living room had been. She made a move towards it.

'No, love.' A brawny hand yanked her back. 'You can't go there.'

'I'll need my clothes.'

'It's not safe. We've dug you out once, we don't want to have to do it again.'

Esme caught a glimpse of torn red taffeta caught on a beam and recoiled.

'Hannah!' She pointed. 'Your birthday present!'

Tears were scalding her eyes for the first time.

'It doesn't matter, Mum,' but distress was making Hannah suck her lips in.

'Oh dear, I am sorry!' Esme had taken her round the big shops in Liverpool to choose a dress length and a pattern, and then a dressmaker had measured her and made it up. Hannah was keen on clothes and these days it was hard to find anything stylish. This way, it couldn't be a surprise, but at least she could give Hannah a dress that really pleased her. Except now that was gone too.

'What about all our bits and pieces?' Esme asked the ARP warden. It had taken her years to furnish her house. It was heart-rending to see most of her things reduced to rubble. How was she going to cope?

'Don't you worry, love.' She recognised Mr Peterson, a pensioner who lived almost opposite. 'If anything can be salvaged, I'll get them to put it in our yard and you can have it later. There's a WRVS van just come into the street – they'll give you a cup of tea.'

His wife said, 'I'd ask you in to our place for tea but we have no water and no electricity.'

'At least we still have a house.' Her husband put his arm round her shoulders.

'The windows have gone and it's full of dust,' she sighed. 'What is the world coming to?'

Hannah pulled her mother up to the van, and Esme accepted the cup of tea pushed into her hand. It was hot and tasted marvellous. Hannah ate a bloater paste sandwich too, but Esme couldn't face food.

'Are you sure you're all right?' one of the women asked. 'We can get somebody to take you to hospital if you've got cuts or grazes that need dressing.'

'No, we're unhurt.' But Esme was at a loss, not knowing where to go. She looked back at the gutted remains of her house. 'We've been made homeless.'

'Go to the Methodist Hall. We'll get a lift for you. Mr Williams, is there room in your car for another two?'

Almost before she knew what was happening, Esme found herself being pushed on to the back seat of a car that already seemed full of people. Hannah crowded in.

The Methodist Hall was crowded too. A brisk middle-class woman of middle age asked if they had relatives who could take them in.

'No,' Esme told her. She didn't want to go to Philomena's house. It wasn't that she objected to giving Philomena a hand when she needed it – she owed her that – it was the thought of going back to live permanently in Grasmere Road, so near to Arnold Goodwin, that was upsetting her.

They accompanied Philomena to the early morning service at church every Sunday and had a big lunch with her afterwards, which took up most of the day. Arnold Goodwin was always in church and his dark intense stare seemed to follow her. Living close to the Goodwin family meant she couldn't forget the painful years of her youth.

Esme and Hannah were given another cup of tea and put into a queue of those made homeless and needing hostel care for tonight. All around them, bedraggled anxious people were talking about the savage raids of the night. Their stories were pitiful. Like Esme and Hannah, most people here had lost everything they'd owned. Many had seen members of their family killed.

'Mum,' Hannah was pulling at her sleeve, 'wouldn't it be better if we went to Aunt Philomena's? I mean, a bed in a hostel, then possibly being evacuated...' Her earnest blue eyes stared into Esme's. 'Aunt Philomena's would be better than that, wouldn't it?'

She was right, of course, and Esme couldn't explain her objections. 'If we could find a phone, I could ask her if she'll take us in,' she conceded.

'The phone lines are all down,' Hannah said. 'I've just heard somebody say so. We'll just have to turn up on her doorstep. This is an emergency, Mum. It's the best thing to do. Just look at this queue for hostel accommodation. How are they going to find beds for everybody?'

'What if Philomena's house has been bombed too?'

Hannah groaned. 'Fate couldn't be so cruel.'

'Right, let's go and see if she'll have us.'

'She will. She wants us there, Mum, you know she does.'

Esme was in despair. She knew she had no choice but to go to Philomena's house – it was the only practical solution – but she felt vulnerable. She told the woman who had greeted them on arrival that she thought she could make her own arrangements and asked the way to the nearest bus stop.

The WRVS woman said, 'The buses aren't running to their normal timetables, I'm afraid. Some of the roads are blocked with rubble.'

'The nearest train station then – that would be almost as convenient. We want to go to Rock Ferry.'

The woman pulled a face. 'There's no train service between here and Birkenhead. Park Station has been bombed; the trains can't get through.'

Hannah had been given a piece of string, and a man was helping her tie her eiderdown into a manageable roll. He told them he was going into Birkenhead and would give them a lift if they could wait a few moments.

It was more than a few moments, but Esme sat back resigned to their predicament. She felt like a zombie, the loss of her house hard to take in. On the journey into town she found the devastation shattering. The man dropped them off and they took a train from Hamilton Square to Rock Ferry. As they came out of the station they saw a bus disappearing down the road.

'We might as well walk,' Hannah said. 'It isn't far.'

After crossing the New Chester Road, they went down St Augustine's Road, passing the church on the corner. The vicarage was round the corner, the first house in Grasmere Road, a large detached villa. The second, Highfield House, was even larger and had been built by Aunt Philomena's forebears in 1855. It had had a classical portico over the front door, giving it an imposing air, but the front of the house had caught the wind off the river, and in an effort to stop the winter draughts, the portico had been turned into an enclosed porch some twenty years later.

Philomena's family had owned a quarry and a brick-making business in New Ferry. They had provided the land for the church and vicarage, and had built both, using the family bricks.

It had been the intention of the family that all the houses in Grasmere Road would be detached and rather grand. However, by 1884 the business was not so profitable and they'd sold off some of the land to a builder. He had erected a row of a dozen large semidetached villas; big houses in the Victorian Gothic style, all to the same design. In the 1930s smaller modern semis with tiny gardens were built facing them on the other side of the road.

It took a long time for anybody to answer their knock, but Esme could hear her sister-in-law shuffling towards them. 'Brenda's gone shopping. You'll have to wait.' The door opened a crack and Philomena's face peered anxiously out at them. 'Esme!'

Hannah said, 'We've been bombed out, Aunt Philomena. Can we throw ourselves on your mercy?'

'Of course.' The door opened wider. 'Come on in. You both look in a sorry state.' She shuffled ahead of them back to her sitting room.

At fifty-four, Philomena was twelve years older than Esme and despite the slowness of her gait, she had an aura of strength and power. She was stout, with a pouter pigeon chest, a large nose and a determined chin; her hair was iron grey, strong and wiry, and cut into a severe Eton crop.

Her pale protruding eyes, behind their rimless spectacles, missed nothing.

'Tea, Esme? Perhaps you'd make it, Hannah?'

'Of course.' Hannah leaped to her feet and went to the kitchen. She was used to helping in the kitchen.

'I'm distraught, Esme. Such a terrible time I've had. Last night was dreadful.' Philomena had to air her worries first, before enquiring about those of her guests. 'Such awful damage. I couldn't believe it.'

Esme had seen no broken windows as she'd walked here. 'At least the bombing wasn't too close,' she said.

'Much too close for comfort,' Philomena complained. 'I feared for my life. Birkenhead caught a packet last night.'

'Wallasey too,' Esme retorted.

'I heard on the news this morning that they'd sunk one of the Mersey ferry boats at its moorings at Seacombe landing stage.'

Hannah returned with a tea tray set with dainty china cups, a silver teapot and milk jug, the way Philomena liked her tea served.

'The *Royal Daffodil,*' Hannah said. 'I heard the ARP men talking about it. I'm sure we heard the explosion.'

Esme said, 'My house has been decimated. We can't live there. The roof came down on us.'

Philomena looked taken aback. 'Well, at least neither of you is hurt.'

'But we've lost everything, our home...'

'Esme, you have only yourself to blame. Haven't I been pleading with you to come back here and live with me? You don't understand what it is to be disabled and alone in this house with these dreadful raids going on.'

Esme did. She hadn't been alone because she'd had Hannah with her, but she'd felt responsible for her safety. 'You can take us in? It's all right if we stay?'

'You know it is. Aren't I always willing to help you when you're in trouble?'

'Thank you, Philomena. I do appreciate what you do for us.'

'You know I can't manage the stairs any more, and I've turned the laundry room into a new bathroom. All the upstairs rooms can be made into a flat for yourself and Hannah. The main bedroom would make a reasonable living room, and we could get a sink and a cooker put into my father's old dressing room.'

'Thank you,' Hannah said. 'It sounds as though we shall be comfortable here.'

'I hope we all will, and if we each have a flat, it will ensure we both have privacy when we want it.'

Esme felt she'd misjudged Philomena. 'I'm very happy to accept. You couldn't be more generous. I'll be able to pay you rent.'

'No need for that, Esme. You are my sister-in-law. What I suggest is that instead, you help me where you can. I have Brenda here every morning, she does the cleaning and a bit of cooking, but in the afternoons and evenings–'

'I'll be only too pleased to do all I can,' Esme said, and meant it.

'I'm sure it will be the ideal arrangement for us

all,' Philomena said. 'Why don't you go upstairs and look round? The place will need cleaning, of course, but you can decide where you'll sleep and make the beds up. I'm sure you'll find enough linen in the cupboards.'

Esme followed Hannah upstairs, the girl bounding ahead, excited at the prospect of a new home. The arrangement sounded better than Esme had dared hope, but there was still the problem of the Goodwin family living at number eight. They would be her neighbours again.

CHAPTER TWO

By midday Hannah was hungry, but with rationing she was wary of asking Aunt Philomena what they could eat for lunch. She was glad when her aunt called upstairs to them that she wanted hers.

'Brenda prepared some soup for me – perhaps you'd heat it up, Esme? There might be enough for us all. She usually makes enough for two days.'

Hannah lit the stove and took over; her mother looked ready to drop with exhaustion. She was too thin, and always seemed in a somewhat anxious state. Today she was worse than ever and, of course, they hadn't had much sleep this last week. Together they'd decided which of the rooms they'd use as bedrooms. They'd even found enough bedding but had not yet had time to clean the rooms or make up the beds.

Between two plates, Hannah found a corned beef sandwich, which had also been prepared for Philomena's lunch. That would definitely not stretch to feed the three of them. But there was margarine and marmalade and half a loaf of stale bread, so she could make some toast.

A bigger problem was what they would eat tonight. She peeped in the oven and found a casserole prepared for Aunt Philomena's dinner, but there seemed to be very little else. Mum wouldn't care – she had the appetite of a sparrow

– but Hannah knew she'd want to eat. She'd have to go shopping. Her first day here looked like being a busy one.

Over lunch, Esme said, 'I should be at work now. Heavy raids make work for us.'

'We've been bombed out, Mum. You could hardly be expected to turn up at your office at nine o'clock this morning.'

Esme pursed her lips. 'I should let them know.'

'You can use my phone to do that later this afternoon,' Philomena told her. 'Tell them you'll be living here from now on, and it won't be possible for you to travel to Wallasey every day. Perhaps they could transfer you to a nearer Food Office?'

'I'll ask them,' Esme said.

'And what about you, Hannah?'

Hannah had been helping out in the infant classes at the convent. She'd decided to start a teacher training course as soon as she was old enough.

'She's going to apply to Chester College for a place in September,' Esme said.

Hannah sighed. 'That was before I realised I'd be directed into war work once I turned eighteen. Anyway, I should be doing something to help the war effort.'

'Such as what?'

'I'd quite like to join the WRNS.'

'Hannah!' She could see her mother was shocked. 'I don't want you to go away.'

She understood. Her mother didn't want to be left here alone with Aunt Philomena. She didn't blame her; already it seemed Philomena wanted to be waited on hand and foot. The new kitchen she'd put in was built to a height she could use from her wheelchair, but that stood empty in the hall as she said she didn't like using it.

'The WRNS?' Aunt Philomena's protruding pale eyes swung to her. 'You'd get a commission?'

'No,' Hannah faltered. 'No, I don't think so. Certainly not to start with.'

'Why not? A nicely brought-up girl like you, convent educated.'

'I have no special skills, Aunt Philomena. I'm a school leaver. They'd have to teach me what they wanted me to do.'

'Then it's quite unsuitable. Goodness knows what the other girls would be like. You're far too young to leave home and do that.'

'But they take girls from age eighteen–'

'No, Hannah. It doesn't bear thinking about. You could land yourself in all sorts of trouble. Your poor mother wouldn't get another full night's sleep. I'd be much happier if you found your war work here and stayed with us.'

Her mother's eyes were pools of distress. 'Please, Hannah,' she said.

Hannah felt she didn't have much choice. She couldn't turn her back on Mum just after this disaster.

Aunt Philomena wanted her to make coffee after lunch and brought out a tin of fancy biscuits to eat with it.

'My favourite,' Hannah told her. 'I haven't seen these for years. Where d'you get them?'

'Brenda finds me little luxuries from time to time. She's very good.'

Afterwards, Philomena went to her bedroom for her usual afternoon rest.

Hannah said, 'Lie down on the sofa, Mum. You need a rest too.'

There was a thick car rug folded over the back of a chair, which she'd seen Aunt Philomena put over her knees on cold Sunday afternoons. Now she spread it over her mother.

'What about you?'

Hannah looked longingly at an armchair, but said, 'I'll go upstairs and start cleaning.'

'I'll come up and help you make up the beds later.'

Hannah was heading upstairs when the front doorbell rang. She went to answer it. The grey-haired woman on the step looked surprised to see her.

'Oh, my dear ... I was expecting to see Mrs Wells.' She wore a grey wool coat, a plain felt hat and gloves.

'Hello,' Hannah said. 'You're Mrs Osborne, aren't you?' She recognised the wife of the vicar who had replaced her Uncle Fred, and who now lived in the vicarage next door. 'I'm Hannah Ashe, Mrs Wells's niece.'

'Yes, of course! I came to see if your aunt was all right. I mean, she lives on her own, but now you're with her...'

'My mother's here too. They're both having a rest. We were bombed out last night, we'll be staying here from now on.'

'Oh, my dear, how terrible for you. Your mother, is she all right? Not hurt?'

'She's upset. We've lost almost everything and

she's very tired.'

'Yes, I am sorry. If there's anything I can do, don't hesitate to ask.' Her expression was benign, full of goodwill. 'I'll leave you to get on. I hope you'll both feel better soon.'

'Thank you.'

Hannah went on upstairs and opened all the windows. She was damp-dusting the room her mother had chosen when the doorbell rang again. She ran downstairs quickly before Mum tried to answer it. There was a young officer in RAF uniform on the doorstep. He was holding out a carrier bag.

'Hello. My mother asked me to bring these few things round to you.'

'That's very kind.'

'I'm Robert Osborne, usually known as Rob.'

'I know who you are – I saw you in church once. Aunt Philomena pointed you out.'

She'd said, 'A very nice young man, he left university in the middle of his course to fight for his country.'

Friendly brown eyes were smiling down at Hannah. He was tall and handsome. His uniform had been recently pressed and couldn't have been smarter. The Battle of Britain had given airforce men more than a touch of glamour. They were the heroes of this war.

Hannah felt a mess when she'd have liked to look her best for him. She still wore the siren suit she'd slept in for some time, and it and her hair were impregnated with gritty dust.

She peeped into the bag, and saw a tin of Spam. 'Just what we need, something to eat tonight. I won't have to go shopping straight away.'

'Mother said you'd be bound to find it difficult, with rationing.'

'Do thank her. I'm so grateful. Mum will be too.'

He half turned to go, then swung back to face her. 'I say, I'm having a bit of a do tomorrow evening, just a few friends round – would you like to come?'

Hannah smiled. He had an engaging manner, which she found attractive. 'I'd like to, but I haven't any clothes. Literally nothing but what I stand up in.'

He laughed. 'Come as you are then. You look fine.'

'I look like a refugee and I feel worse.'

'Do come, I mean it. Seven o'clock tomorrow. We're going to be terribly short of girls. Apart from one cousin, I don't think there'll be another, unless you come. It's my birthday.'

Hannah laughed. 'Tomorrow is your birthday? It's mine too.'

'Then you must come, I insist. I'll be twenty-two.'

'I'll be eighteen.'

'Do please come.'

Hannah went back upstairs, thinking she'd like to, but she'd have to find a dress and some different shoes. She couldn't possibly go as she was.

If only the dress Mum had planned to give her as a birthday present had survived. She hadn't seen it in its finished state, but she'd had a fitting and she'd chosen the pattern. It would have been her first grown-up party dress and she knew she'd have loved it. Mum said she'd left it hanging from the picture rail in her bedroom, and they'd seen torn red taffeta shining like a jewel amongst the rubble, so it hadn't survived. But it was no good thinking about it now.

Later in the day, she told Philomena about the invitation.

'You must go, Hannah,' she said earnestly. 'He's a very nice young man. I thoroughly approve of him. I expect you're dreaming of young men and marriage. He's very eligible.'

Hannah recoiled. 'Not immediately, no,' she said stiffly. She'd rather liked Rob, but Aunt Philomena's whole-hearted approval was turning her off him.

'All girls do. If you're sensible you'll make every effort to know him better. You must take him a nice present.'

'What? There's no time to think of presents. It's tomorrow.' A far more pressing matter was to find a dress she could wear.

'I'll find him a present,' Philomena said. 'You won't have to go empty-handed. You mustn't miss this opportunity. When you're a little older and out in the world, you'll need somebody to look after you.'

Hannah said, 'I need a bath and some clothes. I can't go anywhere like this.'

That drove Philomena to take her and Esme into her bedroom and throw open her wardrobe and chest of drawers. 'You must take what you need to tide yourselves over. There's plenty here. I haven't always been as stout as this, Esme. You'll find clothes nearer your size at the back there.'

She took one out. 'This is a nice warm dress. I was sorry when I could no longer get into it.'

Esme accepted it and seemed pleased. She picked out some underwear.

'I must apply for extra clothing coupons. There's an allocation for those who are bombed out and lose everything; we'll get twelve pounds each too.'

Hannah looked at Philomena's clothes and felt at a loss. There was nothing that she could possibly wear to a party.

'I'll go back to Wallasey in the morning,' she said, 'to see if anything was salvaged from our house. If not, I'll stop in Birkenhead and buy myself a dress and some shoes. I think I'll have enough coupons for that.' Both her mother and Philomena pressed more coupons on her.

Hannah selected a very ample nightdress and dressing gown, then looked at the large pink *Directoire* knickers Aunt Philomena favoured. She sighed, but took a pair. At least they'd be clean.

She felt a little better by the next morning when she'd had a bath and washed her hair. Philomena's knickers came below her knees.

When she went downstairs her mother was already in the kitchen. She kissed Hannah's cheek and put an envelope into her hand. 'Happy birthday, love.' There was a birthday card and three pound notes folded inside it. 'It's the best I can do this year.'

'Mum, thank you, thank you. I didn't expect anything when I saw the frock in shreds. This is very generous of you.'

'Philomena says I must send you in to see her as soon as you've finished your breakfast.'

When Hannah went to see Philomena, her aunt had a card and a small packet for her. She opened it and was thrilled with the gold bracelet inside.

'Aunt Philomena, it's really lovely. I'm delighted with this.' Hannah kissed her soft wrinkled cheek. 'Thank you very much.'

'It isn't new, of course. I used to wear it when I was a girl.'

Hannah snapped it on her wrist.

'Take care of it. It's eighteen carat.'

'I will. It's my first really nice piece of jewellery. I shall wear it tonight.'

'I've asked Brenda to make a birthday cake for you, but it'll have to be sponge because we've no dried fruit.'

Hannah smiled and kissed her again. 'You're very kind. It really does feel like my birthday now.'

Hannah went out into the back garden and put her siren suit over the line. It took ages to beat the grey cloying dust out of it with a carpet beater, but she felt she'd be more comfortable in that than something belonging to her aunt.

When she saw what remained of their house, Hannah felt her guts wrenching. It was not just their house that had been wrecked. Four houses in the middle of the terrace had been reduced to ruins. A lorry was parked in the street and workmen were loading broken window frames and beams on it.

She turned to the Petersons' house, which was almost opposite, and knocked on the door. When

Mrs Peterson came she put her arms round Hannah and kissed her, though she'd never done that before.

'Your poor mother, what she must be feeling...'

'She's all right,' Hannah said, deciding there was no point in saying Mum was exhausted and a bag of nerves. 'But a bit worried because she didn't go to work yesterday.'

'We managed to salvage quite a lot for you. Come and see. Some of it is in our shed, the rest in the back yard.'

'My wardrobe!' Hannah was delighted to see it leaning against the yard wall.

'It isn't up to much now,' Mr Peterson said. 'The mirror's broken and it won't stand up straight.'

'I don't care about that, it's the clothes inside I want,' Hannah said.

'It's locked,' the old man told her, 'so you might be lucky. Have you got the key?'

'I always left it in the door. It was the only way to keep it closed.'

'Well, it's not here now. Shall I break it open?'

'Yes, please.'

'Won't be much good when I've finished with it.'

'It isn't now.'

Hannah thought of Aunt Philomena's well-kept house. She'd probably refuse to let this battered wardrobe over the doorstep anyway.

Mr Peterson forced the door open and Hannah was thrilled to see her clothes again. Most of the hangers had come off the rail and her clothes were in a heap at the bottom. She lifted them out eagerly.

'Everything seems all right, if a little crushed. I'm delighted to have them back.'

There was no sign of Mum's wardrobe but Mr Peterson had collected quite a lot of her clothes together.

'They'll need washing,' his wife said, 'and perhaps a stitch here and there, but most of them are still wearable.'

There was even Mum's blanket chest and her chest of drawers with only one drawer missing.

Mrs Peterson brought out a number of paper carrier bags and her husband helped her tie the rest of her things up into bundles. There were a couple of cardboard boxes into which they'd packed a motley collection of dishes, cutlery, hairbrushes and books.

'Too much for me to carry on the bus,' Hannah said. 'I'll walk as far as the ferry and try and get a taxi. What about this broken furniture?'

'Don't worry about it, love. I can get some morning sticks out of it and the rest I'll put out for the men. They'll take it away on the lorry. A waste really – it was right nice stuff.'

They insisted Hannah have a cup of tea and a biscuit before setting out. They'd been good neighbours; Mum had been fond of Mrs Peterson. Hannah thanked them and went to look for a taxi, then rode home in style with her various belongings piled high all round her. She was pleased she'd have a dress to wear to the party this evening.

When it was time for Hannah to get ready for the party, she was having second thoughts about it.

She hardly knew Robert Osborne, and in fact was unlikely to know anyone else there.

She'd looked through the clothes she'd brought home, and found them all a bit dusty, but she did have a choice. She settled on a sky-blue cotton frock that used to be a favourite. It was clean and still fitted her although it was three years old. She ironed it and it came up crisp and fresh, but she was afraid it looked a touch schoolgirlish for the party she was going to; it had a Peter Pan collar and ruching on the bodice. After all, Robert Osborne was a grown man of twenty-two.

Hannah found being bombed out was proving a big turning point in her life. It had drawn a line between her childhood and her adult life. It meant a new home and her first real job. She'd go to the Labour Exchange on Monday and ask about war work. She didn't know many people round here, and felt she really ought to go to this party and try to make new friends.

'You look very nice,' Aunt Philomena told her when she went downstairs.

Hannah thought she looked fifteen again. Her dress had short sleeves and a full skirt. She was wearing an Alice band on her long fair hair and had left it loose.

'Will you be warm enough in that?' Philomena asked. 'I have a pretty shawl you could borrow. Go and look in my bottom drawer.'

Hannah went reluctantly, but when she found it, she thought it pretty too. It was a darker blue than her dress and went well with it, and it would hide some of the ruching on the bodice.

She felt nervous as she walked round to the

vicarage next door, but as soon as the door opened and Rob drew her in, she felt at ease.

'You've come after all. I hoped you would.' He was smiling his welcome. He had nut-brown hair, brushed straight back from his forehead. He was even more good-looking than she'd thought yesterday.

'Happy birthday,' she said, putting two small packets into his hand.

'You didn't have to bring presents.' He was embarrassed, a little awkward. 'I should have told you. I didn't intend to put you to any trouble, not when...'

'Open them,' she said.

'Gosh, gold cufflinks?' His brown eyes came up to meet hers, full of amazement. 'You're very generous, thank you. Outstandingly generous.'

'They're from Aunt Philomena. Not new – they belonged to my Uncle Fred. Did you know him?'

'My father did.'

'She wanted you to have them.'

'It's very kind of her. I'll write a note to her tomorrow.'

Actually, Philomena had said, 'He might as well have them as leave them lying in my drawer. They're no good to us women.'

'The leather bookmark is from me.' It had been in the box of oddments picked up from the ruins of their home. She'd bought it at a bring-and-buy sale at the convent and never used it. As he took it out of the tissue paper, it looked a bit pathetic.

'The best I could do, I'm afraid.'

'I read a lot,' he told her. 'Fine tooled leather – I shall think of you every time I use it.' He smiled ruefully. 'But it's your birthday too and I've nothing to give you. Sorry, I should have thought of it.'

'No,' she said, awkward too now. 'No, don't worry about that.'

'Come and say hello to the others.' He took her into the sitting room where several other guests were chatting.

'This is Hannah,' he announced. 'It's her birthday too. She's eighteen today. Happy birthday, Hannah.' He went on, 'I'd forgotten that, which is very remiss of me, particularly as Hannah was bombed out of her home only two nights ago and lost almost everything.'

Hannah smiled at the group and said, 'My birthday gift from my mother was to be a party dress, but when I went back to look for it, I saw it torn and filthy in the rubble. I'm lucky to have this one. It survived inside my wardrobe.'

Everyone told her it was very nice.

'For a fifteen-year-old,' she giggled. 'I was fifteen when it was new.' She didn't mind saying that since Rob had told them all she was eighteen.

'This is my cousin, Margaret,' Rob went on.

She was wearing a sophisticated silk party dress in a pretty apricot colour, and was the only other girl there.

'I think you're very brave to come out like this,' she told Hannah. 'I'd still be cringing in a corner if that had happened to me.'

Hannah sat on the large sofa and looked round. This had been Aunt Philomena's home once, and her sharp eyes were going round noting all the changes. She'd come here fairly often when her Uncle Fred had been alive. The room seemed lighter than she remembered, and more comfortable.

There were four men. Hannah thought Philomena would have approved of all of them. Rob's parents had gone out, leaving a real spread on the dining-room table to which everyone could help themselves.

The rugs had already been taken up in the hall. Rob wound up the gramophone and put on a record of Joe Loss and his orchestra.

He turned to Hannah. 'May I have the first dance? Only right we should start things off, as it's our joint birthday.'

Rob held her close as he twirled her round, making it easy for her to move with him, matching her steps to his. She found it exciting to be in his arms like this. The tune throbbed out, giving up its wild energy to Hannah's feet.

'You're a good dancer,' he murmured in her ear. He spun her round with a flourish as the tune came to an end. The two men without partners had been cavorting together, making them all laugh.

'Now it's our turn to have the real partners,' they sang out as soon as the girls were released, and Hannah was waltzed off to music from Henry Hall's band. Neither of the girls had a chance to sit down all evening.

Hannah enjoyed it all immensely, but she was disappointed not to have made new friends in the neighbourhood. Margaret lived in the Lake District and was staying only for a few days. Of the men, Rob had met Mike since he'd joined the RAF and the other two were his school friends who came from Liverpool.

It was after midnight when the party broke up, and they found it was raining.

'Not a night for the bombers,' Rob said, looking up at the overcast sky.

'That's a comfort.'

'I'll walk you home.'

Hannah giggled. 'It's only next door.'

'I need to see you safely inside,' he said gravely.

Hannah led the way up Philomena's path and put the key she'd been given into the porch door. A few steps beyond was the front door, and she opened that too. Rob was leaning against the outer door, a darker curve against the dark sky. She wondered if he'd kiss her, but he made no move to come closer.

'Thank you for coming, Hannah.' He kept his voice low so as not to wake her family. 'It wouldn't have been much of a party without you.'

'And Margaret.'

'Yes, Margaret too. I don't know when I'll see you again. Mike and I have to report back tomorrow. Our leave's over and we're off to Canada for more training next week.'

Hannah was sorry. She'd have liked him to take her dancing again.

'Good luck.'

'Thanks, same to you. For your war work, I mean.'

'Thanks.'

They were running out of things to say but he seemed reluctant to go. Hannah was on the point of saying good night and stepping inside.

Rob said, 'I've had a jolly good birthday.'

'So have I,' Hannah smiled. 'Better than I expected.'

'Good. I wonder where we'll be this time next year.'

'I'll still be here.'

'I'll drop you a birthday card.' She saw his teeth flash white in a smile. 'I won't forget again. Good night.'

He was going, keeping his step purposely quiet. Hannah went in and tiptoed up to her room.

On Monday morning, Hannah woke to find her mother bringing her a cup of tea. She was fully dressed, even to her hat.

'What time is it?' asked Hannah.

'Half-past eight. I'm sorry to wake you so early, but I'm going to the Food Office in New Ferry now. I told you, didn't I?'

'Yes. I want to go to the Labour Exchange this morning to see about a job. If I'm not here when you come back, that's where I'll be.'

'Right. I've been talking to Philomena and her daily help. Brenda's husband is a painter and decorator and she's going to bring him round here this evening to see us. If we can get some paint, he'll buff the place up a bit for us.'

Hannah drank her tea and got up. She was excited at the thought of a proper job. The nearest Labour Exchange was in New Ferry. She'd already discussed getting there with Philomena, who had advised her to walk up to the New Chester Road to catch a bus. She could have gone with her mum if she'd got up earlier.

When she reached the bus stop, a pretty girl with a pert upturned nose was sitting on the low wall behind it.

Hannah asked, 'Can you tell me what number bus I need for New Ferry?'

The girl looked up and smiled. 'They all go through, any bus will do.'

'When's the next one due?'

'It'll come when it's good and ready,' she said, 'and not a minute before. I've been waiting ten minutes. I could have walked it in the time. But look, here's one coming, you're in luck. A number forty-two, that'll do us.'

The bus was full and they both had to stand. Hannah paid her fare and asked the conductor to put her off in New Ferry. More passengers were squeezing on at every stop. The conductor was upstairs when the bus was slowing again. Hannah sensed that this time there'd be a general exodus.

'This is your stop,' the girl said as she made to get off too.

Out on the pavement, Hannah was looking about her. 'Can you tell me the way to the Labour Exchange?' she asked. 'I'm new round here.'

The girl smiled. 'I can do better than that, I can take you there. I'm going myself. Come on, it's down Bebington Road.'

'Thanks.' Hannah told her how she and her mother had been bombed out of their home in Wallasey four nights ago, and had had to come to live with her aunt.

'That was a terrible night. Thank goodness it's

been quieter since then.'

'It's the bad weather. We'll be in for it again when we get a fine moonlit night.'

'This is the Labour Exchange.' The windows had been painted green so it was impossible to see inside. There was a queue.

'Looks as though we'll have to wait,' the girl said, joining the line.

'I'm looking for a job,' Hannah told her. 'War work. After being bombed out, I feel I've got to do something to help. I'm eighteen anyway, so I think they'll make me.'

'I'm looking for war work too,' the girl said quickly. 'I've got a nice job in a dress shop, but ... well, my fiancé is being sent overseas soon. I've got to do something to help too. I want him back home as soon as possible.' Hannah saw she was wearing an engagement ring.

'What sort of war work do you want?' Hannah asked.

The girl shrugged. 'The papers are full of forms to apply for the Land Army or the WAAF or nursing or whatever. If you haven't done that and you come here, I gather they decide for us. It's wherever workers are needed most urgently.'

'Oh!' Hannah had an unwelcome vision of being told to work in a munitions factory.

The girl pushed her dark curls away from her face. 'I don't care so long as it helps and it pays well.'

They didn't have to wait too long. There was a special clerk dealing with local war work. He took them to his office where they found two other girls already there. They were all given forms to fill up. Hannah wrote her name and address and looked at the form her companion was filling in.

'Georgina Goodwin,' she read aloud.

'Known as Gina. What's your name?'

Hannah pushed her form nearer to her.

'You live in Grasmere Road?' Gina was giggling.

'I'm staying with my aunt; that's where she lives.'

'I live there too.' Gina pushed her form in front of Hannah again. It showed her address as 8 Grasmere Road. Hannah started to giggle too. The two other girls joined in. They were called Josie and Grace.

The clerk returned, collected their forms and dealt with them all together. They were told to report to Hooton Aerodrome at eight o'clock the next morning. They would be helping to repair Mosquito planes damaged in battle.

'Your normal working hours are eight to five for five days a week, eight till one on Saturdays and the pay for that will be thirty-nine shillings a week at age eighteen.'

He went on to explain that at present the whole work force was doing regular compulsory overtime of three hours each day and finishing at eight in the evening. There would be extra pay for that. He then gave them each another form to fill in.

'You can take this home with you and do it there. It's about your medical history. The firm has a doctor and you'll each have a medical examination sometime in the first few days. You need to take this form with you tomorrow as well as a reference from your last employer.'

He gave them each a page of written directions on how to get there, told them to wear warm clothing and sensible shoes and ushered them out.

'Phew! What have we let ourselves in for?' Josie giggled. 'A twelve-hour day! I don't know if I'll be able to stand that for long.'

'You'll have to,' Gina told her. 'If you're over eighteen you get directed to work where you're needed.'

She was studying the directions. 'It says it's possible to get there by bus or train. A workmen's bus ticket at a reduced rate is available on all buses before eight in the morning, and there's a special one put on from the New Ferry bus depot that leaves at ten minutes past seven.'

'Gosh, that means an early start.'

Gina grimaced. 'Yes, crack of dawn. Doesn't bear thinking about. There'll be plenty of buses at that time in the morning to get us to New Ferry, but we'd better be at the bus stop by five to seven.'

'It looks as though we'll be seeing a lot of each other,' Hannah said.

'I'll call for you in the morning, shall I? I have to pass your place.'

'Yes, please. I'm glad I've got you to go with. I wasn't looking forward to the first day.'

Gina gave her a radiant smile. 'Makes it easier, doesn't it? Knowing each other first.'

CHAPTER THREE

When Hannah turned into the gate of Highfield House, Gina continued up Grasmere Road, not altogether pleased with the war work she'd just volunteered to do.

She was glad she'd met Hannah Ashe. She liked her and was happy they'd be working together. It was the thought of those long hours she found off-putting. Eight till eight, twelve hours a day!

She reached the gate of her own house, turned and looked across the road to the line of recently built semidetached ones. Number twenty-two was where her fiancé's mother and sister lived.

The Latimers had moved here a few months before the start of the war. Jim had already been in the Army when she'd first met him, he'd come home on fourteen days' leave. It had been love at first sight for both of them and he'd turned all her ambitions upside down. Now she was writing to him every day and he was rarely out of her thoughts. It was three months since she'd seen him.

Gina studied his home. The bay windows were curtained with net. Everything was ultra neat and tidy, but there was no one to be seen.

His mother had let Gina know that she disapproved of the engagement, by saying, 'Jim has always been impulsive; he makes big decisions without any thought. Often, he regrets them later.'

Gina blamed Pa. He'd been too officious and made enemies of their neighbours. He'd banged on their doors and complained they were showing chinks of light through their blackout curtains.

There was a letter from Jim waiting for her on the kitchen table when Gina got inside. She opened it eagerly and started to read. Jim's excited scrawl seemed to jump off the page. 'I've just heard I'll be coming home at the beginning of next month. Embarkation leave this time.'

To think of seeing him again set her heart racing, but then she thought of her new job and was sorry she'd signed up for it. She wanted to thump the table with frustration. She shouldn't have gone for war work just yet. If she was working twelve hours a day she wouldn't be able to see much of Jim when he was here.

Gina started to make herself something to eat, still thinking of Jim. Her family hadn't approved of the engagement either.

'You're far too young to think of getting married,' Pa had told her, 'and you hardly know him. Don't do it.'

Gina wouldn't be eighteen for another few months but she knew Jim was the man for her. She'd gone ahead and accepted his ring though she knew they'd have a long wait before they could be married.

He was twenty-three and seemed grown up and sophisticated. He'd been working in Clapham as a primary school teacher for almost a year before he'd been called up. She knew his sister, Moira, who was a good customer at the dress shop where Gina worked, though she was more of an acquaintance than a friend.

Pouring herself a second cup of tea, Gina heard footsteps coming down the hall. Her elder brother, Eric, came in to slump at the kitchen table opposite her.

'What are you doing here?' she asked. 'Shouldn't you be at work?'

Gina had two brothers: Leslie, who was younger, and Eric, who had turned twenty-one. She also had a little sister, Betsy. Everybody could see she and Eric were brother and sister. They were very much alike to look at, with the same dark curly hair. She was particularly close to Eric. She and Leslie followed wherever he led.

Eric dropped his head in his hands. 'I'm sick. Is there more tea in that pot? I feel as though my throat's cut.'

Gina got to her feet and poured him a cup. Eric's health had to be taken seriously. 'What's the matter?'

'Tonsillitis. I didn't go to work this morning. I went to see the doctor.'

'He's given you medicine?'

'Something horrible to gargle with and some pills.' The doctor took Eric's health seriously too. 'He's signed me off work for a week.'

'That should cheer you up. What about fire watching? Aren't you supposed to be doing that tonight?'

'Yes, but Leslie said he'd take my turn. If I feel better tomorrow, I'll do his for him.'

'I'd have made you something to eat if I'd known you were upstairs.'

He sighed. 'I'm not hungry.'

Eric had been called up for military service at the beginning of the war but had failed his medical examination. He'd had rheumatic fever as a child and they'd told him it had affected his heart. The news had hit him hard, particularly as their mother had died of heart problems when they were children.

Gina remembered clearly how Eric had taken a slip of paper from his pocket when he'd come home.

'Myocardial degeneration, they called it. I copied what they wrote on my forms.'

Gina had stared at the bit of torn paper. The whole family had been in the kitchen that night and had been stunned at his news. Even Cicely, their stepmother, had looked concerned. Gina had seen the colour drain from Leslie's cheeks; he'd had rheumatic fever as a child too. Little Betsy hadn't really understood – she was still a toddler – but she knew they were all shocked.

'What is myocardial degeneration, Pa?'

'I don't know exactly.' For once, their father was at a loss. 'Go and see Dr McPherson. He'll tell you.'

Gina knew Eric had seen their doctor, but all he remembered being told was that he must avoid heavy work and all exertion, that he should get plenty of sleep and regular meals.

'Sounds like I'll be fine if I live the life of an invalid,' Eric had said miserably.

'You're not the sort to do that. Especially if you feel all right.'

'I felt fine until they told me,' he'd retorted angrily. 'Until then I had no idea there was anything wrong with me.'

They had gone to the library together the next day and asked for help to find out what exactly this ailment was. They'd read sections in several tomes.

'D'you understand now?' Gina had asked, when he'd slammed the last one shut.

'Not entirely – they use such long words – but I've got the gist of it and I wish I hadn't. My heart has been damaged and there's nothing can be done about it.'

'That's overstating it,' Gina had said briskly. 'Look at this list of symptoms. You don't have any of them, do you?'

'No.'

'You don't even look ill.' In fact, Eric looked robust; he was a handsome young man. 'You've got years ahead of you. You'll probably live to a ripe old age.'

'You're right.' He'd smiled. 'I'm going to forget the whole damn thing. I was looking forward to joining up. It might have been more fun than the Co-op shoe department.' He'd been working there since he'd left school.

From that time, they'd all been concerned whenever Eric felt off colour, though he was ill no more often than the rest of them.

Now Gina told him about her new job and the long hours she'd have to work while Jim was home on leave.

'I was too keen to get war work,' she said. 'I should have left it until I was eighteen. I was a fool.'

'Go and see the doc,' Eric advised. 'Get yourself a week off. That would solve it.'

Gina pretended to be envious. 'He gives you time off whenever you go to see him, but he wouldn't do it for me.'

'He would if you played your cards right.' He grinned at her. 'I could tell you how to do it.'

'What are you trying to do, Eric, train me into your evil ways? I wouldn't dare.'

Hannah found her mother had returned home before her. Esme was quite excited and said she had been transferred to the New Ferry Food Office, and would be starting work the next day too.

They were getting ready to go to the shops to buy groceries when the doorbell rang. Hannah ran down to answer it and found Margaret, Robert's cousin, on the step.

'Hello, Hannah,' she said. 'Rob's gone back to his unit but he asked me to deliver these.'

'To me?'

'The package is for you, the letter for Mrs Wells.'

'Thank you. Won't you come in?'

'I'm afraid I can't. I want to catch the two o'clock train home. Nice meeting you. Bye.'

Hannah took the letter to her aunt.

'There,' Philomena said, 'I told you he was a nice lad. He's written to thank me for those cufflinks. What's that you've got? Has he sent you a birthday present?'

Hannah could only suppose he had. She took off the wrapping paper. It was a box of chocolates.

'Lovely,' she said. 'I haven't seen chocolates like

this for years.' She opened the note he'd enclosed.

'Very nice, dear,' Philomena said. 'You must write to him and keep in touch. Has he given you his address?'

'Yes, though he said he was going to Canada next week.'

'He'll be glad to have letters from you. All the boys do when they're away from home.'

'I'll write to thank him, of course,' Hannah said as she read his note.

Dear Hannah,
Please forgive me for not having a small gift ready for your birthday.

After hearing how you lost your presents and almost everything else you owned in the bombing, I feel guilty that I thought only of myself when it was your birthday too.

See you again sometime, but don't know when.

All the best,

Rob

For once, Hannah decided Aunt Philomena had been right about Rob. He was a rather dashing pilot and had been kind and friendly. Hannah had liked him but they'd been such a sophisticated lot at his party that she'd felt like a naïve schoolgirl in comparison. He'd danced with her and made much of her because there was no other girl there but his cousin.

She felt a pang of disappointment that Rob was going to Canada. She'd have liked to see more of him. In the middle of a war another continent could almost be another planet.

Hannah shivered. He could be killed. During the Battle of Britain they'd estimated that a new pilot's career lasted three weeks on average. It could be years before their paths crossed again, if ever.

The next morning, Hannah was waiting at her gate when Gina came running down the road to meet her. They were both shivering with cold and excitement as they waited at the bus stop. They met up with the other two new girls when they changed to the works bus in New Ferry. It was a long slow journey as they stopped frequently to pick up other workers. Hooton Aerodrome was about five miles away.

When they arrived the new girls were directed to a small office. Their boss told them that before the war this had been an airfield where flying had been for fun, with small private planes and lessons available. Now, Mosquito planes that had been damaged in battle were being repaired in the hangars.

Hannah was separated from the others and taken to the woodwork department. It seemed a cold and noisy place. There was hammering and sawing close by and a perpetual buzz of machinery from the other side of the hangar where a team of engineers repaired and serviced the engines.

Old Charlie, the foreman, who should by rights have retired some time ago, explained that the plane's frame was built largely of plywood ribs. A team of carpenters was replacing broken ailerons, tail rudders and damaged ribs, and gluing them in position. Hannah was given the job of reinforcing the glue with tiny nails.

Charlie showed her how to insert them in a zigzag pattern about an inch and a half apart.

He said, 'Men find it difficult to work with tiny five-eighths nails – they're always hitting their fingers – but with your little hands you should have no difficulty.'

Monica, the only other girl working in the woodwork department, mixed the glue. Hannah soon mastered the job and was afraid she might find the work monotonous after a time, but wireless programmes were broadcast through speakers high up overhead to keep the atmosphere lively. She particularly enjoyed *Music While You Work* and *Workers' Playtime.*

When the wooden framework was restored, the plane went to the dope room where other girls repaired flak damage to the outer shell with fabric, and painted it over with some chemical solution that set hard and looked like dark green paint. They called it doping. Gina and the two other girls had been given masks to wear and were sent to work in there. The stench of chemicals was overpowering. Hannah thought she'd been given the better option.

Even so, everything seemed very strange, and it was a long hard day. Hannah was weary when at last finishing time came. On the bus going home, she said, 'Another early start tomorrow.'

'Most of the girls cycle in,' Gina told her. 'It would take less time than coming on the bus. Have you got a bike?'

'I did have, but it was one of the things I lost

when we were bombed out.' Hannah bit her lip. 'I'm going to miss it.'

'Couldn't it be repaired?'

'No, it was blown to bits. I saw parts of it in the rubble; the frame was bent and twisted.'

'My brothers are dab hands at restoring bikes. They could build one for you, if you like.'

'Could they?' Hannah was interested. Cycling to work would save money as well as mean they didn't have to get up so early.

'Course, it'll take a bit of time. They rebuilt one for me. It's a real racer with a dynamo and three gears. I love it. It would be cheaper for you than buying new.'

'We passed a bike shop in New Ferry yesterday. They had only second-hand bikes – I looked.'

'Come home with me and see Eric. He was the brains behind the bike-building to start with, and he taught Leslie. He's really keen, always has been on cycling. He buys old bikes and replaces all the duff bits, makes sure everything works properly. It's a sort of hobby and he makes a bit of extra pocket money. He's only fifteen but he does a good job.'

'I would like another bike.' Hannah knew how useful a bike would be now public transport rarely ran to time.

'Come up – it won't take more than a few minutes,' Gina urged.

'Right, I will then.'

They got off the bus and walked home together, passing the vicarage and Highfield House, with its chimneys standing out stark against the night sky. Gina pointed towards the large semidetached villas that had been built in about 1890.

'I live in one of these, a few yards further up. Here we are.'

It was pitch-dark. Hannah strained to see the three-storey house, a black mass against a sky that was only marginally lighter on this rainy night. Two Gothic gables jutted up over the attic bedrooms. The blackout was faultless. Gina took Hannah by the hand to lead her up the garden path.

'We've got thirteen hens and two cockerels now,' she told her. 'We turned this shed into a henhouse.' It was built against the side of the house.

Hannah could just make out the wire netting of their run. 'Aren't they quiet?'

'Shut in for the night. They'll be asleep now.'

A few steps further round the rear of the house, and Hannah was taken into the back kitchen. She found herself blinking in the bright light.

It was a cluttered room. There was a big sink full of dirty dishes and pans, dirty clothes were soaking in a zinc baby bath. Pride of place was given to a modern gas cooker with a frying pan containing two sausages on top. Gina led her through to a larger kitchen beyond.

'This is my big brother, Eric,' she told Hannah. He was scrambling eggs on a much older gas cooker. Hannah thought him good-looking. He resembled his sister, except that his nose was large and straight rather than upturned like hers. He had the same dark eyes but his were challenging, and there was an air of derring-do about him.

'Hello.' He smiled at Hannah.

'Don't get too close,' Gina warned her. 'Eric's got tonsillitis.'
'I'm better today.'
'And this is Leslie, our little brother.'
He was making toast, which smelled delicious. Leslie was neither as tall nor as broad as his brother, so that beside him he looked slight. He appeared neither as handsome nor as confident as his siblings, until Gina told him why she'd brought Hannah home. Then he came to life and talked non-stop about bikes.
Eric drew his pan off the heat and asked, 'Do you want to eat with us?'
'Yes,' Gina said.
Almost simultaneously, Hannah said, 'No, thank you. We've had a meal this evening in the canteen.'
At that moment, the door from the hall suddenly crashed back and a broad-shouldered, barrel-chested man strode to the table.
He asked belligerently, 'How many times do I have to tell you kids to go easy on the butter?' He snatched up the butter dish from the table and retreated to the door.
Hannah felt the conviviality drain away, and she saw Eric straighten up with resentment. Gina's chin had gone up too, but it was Eric who said quietly and politely, 'Butter's finished, Pa. That's marge.'
So this was their father. Probably in his mid-fifties, he was more brawny than his sons and beginning to show a sprinkling of silver through his dark hair but, with his dark moustache, Hannah thought him a strikingly handsome man.

His eyes came to rest on Hannah. 'Who's this?' he demanded.

'A friend,' Gina replied. 'We work together.'

'Hannah Ashe,' Eric said. 'From Highfield House.'

Mr Goodwin's dark eyes were on her and Hannah knew she was being assessed. 'Esme Wells's daughter?'

'Yes,' she said. 'She was Esme Wells once. She's Esme Ashe now. That's her married name.'

'Yes, that's her.' His laugh was cynical. 'I'm surprised she lets you come to our house.' He turned and went, leaving an embarrassed silence.

Leslie began talking about bikes again and pouring cups of tea. Hannah found one placed in front of her.

Their home was very different from anywhere Hannah had lived. If Aunt Philomena saw this she'd lift her nose in the air and say it was dirty and ill kept. Hannah thought it more untidy than dirty. Clothes, crockery and personal belongings were piled on chairs and tables. An ancient coal range almost filled one wall with its big ovens. Once it would have been blackleaded; now it was rusting and the grate was empty. No fire had been lit in it for decades, it seemed. A fierce draught was coming down the chimney.

At home, Mum wanted everything put away immediately it had been used. She wouldn't sit down until she'd wiped every kitchen surface to hygienic perfection. Hannah's home shone with cleanliness.

Putting down his cup, Eric picked up a camera from the clutter on the end of the table, and pointed it at them.

'Well, go on, take our picture,' Gina urged.

'There's not enough light.'

'Get his lamps out, Leslie.' She smiled at Hannah. 'Our Eric's passionate about photography. He's always snapping us.'

'Can you still get film?' Hannah asked him.

'It's in short supply like everything else.'

She was surprised at just how much extra light the lamps did provide.

Eric said, 'You'll have to get closer together. Come on then, Gina, say cheese. Smile, all of you.'

As soon as that was over, Leslie was getting to his feet.

'Where's the torch?' he asked. 'Come out to the shed, Hannah, and I'll show you the bike I put together for Gina. I did one for myself too.'

She stumbled after him and Eric. 'This one's mine and this is Gina's. I put them together from bits and pieces.' There was pride in Leslie's voice. 'This is Eric's.'

It was more staid than the other two. 'I'm not so keen on cycling,' Eric explained. 'What sort of a bike do you want, a racer like Gina's?'

Hannah said, 'More like yours, I think. I'm not keen on low handlebars and a high seat, but perhaps I should have gears? I'm thinking of using it to go to work every day.'

'There aren't any hills between here and Hooton,' Eric told her. 'It probably wouldn't make too much difference.'

Leslie's voice was eager. 'Shall I look out for one for you? See what I can pick up?'

Hannah made up her mind. 'Yes, please. I don't want extras, just an ordinary bike. Not too expensive. This is my first job and there's lots of things I need.'

'OK. I'll undercut anything you can find in a bike shop, won't I, Eric?'

'He will, and it'll be just as good. Anyway, you know where to bring it if you have any complaints.'

'Thanks,' Hannah smiled.

As she ran home she thought of Gina and her brothers. She liked them but thought their father a little strange. What on earth had he meant by his comment about her mother?

When Hannah had gone home, Gina sat down to eat with her brothers at the kitchen table.

'Pa has no idea what a bad impression he makes on visitors,' Eric grumbled. 'He's always so nasty to us.'

Gina pulled a face. 'He doesn't show a lot of affection.'

'There's none there to show.' Eric was matter of fact. 'We're a family divided. It's us and them.'

'And has been since our mother died.'

'Since he brought Cicely here, anyway.'

Leslie said, 'He has a very high opinion of himself.'

Eric smiled. 'He must find that frustrating, when nobody shares it.'

'To hear him talk,' Gina said, 'you'd think the Birkenhead Police would crumble if he wasn't there to direct it.'

'He's still a constable,' Leslie pointed out,

'though he joined umpteen years ago.'

'That doesn't sound as if he's a natural leader of men,' Eric agreed. 'I think he regrets that he ever joined the police. He's made a few wrong decisions in his life and that's one of them. It upsets him.'

'He's always grumpy.'

'He can be very touchy.' Eric reached for another slice of toast. 'You two should be careful what you say to him. You know it doesn't take much to make him fly off the handle.'

At home, Hannah found her mother and Aunt Philomena waiting to hear all about her new job.

When she explained about the Mosquito's plywood ribs and what she had to do, Philomena said, 'An aeroplane made of plywood? It sounds very fragile, especially in wartime. I wouldn't like to go up in the air in that.'

'They say it's a good plane,' Hannah told her. 'The pilots like it.'

She went on to tell them about her new friend Gina, and how her brother Leslie was going to rebuild a bike for her. She'd expected to be congratulated on her thriftiness.

'Do you mean the Goodwins?' Her mum had a horrified expression on her face.

'Yes, that's their name. Do you know them?'

Mum seemed flustered. It was Aunt Philomena who answered.

'Yes, we know them. I don't think you should have anything to do with them.' She straightened up in her chair. 'They're not our class, dear.'

Hannah said, 'I can't help but see Gina – we

work in the same place. Right now, I'm glad to know anyone there, though they're a friendly crowd. Anyway, I like her.'

'There's a collection of old bikes in the garden shed,' Philomena told her. 'On no account buy another from them. Have nothing to do with them.'

'But why?' Hannah asked.

'I've told you.' The irritation was obvious in Philomena's voice.

Later that evening, when she and Mum went upstairs to their own quarters, Hannah asked her what Aunt Philomena had against the Goodwins.

'There was trouble between our two families,' she said. 'A long time ago.'

'Well, Gina doesn't seem to know about it,' Hannah mused.

March was bringing a spate of heavy air raids. On the night of the eighteenth, Police Constable Arnold Goodwin was due to go off shift at ten o'clock, but the siren wailed as he was walking across to the bicycle shed. It was another cloudless night with a full moon, exactly the sort of night to bring the bombers. In the pale silvery light it was possible to see almost as clearly as in daylight. Within minutes, Arnold could hear the throb of enemy aircraft overhead and the ack-ack guns starting to fire at them.

For a moment, he watched the yellow searchlights comb the sky, picking out the great silvery barrage balloons floating eerily overhead. He'd hoped for a quiet night and a good sleep, but already the 'crump, crump' of high explosives was audible. He was afraid he wouldn't get much rest tonight.

All members of the police force were ordered to report for duty whenever there was an air raid, regardless of the hours they were working on the roster. Arnold was strict with himself and kept rigidly to the rules.

He returned to the duty room, and fifteen minutes later he was ordered to a street in Rock Ferry.

Three small shops in the middle of a long terrace had received a direct hit; they were the sort of shops where the owners lived on the premises. His stomach turned over as he looked at the grim scene. The buildings had been gutted. One had been a greengrocer's shop; fruit and vegetables had been flung everywhere, many now damaged and covered with thick grey dust.

Arnold was the first of the civil defence workers to arrive. He'd seen the others in the team engaged in a nearby street where another bomb had exploded, and he knew everybody was stretched to their utmost. He propped his bike against the kerb and started on his own; calling to see if there was any indication of life under the rubble.

He received no reply and was trying to decide on the best place to start digging when he saw a metal strong box of the sort small shop keepers used to store their daily takings. It was damaged on one corner, but the lock had held, and since it appeared to contain money he put it in the saddlebag of his bike to take back to the station. The owner would be able to claim it later. It was the safest thing to do; valuables were being looted all the time despite the notices saying that looting was punishable by life imprisonment or even death.

To his knowledge, nobody had received the death penalty as yet and few were charged. But belongings went on being quietly spirited away while their owners were incapable of looking after them.

By this time, a few of the neighbours were gathering, and gawping at the mess. Arnold took out his notebook and started by asking the usual questions.

'Do you know how many people live in these properties and can you tell me their names?'

'You're wasting time,' somebody said angrily. 'What about getting them out?'

'All in good time. Are these people in the habit of going to a public shelter or do they have their own on the premises?'

'They've got good cellars here, mister. They use them as shelters.'

That was the worst possible scenario, as far as Arnold was concerned. It meant they'd have to dig into the foundations if they were to get anybody out. When the ARP warden arrived with a few spades, Arnold called for volunteers, put on the heavy-duty gardening gloves he carried for this purpose and set about lifting the larger roof beams out of the way.

The smell, which got in his nostrils, was horrible. All bombed buildings smelled the same: of ancient dust, old plaster and lathe, and often of gas.

Arnold was sickened by the dead bodies and

severed limbs he helped dig out from those three shops, some of them children. Not one person had survived. He helped to move ten dead bodies to the mortuary, and by then they'd heard of another bomb site near the park where their help was needed.

They hadn't all been killed on this site, but Arnold felt even more sickened by the terrible injuries, and by his inadequacy when faced with those needing his help. When the injured had been taken to hospital, he pedalled back to Tranmere Police Station, thirsting for a cup of tea. The all clear had sounded some time ago, and by now it was two in the morning. He'd just hand in this cash box and he'd be able to go home to bed.

He was lifting his bike into its slot in the bike shed when a colleague said, 'Goodwin, bad news, I'm afraid. I hear there's been bomb damage in Grasmere Road. That's were you live, isn't it?'

Arnold could feel his gut twisting. 'Yes, do you know what number?'

'Seven or eight, I'm not sure. It's one of those big Victorian semis.'

Arnold felt gripped by terror. Bile burned his throat. Number eight was his house.

'Anybody hurt?' His voice was an unfamiliar falsetto.

'Don't know yet. Frank Tedders has gone to deal with it.'

Arnold yanked his bike down from the stand so fiercely that it bounced. Swinging his leg over, he was off home as fast as he could go, his heart in his mouth all the way. What if it was his house, and his family had been killed or maimed?

CHAPTER FOUR

As Arnold turned into Grasmere Road he came out in a torrent of sweat. He could see an ambulance waiting in the road outside his own house. He got closer and realised it wasn't his house that had caught it, but the one next door, the one attached to it.

His front gate stood open, and he rode up his path, feeling weak with relief. He dismounted to examine his house. Not even a window was broken at the front. Next door, the façade didn't look too bad though all the windows had shattered. He propped his bike against the corner of his house and ran next door, thinking of Percy Edwards and his wife, Alice, who had lived there for as long as he could remember.

They'd brought up a family of four there, but they'd all left home now and Percy must be nearly eighty. Somebody was being stretchered out but the face was completely covered.

'Who's that?' he asked.

'The old lady. We've already got her husband. He's dead too.'

Arnold's stomach was knotting. That had been a close one. The civil defence team were leaving, some with shovels over their shoulders. Someone recognised him and wished him good night. He went through to the Edwardses' back garden and saw that the back wall of the house and part of the roof had collapsed. Some of his back windows had gone too. But the shed Percy had had was now reduced to fire lighting sticks and scattered over the garden. In the roads behind, he could see gaps where previously houses had stood.

Frank Tedders' raised voice ordered everybody off the site.

Arnold then said to him, 'A very close shave for me. That's my house next door.'

'Next door, eh? I knew you lived somewhere near here. It was a bomb in Ottersley Street, blasted a swathe through three streets. Four dead and several badly injured. Your luck was in tonight.'

'Yes, thank God.' Arnold was appraising his house from the back. He thought it relatively unharmed. The roof didn't look too bad where it joined his half of the building.

'The builders will be round to make it safe in the next day or two. They'll see that your roof is weatherproof.'

The crowd of onlookers was slow to move. Frank Tedders drew himself up to his full height and called out, 'Thank you, everybody. We've done all we can. I want everybody out of here now – come along. What's left of this building looks as though it could collapse at any moment, and we don't want any more casualties.' The crowd began to move.

'No looting, mind,' Frank went on. 'What have you got there, sonny?' A lad was trying to sneak past him with something under his coat. 'What d'you mean, just a vase? Put it down. It doesn't belong to you.'

Arnold rocked on his heels, taking deep breaths. 'Thank God, thank God,' he kept repeating over and over to himself like a mantra.

Then he glimpsed a child darting away, threading through the people walking down the path. Recognition dawned and galvanised him to action. He chased after her and swung her round to face him.

'Betsy! What are you doing here?' It was his six-year-old daughter. She was wearing a soiled dressing gown over her nightdress with only ankle-strap carpet slippers on her feet.

'You naughty girl! It isn't safe for you to be running round here in the middle of the night.'

'I wanted to see, Pa.' She was jumping up and down with excitement. 'Such a rumbling crash, it woke me up.' She wasn't frightened, being too young to recognise danger.

'Look at you, you'll catch your death of cold if nothing else. You should have stayed in the cellar.' He clutched her hand to take her home. Betsy was dancing beside him.

He jerked her to a halt. 'Did you come by yourself? Are the others here?' His three older children were unlikely to have stayed in their beds, and he guessed Betsy had come with them.

'Gina and Eric are,' Betsy said. 'Leslie's still out fire watching, but Eric came home.'

'Where are they now?' He was so angry, he could hardly get the words out.

'Don't know,' Betsy sang out. He swung her savagely over the doorstep and into the back kitchen. There was a light on in the main kitchen beyond. Georgina was opening a tin of peaches on the draining board.

'What the hell do you think you're doing?' Arnold spat out.

At almost eighteen, Gina was turning into a real beauty. She was painfully like her dead mother, with a good figure and a pert nose. But Rowena had never been so determined to have things her way. Arnold found Gina the most infuriating of his children – and the one with the sharpest tongue.

'D'you want some, Pa?' Her dark gaze was confrontational. The sweet scent of the fruit was tempting. Arnold was austere by nature, and did not allow himself indulgences.

'I do,' Betsy said, getting out another bowl for Gina to dish some up for her.

'So do I,' Eric said. He was sitting at the table.

'You've looted that fruit,' Arnold accused.

Eric smiled. 'There were tins lying everywhere. I pitched a few over the fence.'

'That is looting. It's against the law.' He hated his children doing things like this. 'Go and throw them back where they belong.'

'No point, Pa. This tin was damaged on the rim. Either we eat them now or they'll go off.'

He knew he ought to insist, perhaps even book them for the offence. That would teach them.

'It's gut-wrenching to have our neighbours killed like this.' Gina shuddered.

'Horrible,' Eric agreed. 'They were kind to us when we were kids. Anyway, I'm sure Mrs Edwards would just as soon we had the fruit as anyone else. Hang on, Betsy, there's some evaporated milk to go on top. Are you sure you don't want some, Pa?'

'Why don't you behave like a normal girl?' he demanded of Gina. 'You had no business taking Betsy into a bombed building.'

'I didn't. She followed me.'

'But you saw her there. She's only a tot, not old enough to look after herself.'

Gina's grin was cheeky. 'I figured if she could get there by herself, she could get back again. Mrs Edwards used to give her sweets. Betsy often went to see her.'

'You should have brought her straight back. Couldn't you see it was dangerous?'

Eric said quietly, 'Gina and I were helping to get the old people out, Pa. Doing our duty like you say we should.'

'Oh, for God's sake!'

He could feel his temper rising again. He mustn't let himself be goaded by them.

'Where's your mother?' he demanded.

Gina shrugged. 'Cicely?' All three had refused point-blank to call her *'mother'*. 'Asleep, I suppose. She didn't get up.'

He was about to go upstairs. 'Mummy was in the cellar with us,' Betsy's piping voice told him.

Arnold turned and skidded down the steps to the cellar. Cicely was stretched out on the camp bed she'd insisted he bought her, a huge mound topped with a lot of fair hair twisted into metal curlers. She was sleeping like a baby. That infuriated him more.

'Wake up.' He shook her roughly. 'I've just found Betsy playing around in the ruins next door. You've got to take more care of her. It's your duty, for God's sake.'

'Whatsthat?' She opened small bleary eyes half hidden by folds of flesh. Piggy eyes, Gina called them. 'What ruins?'

'Didn't you hear it? It must have sounded like the crack of doom. Next door has been blasted in half, part of the roof is off and the neighbours have been killed.'

'What?'

He lost his patience. 'Bombed, for God's sake! The house is gutted! You're lying here like the fat slob you are and your child is climbing round in the ruins watching the bodies being brought out.'

'Oh!' Cicely sat up at last. 'She was here last time I looked.' She nodded towards the little bed he'd made for Betsy from an old deck chair. The blankets had been tossed aside.

Cicely had been a great disappointment to Arnold. She was fifteen years younger than he, and was fat and forty now, but before she'd put on so much weight, he'd thought her rather glamorous.

She'd been ambitious; she could dance and had a clear singing voice, and had had some success in pantomime during the winter, and in end-of-the-pier shows in summer.

Arnold had thought he was saving her from a life of sin. She was disporting herself nearly naked on stage for audiences to gawp at.

But Cicely had screamed at him that she'd imagined he was in love with her, and she'd given up her career to marry him. Her words still rang in his ears.

'I made a big mistake. I threw away my chance of a stage career. I took a wrong turn by marrying you, an old man, a widower with three children.' The dissatisfied droop to her mouth emphasised that.

He'd insisted she get a respectable job and was now working in a creche attached to a munitions factory. But she was lazy, and wouldn't lift a finger if she could avoid it.

She asked now, 'Is Betsy all right?'

'No thanks to you. Why can't you be like other mothers and take proper care of her? It's your duty.'

Cicely's plump face puckered with irritation. 'Duty? I'm sick to death of hearing about my duty. You're very strong on what you do for the general public, but what about your duty to me and Betsy? You're hardly ever home, and if you are, you're asleep in your bed.'

'I have to work, for God's sake; earn a living for us all.'

'Well, you don't earn any fortune,' she spat out. 'We'd never make ends meet on your wage. I work too, remember? But you expect me to keep the house spotless and look after your tribe of kids as well.'

Arnold couldn't help himself – his frustration boiled over. He drew back his large hand and landed a heavy swipe across her face. She gave a little yelp of pain and collapsed back on her pillow.

'You do nothing to help here,' she sobbed. There was a trickle of blood on her lips; she'd bitten her tongue. 'You expect miracles but I can't do everything.'

'The all clear's gone. I'm going upstairs to bed.' Arnold turned and went up. Eric and Gina were drinking tea in the kitchen. Three used bowls and an opened tin of peaches showed they'd feasted on what had recently been in the Edwardses' larder.

No doubt they'd heard most of the argument he'd had with Cicely. He grabbed the teapot and poured himself a mugful. The clock showed it was ten minutes to four.

'Where's Betsy?' he demanded, still anxious about her.

Eric said, 'We've sent her upstairs to bed.'

Arnold blamed Eric for most of his family troubles. After Rowena died, he'd turned into a right little street Arab, always out and up to mischief. He pretended to be more amenable these days, but Arnold knew he led the other two in a private war against him.

He could see Eric's ten-year-old face now, white and fear-stricken, yelling at him, 'Don't hurt my mam. Please don't hit her. I won't let you.'

His mother had been in bed, and Eric had thrown himself between her and the arm Arnold had raised. He'd belted the child – he had no right to come into their bedroom. Then he'd thrown him so hard that his head had hit the wall.

Rowena had screamed, 'Don't hit Eric. Don't you dare lay another finger on him!'

Eric had run to her arms but he'd been looking at Arnold when he'd sworn, 'When I'm grown up, I'll fight you. You'll pay for this.'

Even worse, on the night Rowena had died, Eric's dark eyes had sparkled with hate.

'You've killed her,' he'd accused, rounding on

his father in fury just when he'd expected the doctor to arrive. 'You've killed our mam.'

It wasn't true, of course, but Arnold had never been able to banish that from his mind. He admitted to himself that he'd shed a tear when they'd found out about Eric's heart condition after he failed his medical for the Forces. It was a love-hate relationship he had with his first-born.

He asked Eric, 'Have you had a bad night?'

'Heavy, fires everywhere. A bomb burst the water mains in Birkenhead and they couldn't be put out.'

'Go to bed,' he advised. Eric should not overtire himself.

Arnold went upstairs to sit on his bed and drink his tea. Cicely was already snuggling down in it. She'd failed him. She'd not brought up Rowena's children as well as he'd hoped. He couldn't get close, couldn't reach any of them; he wanted to feel more love for them than he did.

He thought of himself as a God-fearing man, law-abiding and dutiful. He believed in doing his duty; did not drink, or swear in public, and looked down on men who lacked the self-control to do likewise. He wanted his children to love and respect him and follow in his footsteps but he knew Eric was leading them into all sorts of mischief and he didn't know how to stop it.

He shouldn't have hit Cicely, but there was an incompetence about her that made his hackles rise, a brashness that he'd never liked. And she had far too much lip and knew how to provoke him.

Arnold had to admit that if he had a fault, it

was his temper, but his family would try the patience of a saint. Gina had the sauce to tell him he was often grumpy, but if he was, it was the war and all the extra hours he had to work that made him like this.

He was starting to get undressed when the air-raid siren started to wail. Not again! He was tired out, past being able to help anybody. But all police officers were ordered to go on duty whenever there was a raid. He let out a string of expletives, pulled his braces back up and padded out to the stairs.

Gina was running up to meet him.

'Take Betsy down to the cellar,' he ordered.

'Why else would I be coming upstairs?' she yawned.

'Where's Eric?'

'He's gone to bed, like you told him to. He reckons the bombers should be on their way home by now. It's too near daylight for them.'

Arnold snarled, 'Eric can always think of some reason why he needn't do his duty.' The air-raid siren was still whooping up and down. It never ceased to send a shiver down his spine.

He reached the police station at Tranmere, where he was based. Most of his colleagues were collecting there waiting for orders, but this time there were no reports of falling bombs.

They were sent out on their normal patrols. Arnold could barely drag one foot after the other. An hour went by before the all clear sounded and he could go home. It seemed Eric had been right: this time it had been a false alarm.

It was dawn, the sun was just coming up into a

pearl-grey sky. It would be another fine clear day. Arnold felt so exhausted as he made his way home that he could hardly pedal. His bike kept swooping first to the left and then to the right. The road was swirling in front of his eyes.

He tried to work out how many hours he'd been awake but kept losing count. There had been five or six raids during the night. Wave after wave of enemy bombers had come over, killing and maiming, and causing yet more devastation. With the very heavy raids, since the beginning of the month he'd already worked more hours than he would normally do in a whole month.

He was a strong man, but even so, his strength was spent. His muscles ached with digging and trying to move heavy slabs of masonry to free people trapped beneath them.

He was glad to see his own garden gate and pushed his bike into the shed. His family were getting up, Cicely looking rather subdued. He was relieved that the slap he'd given her had left no mark on her face.

'I'm sorry,' he said stiffly. 'I should not have struck you. What have you got for my breakfast?'

She made him a bacon sandwich and a cup of tea before setting off to work. Then he went upstairs and drew his bedroom curtains. It was bliss to take off his clothes and get into bed at last.

Hannah was waiting at the gate of Highfield House for Gina to come the next morning. A workman she'd seen before came rushing past.

'A dreadful night,' he panted. 'The poor old

Edwardses copped it. Terrifying, isn't it? Could be our turn next.'

The sirens, bombing and ack-ack guns had woken Hannah in the night, but she'd managed to sleep in between the raids. She didn't know who the Edwardses were, but she walked up the road to see what he was talking about. Even though bomb damage was becoming a familiar sight, the wanton devastation never failed to shock her.

Gina came rushing out. 'We're late. Come on, don't stand staring or we'll miss the bus.'

'That was terribly close to you. Were your neighbours hurt?'

'Killed.' Gina's lip quivered.

'How awful!' It made Hannah feel sick.

'I was fond of old Mrs Edwards – known her all my life.'

'And their house was attached to yours!'

'I don't need it any closer. A bomb fell in Ottersley Road – you know, three streets behind us that way.' She jabbed with her finger. 'The blast took out quite a few houses. Next door took the tail end of it. I really thought our house was collapsing over us. The noise was deafening.'

'It almost did. Is there any damage?'

'A few windows went at the back, but Pa says the Government pays for them to be replaced.' Gina yawned. 'We were up half the night, were you?'

'No, not really. We spent the night in the cellar. It's been fitted out as a shelter.'

'That's where we go, but it's a horrible place. I never sleep as well there as in bed.'

'Aunt Philomena goes in for every comfort. She

had a double bed taken down, but then found the cellar steps too steep for her to manage. She said she was afraid of falling. The day we arrived, she said, "I'm staying in my own room and my own bed. If the Good Lord decides my time has come, then so be it." So Mum and I are more comfortable sharing her double bed there than we were in our Morrison shelter at home. She even has reading lamps and a little stove down there, so we can make tea.'

Gina sighed. 'You must have heard the explosion when the house next door to us caught it?'

'Oh, yes, it shook the foundations. Mum sent me upstairs to see if Philomena was all right. She didn't answer when I spoke to her. I was worried and stood in the doorway of her room, listening for her breathing, but she'd pulled her eiderdown over her head. She was frightened. Mum got up to soothe her while I made us all a cup of tea. We had a good look round afterwards to see if there was any damage but there wasn't.'

When they changed to the works bus, Gina went to sleep with her head against the window.

Esme heard what had happened to the Edwardses' house from Brenda. She could hear the daily help telling Philomena, her voice shrill with horror. To get here, she'd had to walk along Grasmere Road and pass the damaged house. Esme ran down to find out more. 'There's bomb damage in this road?'

'Yes.' Brenda wore a red headscarf round her head, under which the bumps made by her curlers could be clearly seen. 'Further up, one of the big semis on this side, number seven or eight.'

'The Goodwins' house?' Esme was startled. Had luck been on her side for once? If they'd been bombed out, she might have less chance of seeing Arnold. Not that she'd have wanted to see his family hurt, of course.

'No, the next house to theirs, the one attached to it. It blew out their windows at the back.'

'Oh! They can still live there?'

'Yes, their half of the building looks all right. I'm sure they can.'

Esme had hated coming face to face with Arnold Goodwin at church. His eyes had stared into hers, discomforting her, letting her know he knew all her secrets. He was the church sexton so he never missed a Sunday.

She told herself she was being silly; she mustn't think like that.

Arnold didn't sleep well. He woke up several times, shuddering at the close shave his house had had in the latest air raid. It left him cold with horror that he'd very nearly lost his house and family.

Every time he closed his eyes he thought of Mr and Mrs Edwards. He'd known them all his life and his parents had before him. They were part of his world. He'd had closer contact with many people killed in raids, but to have it happen to people he knew was quite different. He was flooding with pity and grief – and cold terror that such sudden death could happen to him and his family.

It was mid-morning before he fell into a deep sleep. When his alarm went at half-past twelve, his head felt fuzzy and his limbs ached with exhaustion. The house was quiet. Betsy was at school and the rest of the family at work.

With a shiver, he remembered his home had been damaged last night. He sat up and looked round his bedroom. There was a fall of soot in the grate and a thick layer of dust covering everything. He got up and pulled back the curtains. The glass in the window was broken and there were slivers everywhere.

He pulled on his clothes and went through the other rooms. All those at the back of the house were in much the same condition. He went outside then to look up at the roof. It was frightening to see the damage to the end gable of the Edwardses' house. If that bomb had fallen just a few yards further to the west... Arnold felt sweat breaking out on his forehead.

That fear released all the others that had beset him these days; a thousand demons hammered in his mind. He was scared stiff of air raids but dared not show it. A policeman needed to appear strong at all times but his confidence had ebbed. He felt a coward, barely coping with anything.

According to the roster he was due back at the station at two o'clock. He needed a wash and something to eat first. He thought it would help calm him to do what he usually did – fry some bread and a couple of eggs to go on top. He switched on the wireless, wanting to chase the worries from his mind, but *Workers' Playtime* was puerile stuff and he switched it off and started to list the damage to his house on the back of an old envelope. To apply for Government help with the repairs, he'd have to fill up several forms. Fortunately, he had a plentiful supply of those at work, but the lead in his pencil broke and he found he couldn't think clearly.

It came to him suddenly that he'd done nothing about the cash box he'd put in his saddlebag. Neither had he made an entry in the book the police kept for logging lost property; he'd forgotten all about it. The delay would be considered remiss of him, and Arnold could feel panic rising in his throat as he rushed out to the bike shed.

He decided he might as well find out if there was any money inside. If not, he might just as well put the box in his dustbin. It was the standard sort of cash box made of green metal. He shook it: it didn't rattle and it wasn't heavy, so there were no coins in it. It had a strong lock and he found it quite a struggle to force the box open. After trying several tools he took the claw end of a hammer to lever up the lid. The lock snapped at last and the lid fell open, cascading banknotes on to the shed floor.

Arnold straightened up, profoundly shocked. Pound notes were fluttering everywhere and there were bundles of five-pound notes done up with elastic bands. He'd only rarely seen a five-pound note before.

He slammed the shed door shut and stood looking down at the money. His heart was hammering: this was real wealth. If added to his pension, it would make a big difference to his family.

Nobody need know. He was fairly sure nobody had seen him put the box in his saddlebag. The money had come from that terrace of small shops, where nobody had survived, so its owner would be dead. Arnold felt paralysed, unable to move for a few moments.

Then, in a panic, he started snatching up the money and trying to count it before pushing it back in the box. His fingers were shaking, making him drop some on the floor again. He thought there was over five hundred pounds, but he wasn't sure just how much more.

He knew he ought to take it back to the station with him, hand it over and report how it had come into his possession. The trouble with being in the police force was that he saw how many people did feather their own nests and get away with it – even some of his colleagues. This would be almost too easy. That was what made it so tempting.

He'd never earned enough to be able to save. The house he'd inherited from his parents was the one thing of value he still owned. They'd left him some money but that was running out and he didn't expect to inherit anything else. He'd never seemed to have enough money to cover his needs since the thirties depression when police wages were cut. He had no savings, no other security and he was afraid that promotion had passed him by. He longed to get out of the force yet was worried about how he and Cicely would survive on his pension. Especially as he'd have Betsy to support for a long time yet.

As Arnold saw it, the hand of fate was holding out this cash box to him, a gift when he needed it. Of course he'd keep it. He'd be a fool to turn it in.

With a cushion of money behind him he could still his fears of what might happen in the future, banish the feeling that he was a failure, and even provide a few luxuries. He sat down on the stool he kept there. If he did hang on to the money, he'd have to hide it properly. He didn't want Cicely or Gina to get their hands on it. But dare he?

Where was the best place to hide it? The children had their fingers into everything. His own bedroom was the only safe place from them, but Cicely might just put her hand on it if he hid it in with his socks or underwear. He looked round – here in the shed? But all the children had bikes and kept them here. The shelves were open and laden with puncture repair kits, oil cans and other bicycle paraphernalia, as well as his gardening equipment. Not here.

Out in the garden, that was the safest place. Nobody ever helped him in the garden. He couldn't ask Eric, who must do only light work. Arnold looked down the length of his garden to the back boundary. It was a large plot, with rows of plants growing in straight rows. He was proud of his work. His eye stopped at the compost heap down in the far corner. That was it: he'd bury it under that. Nobody would think of looking there.

He set about it right away, forking the compost out of the way and then digging into the soil beneath. The ground was cement hard, the compost having always been there to soak up the rain. Arnold stuck at it; he'd had plenty of practice at digging recently.

When he had a deep enough hole, he went back

to the shed to get the cash box. He couldn't resist opening it again to let his eyes linger over the mass of banknotes. This hoard would give him security and allow him to do all sorts of things once the war was over.

It occurred to him then that it wouldn't be easy to get at it again, that he'd need to wait until all the family were out of the way. And he'd need fine weather; the neighbours might get ideas if he was seen digging up his garden on a wet day. Not that he meant to fritter the cash away. This was his nest egg for retirement. It was no good expecting Eric and Gina to help him when he was too old to work.

He might need just a few pounds from time to time. He took out a handful of notes. It made sense to keep some more easily to hand. He looked along the shelves in the shed until his eyes settled on a cocoa tin he'd brought out a week or so ago, thinking it might come in useful to keep nails in.

He prised it open. It was shiny inside and still smelled strongly of cocoa. Hurriedly, he pressed the handful of pound notes into it, then added a second. He would think of this as his current account. The larger amount in the cash box would be his deposit account. He took that back to the compost heap, keeping it carefully under his jacket. He felt much safer once he'd forked the garden rubbish back on top of it. It would be safe there for years.

Back in the shed he thought again about the cocoa tin. He couldn't risk leaving it there. He glanced at his watch and was surprised to find it was almost time for him to leave for work. He had several large plant pots upturned round the back of his shed. Underneath one, he scraped back the soil far enough to cover the tin and let the plant pot fall back in place. There was rank grass growing all round it, and it looked as though it hadn't been disturbed in years. It would be easy enough to put his hand on that if he needed it. Nobody would be able to see what he was doing behind his shed.

Seconds later, he was panicking again in case he was late. He shot back indoors to get his tunic and helmet.

CHAPTER FIVE

Eric got out of bed and yawned. He felt much better; his sore throat had gone and he could see his sick leave as an unexpected holiday. It was after midday and he'd enjoyed a lazy morning, dozing and reading in bed.

It had been a dreadful night. He'd gone to do his fire-watching stint and pinpointed the start of several fires, only to hear there was no water to put them out. He'd felt the frustration just as the firemen had. When the all clear sounded, he'd come home, only to find the house adjoining them had been hit. He'd helped dig the Edwardses out. To know they'd both been killed made him feel that all their lives were hanging by a thread.

He hadn't realised at first that Gina was digging too. Afterwards, it had taken him a while to calm her down. She'd had the shakes, poor kid.

Leslie had woken him when he'd got up to go to work and Eric had dragged himself down to the kitchen. Leslie had started in the Acme Dry-Cleaning Centre at the bottom of Bedford Road when he'd left school and liked the work. He could cycle there in five or six minutes, and Harry Oldshaw, the manager, maintained a relaxed and happy atmosphere in the shop.

Eric had dropped in from time to time to see his brother and had become friendly with Harry.

He thought him a great guy who knew how to put his hand on anything he wanted.

Eric had had breakfast with Leslie and then returned to his bed and gone back to sleep. He knew Pa had come home and was on the two-till-ten shift. He'd found the easiest way to cope with Pa was to keep out of his way, and he decided to stay where he was until Pa went back to work.

Eric knew now that Pa was getting up – he was banging about in the bathroom. He heard the back door slam, though his clock told him it was too early for Pa to be going to work. He got up and went to the window, seeing for the first time that it had been badly cracked in the night but the crisscrossed paper was holding the glass in place. He peered out between the curtains. There was a good view of the back garden from his second-floor bedroom.

Pa was out gardening and that surprised him. After what must have been a busy night, Pa usually spent all the time he could in bed. He never stopped complaining about the long hours he had to work and his lack of time off.

Eric could see his father working on his compost heap, but every so often he stopped and looked round in a somewhat furtive manner. Eric moved back into his room, watching through the slit between his curtains. It almost looked as though Pa was up to something, but no, he was strolling back towards the house.

Eric was on the point of going back to bed when he saw Pa returning to the compost heap with something under his coat. He guessed then that Pa meant to bury whatever it was, and it must be important for him to take this much trouble over it.

In the end, he didn't quite see what it was. Pa popped it quickly into the hole he'd dug and started to fill it in. He had something he wanted to keep hidden from the family, and by now Eric was almost overcome with curiosity about what it could be.

At a quarter to two, Eric started to dress. A few minutes later, he heard the back door slam again and he rushed down to Gina's bedroom, which was at the front of the house on the floor below.

Pa pushed his bike down to the gate and pedalled off. Eric knew then that he had the house to himself until Betsy came home from school.

He'd meant to cut himself a sandwich, but decided to see what Pa had buried first. Pa had left his Wellingtons, now heavily encrusted with damp soil, just inside the back door. Eric pushed his feet into them. In the shed, he found the garden fork Pa had used and took that down the garden with him.

It was an easy job, since Pa had loosened up the soil. Within a few minutes, his fork grated on metal. Eric bent to sweep the soil from it and saw a cash box. If this belonged to his father, he'd never seen it before. He pulled on the handle to get it out and the lid swung up. He gasped when he saw it was full of banknotes. He staggered back and stood staring at them. Eric could hardly believe what he was seeing. There must be several hundred pounds here!

He gripped the sides of the box and yanked it

out. The lock had been forced open and damaged. It looked as though Pa must have done that!

He could feel himself quivering with shock. He'd thought Pa was honest! A stalwart of the Church, he upheld the law and did his duty. He was a police officer, for heaven's sake!

Pa was always lecturing him on integrity and moral fibre. He kept going on at him for quite minor misdemeanours, pointing out that he would never take such liberties. Not that Eric had ever stolen money on this scale – he'd never had the chance. He'd never seen so much money collected in one place before.

If he hadn't seen Pa bury this with his own eyes, he wouldn't believe he could have done it. Pa was so stiff and self-righteous, so easily disgusted by other people's failings. Eric felt utterly dumbfounded. He'd have sworn Pa was as honest as the day was long. Pa thought of himself as being whiter than white, but it seemed he did bend the rules when it was to his advantage.

If he left this money where it was, Eric guessed he'd see nothing of it. Pa would not steal to benefit him, Gina or Leslie. He'd spend it on himself and possibly Betsy. He doubted Cicely would get much of a look-in either.

Eric knew he couldn't stand up to Pa's filthy temper. These days he watched his tongue, was careful not to rile his father and showed more deference than he felt in order to placate him. His war with Pa was fought largely in underground battles. To remove the money Pa had stolen was an idea that really appealed to him. Pa would have no idea who had taken it.

Suddenly Eric pushed the soil back into the empty hole, stamping it down and tossing the compost back over it. He meant to find a better place to hide the box, somewhere where Pa wouldn't be able to get it back.

He was careful to put Pa's fork and Wellingtons back exactly where he'd found them. It was starting to rain, a heavy shower, perfect weather for his purpose. There'd be no sign that anything had been disturbed after this.

He went upstairs to his bedroom, tipped the contents of the box out on his bed, and counted it. There was a prodigious amount of money. He found an old pillowcase and stuffed the notes in, then hid it under his bed.

He decided to get himself something to eat and then take a walk and get rid of the cash box. He hid it inside a brown paper carrier bag and walked down to the promenade, thinking he could pitch it into the Mersey mud. Nobody would think anything of it if they saw it there. There was all sorts of flotsam and jetsam along the tide line, especially since the bombing had started, and there'd be even more now a ferry boat had been sunk on its moorings.

It started to rain again. There was hardly anybody about, but it was high tide. Eric feared that if he threw the box in here, it would be left high and dry on the stones as the tide receded. It would be better if he could get it further out into the river. He looked at the pier.

The ferry service from Rock Ferry had been discontinued since just before the war. There were notices forbidding access to the pier, saying it was no longer safe. A barrier had been placed across the entrance but Eric leaned against it and moved it far enough to squeeze himself through to the pier.

The ferry buildings would shield him from view of anyone on land until he got some way along, but he could be seen from the river and it was busy with shipping. Eric realised that the ships kept to the deep water channels, and would see only a distant figure. Luckily the rain was heavier now and cutting visibility.

He set off at a trot across the slippery timbers, now green with moss. Some of the boards were rotting and others missing, but to go where others dare not gave him a thrill. When he was near the end, he dropped the cash box through a gaping hole and heard it splash into the brown waves below.

Eric went home feeling exultant. Tomorrow, he'd open some bank accounts and pay some of the money in. Not all at once – that might attract attention – but a little at the time. He'd be paid interest on it too. He felt a rich man.

The following night there had been no air-raid warning by bedtime. Arnold put off getting undressed, expecting to hear the siren at any moment. He was exhausted when he got into bed. Cicely had been asleep for some time. All day remorse had been nagging at him, he hadn't been able to concentrate on anything. Now he felt overtaken by despair.

He was an honest man and he despised the

criminals he had to deal with for being weak and giving in to temptation. He didn't know what had come over him. Looting was theft whichever way you looked at it, and it was his job to protect those injured by enemy action from the further injury of having their possessions looted. Yet, he'd looted himself.

He hadn't intended to, but once he'd found the cash box contained a lot of money he'd been unable to help it. He couldn't believe he'd do anything as dishonest as that. He'd been too tired to think clearly; he hadn't been himself.

Once he'd seen the contents of a hat shop blasted a quarter of a mile to end up damaged and dirty in the ruins of somebody else's house. Usually, the goods exposed as a result of bombing were of little value to anyone – just the odd book, or a dented saucepan that no longer appeared to belong to anyone, but now he understood how tempting they could be.

Arnold knew he was tossing and turning. He woke Cicely up.

'What's the matter?' she asked, but she was asleep again before he could reply.

He knew he'd been very foolish. Could he take the stolen money to the station now; say he'd forgotten about it?

No, police officers were not supposed to forget things like that. He'd lose face. He had to appear on top of the job. Shame like a heavy cloak had been on his shoulders all day. He wanted to be upright, a pillar of society. How could he have been so stupid? What was he to do with all that money? He wanted to be rid of it. It now felt like a weight on his conscience.

He could never forgive himself for hitting Cicely either. How many times had he vowed he'd never do it again? And somehow the demons within him forced him to do it.

He went to church every Sunday morning and prayed for forgiveness for his lapses and asked for the strength to keep his temper. He tried to atone by helping to look after the church buildings and grounds. It was a job he felt he could do.

But nothing helped. He writhed in agony that he'd raised his arm in anger yet again. If the neighbours knew, they'd despise him. Philomena Wells and Esme Ashe did know; he thought Rowena must have told them. Arnold felt the heat of their hatred whenever they came face to face.

He loathed himself: he was unlovable, he was cruel to his family. He was thoroughly ashamed of himself.

The next morning, while he was eating the breakfast Cicely had cooked for him, she said, 'I need some money to get Betsy another pair of shoes. She could do with a new mackintosh too; she's growing so fast.'

Normally, Arnold would ignore such pleas. He gave her an adequate allowance for housekeeping and such expenses, and anyway, she was earning herself. But now he had plenty of money.

'Wait till payday,' he told her. 'I'll see what I can do.'

Cicely seemed quite pleased at that. Arnold felt it was one way he could atone for the theft.

The next time he was alone in the house, he dug up the cocoa tin from under the flowerpot and put the money in his wallet. The tin went into the dustbin.

He was more than generous to Cicely. He gave her three pounds extra on payday. She was delighted and sniffed at the notes, saying they smelled of chocolate.

When the vicar gave him some notices about a church fête and asked him to put them up, Arnold volunteered to help on the white elephant stall and added ten pounds to the money it earned. He felt much better after that, and Mr Osborne was very pleased and congratulated him on his efforts.

Arnold told himself he'd made amends; everybody was pleased with him. He'd been a fool to let himself get nervous and have nightmares about that cash box and he'd be an even bigger fool to give the money away. He'd had a crisis of confidence but he was over that now.

The money was safely hidden. It was his nest egg.

One morning a week later, Eric was shaken awake by Gina.

'Do me a favour,' she said. 'Go and tell Hannah I won't be going to work this morning. Pretend I'm ill – make something up, will you? Otherwise she'll come up here looking for me.'

Eric had liked the look of Hannah and welcomed the chance to get to know her. He felt cheerful. He'd recovered and still had another day off work. As he strode down the road he could see her waiting at her gate. The early morning light was shining on her fair hair.

'What's the matter?' she called as he drew nearer. 'Isn't Gina coming?'

'No, she twisted her back last night. She's going to see the doctor. Will you let them know at work?'

'Of course, poor Gina. Is she in pain?'

'Yes, never stops complaining.'

She smiled. 'Just like a brother to say that.'

'How would you know?' he teased. 'You haven't got a brother.'

'No, it's just how I imagine...'

'Actually, she can hardly move,' he said more seriously.

Hannah turned to go for her bus. 'Tell her I hope she'll be better soon.'

Eric watched her round the corner before returning home.

Gina had cooked him egg and bacon, and he sat down to eat with her. She asked, 'How did she take it?'

'Fine, she's a damn good-looking girl.'

'She's not your type, Eric.'

He rather fancied her. 'Why not? I thought you liked her?'

'I do, but she's ... you know, rather prim and proper. The last vicar was her uncle. She wouldn't like some of the things you do.'

'Oh, I don't know. Hannah likes you and you do bad things too.'

'Only because you egg me on. Anyway, if I want to spend time with Jim, it's the only way. But I don't want her to know about this. It's between you and me. Tell me again what I've got to say to the doctor.'

'Before you go, learn off by heart the signs and symptoms I wrote down for you.' He'd been to the library for her yesterday, and knew by now where to put his hand on the medical books.

'If you hadn't put your spoke in, I'd just not have gone in to work.'

'This way, you'll get more time off and no black marks from the management. And it gives you a bit of a kick to know you can twist the system, doesn't it?'

'I've got to pay the doctor, haven't I?'

'Here, he charges three and six if you go to his surgery. Have it on me.'

Gina smiled. 'You're not mean, I'll say that for you. Still, I think Eileen Harris is more your sort.'

Eric pulled a face. 'I'm not so sure.' He'd been going out with Eileen for the last eighteen months and somehow the affair was going off the boil. 'She's talking of joining the WRAC. That means she won't be around much longer.'

'Don't tell me you're looking for a replacement before she's gone?'

He smiled. 'I wouldn't put it quite like that, Gina.'

When Leslie and Betsy got up for breakfast and more tea was made, Eric took up a cup to Cicely, who was staying in bed. Last night she'd raved at him because she'd caught his sore throat and he knew how she must be feeling. He needed to build up some goodwill with her.

Eric had a lazy and enjoyable day. Late in the morning he took some of the money from under his bed and opened two savings accounts in the National Provincial Bank, one in Gina's name and one in Leslie's, though he hadn't mentioned it to them and didn't intend to. He was given forms they must each sign, he'd get them to do it but he wouldn't tell them what it was for. Then he opened savings accounts for himself, one in the Temperance Permanent Building Society and another in the Liverpool Savings Bank. He'd feed more into all of them from time to time.

He called into the Acme Dry-Cleaning Centre in Bedford Road next. His younger brother, behind the counter, serving a customer, looked up and nodded to Eric. It was a neat clean shop, with two long racks of newly cleaned and pressed clothes awaiting collection.

Eric gave Leslie a wave and went through to the room behind. This was larger and not nearly so tidy. The machine that did the cleaning was the focal point. It was churning noisily and giving off a strong chemical smell, which the staff tried to overcome with tobacco smoke.

A heap of garments awaiting attention had been tossed on the floor beside it. There was a large table on which clothes could be spread out and pressed flat, together with a standard ironing board and several irons standing on their heels giving out heat.

A small shabby desk was wedged into one corner. With his feet up on it and his chair balanced on its two back legs, Harry Oldshaw, Leslie's boss, was studying the racing results in a newspaper, looking very relaxed.

'Eric, how are you? Come on in.' He rocked his

chair back on its feet and got up to crash his palm against Eric's shoulder. It was his way of showing he was pleased to have his company.

Harry was some ten years older than Eric, shorter and more slightly built, with sharp features and a lot of straight brown hair in need of a trim.

Eric sat on the edge of his desk.

Harry was always ready for a natter. He had a failed marriage behind him as well as a daughter. His wife had taken the child and gone to live with her mother, and he'd gone home to his. Harry's mother lived a short walk away and he usually went home for his dinner. Eric wished his boss in the Co-op shoe department was more like Harry.

'A cup of tea?' Harry suggested.

Mindful of his new wealth, Eric said, 'It's near enough dinner time – how about a drink at the Coach and Horses?'

'You bet.' Harry took his wide-brimmed trilby from its peg on the back of the door.

'Just popping out for a bite to eat,' he said to Leslie, who had more customers in. Eric knew his brother would be envious, but he was too young to take to the pub and somebody had to mind the shop.

Harry always had plenty of money himself and always some scheme in hand for making more. Eric was fascinated by the sheer range and novelty of his ideas and the fact that they worked. He didn't tell him about the money Pa had hidden under the compost heap. Eric knew when to keep his mouth shut.

He went home afterwards and spent the rest of

the afternoon in the cellar where he had a dark-room. He'd developed a roll of film a day or two earlier, and today he pottered about printing the pictures. There was the one of Gina and Hannah Ashe he'd taken in the kitchen, but it didn't please him. He wanted a better picture of Hannah.

He went up to the kitchen to get something to eat and the poor image of Hannah niggled at him. Later in the evening, he returned and tried to enlarge it but the result wasn't clear. His exposure hadn't been quite right; there wasn't enough contrast. He was dissatisfied with the standard of his photography.

Later still, Eric was in the kitchen with Leslie when he heard a knock on the back door. When he answered it and saw Hannah Ashe standing there, he was disconcerted.

'How is Gina?' Her blue eyes looked into his.

She'd been in his thoughts since he'd seen her waiting for Gina this morning. Why hadn't it occurred to him she might come up and ask how she was? Be careful, he reminded himself. Gina doesn't want her to know.

He tried to appear sympathetic. 'Not too good. The doctor said she must rest. He's given her a week off.'

Hannah was showing genuine sympathy. 'I thought she might like something to read. I've brought her some books.'

Eric felt at a loss. Did she expect to be invited in to see Gina? Normally, he would have asked her...

He said, 'Would you be good enough to take her sick note in to her boss?'

'Yes, I'd be glad to.'

'Now where did she put it?' Eric retreated to the kitchen and she followed him in. Leslie was reading at the table.

She asked, 'Is Gina in bed?'

'Yes,' Eric said hurriedly.

Oh gosh, she was out with Jim Latimer, had been all day. For all he knew, she could be coming back up the road this minute. 'She's asleep. Leslie went up to see if she wanted anything just a few minutes ago.'

'It's on the mantelpiece,' Leslie prompted him, 'Gina's sick note.'

'Oh, yes.' He gave it to Hannah and took the books she offered.

'Tell her this Georgette Heyer is good.'

'Yes.'

'And tell her I missed her chatter in the bus and the canteen and hope she'll be better soon.'

Eric was finding the situation difficult, and wanted to bring the conversation to an end.

Leslie came to his aid again, saying, 'D'you want to see this bike we're building for you?'

'Yes, yes please.'

Eric was still uneasy. He wanted her out of here safely back in Highfield House before Gina came. It would be awful if they met in the road. There was more delay while they looked for a torch.

'Be careful,' he warned Leslie. 'There's no blackout on the shed window.'

He was embarrassed at all the white lies he was having to tell for Gina, and would have liked to sink down on a chair when Leslie took her out, but he had to follow them to try to speed this up.

Eric pulled the shed door closed behind them and stood with his back to the window. Leslie played the torch over the bike. 'I need to find a saddle for it, then it'll be finished.'

'It's just what I want,' Hannah said with obvious delight. 'And it looks new.'

Eric said, 'The back wheel is and the chain mechanism. The front wheel seemed all right. Leslie's put a new tyre and inner tube on it.'

Leslie was proud of his work. 'I've painted out the scratches on the frame and polished up the chrome bits. It was damaged in a raid.'

'I'm thrilled with it.' She clearly was.

'I've got a new bell to put on and a pump. When I get the seat, I'll let you know.'

When Hannah went, Eric used the torch to light her way down to the front gate. He waited on the pavement until he heard the front gate of Highfield House swing shut.

Relieved, he went back to the kitchen. 'She's a real smasher, isn't she?' he said to Leslie.

Sitting in the cinema, Gina could feel her heart racing. She found it hard to drag her gaze from Jim's profile. He had a large Roman nose and a determined chin, but with his short wiry build, he was not the obviously handsome heart-breaker. His hair was brown and nondescript, but he had an attractive cleft in his chin and his eyes were full of love when they looked at her.

He was holding her hand. Every so often he'd give it a squeeze and smile at her in the half-light. His uniform sleeve felt rough against her wrist. She felt full of love for him.

He let go of her hand, slipped his arm round her shoulders, pulling her closer. Gina sighed with satisfaction. He wasn't paying much attention to the film either, but they'd had to come inside when it got dark because it had grown colder.

Jim was a very serious young man, not at all like her brothers. He wasn't out for a good time; he wanted to do his duty, pull his weight and fight for his country. Gina was proud of him. He was the sort of man who was easy to trust, and she felt ready to put her whole future in his hands. She knew he wouldn't let her down – he wasn't the sort to let anyone down.

She hadn't told him about going to the doctor's this morning, pretending to have a bad back. He would disapprove as strongly as Hannah would. Gina had been nervous at the time, but now she was delighted that Eric's ruse had succeeded and she had a whole week to spend with Jim.

She'd told him she wasn't starting her job at Hooton until after his leave was over, but she'd had to go in for a couple of days of training first.

'That sounds unlikely,' Eric had chuckled, but Jim had accepted it.

After she'd seen the doctor, Gina had gone home to change into a smarter outfit and had been out with Jim since late morning. She'd suggested the fish and chip shop in New Ferry, where you could sit inside and have mushy peas with it and a cup of tea afterwards. They'd sat over the meal for a while, while he talked of facing the enemy for the first time.

'Mam told me the Snellgroves heard only last

week that their son Sidney had been killed. Did you know Sidney?'

'Yes,' Gina said, shuddering, 'to say hello, but not very well.' The Snellgroves lived next door to Jim's family.

That brought home to them both that Jim would be in constant danger once his leave was over. She'd been able to feel his fear, which was a hard edge in the back of his mind all the time. He said he was afraid he'd be found wanting, unable to do what was asked of him on the battlefield. She knew he must also be afraid he'd be killed. Not that he said so – he was the sort to keep a stiff upper lip – but she knew just the same.

Gina didn't blame him. She'd be terrified if she were in his shoes. She wanted to put her arms round him and comfort him; she wanted to protect him. She knew his departure would be almost impossible to bear. She wasn't going to think about it during this lovely week. But this was what war meant. Everybody had to face whatever lay ahead, however much they dreaded and feared it.

Gina had felt better out in the fresh air afterwards. They'd taken the bus to Thurstaston and walked up on the Common. It had been a fine but blowy afternoon, with transient sunshine, but they'd been able to get out of the wind in a small hollow. There was nobody about, Jim had spread his mackintosh on the ground and they'd laid down on it with their arms round each other.

Gina had thought a lot about love recently. She'd wanted to show Jim how much she loved him. He ought to experience the good things in life before he had to deal with the bad. She wasn't going to deny him anything. In fact, looking back, she'd encouraged him to make love. There was no point in withholding the great experience from him. She'd never gone the whole way before and he said he hadn't either. They'd sworn undying love for each other and she'd promised she'd wait for him however long it took.

Jim had treated her to a lovely supper in the Woodside Hotel before coming to the pictures. He'd said he didn't care what he spent on this leave, they were going to enjoy themselves.

Towards the end of the week, it seemed to Gina that the days were flying past and the end of Jim's leave would be here all too soon. The doctor had told her to come and see him again when her sick note was running out. She did that and was told she was well enough to return to work. Instead, she took two extra days off to squeeze every moment she could to spend with Jim.

The early days of his leave had been full of thrills and pleasure, but now Gina felt clamped in misery. She went to see him off on the train and couldn't keep the tears away. She caught the bus home, feeling bereft and scared of finding herself pregnant.

If she was, there was no way Jim could come home again to make an honest woman of her. She'd be on her own, and the thought of having to tell Pa terrified her.

CHAPTER SIX

On duty a few days later, Arnold Goodwin was glad to take off his police helmet and place it on the bar of the George Hotel. The helmet was heavy and he had a headache. He opened his notebook and placed it beside his helmet.

'We've had two complaints about you keeping a noisy house,' he told the landlord. 'Last Saturday night, around closing time.'

'There was a crowd of sailors in from a ship in Morpeth Dock.' The landlord looked fed up. 'They were just back from an Atlantic crossing – can you blame them? It didn't last long.'

'Three-quarters of an hour, according to the complaints. You had plenty of ale in?' Arnold ran his eye along the bottles behind the bar. Many were empty and there wasn't much in the others.

'Not enough. I took delivery of two barrels of bitter the day before.'

There was a pause while Arnold wrote that down.

'Can I offer you a drink?' the landlord asked. 'Whisky perhaps?'

'No thank you.' Arnold didn't drink. 'Police officers do not drink on duty.'

He stepped behind the bar to see how much liquor was kept hidden. There was one whisky bottle about a third full.

The licensee knew what he was doing and tried

to smile. 'For special customers. No law against that, is there?'

Arnold was not amused. 'I'm going to caution you against keeping a rowdy house.' He went into his preamble, which he knew by heart. 'Any further complaints and you may have your licence taken away.'

Out on the pavement he took a deep breath. He was feeling frustrated and out of sorts. Nothing was going right in his life. He now had to visit the Red Lion and the Wellington Hotel for the same reason. Then there was a woman living in Brassey Street who was having her Co-op milk coupons stolen from her doorstep.

All this, when he knew very well the war had opened up a whole series of new money-making schemes for criminals. The black market was flourishing in every district in Britain, including here in Birkenhead. And it wasn't just the known criminals who were getting involved. It seemed to Arnold that half the population was at it.

The police were being kept on their toes. They couldn't keep up with the imaginative ideas of those bent on making a fortune while times were hard. It stuck in his throat when decent young men were fighting and giving their lives for their country.

Arnold felt thwarted at being kept on routine duties such as these. If there was a pub brawl or a problem with stray dogs, it seemed to be his lot to sort it out. Occasionally, the police had to turn out in force on a case, and then he'd be the one doing the ground work. At a time when every pair of hands was said to be needed, Arnold was afraid he was being passed over. Perhaps he wasn't cut out for police work.

He'd thought much the same about the business he'd inherited. His father had set himself up as a funeral director and made a success of it. Arnold had been drawn into it as a youth, but had not liked attending to the dead. His father had always criticised what he'd done: he didn't handle the relatives with enough sympathy; his manner was arrogant; he didn't take enough care. Father had told him many times he was useless.

When his parents died, Arnold had inherited the funeral parlour and thus a means of earning his living. He still didn't care for it but Rowena had shrugged and said somebody had to do the job.

Few had much money to spend on their dead relatives in the twenties and thirties, and the income from it dropped. In 1933 the Co-op had offered to buy his business; he'd sold it for a pittance and joined the police force. He regretted it now. With the bombing, the funeral business was so brisk he'd heard they were using cardboard for coffins and everybody was making more money.

Arnold had never liked the large sprawling Victorian house he'd inherited from his parents. He hadn't been able to keep it in good condition and now it needed a lot doing to it. Cicely was always complaining that it was too large, draughty and unmanageable, and kept the main drawing and dining rooms shut up.

Arnold was glad of the large garden. He spent what spare time he had growing potatoes, soft fruit and vegetables, and keeping hens to eke out their rations. It wasn't a happy home. For Arnold, things were as bad at home as at work.

Today, when he got home and saw the squalor Cicely never bothered to clean up, he was enraged. He threw himself on his armchair and started to fantasise about how he'd make her pay for her laziness.

Cicely had never been such a good wife to him as Rowena had. He wanted to look smart but she wouldn't press his clothes, sometimes she didn't even do the weekly wash. He often had to put his clothes to soak in a bucket and stand it in the back kitchen sink as a hint to Cicely that she was neglecting her duties.

He rampaged upstairs to his bedroom to collect his dirty washing and saw a row of neatly ironed shirts hanging in his wardrobe. It made him feel despicable. Cicely did try.

Had she been at home, he might have hit her. What was the matter with him?

He would fight the demons in his mind that drove him to violence. He promised himself he would never hit any of them again; not Cicely, however provoking she was; not Gina, who goaded him; not Leslie either.

Leslie was weak and, like the rest of them, wouldn't face up to his responsibilities. Betsy, too, was going the same way. What could he expect when the older ones were encouraging her to give cheek and flout his authority? And her mother sat back and did nothing, letting it all flow over her.

Arnold shuddered. He was afraid for them and for himself.

Eric eased an old lady's gnarled foot into a shoe, laced it up for her and straightened up. He watched her take a few steps.

'No,' she said. 'I don't think so. They're too heavy. Do you have a lightweight shoe?'

Already she had eight pairs spread round her chair. They had very little else in her size. Eric turned back to the shelves, and asked himself if he meant to spend the rest of his life doing this. It was all right as a job, but it was leading nowhere and it was beginning to bore him. Mr Hornchurch, the manager, was sympathetic about his dicky heart and made allowances for him if he was late or took time off, but Eric wanted a more interesting job. He'd expected to be in the Army by now, doing exciting things.

He kept thinking about his new wealth. He could use it to start his own business. What he'd really like to do was become a photographer. He'd fancied a job in a photography shop when he'd left school and had applied for one, but Cicely had had a friend working in the Co-op department store and thought that would be a good place for him to start. He'd got a job offer from them quite quickly and Pa had pushed him into it.

'Photography is a good hobby,' he'd told him, 'but you need to earn your living. This is a first-class opening.'

Now Eric wondered if he'd be able to open a photography shop of his own. He'd have to wait until after the war, of course. Film and cameras were no longer being made for civilian use; shops selling that sort of thing had had to close down, but when they eventually came back on the market, there'd be good opportunities for someone like him. If he had enough money to do it.

'Hello.' Harry Oldshaw had come into the shop and was standing close behind him. 'Are you doing anything tonight?'

'Nothing special.'

'Something's come up. I've a friend who's asking for a favour. Meet me in the Coach and Horses and I'll tell you about it. There'll be money in it for you. Eight o'clock all right?'

'Yes, fine.'

Eric took another pair of shoes to the old lady and watched Harry leave the department. He reckoned Leslie had more fun working for him than he had here. With his wide-brimmed trilby on the side of his head, Harry looked a bit of a spiv. Pa had taken one look at him, and said, 'Don't bring that fellow to my house again. I don't want him here.'

'Why not?' Eric had asked, making a mental note not to mention he was Leslie's boss.

'He's a shady character, not suitable company for you.'

'Don't tell me Harry's got a police record?'

'As a police officer, I have to keep myself away from the criminal elements, and that goes for members of my family too.'

Since he'd watched his father bury that money, Eric was beginning to see him in a new light. Up till then, he'd taken Pa's high opinion of himself as being an accurate one. Now he'd put his mind to it, Eric began to think that Pa had made a mess of his life. He'd been left a business by Grandpa.

Eric saw that as a marvellous inheritance, a huge advantage to be given, but Pa had sold it off instead of working at it. He gave up too easily. In his estimation, Pa was a failure.

Eric wondered how soon he'd find out his money was missing. He'd had no compunction about taking it. He knew he'd left no clues and he'd told no one, not even Gina. Pa had had the upper hand for far too long, and he'd let them all know he had it. This would even things up.

As children, Gina and Leslie had been frightened of him, and Eric had had difficulty standing up to him. Since he'd grown up, it had become a power struggle, but Eric reckoned *he'd* got the upper hand now. Theirs was not a happy family and hadn't been since their mother had died.

He was glad to be going out for a drink tonight. It made a change, and what Harry had said about there being money in it for him had intrigued him.

When he arrived at the Coach and Horses, he saw Harry up at the bar with a pint in front of him.

'What's all this about then?' he asked.

Harry insisted on buying a pint for Eric, then took him to a seat in the corner.

'It's like this,' he said, moving closer to him. 'I know a man who doesn't want to be called up. He's willing to pay you to impersonate him when he goes for his medical exam.'

'What?'

'He gives you his papers and you pretend to be him. With your dicky heart you'll be found unfit and he's off the hook. What d'you reckon?'

Eric smiled. 'Could be a bit of fun, couldn't it?'

'As long as you aren't rumbled,' Harry sniggered.

'I'd be careful. Is that how you've managed to avoid it? I mean, there aren't many men of your age doing their own thing, are there? Dry-cleaning is hardly a reserved occupation.'

Harry grinned at him. 'No. The Forces don't want men who are convicted of such things as burglary. I know of some who go out to steal and plan to be caught. They reckon three months in borstal is better than fighting out the war.'

'Is that what you did?'

'I got three months inside, but I didn't deliberately seek it. The bobbies made a mistake, got it all wrong. I was innocent, but I'm not complaining now.'

Eric went to the bar to get two more pints, though it was weak stuff and tasted as though it had been watered.

'Why doesn't your friend do that then?' he asked when he came back. 'He wouldn't have to pay anybody, would he?'

'It leaves a blot on the character, Eric. May spoil a career. A dicky heart now – that would bring him sympathy, and if he doesn't moan about it, he's thought to be brave. If he puts himself out to do a bit of war work, he's thought a ruddy marvel. Some reckon that's worth paying for. He's offering twenty quid – will you do it?'

'Yes, but perhaps you should tell him my price is twenty-five.'

'You're learning.' Harry sniggered into his beer. 'I think he'll cough up, and maybe you could ask for expenses too. You'll have to get yourself to Bootle.'

'When is it?'

'His appointment is this Thursday. This is what you have to do...'

Eric walked home slowly in a pensive mood, dreaming of riches. Real wealth might be possible. He'd be a fool not to jump at a chance like this. He'd hang on to all the money he could; the war was making it difficult to spend much now anyway. No point in buying a house when they were being bombed left, right and centre, but afterwards, there'd be big opportunities.

He'd set himself up in a nice business and a good house, perhaps retire at forty. He had to accept that, with his dicky heart, he might not live to a ripe old age, but he was going to forget the problems with his health. He felt fine and was going to enjoy his life, have the best time he could. He was going to do things very differently from Pa.

On Thursday morning, Eric got up, ate some toast and left the house at the time he usually went to work. He always left before Betsy went to school, and he didn't want to be around today and have her asking awkward questions.

He caught the same bus into Birkenhead that he usually took to work, but stayed on to the Woodside terminus. There he took the ferry across to Liverpool. It was crowded with office workers circling round the deck to get a little exercise during the ten-minute crossing. Eric sat and watched them and the gulls following the boat.

At the Pierhead, he took another bus out to Bootle on the west side of the city. He was enjoying himself. This trip out made a nice change from the monotony of the Co-op shoe department. He thought of Hannah as the bus rattled through unfamiliar streets. He'd never met a girl he fancied so much. He'd asked her if she would go to the pictures with him on Saturday night.

She'd said her mother didn't like her going out to such places, not while they were having so many air raids.

'It would worry her stiff. Did you hear there was a direct hit on a cinema in Liverpool the other night?'

He had – it had made the headlines in the local papers. 'We'll leave it for a while then?' he'd said. 'Perhaps when things get better?'

'Yes, that would be best.'

She'd smiled and Eric counted that as a show of willingness that one day she would. He'd keep on at her.

The conductor caught his eye. 'Your stop,' he said.

Eric had asked to be put down at the top of Balfour Road. He'd never been to this part of the city before. He got off and stood looking round for a moment, counting the trip as something of an adventure. Then he got out the instructions he'd been sent and read them again.

'Go round the corner and turn left. Fifty yards down on your left, find the Brown Cow Milk Bar.' John Hugh Morris had written that he'd be sitting in the café window.

Eric found the milk bar without any trouble; it

was in a suburban shopping parade, a shabby place converted from a small shop. There were no customers in at all, but he was forty minutes too early. He walked on, looking in shop windows, bought himself a newspaper and read the headlines. When he came to a small branch of Woolworths he saw a short queue for sweets. He stood in line and bought fruit pastilles for Betsy.

When he went back to the milk bar, both the tables in the window were occupied, each by one man. Eric went in and stood at the door, trying to decide which of them he'd come to meet. The younger of the two met his gaze and nodded. Feeling the first fluttering thrill he went over to join him.

'John Hugh Morris?' he asked.

'That's me.' He stood up, a well-built youth with a healthy colour in his cheeks. 'What'll you have? Not that there's much choice. Milk shakes are off and so is coffee.'

'A cup of tea will be fine.'

'I'll get the tea. Let's sit at a less prominent table.'

The youth was turning to the counter when Eric asked, 'You've brought your papers? I'd like to have a look at them first.'

He sat down at a table in the corner, popped the papers inside his newspaper and started to read.

'John Hugh Morris. Date of birth: 4 February 1922. Age: nineteen.' He was two years younger than Eric was himself, but he'd get away with that. People developed and matured at different rates. 'Address: 17 Willesden Street, Bootle, Liverpool.'

Eric set about committing these facts to memory. Then there was the list of illnesses John Morris had suffered in childhood. He needed to be familiar with those too.

Morris returned with two cups of tea. 'I haven't filled in all the form, not the part about recent medical history. What should I write there?'

Eric got him to add rheumatic fever to his list of illnesses and dictated a line or two of recent medical history that would fit in with his own.

'I'd better sign it,' Eric said. 'They'll give me other papers to sign when I'm there.'

It was quite fun really, cheating the bureaucratic state. Not like cheating another person.

'Have you brought the money?'

'Yes.'

Eric accepted the agreed payment of fifteen pounds before the exam, and was pleased to see the youth had the other ten to complete his payment when it was over. It was all in used notes. Harry had told Eric he wasn't the only one doing this. He'd heard some men found clients who would pay as much as seventy pounds– 'But you have to charge what you think your client can afford.'

'I need to borrow your identity card,' he told John Morris, 'in case I'm asked to show it. Better to be on the safe side.'

Eric ran through the details he had to memorise again.

'They ask questions, like what is your job? Are your parents still alive? They asked me what school I went to.'

As he noted the answers, Eric could feel his

excitement growing. He could see this as his war work. Perhaps he and Harry could find other lads who'd be prepared to pay for this service.

'Where are they holding these medicals then?'

'The address is on the form, but I'll show you. It's behind here, a few streets away. It used to be an ice-cream factory, but they can't get the stuff to make it any more.'

Eric had heard rumours that it would soon become illegal to make ice cream anyway.

'I hear they're thinking of tinning carrots in there, but they haven't started yet.'

It was getting near to eleven o'clock, the time of John Morris's appointment. 'We'd better be going,' Eric said. 'It'll be safer if we aren't seen together when we get closer. We don't want to jog the memory of any acquaintances you might have. You lead the way, I'll follow twenty yards behind you. See you back here, shall I?'

'No, I'll wait round the corner for you,' John Morris said. He looked more nervous than Eric felt himself. 'Can't hang about in this milk bar for too long.'

It was a five-minute walk away. They left the shops behind, and now the street was bordered by warehouses and machine shops. Morris indicated that the premises were round the next corner and turned in the opposite direction.

Eric saw two uniformed soldiers standing one each side of the door and a large notice told him that Army Medical Examinations were being held upstairs. There were other men going in. Feeling a swirl of excitement in his stomach, Eric trailed upstairs behind them and found himself in a queue. A large number of recruits had been invited to attend at eleven o'clock, but he'd half expected that; it was what had happened at his own appointment.

When his turn came, a corporal took the form and barked, 'Name?'

Keeping his voice low, he said, 'John Hugh Morris.' He was afraid there might be somebody within hearing distance who knew the man, but nobody challenged him.

Eric had all his details in the front of his mind and reeled them off while entries were made in a ledger.

'Strip down to your underpants,' the order came. Eric knew he'd be told to drop those later. He could see the humiliating routine going on all round him. Men were told to cough and bend over.

'Leave your clothes over there.'

Eric hung them all precariously on the only peg available and joined the line of shivering men. Some had kept their jackets round their shoulders.

There were two doctors on the job, resplendent in their RAMC uniforms, one a captain, the other a lieutenant. Each had a corporal acting as his clerk. Eric had learned to recognise the rank badges. The queue moved along at a moderate pace.

When John Morris's name was called, Eric stepped in front of the lieutenant and could feel himself quivering with an inner thrill he mustn't show. He was told to open his mouth and a spatula was jammed against his tongue, making him gag. Seconds later a stethoscope was held against his chest.

'Deep breaths.'

There was a pause. The stethoscope moved an inch, then another inch, Eric noted the concentration on the doctor's face. He turned to consult the list of previous illnesses on the form.

'You had rheumatic fever as a child?'

'Yes.'

'You were in hospital? For how long?'

'Two months, then a convalescent home.'

The stethoscope clamped back on his chest. 'Are you well now?'

'Yes, sir.'

Eric was exultant. Things were going according to plan. It would never do if the doctor failed to pick up his condition. He wouldn't get paid and John Morris would be in the Army.

'Stay here a moment.'

Eric was pushed to the head of the queue waiting to be examined by the captain. They whispered together. It seemed he merited a second opinion. The captain examined him, looking grave.

'What work do you do?'

'Accounts clerk, sir.'

'Mmm. The illness you've had has damaged your heart. See your doctor about it.'

Eric did his best to look taken aback at the news. 'What does that mean?'

'See a civilian doctor.' The lieutenant was scribbling hard.

The examination had come to an abrupt end. The corporal pushed a form in front of him.

'Sign here and again here.' Eric wrote the name

John Morris below the stabbing forefinger.

'Right.' The doctor handed a certificate to him. 'You can get dressed and go.'

Eric read it quickly. John Hugh Morris was assessed as being Class IV, and unfit for military service. The reason given was cardiac deficiency.

Eric pulled on his clothes in a triumphant haze. Doing this made a swell day out. He'd go to the pictures this afternoon and enjoy the rest of the day.

Gina was filled with relief on one count: she was definitely not pregnant, and she wrote to tell Jim. Luck had been with her on that, but he was now in the North African desert with the Eighth Army and she was frightened he'd be killed in battle.

Eric came downstairs and saw her listening at the living-room door to the news on the only wireless in the house.

'I'm scared for Jim,' she told him. 'All these battles with Rommel – he could be wiped out at any moment.' She followed him to the kitchen table and sat down.

'The awful thing is, I won't know anything about it, not for ages, not even when there's a big battle. With us three banished to the kitchen, and Pa hogging the wireless in the living room, I can't even keep up to date with the campaign.'

Eric said, 'I've been thinking for some time that we should get our own wireless.'

'That would be marvellous.' Just the thought of it made Gina feel she was doing more to keep in touch with Jim. 'I've commandeered the atlas, so

I can see where these strange-sounding places are.'

'I tell you what.' Eric beamed down at her. 'You do something for me and I'll ask Harry if he knows where I can get a wireless.'

Gina was suspicious. 'What d'you want me to do?'

'Ask Hannah to come out for a bike ride with us next Sunday afternoon.'

'That's all?'

'She'll come if you ask her. She'll make some excuse if I do.'

'As a threesome?'

'Leslie will want to come too.'

'She'll come all right. Leslie's just finishing off that bike for her – she'll want to try it out.'

'That's what I thought.'

'You fancy her!'

'What if I do? It's not that easy to get friendly with her.'

'I had no trouble.'

'Ask her, will you? If the weather's fine we could go to West Kirby.'

Gina did, and reported that Hannah now had her new bike and was keen to try a cycle ride.

Eric brought a wireless home and found a spot for it on the kitchen dresser. It was very smart, a Marconi, covered in black leatherette with chromium knobs and trim.

Pa noticed it immediately and twiddled the controls. 'This must have cost you a pretty penny.'

'It's second-hand,' Eric told him.

'Does it work properly?'

'It will.'

'Pa's envious,' Gina whispered when their father had gone. 'It's better than his.'

'Harry's found an engineer who'll fix up an aerial in the loft for us,' he told her. 'He's doing it as a foreigner, so it'll probably be Saturday afternoon.'

Leslie came in and saw the wireless for the first time.

'Have you bought that for us, Eric?' he asked excitedly.

'Yes, so you can sing along with Vera Lynn,' Gina teased.

CHAPTER SEVEN

Eric felt victorious. He'd got what he wanted. The breeze was buffeting his face and blowing through his hair. Beside him, Hannah was pedalling her new bike.

She glanced at him and said, 'It's a marvellous feeling to be out in the open air after being cooped up for days in that aircraft hangar.'

Eric felt he was pedalling hard, though Leslie would say it was a sedate pace. He and Gina were now some way ahead. 'Or in a shoe shop,' he said. It was a sunny spring afternoon.

'I'm so glad Gina's recovered from her backache.'

Eric watched his sister swoop round a distant corner, looking more like an athlete than an invalid. He should have warned her. Did Hannah suspect?

'Aunt Philomena says there's nothing worse than backache for making you feel miserable.'

'Gina let us know she was miserable. Very down in the mouth.' Especially the day she saw Jim off, Eric thought to himself. 'But she's young and healthy; she's got over it quite well. It's much harder for your aunt.'

'Leslie's done a wonderful job on this bike. It was kind of him to fix me up with lights and batteries too.'

'Those were Gina's orders. She's talking of

cycling to work. Will you do that too?'

'Yes, that's why I wanted it.'

'Then you'll need the lights. Gina told Leslie he had to put them on. She made him come with us today too, so if it breaks down he's on the spot to mend it.'

Hannah laughed. 'I tried it up and down the road on Thursday night when he brought it round. It was already dark and I was tired, so I didn't go far, but I knew it would be fine.'

Leslie had come home and told Eric that Hannah had shown him some ancient bikes stored behind the gardening tools in her shed.

'Aunt Philomena thought I could use one of these,' she'd said.

Leslie had thought it a bit of a joke. 'They dated from the turn of the century and all the rubber had rotted. I could almost tear the tyres apart.'

Hannah had said, 'I didn't want to. They look old-fashioned, with this curved frame and the stringing over the back mudguard.'

'To stop your skirt catching in the wheel,' Leslie had told her. 'Not worth refurbishing. They'd be very heavy to pedal. You're better off with a more modern frame.'

Hannah smiled at Eric now. 'I love all these country lanes. It's another world; seems miles away from the war and the air raids.'

'Gina and Leslie often come out for a spin. They know their way round. This little town is Heswall. We can go down to the shore here, but it's a bit of a pull back up the hill.'

'This is smashing,' Hannah breathed as she caught sight of the sun sparkling on the River

Dee with the tide full in.

'There's a café on a bend near the bottom,' Eric said. 'It's a good place to stop and rest.'

They rode down the steep hill towards it in single file and caught the other two up.

'We can sit outside here,' Gina said, leading the way to one of the tables.

'Lovely.' Hannah sat back with the sun on her face. Her hair sparkled like burnished gold. 'So much nicer than sitting at home with Mum and Aunt Philomena.'

Eric smiled at her. 'We do it quite often in the summer. You must come again. Come as often as you like.'

He saw that that disconcerted her. 'Why not? You work hard all week, you should get out and about on Sundays, have a bit of fun.'

The waitress came and Eric ordered tea and fancy cakes.

'We have only tea cakes or scones. I'm sorry.'

They decided on the scones, and they came with a tiny blob of jam to scrape on them.

'Why not come with us?' Eric pressed.

Hannah was looking round the table, no longer at ease.

'It's difficult being an only child,' she said slowly. 'I wish I had brothers and sisters. A father, too, would be nice.'

'You can always share mine,' Eric replied. 'You'd soon get fed up with them.'

'Course I wouldn't. What I'm trying to say is that Mum wants me to be with her.'

'All the time?'

'There's only Saturday afternoons and Sundays

now. With all the raids, she's afraid to let me out of her sight. She hasn't got over being bombed out, and she's still nerve-racked. She doesn't think I'm old enough to have friends of my own.'

'And certainly not boyfriends,' Gina smiled at her. 'You must tell her she's wrong. You're older than I am, and I'm engaged to be married.'

'You know what Pa thinks about that,' Leslie put in.

Eric saw a faint blush run up Hannah's cheeks. She was serious and wanted to explain why things were different for her.

'Mum brought me up alone. It's made us close. She's all I've ever had, and we've always clung together. It's been us against a cold world. I know she feels responsible for me, but suddenly I'm beginning to feel the boot's on the other foot and I'm responsible for her.'

Eric could understand that, as he'd always felt a responsibility for Gina and Leslie. After all, Pa seemed to think only of Cicely and Betsy.

Hannah went on, her face showing the intensity of her feelings as she sought for words, 'I want to help Mum get over what happened. Losing our home was a terrible shock to me, but it's worse for her. She spent years building it up and she's lost the place where she felt safe. She's always done her best for me, and now I want her to get back on her feet, feel better and be happy. I can't just go off with my own friends and leave her by herself.'

'She wouldn't be alone,' Gina pointed out. 'She's got your Aunt Philomena there.'

Hannah sighed. 'Well, I'm not sure how fond she is of Philomena. She can be a bit demanding at times.'

Eric could sympathise with her. She was thoughtful for others. The more he saw of Hannah, the more he liked her. He wanted her to be part of his future. Once this war was over, he could see himself married to Hannah. Not that he'd mention anything like that to her yet – he didn't want to frighten her off. He made up his mind to take things slowly, not rush her, but once her mother was over this shock and Hannah was used to coming out with the three of them, sooner or later he'd let her know how he felt.

When they turned into Grasmere Road on the way home, he stopped at her gate to say goodbye.

'Your mother doesn't forbid you to come out with me?' The thought had come to him on the way home that they would think he wasn't good enough for her, or that they knew of his dicky heart and thought he'd eventually be a burden to her.

'Oh, no, Mum doesn't forbid anything. She has other ways of letting me know what I must do.' Hannah was smiling at him. 'But Aunt Philomena does. I don't let that stop me, though. She has some very funny ideas.'

'Come out with us when you feel like it,' Eric said gently. 'I shall look forward to the next time. Don't let it be too long.'

Hannah felt totally captivated by Gina and her brothers, particularly Eric. He was showing an interest in her, he was kind and he was handsome. She was enjoying their company and wanted more of it. She knew Mum and Aunt Philomena disapproved strongly, but they were not telling her why. They'd dropped hints about the family, but hadn't given her any real reason.

Over the following weeks, she felt she was settling in to her new job and her new home, and mercifully, once June came, the air raids were far fewer.

Hannah thought Aunt Philomena was a tyrant and her mother was slower to recover from being bombed out because of her demands. But at least Philomena and Brenda knew how to obtain scarce services. With the help of a builder, a plumber, an electrician and a decorator, the upstairs flat had become more comfortable.

After working until eight, there wasn't much she and Gina could do before bedtime. It had become a habit for those of their workmates cycling to work, and who lived in the same direction, to stop for a drink on the way home. They'd chosen the Grapes Hotel on New Chester Road in New Ferry.

'It's just an hour to relax with friends before going home,' Gina said. 'Stop off with me. One hour won't matter, will it?'

Hannah knew crossing the threshold of any pub was enough to incur her family's disapproval. Aunt Philomena said, 'Young ladies do not go to public houses.' But as Hannah had no idea what the inside of a pub was like, she was curious. Everybody else seemed to like going to them.

She found the Grapes smoke-filled and rather shabby. The lads said the beer was watered, but the girls usually drank whatever pop they had available. Hannah enjoyed their banter.

'One good thing about this job,' she said to her workmates, 'we're well paid. Most of us have never been paid this much before.'

'But there's nothing to spend the money on,' they chorused, 'except an extra day off.' Her workmates didn't always turn up for work. An impromptu holiday was one luxury they could have.

Hannah went on, 'Another good thing is we're allowed two meals a day in the canteen.' Tonight, it had been corned beef fritters with chips. But after being on this grinding routine for some months, they all longed for a job with shorter hours, good food or not.

Gina said, 'If I say anything about the long hours in Pa's hearing he says, "It's your duty. Don't you know there's a war on?"'

'As if any of us could ever forget it.'

'It's depriving me of everything that makes life worth living,' Gina went on. 'I've none of the things I want.'

'Such as what?' Hannah asked. She thought Gina had lots of freedom at home and could have good times with her brothers.

'I long for really smart clothes, not this utility stuff. I'd love to have some decent cosmetics and French perfume.'

'A holiday by the sea,' Hannah said, 'that's what I want. A whole fortnight with nothing more to do than sit on a beach and go for walks.'

'I'd be grateful for enough time to go to the hairdresser's,' another girl said. 'I need a hair cut, and it's hard to find time to see a film. Oh, and I haven't been to the theatre in ages.'

'I've heard the carpenters saying that our

overtime might soon be cut,' Hannah said. 'We aren't so desperately busy, are we?'

'Roll on the day.' Gina's face lit up at the thought. 'And I'd like lots of lovely food with more chocolate and lovely fruit – oranges and bananas – but most of all I want more fun – more parties and dances. Hannah, what d'you want most?'

She thought for a moment. 'I want the war to be over. Then we'd have all those other things.'

'Yes, Jim would come home.' Gina sighed with pleasure at that. 'I feel as though my life is completely on hold. I don't know whether I've got a fiancé or not. I mean, he could be killed at any moment. I can't bear to think about that. And even if he survives, it'll have changed him.'

Hannah went with Gina to the pub two or three times a month. On other nights, Gina would often say as they turned their bikes into Grasmere Road, 'Come on up to our place and have a cup of tea. Eric told me to ask you.'

So, on one or two nights each week, she would pop in to see her mother and tell her where she was going. She didn't want to make a secret of it, but she knew Mum didn't like it. Then she'd go up to the Goodwins' house to drink tea at the kitchen table with Gina and her brothers. She liked all three of them. By now she'd met the other members of the family.

Little Betsy often joined them in the kitchen, but if her mother, Cicely, walked through the kitchen while Hannah was there, she gave no sign that she saw her. She had an unlined podgy face with a mouth that was dissatisfied and drooping. Her eyes were deepset in pits of flesh and seemed unhappy and half hidden. Gina and her brothers made no secret of their feelings for Cicely. Hannah could feel their dislike of her welling up and settling like frost between them.

Eric told her that their mother, Rowena, had died when he was ten. Hannah had asked why, and it seemed she'd had some heart problem too. He said Pa had married Cicely far too quickly, before they were over their loss and she hadn't tried to meet them halfway.

'If we did anything wrong, she called on Pa to discipline us. He ordered us to love and obey our stepmother, as if we could love to order. Her coming split our family in two.'

'Eric made us close ranks and present a united front,' Gina said. 'Cicely is resentful about having us in the house. She's not going to cook and clean for us. If we want anything, we have to get it ourselves.'

Hannah said, 'Your father isn't nearly so fussy about everything as my mother. And not so strict as my Aunt Philomena. You're allowed to do what you want.'

Eric smiled. 'Only because we've fought tooth and nail to do that.'

'But things seem more relaxed here than in my home.'

'Relaxed is the last thing it is,' Gina retorted, tossing her dark head. 'Haven't I told you about the endless rows Pa causes? There's always one of us in trouble. Every so often, Eric starts looking for rooms so we can get away from him, but there isn't a hope. If anything to rent comes on the market it's snapped up in five minutes.'

That evening Hannah went home feeling guilty because she'd done something of which her family disapproved. When she let herself into Highfield House all was silent, though it wasn't yet ten o'clock. She found her mother dozing in an armchair in front of a dying fire.

'Better if you go straight to bed, Mum. You work very hard.' Apart from her job at the Food Office, Esme was doing more and more for Aunt Philomena in the evenings. When Hannah had filled the hot-water bottles and made two cups of cocoa she took them in to her mother's bedroom on a tray.

'I've brought mine in to have it here with you,' she said. 'I hardly have time to talk to you these days.'

Then inexplicably, she didn't know what to talk about. As she sipped at her cocoa, her gaze went to the photograph on Mum's dressing table.

'I wish you'd tell me more about my father. You never talk about him these days.'

'He died a long time ago, dear.'

She sounded reluctant, and Hannah wondered why. Surely a loved husband and father would be remembered always? 'I know hardly anything about him.'

'There he is.' Esme waved towards the photograph. 'A handsome man, wasn't he?' He was wearing the uniform of an army captain in the Great War.

'He was fighting in the trenches?'

'Yes.'

'But he came through the war, didn't he? I was born long after that.'

His eyes were looking straight at the camera.

He looked confident, as though he'd made a success of everything in his life. 'What did he die of?'

'A bad cold turned to pleurisy, then to pneumonia. He seemed so strong; I didn't think he'd go so quickly.'

'You'd have had a much better life if he'd have lived,' Hannah said.

'So would you.' Her mother seemed uncomfortable, as though she wanted no more of this.

'For how long were you married?'

'Er – two years, dear.'

They'd drunk their cocoa. Hannah got up and kissed her good night. Mum was too tired to talk. She wasn't going to learn anything new about her father tonight.

When the shorter days of winter came, it was dark both in the mornings and at night, but Gina insisted that she and Hannah continue to cycle to work because it meant an extra half-hour in bed in the morning.

Blackout regulations required all bicycle lamps to be partly covered with black tape so the beam from them was pencil slim and lit up little of the road. There were many more accidents as a result of the blackout, despite the reduced traffic on the roads. Both girls were very careful to keep their eyes and ears open.

Hannah had been out for cycle rides with Gina and her brothers on several Sunday afternoons during the summer, but now it was cold and the days were dark, not the weather for cycling for pleasure. Gina was always pressing Hannah to go home with her after work.

She said, 'Eric says he hardly sees you these days.'

Hannah enjoyed going to sit at their kitchen table and drink tea with the three of them. She was careful to tell her mother where she was going.

Whenever she came face to face with Eric, his dark eyes would look at her with burning intensity. Hannah found herself thinking about him more and more when she was alone. He was pulling her to him like a magnet.

As for Gina, friendliness bubbled out of her. She confided in Hannah all her hopes and worries. Hannah was not as open with her, though she counted Gina as her best friend.

One evening, when Hannah got up to leave, Eric came to the back door to see her out.

'I wish you'd come with me to the pictures or a dance or something on Saturday night,' he said. 'It's my birthday soon and I'd like to do something for that. Anyway, a night out would do us both good and what's the harm in it?'

This time Hannah felt her heart race that he wanted to see more of her.

'I'd really like to, you know that.' She felt awkward; it seemed so silly. 'But it'll upset Mum if I do. Not to mention Aunt Philomena.'

'Would you come if I were to persuade Gina and Leslie to come too?' His dark eyes were pleading with her. 'Your mum wouldn't object too much if it was a foursome? She doesn't on Sunday afternoons, so why not on a Saturday night?'

Hannah felt heady with joy. 'Perhaps,' she said cautiously. 'Yes, why not?'

Eric's eyes were shining. 'I'll take great care of

you, Hannah. I'll pick you up from your front door and return you back safely. I promise you'll come to no harm with me.'

Eric went back to the kitchen table making big plans for a night out. 'Next Saturday,' he said to his brother and sister, 'you must both come. We'll go dancing. What about Reece's?'

Gina said, 'No, I can't. I told you about the American. I'm seeing him. On business.'

'Oh, Harry's friend?'

'Yes. His name's Spike O'Hanlon. I agreed to meet him on Saturday. It's all laid on. He said he'd take me to the Bear's Paw for dinner.'

'We could all go,' Eric said, full of enthusiasm. 'It's my birthday next week, so why not? Ring him up and tell him we'll meet him there.'

'I think it's quite an expensive place.'

'Don't worry, Gina, I'll pay my whack. Tell him I'll book a table for five.'

'All right.'

'Did he say he'd bring you back home?'

'Well, yes, he has to, to bring the stuff.'

'Is there room in his car for three more?'

'Yes, you should see it – it's enormous, big enough to hold a dozen.

At dinner time the next day, Hannah and Gina were sitting over a cup of tea in the canteen, when Gina said, 'You must know Eric's besotted with you? You keep saying no when he asks you out, but he isn't going to give up. Eric isn't the sort to give up on anything he wants.'

Hannah felt she knew him better than Mum

and Aunt Philomena did. They were wrong, and would have to accept that she was old enough to make her own decision about him.

'He's in love with you, Hannah. He can't stop talking about you. He's arranged a big night out for us all on Saturday to celebrate his birthday.'

'I'm looking forward to it,' Hannah said.

On Saturday, they had a marvellous evening, like no other Hannah had ever known. She danced with Eric, felt his arms holding her close. At the end of the evening, when Spike pulled his car up at the gate of Highfield House, Eric got out with her and the car moved further up the road.

Eric's arm was round her waist as they felt their way up the dark path. Hannah unlocked the porch door and drew him inside, feeling his arms tighten round her in a hug of joy. His touch sent thrills like sparks circling round her body, she felt truly alive. He kissed her for the first time.

'You're beautiful,' he whispered into her hair. 'I've dreamed of getting to know you really well for ages. You wouldn't let me near you.'

He kissed her gently all over her face before his lips settled on hers again. She thought his strong features handsome. Once Gina had told her Eric was in love with her, she couldn't help but feel attracted to him.

'We mustn't make a sound,' she whispered, 'or we'll disturb Mum or, worse, Aunt Philomena. She sleeps in this room here on the ground floor.'

'They'll both be fast asleep by now,' he said.

Even in the darkness, she caught the flash of his smile and shook her head. 'Mum won't be able to settle till she knows I'm back. I ought to go in. I'm afraid she'll be getting anxious.'

Hannah was torn in two, really wanting to stay with Eric.

'I've loved you since I first set eyes on you,' he told her. 'I want to spend the rest of my life with you.'

To Hannah, it seemed a miracle that he could care this much about her. She melted into his arms for one last moment.

She was bowled over by him, in love for the first time, but she was apprehensive about how her family were going to take the news.

Esme Ashe was on edge and felt miles away from sleep. She got out of bed to peep through the blackout curtains. The road was bathed in silvery moonlight and there was nobody about. The glitter of frost made the outside world beautiful.

Tucking the curtain back in place, she put on the light and gave her alarm clock a worried shake. It really was ten minutes to one. Hannah had told her she'd be late home, but this was ridiculous.

She'd heard a car drive up the road three-quarters of an hour ago and had thought it might be bringing her back. For the fourth time she went to her daughter's room to check that she hadn't crept in without being heard, but her bed hadn't been disturbed. Where could she be?

Before setting out, Hannah had said, 'I don't want you to worry. You've brought me up very well. You can trust me to look after myself from now on.'

But Esme knew that Hannah didn't heed the

advice she and Philomena gave her. She didn't believe that some people could lead her astray. She was only just turned nineteen and that wasn't old enough to stand on her own feet.

It frightened Esme to know she was out with the Goodwins. Hannah couldn't see that they might be a source of trouble – not nice people at all. Quite dangerous for her, really. She was too innocent to be out at this time of night. With her glistening blonde hair and fun-loving smile, she was too attractive to men.

Esme glanced at her reflection in the mirror and grimaced. She wore a thick pink hairnet tied over her head to keep the waves of her recent perm in place. Her brown hair was barely visible through it. Lines of resentment and mortification were etched only too clearly on her face, but she'd never been quite as pretty as Hannah was now.

It pleased her that in looks her daughter took after her, but there was quite a lot of her father in her temperament and that made Esme nervous. Hannah certainly shouldn't trust Eric Goodwin an inch.

Esme switched out her light and lay back on her pillows, feeling awash with worry. It was thoughtless of Hannah. She must surely know it would be impossible for her mother to sleep until she was safely home and in bed.

At that moment she heard a soft click from below. Was it the front door? She sat up to listen. Yes, that was the creak of the bottom stair.

Esme shot out of bed to switch on the landing light.

Hannah, shoes in her hand, blinked up at her in

the sudden brightness.

'Aren't you in bed yet, Mum?'

Esme couldn't stop the words rushing out. 'Where've you been till now? You must have known I'd be worried stiff.'

'Mum! I told you I'd be late and I'd be perfectly safe with Gina and her brothers. There were five of us together.'

'But at this hour? Everything closed down ages ago.' Esme's face screwed up with concern. She shivered and pulled her flannelette nightdress closer.

Hannah seemed full of remorse, and said gently, 'I told you it was Eric's birthday and we were going to the Bear's Paw for dinner. It's a great place – there's a little dance floor. It was a lovely, lovely evening. I've had a marvellous time.'

Esme could see she had. Her eyes were sparkling, her smile radiant. All the more reason to worry. 'It's a nightclub? You didn't tell me that!'

'I didn't want you to work yourself into a state.'

'Over in Liverpool? A dinner dance?'

'They call it a supper dance, really.'

Esme didn't approve of nightclubs. Hannah was too unworldly for that sort of place and she wanted to keep her that way.

'It must have cost a lot. Who paid for that?'

'Eric and Spike split the bill.'

'Eric can't afford places like that, and who's this Spike?'

'A friend of Gina's. Eric said it was a double celebration because well, he says he loves me, and I feel the same way about him.'

'Oh, my God!' Esme was shocked. This was

what she'd dreaded all along.

'I want you to be happy for me, Mum.'

'I can't,' she gasped. The same catastrophe that had overtaken her could overtake her daughter. 'Don't let him lay a finger on you, d'you hear?'

'He wouldn't!'

Esme gulped. 'You've been drinking,' she accused. 'I can smell it on your breath.'

'Mum, you like a glass of sherry yourself. I've only had one or two.'

'But how did you get back? The boats and trains stop running before midnight. I was afraid you'd be stranded.'

'Gina's friend is an American; he has a car and ran us back. I told you it was all arranged and that you mustn't worry. I mean, the Goodwins live down the road...'

'Gina's friend? Boyfriend, you mean? I thought she was engaged to Jim Latimer?'

Esme had been brooding on Georgina. It shocked her that she openly went out with other men. 'There's Jim fighting for his country with the Eighth Army and she's going out with other men. Where does she meet these Americans?'

'Through her brothers, I suppose. It isn't like you think. We were all together – where's the harm in that?'

'Who knows what it's going to lead to? Anyway, where does he get the petrol for jaunts like this? It's rationed, nobody can run you about these days.'

'I've told you, things are different for the American Forces.'

'He's stationed at that big base...?'

‘Yes, Burtonwood.’

‘That’s miles outside Liverpool!’

‘With a car, it isn’t far.’

Esme lost patience. ‘I hoped you wouldn’t take up with Eric Goodwin. You can see how easy it is to meet all sorts of other men through him. They could be criminals. There’s a war on, Hannah. I didn’t expect you to be this late. Of course I worry, and I think I’ve good reason. What if there was an air raid?’

‘Mum! We haven’t had a raid since last summer. There’s no reason to worry. You haven’t got over being bombed out, that’s the trouble. That’s still playing on your nerves.’

Esme sighed. Hannah didn’t understand. ‘Well, you’re home now. Let’s get to bed. It’ll be hard enough to get up in time for church tomorrow.’

‘Mum, I want to sleep in tomorrow. I’ll give church a miss. All right?’

Esme suppressed a shiver of vexation. She said to her daughter, ‘You know I think you should attend church regularly, dear. It’ll upset Philomena if you don’t. You know she likes you to come with us.’

She heard Hannah sigh. ‘Surely it won’t hurt to miss one Sunday?’

‘Perhaps if you went to evensong instead...’ she allowed.

‘I’m sorry, Mum.’ Esme could see Hannah squaring her shoulders to tell her. ‘Eric Goodwin is calling for me around three. I said I’d go out with him tomorrow.’

‘Eric Goodwin indeed! I thought you were interested in Robert Osborne? I don’t think it’s very nice of you to go out with Eric while Robert's away.'

'Mother! There's nothing between me and Rob. I haven't seen him for over a year.'

'But he wrote to you and you wrote back.'

'We share the same birthday so we sent each other cards. It doesn't mean anything. Tonight was the first time I've been out. I bet you went to parties and dances when you were young. Our generation is missing all that. We long to have a bit of fun.'

'Fun? There's a war–'

'I know, but I'm doing my bit for the war effort.'

Esme suppressed a shudder. 'It's the people you have to mix with.'

'Mum, they're good company. I enjoy working there.'

'But Eric Goodwin...'

Esme saw the light go out of her daughter's face. 'I'm too tired for this. I want to go to bed – I think we both should. Good night, Mum.'

'Good night, dear. I put a hot-water bottle in your bed, but it'll be cold by now. I do hope you aren't going to make a habit of being this late.'

Esme went to her own bed and pulled the blankets up around her neck, but she felt miles away from sleep. She was afraid for Hannah, afraid she'd find herself in trouble as she had. Hannah was getting too involved with the Goodwin family. She didn't realise that could be dangerous.

CHAPTER EIGHT

Hannah awoke the next morning to see her mother at her bedside. 'I've brought you a cup of tea, dear,' she said.

It was an effort for Hannah to open her eyes. 'Thank you, Mum.'

'It's half-past ten. You've had a good lie-in. As you'll be home to cook the lunch today, Philomena decided she'd prefer the eleven o'clock service to the nine.'

'Right, I'll see to it.' It was part of Hannah's routine to help to cook the Sunday lunch, the one meal of the week they ate together.

'It's almost time to put the oven on, say in fifteen minutes.'

'OK.'

'I do wish you wouldn't use that silly expression, dear. Very American.'

Her mother's lips were straight and stern. Hannah knew she'd upset her last night by telling her she'd fallen in love with Eric. She hadn't been able to help herself. Her mother went out, closing the door quietly to show further displeasure.

Hannah closed her eyes and lay back, listening to the noises of the house: her mother's heels running downstairs; the squeak of Aunt Philomena's wheelchair as Mum pushed it up the hall.

Their voices drifted up, agreeing they must wrap up, it was a very cold morning. Then the front door slammed and she was alone.

Hannah's mind was still whirling with the events of the night before. She'd only to think of Eric to feel thrills swirling through her. Mum didn't realise she'd spent the best part of an hour in the porch with Eric's arms round her.

Poor Mum – she was always tense, always on her best behaviour. Hannah wanted her mother to relax and enjoy the little things that were still available to them. She felt herself nodding off again and opened her eyes with a jerk. One look at her clock, and she shot out of bed and down to Philomena's kitchen to put the oven on. The meat was there on a plate, a joint of topside that Brenda had brought, smallish but far more than the ration for one person. The Yorkshire pudding batter was prepared, the potatoes peeled and the cabbage chopped in readiness.

The lino was cold to Hannah's feet. She ran back to her bedroom and jumped in bed to drink her tea. That was cold too. She had to hurry then to get dressed and get the meal on.

The next thing was to spread a clean starched cloth on Aunt Philomena's dining table. She set out the silver cutlery, table napkins and the large cut-glass cruet set, and made sure the fire had been banked up in her sitting room.

Back to the kitchen to make an apple pie and a milk pudding. Every Sunday was like this. Hannah turned on her aunt's wireless and found a dance band, but it would have to be off before they came home.

She timed it right, and was at the door to help get Philomena's wheelchair up the ramp and into the hall, where she unwrapped the rugs from her.

'Good morning, Hannah.' Philomena rolled her chair into her bedroom and unpinned her felt hat. 'You and I need to have a little talk. It grieves me when you don't come to church and it upsets your poor mother. We can forgive you this once, but I want you to promise not to make a habit of this.'

'Not a habit, no, definitely not a habit.'

'Your mother wants to think she's brought you up properly.' Mum was divesting Philomena of her coat and wouldn't look at her.

'She has, Aunt Philomena.'

'We want you to be a respectable young lady and not let the family down.'

Hannah followed her mother and the wheelchair into the sitting room. 'I'll do my best not to.'

They were in the original drawing room of the house. Much of the furniture was still here. It had a faded elegance, and was bigger, warmer and altogether more comfortable than their living room upstairs.

Philomena expected total obedience from both Mum and her. Hannah had learned that the best way to get through her little talks was not to put her own point of view, but today that wouldn't be possible. She had to spell out to her aunt that things had changed. Otherwise she'd accuse her of being secretive.

'Perhaps you'd pour the sherry, Esme. I do think a glass before lunch does us good.'

Hannah fetched the cut-crystal glasses. Aunt Philomena's wine merchant didn't let her down, even now when sherry was in short supply. She came from a stratum in society that had always had the money to live comfortably.

'You missed an uplifting sermon this morning, Hannah.' It was routine to talk of the sermon at this time. Usually, it was said to be good, but not quite so good as Uncle Fred would have given.

Hannah said, 'Aunt Philomena and you too, Mum, I want to say that I know the Goodwin family better than either of you, and I think you're wrong about them.'

'Nonsense!' Philomena let out a roar of protest and jerked her glass so violently that some of her sherry spilled down her dress. 'Now look what you've made me do.' Her attention was deflected as she mopped at her bodice.

Hannah was determined to have her say. 'I don't want you to think that I'm going behind your backs. For a long time, I've been making excuses when Eric's invited me out. I've always said no, and I've tried to respect your wishes and do as you thought best. But I like him and he likes me, and I very much want to go out with him. Last night, he asked me to go to the pictures this afternoon and I've agreed.'

'The pictures!' Philomena's mouth dropped open.

Hannah escaped to the kitchen to dish up the vegetables into china serving dishes. She'd left a stunned silence, and there was still no sound from the sitting room. She took the small joint to the dining room for her mother to carve.

It was one o'clock, the time Aunt Philomena decreed Sunday lunch was to be served. Her face was like thunder as Hannah pushed her wheelchair to the head of the table. After she'd said grace, she and Mum sat one each side of her, with acres of white cloth spreading over the length of the table, which was never used.

'I'll not have any member of the Goodwin family in my house,' Aunt Philomena said. 'I don't want that lad to come calling here.'

Hannah's heart sank. This was awful. 'I meet Gina at the gate every morning,' she said. 'I can do the same with Eric.'

Philomena's lips tightened, and Hannah understood that that wasn't good enough.

'I don't mean to upset you,' she said, 'but I must be allowed to choose my own friends.'

They were both giving their food their full attention.

'Mr Goodwin is a policeman and the church sexton,' Hannah went on. 'Very respectable, I'd have thought.'

'All the same, dear...'

'What have you got against them, Mum?'

Her mother wouldn't look at her. 'You know what I think of the Goodwins.'

It was the sort of thing they always said to mould her to their will.

'I'm shocked,' Aunt Philomena said. 'You must drop him. I thought you had more sense than this.' And she kept nagging at her until it was time for her afternoon rest.

Hannah felt churned up as she went to wash her face and get ready to meet Eric. She'd made up her mind that nothing Mum or Aunt Philomena said would persuade her to drop him.

She dabbed at her face sparingly with a powder puff. Her complexion was very fair and her cheeks had a natural pink colour so she didn't need much make-up. She applied pink lipstick lightly, just enough to enhance.

It was raining so she'd have to wear her old mac, which had survived the bombing. Getting her best hat wet would spoil it. Philomena said no lady would go out without one, but most girls wore headscarves or snoods these days. She bundled her hair into a snood. Gina had persuaded her to buy a black one.

'The gold of your hair will shine through and look lovely,' she'd told her. It suited her to have it drawn back from her face so that the planes of her high cheekbones stood out clearly.

Hannah was ready. She watched from her bedroom window until she saw Eric coming down the road, his step jaunty and his head held high. She called goodbye to her mother and ran downstairs.

Mum's voice followed her. 'Don't be late tonight, dear. Remember you have to get up for work in the morning.'

Eric was just lifting his hand towards the doorbell when she went out. She pulled the door shut behind her and shot into his arms. He swung her round the porch in a bear hug.

'Lovely to see you, Hannah.'

As they walked sedately down the garden path, Hannah kept a clear yard between them in case her mother was watching.

'I don't want to upset her,' she explained. 'But somehow I always do.'

As she closed the garden gate he took her umbrella from her and opened it over them both.

Standing well back from the window in case Hannah looked up, Esme watched her walk down the garden path with Eric Goodwin. Appalled, she dropped the curtain back in position.

At that moment, there was a heavy thumping beneath her feet, which made Esme jump. The sound was only too familiar and was the last thing she wanted to hear. Philomena was banging the ceiling with the broom handle she kept for the purpose. It was to tell her to come down, that she wanted something.

Esme guessed she'd seen Eric call here and Hannah go out with him. She didn't want to discuss it – it wouldn't help – but she daren't ignore the summons. It came again: thump, thump, thump. She ran down, but Philomena had already wheeled her chair into the hall to meet her.

'I'm shocked, Esme. I think he kissed her in the porch!' Her cheeks were flushed with anger. 'They were sauntering down the path as bold as brass. He took Hannah's umbrella with a very proprietary air and put it up over both of them. No doubt she took his arm. I couldn't help but see from my bedroom. They were laughing and chattering in the porch, disturbing my afternoon rest.'

Esme felt there was nothing she could say.

'You do realise what's happening?' Philomena boomed at her. 'You've got to nip this in the bud, before it goes any further. This could be history repeating itself.'

Esme flinched at that. 'I've tried to warn her,' she said. 'I did ask her to stay away from that family.'

'Then you'll have to be stronger.'

'Do you think I should tell her? Explain...?'

'No! Absolutely not! There's no need. Far better if she's kept in ignorance. A young girl like that should do as she's told. Forbid her to have anything to do with them.'

'It would only put her back up.'

'Better that than she finds herself in the position you did.'

Hannah couldn't keep her eyes away from Eric Goodwin. He was tall, with shoulders that were broadening out. She thought he had dazzling good looks.

'There's a good film on at the Palace,' he told her. 'I've seen it advertised. Let's go there. It's called *Casablanca*. Humphrey Bogart and Ingrid Bergman are in it. Everybody's talking about it.'

It was only when they reached the cinema they realised that the usual programmes were not shown on Sundays. They ran old films instead, and it was to be a cowboy film entitled *Desert Guns*.

Eric was dubious about going in. 'Shall we go into Birkenhead and see what's on there?' He believed in enjoying himself and having fun where he could get it in these hard times.

Hannah said, 'I don't care what it is. I just want to be with you.'

He laughed and led her towards the box office.

They found seats on the back row; the show hadn't yet started. As soon as the lights went out his arm came round her shoulders and pulled her against him. Hannah felt his lips come down on hers in a searching kiss. He could make her tingle. Her mother and Aunt Philomena would be heartily shocked if they knew she was necking like this in the pictures, but it was lovely.

These days, they didn't have separate performances. It was possible to go in at any time and see the show round – even stay longer, if they wished. They came out to find it was a dark, overcast night and raining hard.

'It's only just gone seven,' Eric said. 'What shall we do now? How about a drink? We could walk to the Coach and Horses in Bedford Road.'

'A pub?' Hannah stopped dead. 'I'm not in their good books after telling them about us. Mum will think you're getting me into bad habits.'

'But you go to the Grapes with Gina.'

'Yes, they don't like that, but they'd see it as more of a risk to go with you.'

'Don't tell them. I don't tell my pa anything that's likely to upset him.'

'Mum will smell it on me – the drink. She did last night.'

Eric laughed. 'You can have lemonade if you'd rather.'

Hannah was tempted. 'No, better not. Unless you want to...'

'No, Hannah, if you don't want to, we won't. What about a café? I'm hungry; I've missed my tea.'

Hannah had too. 'There's one there on that corner but it's closed. They're mostly closed on Sunday nights.'

'Come home with me then. I'll cook something for us.'

'Don't you have to ask permission before taking friends home to eat?'

'No, do you?'

'Always. Are you sure? I know I'm always round at your house drinking tea and eating biscuits, but a cooked meal – it's not easy to stretch the rations.'

'We keep hens so there's always eggs in our house. Gina and Leslie will probably be in.'

They turned into Grasmere Road, and had to pass Highfield House. Hannah hurried him past, thinking it looked rather grand with its chimneys standing out starkly against the night sky. Not a chink of light showed anywhere.

Eric chuckled. 'It's too dark to be seen. Anyway, we're doing nothing wrong.'

Hannah knew, as far as her mother and Aunt Philomena were concerned, just holding his arm would be wrong.

Eric took Hannah's hand to lead her up the dark garden path and round to the back door. Gina and Leslie were in the kitchen, preparing their supper.

Leslie said, 'Might have known you'd turn up, Eric. You always do when we're about to eat.'

Gina was all smiles. 'Hello, Hannah. Are you hungry?'

'We're both starving,' Eric told her.

'How was the film?' Leslie asked. 'I wanted to come with you, but Gina said I'd be playing gooseberry.'

Hannah said, 'It wasn't *Casablanca.*'

'They showed an old cowboy film instead.' Eric grinned at him. 'It wasn't any good.'

Gina was cracking eggs into a bowl. 'Poached all right for you, Hannah?'

Hannah studied the trio. They shared a strong family resemblance: all had big brown eyes. Gina's bubbled with life, while Leslie's were soulful and melting. Eric's eyes were full of adoration when they looked at her. Being with them was much more fun than being at home.

Leslie was cutting slices of bread while Gina filled the kettle for tea. Hannah watched them working together and wished she had brothers and sisters. They would make her home a far more interesting place. Within a short time, the four of them were sitting down to poached eggs on toast.

They never stopped talking. 'I'd like to have a photo of you,' Eric told Hannah. 'Let me take one – I've got film in my camera.'

'Not now,' Hannah protested. 'My hair's all over the place.' It was hours since she'd put her lipstick on and she was tired. 'I feel a mess.'

'You look very nice to me. No? Another time then, when you're feeling your best?'

'Yes, I'd like that.'

'Or if you've got a favourite picture at home, I could enlarge it, make a portrait to hang on the wall. I'd make a copy for you too.' Eric had already told her that he'd set up a darkroom in the cellar.

'Can you get all the chemicals and things you need?' she asked.

'It's difficult, but that photographer in Grange Road went out of business a few months ago. He retired, said it wasn't worth carrying on, and I bought a lot of stuff from him – tanks and an enlarger.'

Leslie got up to fetch a photograph to show Hannah. It had been propped up on a chair.

'I've just finished framing this. It's our mother, taken when she was young. She was with someone else, but Eric cut the picture in half and blew up the part that showed Mam.'

'And I coloured it,' Gina said proudly.

'It's lovely,' Hannah said. The colours were pale, almost like watercolours. 'You said you painted the colours on?'

'Yes, with a brush. You've got to have special paint, though.'

'And you can still get it?'

'Eric got some for me.'

'I don't know if I'll be able to get any more.'

'It's to hang on my bedroom wall,' Leslie said. 'If you've finished eating, come and help me do it. I've got some picture hooks.' He tipped them out of a jar standing on the kitchen cabinet. 'They're a bit rusty but they'll do.'

While Gina dumped the dirty dishes in the sink, Eric looked for the hammer, which was retrieved from under some clothes waiting to be ironed, then Hannah trailed upstairs behind them. Leslie's bedroom was on the attic floor and was untidy, with the bed still unmade.

Hannah's gaze came to rest on the dress hanging from the picture rail. She was surprised to see it in Leslie's room. It was the one Gina had worn last night.

'I love your dress, Gina. It really suits you.' Hannah fingered the hem of rose-coloured silk. Hannah had worn her plain grey wool with the white collar, which her mum had bought her, saying she'd get a lot of wear out of it.

'It isn't Gina's,' Leslie laughed. 'I brought it home from the shop.' Hannah didn't immediately understand. 'A customer brought it in to be dry-cleaned,' he explained. 'It's there to remind me to take it back in the morning.'

Hannah's gaze met Gina's. 'It isn't yours?'

'No, I just borrowed it for the night.'

Leslie said, 'Gina came in to see me at the shop and this caught her eye. She tried it on in our back room.'

'I couldn't have done better,' she laughed. 'Not if I'd gone to the best shops in Bold Street.'

'But...' Hannah had to giggle at the audacity of it. 'You shouldn't. It's somebody else's property.'

'They'll never know.' Leslie giggled with her. 'I'll dry-clean it again and give it a special pressing.'

'It was Eric's idea,' Gina said. 'I wanted something special, but there's nothing but utility clothes in the shops.'

'It's probably prewar,' Eric said, 'and must have cost a lot.'

'I couldn't afford a dress like that,' Gina smiled at Hannah, 'and even if I could, I don't have any coupons left.'

To Hannah, it seemed a daring thing to do, and so outrageous she couldn't help but be amused. But her mother would not be. She and Aunt

Philomena would be down mercilessly on anything like that. They were strait-laced and very proper. Was this the reason they didn't like the Goodwins? But they were wrong to condemn them for this sort of thing. It was just youthful high spirits. After two and a half years of war and deprivation, it wasn't possible to buy clothes like that any more.

Hannah couldn't stop giggling. 'Aren't you afraid of being caught? Afraid of Leslie being caught?'

'Oh, no. Harry was there; he said it would be all right,' Eric said easily.

He jumped down from the chair, carefully straightened the picture, then stood back and studied it.

'Pity about the wallpaper. It doesn't look its best against those cabbage roses.'

'Eric's got an artistic streak,' Gina said as they prepared to go downstairs. 'He's very good at this sort of thing. Come to my room for a sec, and I'll show you the original photo he took it from.'

Hannah had been in Gina's bedroom before, which she kept tidy. She took a leather-covered photo album from her dressing table and flicked through it.

'This is it.'

Hannah looked over her shoulder. The picture had obviously been posed. Two girls in the sort of muslin dresses fashionable twenty or so years ago, were sitting side by side on a fallen tree trunk. A small white dog was perched beside them. Woodland and fields stretched away behind.

'It looks like a painted backdrop,' Eric said,

scrutinising it too. 'It was taken indoors.'

'You've made it look so real in the portrait,' Hannah told him. She stared down at the photo, hardly able to believe her eyes, then took the album directly under the light. 'Who is this with your mother?'

'We don't know.'

She looked up, feeling shocked. 'Do you think it looks like my mother?'

Gina took the album from her to study the picture more closely. 'I'm not sure.'

Eric pushed closer. 'It can't be.'

'No, perhaps not, but it looks like her.'

Leslie said, 'That girl's too pretty to be your mum.'

'It was taken a long time ago,' Eric reminded him.

'Do you know exactly when?' Hannah asked.

He slipped the photograph out of the corners holding it in the album. 'There's no date on it, but I think in the early twenties.'

'Anyway,' Hannah said, 'your mother and mine – they didn't know each other, did they? It can't be her.'

'You could show her the photo,' Gina suggested, 'and ask her. Eric made a copy of this. I was going to cut it up and put it in a locket, but I've never got round to it.'

'I remember copying it,' Eric said. 'It'll be down in my darkroom. Do you want it?'

'Yes, please.' Hannah was eager. Her mother had very strong opinions about the Goodwins – perhaps she'd known them well. But no, she'd have said so, wouldn't she? She'd only known them as neighbours living in the same road.

Eric was looking for a torch; there was no electricity down in the cellar. He opened up a door in the scullery, and Hannah saw the stone steps going down into a black abyss. He put the torch in her hand, 'So you can light your way.'

'We're staying up here,' Leslie said.

The air seemed dank and was heavy with the smell of chemicals. The torch beam caught spiders on the walls and beetles on the floor. Hannah kept a firm grip on Eric's hand.

'This way,' he murmured. They were in a big square room with a washing line crossing it, to which a row of photographs had been pegged. 'I hang them up to dry here,' he said.

Hannah shone the torch upwards to look at them, but the place was pitch-dark and she cannoned into a battered armchair. She lowered the beam. The room was furnished with an old couch, a camp bed and a collection of deck chairs. There was a big table with photographs of all sizes heaped on it.

'This was our air-raid shelter,' Eric explained. 'And my darkroom is here.' He threw open another door and here the stench of chemicals was strong enough to sear Hannah's nose. She caught a glimpse of a dripping tap over an old-fashioned stone sink.

'You see, I've got everything I need, even running water. This is where I do my developing.'

'You do all that yourself?'

'Yes, it interests me.'

He led her to the table and started to sort through the prints. He had many portraits of his family and pictures of his house, as well as local views of the river and the Liverpool water front.

'I don't suppose you've any different pictures of that girl?' Hannah asked.

'Not here. I'd remember if I'd enlarged them. There might be more upstairs. I had an uncle who was keen on photography and we've got a lot of his stuff here. You could ask Gina to look through the albums.'

'These are beautiful pictures, Eric. I didn't realise you were this good. Wouldn't you like a job with a photographer?'

'I wish I could get one. I'd love it. But with the war … well, they're all going out of business. They can't get the film and the cameras. I'd like to set up on my own, with my own shop.'

'When it's all over, perhaps you will.'

'I'm certainly going to try,' he said. 'I'm fed up with the shoe department at the Co-op. Here's the photo we're looking for.'

'Thank you.'

Hannah was glad to get back to the light and warmth of the kitchen. Regretfully, she said, 'I ought to go home. I mustn't be late two nights on the run.'

Eric was failing to find an envelope large enough to put the photo in. He tipped biscuit crumbs out of a paper bag and put it in that.

'I'll walk you home,' he said and smiled at her. It was still raining as they ran down the road together.

Hannah unlocked the porch door and pulled him in behind her.

'You've got a smashing porch on your house,' he said. 'A marvellous place to say good night. And a convenient place to keep umbrellas and mackintoshes.'

Eric undid the buttons on her mac and hung it up. He kissed her and wrapped his arms round her in a hug.

'Hannah, I'm in love with you,' he whispered. 'Do I stand a chance?'

She could barely make out his face in the darkness, although it was only inches from her own.

'You know you have every chance,' she said. Tonight, she found tearing herself away from him half an hour later was even harder.

CHAPTER NINE

Hannah was fizzing inside when she let herself into the hall. As she ran upstairs, she heard her mother turn the wireless down in the living room and call, 'Is that you, dear?'

'Yes, Mum.'

She went to her bedroom to change her shoes, and looked again at the photograph. She didn't think it could be her mother, but who could say what she'd looked like twenty-odd years ago? She put it back in the paper bag and went to the living room.

The Palm Court Orchestra was playing on the wireless, just as it did every Sunday night. Her mother was knitting coloured squares to make blankets for the First Aid and Casualty clearing posts. She looked severe.

'I thought you'd be back for your tea before now.'

'I told you, Mum, not to worry about me. I had poached eggs on toast at Eric's.'

'He took you home?'

'Yes. I didn't see anybody but Gina and her brothers.' Hannah could see her mother was agitated. Both she and Aunt Philomena joined in the social life of the Church. They seemed to get on with the rest of the congregation, so why not the Goodwins? Her mother's lips were set in a hard, straight line.

Hannah asked, 'Did you know Eric's mother? A long time ago, I mean, when you were young?'

'No! What makes you ask that?' She seemed to be backing away.

Hannah took the photograph out of the paper bag and handed it to her. 'Is this you?'

Her mother gave a little start of surprise and slammed it down on the occasional table beside her. 'No,' she denied. 'No. Did you think it was?'

Hannah stared at her. She was sure she could see guilt on her face. 'Yes.'

'It isn't.' Her hand came out to pick up the photo again. It was shaking slightly. Perhaps there is a vague likeness,' she allowed, 'but I was never as good-looking as that.'

Hannah was almost sure that was a lie – Mum wouldn't look her in the face. Yet Philomena and Mum had always prided themselves on setting a good example to her. They rated truthfulness very highly. It was unbelievable that she'd tell a lie.

Hannah heard the familiar thump, thump, thump against the ceiling below. Her mother was scooping up the few crumbs she'd let fall from the paper bag. The thumping sounded again more loudly.

'Philomena wants me.' Her mother got up and ran downstairs. Hannah was left staring at the photograph. She didn't hear her mother coming back until she was in the room with her. She looked pale and drawn, yet determined.

'Philomena would like a word with you.'

That was like a royal summons. 'What about?'

'The Goodwins.'

Hannah followed her mother down, knowing

she was in for a ticking-off.

Philomena looked haughty. 'Sit down, Hannah. Esme, get yourself a glass of port if you want one. You can refill my glass, if you would.

'Hannah, we are older and have more experience of this wicked world than you. We are trying to help you. You must heed our advice.' Philomena sipped at her port. 'I watched you walk out with that Goodwin lad this afternoon. I really can't fathom what you see in him, an assistant in a shoe shop. What exactly is the attraction?'

Hannah was bristling with indignation. 'I like him very much, and I think he likes me. I find him very attractive – I find them all attractive. As soon as I met Gina–'

'Who, dear?'

'Georgina Goodwin. I was drawn to her right from the start. She's bubbly, good fun. We just paired off. It seemed a bonus that we lived so close and could travel to work together.'

'Hannah,' Aunt Philomena was at her most formidable, 'she's not a suitable friend for you. There must be other girls you could like. We're telling you to drop the whole family, including her.'

'How can I? I work in the same place. We'd still see each other every day.'

'A change of job, dear. I've never thought the aeroplane workshop suited you.'

'Aunt Philomena, don't be silly.'

'Hannah, dear!' her mother protested.

'Remember who you're speaking to, young lady,' Philomena thundered.

Hannah knew she'd overreached herself. Nobody was allowed to tell her aunt she was silly.

'I'm sorry, but you know it's war work and I was directed into it. So was Gina. We can't leave.'

'If you wanted to do other war work, you could get permission to leave.' Philomena's sharp eyes stared into hers.

'Perhaps. It would depend what it was. I'd have to ask.'

'Why don't you apply to join the WRNS? You were interested in doing that at one time.'

Hannah took a deep breath. She was finding it an effort to keep calm.

'Yes, when I first came here. You were against it; you said it wouldn't be wise.'

'You're older now,' her mother stammered. 'You'd cope better.'

'I'm happy where I am, thank you. I'm happy with the friends I've made. I don't want to change.'

'Hannah,' Philomena's cheeks flushed with anger, 'you must listen to reason.'

'You aren't giving me any reason. You're just saying do this, do that.' She handed Philomena the photograph she'd been holding all this time. 'Is this the reason?'

'I'll need my specs, dear.' Hannah moved them from the table to her aunt's knee.

'Mum, is there some connection between us and the Goodwins you don't want to talk about? Something you want to keep hidden? If so, I need to know now.'

Philomena was studying the photograph.

'It is Mum, isn't it?' Hannah insisted.

'No,' her mother said. 'No.'

Hannah saw her aunt take a deep breath.

'Sufficient for you to know your mother was very gullible in her youth. I'm sorry to say I think you may have the same trait. The Goodwins let her down badly.'

Hannah gasped with surprise. 'They let her down? In what way?' Her mother looked defeated; Hannah could see her folding up.

'She needed a lot of support from your Uncle Fred and me, which we gave gladly. I don't think I could do the same for you if you turned out to need it. I'm too old for that now. Drop them, Hannah. They'll be no good to you. In particular, don't go out with that lad again, what's his name?'

'Eric.'

'Yes, Eric. There's no reason why you can't drop him. Just say no, and don't go to their house again.'

Hannah stood up, feeling a surge of anger. She loved Eric, and the Goodwins were her best friends.

'Aunt Philomena, if you won't tell me what you've got against the Goodwins, I shall have to do as I think fit.'

She ran up to her own bedroom and started to get ready for bed. She knew Mum would think she'd gone too far – she'd seen tears of distress welling up in her eyes. Hannah knew she was mentally tougher than her mother: emotionally more stable and definitely more determined.

She put on her dressing gown and went to make some cocoa. They usually had a hot drink before going to bed. She knew her mother couldn't come up to speak to her just yet. Philomena expected help with her bedtime routine.

Mum came at last to slump on to a chair near the dying fire in their living room.

Hannah took the cocoa in. 'Mum,' she said, 'you let Philomena treat you like a doormat.'

She knew that was the wrong approach when she saw the tears that had threatened earlier run down her mother's cheeks. She put her arms round her.

'I'm sorry but I had to stand up to her. I can't let her dictate how I'm to live my life. Why don't you tell me what you've got against the Goodwins?'

Hannah felt her mother shudder. 'I can't. Philomena thinks it's better this way.'

It was only too obvious her mother didn't want to tell her any more, but her desire to know the truth was growing stronger every day.

The following evening, Hannah was sitting with her friends round their kitchen table, while Gina was making them laugh. She was telling them how she'd spilled dope on the hangar floor and everybody had stuck to it, when her father happened to come through the kitchen.

Hannah could hear him brushing his shoes in the back kitchen. He spent ages on them, during which time they fell silent. At last he was coming through to the living room. He paused at the table to whip away the *Evening Echo* that Leslie had been reading.

He ignored Hannah, but she studied him at close quarters. He was not a man with charisma.

'I do wish you wouldn't take my newspaper,' Mr Goodwin complained. 'I've been looking for it. Why can't you buy your own?'

When the hall door shut behind him, Hannah said, 'I think my mum's frightened of your father.'

Leslie sniggered. 'Nothing unusual about that – we all are.'

'Why?' Hannah asked. Her mother was going to great lengths to avoid him, and wasn't recovering her nerve after the bombing. Surely by now she should have put it behind her and be back to her normal self?

'Pa used to wallop us when we were young,' Gina said. 'Really thrash the living daylights out of us. If we get on the wrong side of him now he'd still hit us.'

Hannah shivered. She couldn't remember ever being thrashed. 'What, now you're grown up?'

Eric said, 'Yes, he's free with his hands. Loses his temper. He hits Cicely.'

'His own wife?' Hannah was shocked. 'Aunt Philomena would disapprove of that. Mum too.'

Leslie said, 'He keeps a birch to hit us with. It's behind the mirror over the mantel in the living room.'

Hannah felt appalled. 'Does he still hit you, Eric?'

'No, I'm careful never to upset him. I bend over backwards to stay on good terms with him. It pays off.'

Hannah tried to think. 'Would my mum and Aunt Philomena know he hits Cicely?'

'No,' Gina said. 'She doesn't advertise it. We none of us do. If Cicely gets a black eye, she's the sort who says she's walked into a door.'

'That's awful!'

'When I was small and he'd been cross with

me, I used to lie in bed and shiver when he came upstairs,' Gina said. 'I couldn't relax until he closed his bedroom door behind him.'

Eric said thoughtfully, 'I don't think Pa means to hurt any of us. He sees himself as responsible for us, and thinks we should follow his example, be upstanding in every way. When we fall below his standard – well, it's his way of disciplining us. He thinks it'll make us behave better in future.'

'What does Cicely do wrong?' Hannah asked, looking round at them. 'Why does he hit her?'

Gina said, 'Lots of things. Doesn't keep the house tidy, won't clean his shoes for him.'

'He's never satisfied,' Eric said slowly. 'Not with what any of us do. He's not a happy man. I'm afraid we all disappoint him.'

'What about our mother?' Leslie asked. 'Did he hit her?'

Gina shook her head. 'I don't know.'

'Yes,' Eric said, pursing his lips. 'Yes, I'm older than you two. I was ten, I can remember... I think she was afraid of him too.'

Hannah let out a gasp of horror. 'That's it then. Mum knew Rowena. She says she didn't but I'm sure that was her photo. She and Philomena must know he used to beat his wife and children, and that's why they're so much against him. And why they don't want me taking up with Eric.'

'In case he turns out like Pa?' Gina laughed. 'Eric would never lift a finger against anyone, would you?'

Eric shook his head.

'He and Leslie are gentle.'

Hannah said, 'You don't need to tell me that.'

She smiled at Eric. 'I've known you long enough to learn what you're like. I've made no secret to Mum that I'm coming here and seeing you all. It's a sort of family feud, isn't it?'

Eric was frowning. 'Except that Pa doesn't seem to worry much about your family. He ignores both you and them. I wonder why.'

Esme was crossing the hall with Philomena's bedtime malted milk, when Hannah let herself in.

'Hello, Mum.'

Her daughter was making for the stairs when Philomena's voice, thick with disapproval, rang out. 'Is that Hannah just coming in now?'

'You'd better come and say good night to her,' Esme whispered, and took her in.

Philomena was sitting up against a bank of pillows in the middle of her double bed. She said to Hannah, 'A young lady like you should not be coming home alone in the dark at this time of night.'

Esme knew Hannah had been escorted into the porch by Eric Goodwin. She'd heard the door click and the soft shuffling noises. It was only too obvious what they were doing there and it worried her. Tonight he'd only stayed for five minutes, but she knew it wouldn't help to point out any of this to her sister-in-law.

'I wasn't alone,' Hannah said, 'and I'm used to the dark. I have to cycle to work in the blackout.'

'Esme, a couple of biscuits, dear. Do we have Rich Tea? Keeping young girls like you at work till this hour, then having to cycle home in the blackout – it isn't safe.'

'We go in the blackout too, Aunt Philomena,' Hannah told her. 'There's a war on.'

'We all know that, dear.' There was no mistaking Philomena's irritation.

Esme was glad her daughter hadn't pointed out that she'd been up at the Goodwins' for the last hour, but she hadn't handled things as well as she might. It would be better if they left Philomena to sleep. Esme fussed round, moving the bedside light nearer to her and putting her book and spectacles within reach.

'If you have everything now, we'll say good night.'

She ushered Hannah out. As they climbed the stairs, Esme said, 'I think I'll go straight to bed myself and read for a while.'

'You look tired.' Hannah's blue eyes gazed sympathetically into hers. 'Shall I make you some malted milk?'

'There's only cocoa left, but yes, I'd like a hot drink. The hot-water bottles need filling too.'

'You get into bed, I'll do them and bring yours in.'

Esme felt bone weary. She undressed slowly and listened to Hannah rattling cups in the kitchen. She'd felt the bond between them tonight. Hannah had been responsive to her feelings, but these days she wasn't always like this.

Esme knew she ought to tell Hannah the full story, give her the reasons why she should avoid Gina and Eric. How could she understand if it was kept from her?

Philomena was dead against her doing that. 'Hannah won't respect you if you tell her the truth. Tell her to have nothing to do with the Goodwins. Make her obey you. You're her mother – surely you can do that?'

Esme sighed as she got into bed. Philomena didn't understand that today's girls were much more independent than in their day. Or at least, Hannah was.

She came in now and pushed a lovely hot-water bottle into Esme's bed. Moments later she was back with two mugs on a tray.

'Mum,' she said. There was something about her manner that warned Esme of what was coming.

'Tonight I got talking to the Goodwins about why you and Philomena don't approve of them.'

Hannah's good intentions, shining in her eyes, made Esme cringe. 'Better if you don't discuss such things with them, dear.'

'Mum, I'd like to clear this up. Is it because Mr Goodwin thrashes them? They told me he knocks his wife about too.'

Esme closed her eyes. Of course, she'd known about that. 'Arnold Goodwin is an evil man, Hannah. We've both tried to tell you that.'

She'd talked to Philomena about telling Hannah the truth more than once, but her sister-in-law was adamant.

'Better if you draw a veil over your sins, Esme,' she'd told her.

'But won't you tell me why?' Hannah pressed her now.

She shook her head wearily and was relieved when Hannah kissed her cheek and left the room, but she wouldn't be able to hide the truth from her daughter for ever.

It was a week later. Hannah went home after work with Gina and followed her into the kitchen. Mr Goodwin was standing over Leslie and Eric, who had an open photograph album in front of them.

Leslie had slipped one photograph out of its corners.

'Is that your mother?' Arnold asked, picking it up to examine it. 'Yes, she was a good woman, but she spoiled you rotten. You were her favourite, Leslie.'

Eric said to Hannah, 'Leslie's found another picture of our mum with that girl who looks like your mother.'

Hannah asked Mr Goodwin, 'Is that my mum?'

Arnold's intense gaze fastened on her face. 'Yes, Rowena and she were friends. It's Esme Wells, your mother.'

Hannah's stomach turned over; she felt sick. Why had Mum denied it when she'd shown her the first picture?

Mr Goodwin was pushing the picture into her hand. It showed a man too, with an arm round each of the girls. 'And that's your father with them.'

One glance was enough for Hannah. 'No it isn't,' she laughed. 'That's nothing like him.'

He raised one supercilious eyebrow and said, 'Take my word for it, he was your father.'

Eric said in a shocked voice, 'He was our Uncle Tom, wasn't he?'

'One and the same. The black sheep of the family.'

Arnold lost interest and scooped the biscuit tin

up from the table.

'Is this all that's left? It was almost full last night. You're like a flock of gannets, eating every crumb.'

Hannah could hardly get the words out; she sounded breathless as she said, 'Does that mean I'm related to your family?'

'From under the blankets, so to speak.' He tucked the biscuit tin under his arm and strode off up the hall towards the living-room fire.

Hannah was fighting for breath. She could feel beads of sweat on her brow. So this was what Mum had deliberately kept from her! It was the reason she didn't like her coming here. She was afraid Hannah would find out the truth.

She could feel her heart thudding as she jabbed her finger at the man in the photograph. 'He was your Uncle Tom?' she asked Eric.

'Yes,' Eric said. 'He was our mother's brother.'

'And your father?' Gina said. 'I'm flabbergasted. We didn't know. We must be cousins.'

Hannah shuddered. Why had Mum kept this from her? Could this be true? She burst out, 'Mum told me someone else was my father.'

'They couldn't have been married,' Eric said, his eyes soft with sympathy, 'your mother and our uncle.'

'But my name's Ashe. My mother was married.'

Eric got up and put an arm round her shoulder. 'This has come as a shock. A terrible way to find out.'

'What happened to him?' Hannah asked. 'Your uncle?'

'I don't remember. I know he came here a few

times, but I was very young. I don't remember anything about him.' Eric was frowning. 'I heard Mam and Pa talk of him, that's all. He died ages ago.'

'What did they say about him?' Hannah demanded. 'Why was he the black sheep of your family?'

She looked round at them, but they were all shaking their heads. 'We don't know.'

'Gina, do you remember him?'

'No.' She was biting her lip. 'I don't even remember seeing him. I knew we had an Uncle Tom, but that's all.'

'You can't remember anything your family said about him?'

'No.'

Hannah jumped to her feet. 'I've got to go home. Can I take this photo with me? I want to show it to Mum.'

'Of course. I'll walk with you.'

'No, Eric, not tonight. I'm too het up about this. I'll see you tomorrow.'

He saw her to the back door. 'I'll be late getting home tomorrow. Could we leave it?'

'Oh?'

'I've got to see somebody … late in the afternoon. Co-op business.'

Hannah was too distraught to think about that either.

Eric said, 'We'll go to the pictures on Saturday, yes?'

'Yes ... yes ... of course,' she agreed distractedly over her shoulder as she hurried away.

CHAPTER TEN

Hannah pedalled the hundred yards home as fast as she could. She was angry. To keep facts like these from her and let her find out in this way was horrible.

When she let herself in, she could hear Aunt Philomena's wireless. She ran upstairs and went straight to the living room without taking off her coat. Mum had their wireless on too. The nine o'clock news was coming to an end. The fire was almost out.

'Hello, dear,' her mother was smiling. 'You've come straight home tonight after all.'

'No. I told you I'd be going home with Gina for an hour. I didn't stay. Leslie gave me this.' She slapped the photograph down on the arm of her mother's chair.

The newsreader, Alvar Liddell's, measured tones announced, '...great damage was done. Four of our planes did not return. On the eastern front there has been...' Hannah switched off the wireless. Her mother looked dazed.

'Look at it, Mum. It is you, isn't it? Mr Goodwin said it was, and he said that man was my father.'

Her mother made a choking sound. Her hands were covering her face.

'Well? I've got to know. Is it true?' Hannah had to wait for an answer. In the silence she could hear the coals dropping in the grate.

'Yes.' Her voice was a whisper, she wouldn't look at Hannah. 'I must get a handkerchief.' She jerked to her feet and rushed to her bedroom. The photograph fell on the hearth rug.

Hannah followed slowly. Her mother was sitting on her bed mopping at her eyes. Hannah sat down beside her.

'Mum, I'm sorry, but I have to know.'

The silence dragged. Hannah could see sobs shaking her mother's body. She put an arm round her shoulders and pulled her closer.

'Who is that man?' She nodded towards the silver-framed photograph on the dressing table. 'You told me he was my father, but he isn't.'

'No.'

'Mum! I used to kiss that picture good night when I was small. When other girls spoke of their fathers, it was his face I saw in my mind's eye. Who is he?'

'A relative of Philomena's, a distant cousin. He died a hero in the last war.'

'He looks every inch a hero. Upstanding, proud of what he's achieved.'

'That's what Philomena said.'

Hannah burst out, 'To hell with Philomena. Why did you tell me such blatant lies?'

That made her mother break down in gulping sobs. 'I've never had a husband. I was never married, Hannah. You know what that means?'

'I'd come to that conclusion.' What other explanation could there be? 'So I was a love child?'

It hardly seemed possible that her mother would dare. She was the shy and retiring sort, the conforming type, who would never do anything wrong. With her tear-stained face and red eyes, it was hard to believe any man could find her attractive, but once she'd been pretty. She was pretty in the old photographs.

'How could I tell you? I didn't want you to be hurt. I had to protect you. I am such a bad example to you. I was afraid you'd do the same thing, and it can lead to great unhappiness, blight your whole life. Philomena said it was in the blood...'

'Rubbish. Don't listen to her.'

'She thought it best to hide it from you – and the congregation too, of course. Philomena said I was gullible because I was in love with Rowena's brother and couldn't see what he was like.'

'What was he like? Tell me about him.'

It took Esme some time to tell her. 'Tom served in the war, three years in the trenches. He was a war hero too. When it was over and he came home, we wanted to get married. It took a while for him to be released from the Army. He had a little money and he wanted to set up a photography business...'

'Photography!' Hannah was trembling, the coincidence was uncanny.

'Yes, to earn his living, to support us. He was swindled out of his money by a con man, so I suppose you could say he was gullible too.'

'Swindled? In what way?'

'Tom was enquiring from estate agents about buying a photography business, but discovered that most dealt only with residential property. Then a clerk in one of the offices gave him the name and address of a solicitor who, he said, handled the sale of businesses.'

Her mother mopped at her eyes. 'We went to see him together, the solicitor showed us details of a photography shop and arranged with a clerk in his office to show us round. We went to see it.

'It was a Sunday and all locked up, of course, but it seemed to be exactly what Tom was looking for. This solicitor had told us the photographer was ill and that was the reason he wanted to sell. He was in hospital at that moment and a relative was keeping the shop running. There was living accommodation above, which seemed ideal for us. Tom was very keen to buy the goodwill of the business, the stock at valuation and take a lease on the premises.' Mum sighed. 'It's a long story.'

'Go on.'

'Tom hadn't enough money, we knew he'd have to take a loan from the bank, a big loan. In the meantime, the solicitor said he'd have the papers drawn up and negotiate a new lease. Tom paid the money over to him. He said he'd hold it in a special account he had, until the contracts were signed.

'We waited then for the papers to come so we could sign them. The solicitor always had some excuse for the delay, but we were not suspicious at first. We walked past the shop several times. It was only when we went in and spoke to the man behind the counter that we heard it had been withdrawn from sale months before. The owner had been ill but his nephew had taken it over and meant to carry on. That was when Tom began to think he'd been swindled.'

'You went back to the solicitor?'

'Yes, that same day, but the office was empty. He wasn't a solicitor, he'd just pretended to be.'

'You went to the police?'

'Yes. It seemed Tom wasn't the only one swindled out of money by that man. He was very plausible, but it didn't help us.'

'And that was the last Tom saw of his money?'

Esme nodded. 'It was a disaster for him. It meant he had to give up the idea of a shop. He started looking for a job, but there were dozens of ex-servicemen all trying to find work. The best he could get was barman in a pub.'

'Which pub?' Hannah shook her head – as if that mattered.

'It was the Grapes on New Chester Road.'

Hannah gulped: the one pub she knew well.

Her mother shuddered and went on slowly, 'On what Tom earned, he'd never be able to pay off his debt to the bank, but at least he had money for food and rent.' Esme looked up, her eyes full of anguish.

Hannah said, 'That blighted your lives, but you were still going to be married?'

She shook her head. 'Things got worse. One night the man who'd pretended to be a solicitor came in to the pub with a number of his friends. Tom recognised him, though his hair looked different and he'd lost his moustache.'

Hannah gasped. 'He demanded his money back?'

'Yes, he was angry. The man pretended he didn't know what Tom was talking about, that he was mistaken. Tom punched him and before he knew what was happening, he'd started a wholesale fight.

'The landlord called the police, Tom was charged with assault and causing an affray and he got the sack. A few months later, he was found guilty and fined for that.'

'Oh, Mum!'

'Nothing seemed to go right for us. Tom spent his days looking for another job. He was reduced to begging from his relatives. I tried to help and so did Rowena.

'She helped him find a job in a jeweller's shop. I thought our problems were at an end. I was looking for rooms to let and we were making plans to be married, but a gang of thieves broke in to the shop and cleared out the most valuable pieces.'

Hannah could see scarlet patches on her mother's cheeks. 'You don't mean...?'

'It seemed Tom was implicated. Anyway, he was charged with theft.' Her voice faded to a whisper. 'We were waiting for his case to come up when I realised I was expecting you. He was sent to prison.'

'Oh, Mum!' Hannah writhed in agony at what her mother must have gone through. 'What did you do?'

'I was working in the council offices and living in lodgings. I knew I wouldn't be able to go on working for long. Tom didn't have much family. Rowena was his closest relative and she couldn't help with money.'

'But your family...?'

'My parents were already dead but I had a brother.'

'Uncle Fred?'

'Yes. Well, you know what happened. He was the vicar of St Augustine's, round the corner here, and Philomena's husband. Philomena wanted me to have you adopted.'

Hannah went cold at the thought.

'I refused, of course, I couldn't do that. You were Tom's child.'

'Uncle Fred helped you?'

'Yes, though it was Philomena's money that made it possible. They said they'd look after you and me if I promised to have no more to do with Tom.'

Hannah felt another spurt of anger. 'But that was almost as bad. Was it because he was in trouble with the police?'

'Yes. Fred and Philomena took me under their wing, but because he was the vicar I had to keep my secrets. Philomena didn't want his parishioners to know his sister was a fallen woman, it would have sullied their reputation.

'They said Tom was no good and never would be, and I'd be better off without him. Your Uncle Fred wanted me to wear a wedding ring and change my name. After all, I couldn't use my maiden name of Wells, could I? Everybody would have known I wasn't married. It would have marked you out too.'

'Is our name really Ashe?' Hannah was suspicious of everything now. The truth was worse than she'd imagined.

'Yes, it was my mother's maiden name. I took it by deed poll.' Esme mopped at her eyes again. 'Really, I wanted to take Tom's name of Caxton.

He would have wanted you to have it, but the local papers reported his court appearances and Philomena was against that. "Too dangerous," she said. "We don't want people to make that association. Fred must have no connection with crime."

'I was told to drop Rowena Goodwin as well as Tom. She knew the truth, you see. Fred took me into his home until you were old enough to go to school. Then I found a job to support us and rented that little house in Wallasey. There were nearer churches I could have gone to, but I still attended Fred's church.'

'We went every Sunday and had our dinner with them too,' Hannah remembered.

'Yes,' Esme sighed heavily before going on. 'Philomena said we must all keep as aloof as possible from Arnold Goodwin, but I think Fred found it difficult because Arnold was the church sexton.

'But things only became impossible when we were bombed out of our home. I didn't want to bring you back here so close to the Goodwins but, as you know, I had no choice.'

Hannah said, 'Philomena wanted you here to run round after her.'

'I have to repay her for all the help she gave me in the past.'

'I suppose so.' Hannah felt overwhelmed with sympathy for her mother and at the enormity of what she'd heard. 'I still can't see what you've got against the Goodwins. It was Philomena and Uncle Fred who split you off from them.'

'They had their reasons for that.'

Hannah said, 'I can understand that they had to make conditions, but they split you off from Rowena too. She was your friend. You must have known Eric and Gina?'

Her mother's troubled eyes met hers. 'Her children were lovely when they were young.'

'Surely you can understand why I'm attracted to them? They're my blood relatives. You didn't want me to know that. What happened to my father?'

Her mother was mopping at her eyes again. 'Tom was so upset when I told him I wanted no more to do with him that he didn't seem to care what happened. I read about his convictions in the paper from time to time.'

'How did you find out that he'd died?'

'Arnold Goodwin told me at Rowena's funeral. He just came out with it.'

'How awful for you, Mum!'

Hannah thought about her father. 'How different our lives would have been had he bought his photography business and married you. How happy and normal.'

She could understand now why her mother had never spoken of her father, but to have been given a fairy story and have a stranger foisted on her in her father's place – that was too much. She blamed Aunt Philomena for that. To cut Tom out of her life and never speak of him must have been very hard for poor Mum.

'I'm no longer a child,' Hannah said. 'I need to know these things. You kept up the façade far too long.'

'I know, but Philomena thought you should be

kept in ignorance of all this. She said, "Hannah's an innocent child and mustn't know of the evil ways of the world."'

'She's never had any children of her own,' Hannah burst out. 'She doesn't realise we grow up, and can't be forced to do what she wants. We all have to live our own lives, make our own decisions.'

'But we were horrified to find you taking up with Eric. It was like history repeating itself.'

Hannah thought about Tom's ambition to own a photography business. She couldn't tell Mum that Eric wanted the same thing, not yet. She could understand now why Mum had been upset to hear she loved Eric.

Her mother's voice was little more than a whisper. 'There was another thing. Rowena was not above taking chances, you know, bending the law a little. Can we expect her children to be any better?'

'They don't take chances, Mum!'

As soon as the words were out of her mouth, Hannah realised that perhaps they did. What about borrowing the party dress from the dry-cleaners? She couldn't mention that.

'That's as maybe. I owe Philomena so much that I have to take heed of her wishes. She provided money to support us for years.'

'She's a strong woman, Mum. She's got her fingers in everything.'

Philomena was still acting as treasurer of the church fund and was directing the lives of many as they ran round after her. Hannah wanted to say she thought Philomena manipulated the ladies of the parish, had absolute power over her mother and wanted power over Hannah too, but she'd said enough against her.

Her mother said, 'We have only your wellbeing at heart, Hannah. We wanted to keep you safe; prevent you from making the same mistake I made.'

Hannah loved her mother and wished she could give her a better life. This revelation had gone some way to clear the air between them.

Esme asked, 'Now you know, will you give up Eric Goodwin?'

'Mum!' Hannah wanted to reassure her, but couldn't do it. 'I love Eric, I trust him. He knew nothing about his Uncle Tom and you.'

There was a lot more she wanted to say but she held her tongue. Why should your anxieties be pushed on us? We're different people. Eric and Gina were not the sort to be conned out of money. They were both street-wise, with their wits about them, and used to holding their own at any level.

'I can't get over that I'm related to Eric and Gina.' Hannah could understand now why she'd been so drawn towards them: they were her own flesh and blood. 'You've always seemed sorry that Aunt Philomena is our only family.'

'I can't count the Goodwins as family.' Mum showed a flash of indignation.

'But if Tom Caxton was my father, they are.' Poor Mum, it must have been a nightmare, finding herself pregnant. Hannah went on, 'You and I should run our own lives, Mum, not allow Philomena to influence our thinking so much.

She needn't know. We'll continue to look after her just as we always have.'

When Hannah had put out her bedroom light and settled down to sleep she began to think more about her father. Mum had loved him so he couldn't have been all bad. He'd been very unfortunate to be defrauded out of his money, and one disaster had led on to others. He'd been sliding down a slippery slope when Mum had been persuaded to have no more to do with him.

Aunt Philomena had meant well, helping them as she had, but things might have been better for her mother if Uncle Fred and Aunt Philomena had tried to help Tom too. He'd had his own nightmare to cope with and it seemed he'd been left to do it alone.

Hannah wished she knew more about him. The only person who might be able to tell her was Arnold Goodwin and he might choose not to. She wasn't sure how to go about asking him.

Hannah didn't sleep well. When she got up the next morning, she still felt haunted by what her mother had told her. Mum had been really upset when she'd said she hadn't changed her mind about Eric. Hannah felt really bad about that.

It was Monday, the night she and Gina usually stopped at the Grapes with the lads from work. Hannah had half decided to go straight home to her mother, but as they cycled to the aerodrome, Gina told her that Eric was planning to meet them at the pub tonight.

'He wants to know what happened. Whether your mum told you anything more.'

Hannah worried about her mother all day, but by the time they were cycling home, she was looking forward to seeing Eric.

He was waiting in the bar when she and Gina arrived at the Grapes. After he'd been introduced round their workmates and they'd bought their drinks, she sat down with him a little apart from the others. It was almost like being alone with him. With the buzz of other people's chatter in her ears, she told him her mother's sad story.

Eric said, 'It's unbelievable, isn't it? That we're related? I suppose it must be so, but I think of you as my girlfriend, not as a cousin.'

Hannah was looking round. 'Mum told me my father worked in this pub once.'

A barman was collecting dirty glasses and emptying ashtrays. She tried to imagine her father doing the same things all those years ago. This was an old and shabby place now. One of the glass panels in the door, etched with bunches of grapes, was cracked and had been taped up.

He smiled. 'Your Aunt Philomena wouldn't have approved of that.'

'Mum says she disapproves because she sees Tom as a criminal.'

Eric shook his head. 'Pa told me he was brassed off with him too. Uncle Tom was found guilty of starting an affray, but that makes no difference to us now.'

Hannah shook her head. 'There was more trouble than that. Mum thinks he let her down. She's afraid you and Gina might turn out the same and that's why she doesn't want me to have anything more to do with you.'

He said seriously, 'How do any of us know how we're going to turn out? It depends on how life treats us, doesn't it?'

'I've told her I'm not giving you up.' His fingers tightened round her hand, holding it close. 'What does your father say about us?'

Eric paused to think. 'Well, he's derisory about your family. He says things like, "that saintly crowd living next door to the vicarage". He tries to ridicule you. Is that what your mother does to us?'

'No, she's afraid ... of your father, I mean.'

It was only when Hannah had Eric in the porch with his arms round her that, haltingly, she told him what her mother had said about the photographs Eric had given her.

'To start with she denied it was of her. To tell a lie like that...' Hannah bit her lip and shook her head. 'I found it hard to believe. She's always been so strong on telling the truth.'

'She's not such a saint after all?'

'Eric, she had me when she wasn't married. That's a terrible sin now, but twenty years ago... You can understand why she's afraid for me.'

'She doesn't think...?'

'She's afraid we'll do the same thing. That what happened to her will happen to me.'

'I wouldn't...'

'She thinks you'll get me in the family way and then desert me. That I'll have the same unhappy life she's had.'

'Hannah, I'd never do that. I love you. I want to be with you whatever happens.'

'I want you to promise me that we won't go the

whole way.'

His arms tightened round her. 'I have to admit I want to, but I promise, no persuasion, no pressure. I never would unless you're willing. You'd have to be willing for it to be any good, you know that.'

Gina rested her forehead against his shoulder.

'I can promise you one thing,' he murmured. 'I'll never let you down, Hannah.'

She was blinking back tears. He loved her, she loved him. That Mum wanted to part them was a terrible problem, but they wouldn't let it happen.

The war was dragging on. There were no more air raids on Merseyside, but the shortages were growing more acute. By the middle of 1942, rumours were going round the hangar that there was to be a cut in the length of the working day. Hannah and Gina were elated when the rumours proved to be correct and they were told that in future the working day would finish at five o'clock. It didn't please everybody.

They heard several of their workmates say, 'It'll mean a big drop in pay, a cut of three hours a day.'

'We'll be able to go to the pictures any night we want,' Gina told them, 'and see a bit more of life. It must mean we're nearer to winning the war.'

Big bombing raids were still being carried out over Germany and the Mosquito was being used as a light bomber, and for pathfinding and reconnaissance.

'We haven't been so busy lately. It must mean fewer planes are being damaged.'

Hannah had got to know their next-door neighbours at the vicarage better. The vicar and Mrs Osborne were friendly and helpful to Aunt Philomena and Mum. They often spoke of their son, of whom they were very proud. They told Hannah that Robert had finished his flying training in Canada and had joined a pathfinder squadron based in Kent, and was now flying Mosquito aircraft on missions over Germany.

It was 1943 when Hannah first noticed that Colin Lewis, one of the carpenters, was taking a lot of interest in Gina. He was always trying to chat her up in the canteen, and even trying to persuade her to call in at the Grapes more often.

'He wants me to go dancing with him,' Gina confided.

'Will you?'

'Yes. I'm dying to get out and have a bit of fun. You don't know how lucky you are having Eric here with you.'

'Do you like Colin?'

'I'm not crazy about him but he's a good dancer. All right for a night out. If Jim were here it would be different.'

When 1944 brought D-Day and the Allied Forces were invading Europe, everybody began to feel the end of the war was at last in sight.

'We're on the last lap.' Hannah was excited. 'Our soldiers are invading Germany and the Russians are closing in from the east.'

Gina sighed. 'But rations are being reduced again, and there are greater shortages than ever. It doesn't feel as if the end's in sight.'

BOOK TWO

CHAPTER ELEVEN

November 1944

Hannah was well used to getting up early to go to work. Every morning, she took her mother a cup of tea in bed, then turned on the wireless in the living room to hear the latest war news, while she ate a hurried breakfast. She always listened out for details of bombing raids and particularly whether any planes had been shot down.

It was dark this winter morning as she pushed her bike out through the garden gate. Seconds later Gina was pedalling down the road to join her. They wore trousers with cycle clips, heavy pullovers and yellow cycling capes on top to keep out the wind and rain.

'No mention on the wireless about the Eighth Army this morning,' Gina reported. 'I hope Jim's all right, I haven't heard from him for a week.'

Hannah was sympathetic. 'That means there's been no major battles. Good news, surely?'

'There's bound to be fighting, the Eighth Army's pushing its way towards Germany,' Gina went on. 'The trouble is, I don't know exactly where Jim is. Austria, I think, but he's not allowed to tell me anything like that in his letters. If he puts it in, the censors block it out.'

'It said there was a raid over Düsseldorf last night,' Hannah reported. She had Robert

Osborne in mind, and dreaded to hear that he hadn't returned from an op. The news didn't help that much. The pathfinder planes were hardly ever mentioned so it was impossible to work out whether he could have taken part. Sometimes she heard the weather had been too bad for any raids to take place and she could be sure he was still safe.

When they arrived at the aerodrome, the small cloakroom was full to overflowing with chattering girls changing out of their outdoor clothes. Those working in the dope room were pulling on old dungarees and heavy boots. Hannah parted company with Gina, arranging to meet her in the canteen at dinner time.

Hannah had been doing the same job for a long time, but the workshop was not as busy and it was easier now the workers finished at five o'clock instead of doing overtime every night. She found her job monotonous, but it gave her plenty of time to think about Eric.

She felt very close to him, though Mum and Aunt Philomena had not changed their minds about him. Hannah was not allowed to take him home, but they'd had to accept that she was seeing him often. She thought him very generous. He was always taking her to theatres and cinemas and would never let her pay her share. He bought her chocolates using his own sweet coupons, as though he was trying to show her how much he loved her.

She was also going regularly several times a week to see him after she'd had her tea. To spend an hour or so in his company was the highlight of the day. In summer, they went for walks but now it was winter again, and if they weren't going to the pictures, they spent the time chatting round the kitchen table. Tonight Gina and Leslie had been at home and they'd had a good laugh. Eric saw her back to Highfield House afterwards.

'I'm afraid I won't be able to take you out on Saturday night after all.' Eric was apologetic. Earlier in the week he'd suggested they go to the Savoy to see Lauren Bacall and Humphrey Bogart in *To Have and Have Not*. She'd been looking forward to it.

'I have to go to Preston on Saturday afternoon,' he told her, 'and I'll probably be late getting back. The trains don't run on time any more.'

Hannah was disappointed. 'What are you going to Preston for?'

It seemed that Eric travelled about a fair amount, despite the fact that there were notices everywhere asking, 'Is your journey really necessary?' He'd been to Southport in the middle of last week and to Ormskirk the week before.

He said, after a short silence, 'It's hush-hush.'

She asked, 'Something secret, not to be talked about? Something to do with the war effort?'

'Exactly,' he smiled. 'Can I see you Sunday afternoon?'

Hannah agreed. Everybody understood that in wartime there were things going on that couldn't be talked about openly. She was delighted to know Eric was doing something important for the war effort. They spent longer than usual in the porch saying good night and she was late going in.

As usual on Sunday morning, Hannah pushed Aunt Philomena to church in her wheelchair. She always insisted on being helped out of it in the porch and it had to be folded back out of the way. She was leaning heavily on Mum, waiting to be helped to her pew when Mr Goodwin came striding past them in his self-important way. Usually, they pretended not to notice his presence, but in the confined space of the church porch that was hardly possible.

'Good morning,' Philomena said in her frostiest voice, as she set off down the aisle ahead of him with a steadier step than usual. Hannah knew she'd intended to emphasise the social distance between them, but Betsy Goodwin was two steps behind her father and rather spoiled it.

'Hello, Hannah,' she said. 'You were right about that book *The Blue Lagoon*. It's smashing. I can't wait to get back to it.'

Hannah sat down, feeling Philomena's disapproval. 'You're altogether too intimate with that family,' she whispered, but nevertheless the bag of peppermints her aunt liked to take to church was offered to her.

As the congregation gathered, Hannah looked round. She'd not missed coming since the Sunday after Eric had taken her to the Bear's Paw; she'd not dared cause such an upset again. Her gaze came to rest on Betsy, with her thin brown pigtails coming from under her navy felt hat. She was sitting beside her father, on the other side of the aisle. Mr Goodwin was always here too, as befitted the church sexton.

The rift between her family and the Goodwins

was no nearer being healed. Hannah watched Mr Goodwin turn to whisper something to Betsy. Eric said his father was unbending and wouldn't give an inch on anything, and that he was perennially bad-tempered.

The service started but Hannah ruminated on the Goodwin family. Eric was ambitious and talked a lot about his plans for the future when the war would be over. He hadn't yet spoken of marriage, but everything he said seemed to infer that he meant her to share the future with him. He was rarely out of her mind.

Her mother was flicking through Aunt Philomena's hymn book to find the last hymn for her. Hannah stood with them to sing.

They had to wait for most of the congregation to leave before them because getting Aunt Philomena back in the wheelchair would hold everybody else up. Hannah could feel her aunt seething with impatience and knew she hated waiting, but at last they were on their way. Mr Osborne had shaken hands with his flock as they'd filed out and was waiting for the women from Highfield House.

He said with a smile, 'We're expecting Robert home on leave. He's hoping to be here on Thursday. We're so looking forward to seeing him again. He's completed his second tour of ops, making sixty in all.'

As he shook Hannah's hand, he added, 'Rob asked me to be sure to mention his leave to you.'

Aunt Philomena said, as soon as they were out of earshot, 'There you are, Hannah. You mustn't turn your back on Robert Osborne. You'd be far better off with him than with Eric Goodwin.'

Having been out with Eric on Thursday night, Hannah was creeping upstairs with her shoes in her hand. Before she reached the landing she heard her mother call, 'Hannah, is that you?'

'Yes, Mum.'

As her mother was awake, she went in to see her. She was sitting up in bed.

'Robert Osborne's home. He came round to see us this evening.'

'Oh! How is he?'

'Very well. Such a pleasant young man. He's invited us all round to afternoon tea at the vicarage on Saturday. You will come, won't you, dear? You haven't arranged anything else?'

Hannah knew she meant with Eric Goodwin. 'No, Mum. Eric has to go to Preston on Saturday.'

'I'm glad you'll be coming. Robert was disappointed not to see you, but I gave him pencil and paper and he's scribbled a note. I put it on your dressing table.'

Hannah was not unhappy now that Eric had cancelled their arrangement for Saturday. She was quite looking forward to seeing Rob again. She'd thought him good company. She kissed her mother good night and went to her room to tear open the envelope.

Dear Hannah, *she read,*

Such an age since we met, it seems almost another life. Would you take pity on my lonely state and come to the theatre with me on Saturday night?

I'm told the show at the Liverpool Playhouse is good. If you haven't seen it and would be willing to try it with me, push a note through my door so I can book.

Hope to see you at Mother's tea party in the afternoon. Come and make it bearable.

As ever,

Rob

Hannah wanted to laugh. A happy coincidence that she was free to accept. She'd be in hot water here if she'd turned him down. She wrote a reply there and then, knowing she'd have no time in the morning.

As she got ready for bed she thought of Flight Lieutenant Robert Osborne. Really, she hardly knew him.

Mum and Aunt Philomena favoured him, and had tried to make her see him as a boyfriend. Heaven knows what he'd have thought of that. Despite everything, she'd quite liked him when she was eighteen. But who was to say she still would?

By four o'clock on Saturday, Hannah had brushed her blonde hair until it shone. She let it hang loose and back from her face with an Alice band. She wished she could roll it over a ribbon into the sort of thick roll round her head that was so fashionable, but somehow the style didn't look right on her. Her hair was fine and she ended up with a roll that was too thin. Another popular style she admired was to pin the front hair up in bangs round the face. Gina had done it that way for her once but her hair had soon broken free from its clips.

Keeping it loose was the safer option, but it made her look younger and more innocent than she wished, especially for going out with Robert Osborne. Hannah was envious of Gina's thick hair, which lent itself to more up-to-date styles. She longed to have her air of sophistication.

Hannah changed into her green dress and decided that was the best she could do. Accompanied by her mother, she pushed Aunt Philomena's wheelchair up next door's garden path.

'Help me out,' Philomena demanded, as soon as they'd rung the doorbell. 'I don't want to make dirty tyre marks on their carpet.'

Rob came to the door. He beamed at Hannah as he assisted her aunt into the hall. 'I'll just let Dad know you've arrived.'

'How nice to see you,' his mother, grey-haired and gracious in manner, was waiting to divest them of the hats, coats and gloves they'd worn to walk the few yards. 'I'm so pleased you could come.'

The Reverend Francis Osborne was brought out of his study to welcome them. His dark hair had a sprinkling of grey and his manner was kindly. The visitors were ushered into the sitting room.

Philomena reminded her hosts that this had once been her home. Hannah thought it looked lighter and brighter than it used to. Rob came to sit in the other corner of the sofa and she was able to study him. He'd changed. There was a calm quietness about him and he seemed to have an inner strength. His shoulders had broadened out, and he seemed more manly and more confident. He smiled slowly at her, the sort of smile that went up to his brown eyes. He was wearing his uniform and had developed a noticeable military bearing.

Mrs Osborne enquired after Aunt Philomena's health, which resulted in a long account of her symptoms and discomforts. Esme tried to change the subject to the weather, but the vicar felt strongly about the effect the war was having on them all and started to talk about that.

Hannah thought it was all rather stilted until Robert brought him to a halt by saying, 'Let's allow ourselves two minutes each on the war and then move on to lighter things. You've already had a go, Dad, so you can have only thirty seconds more. I want to forget the war while I'm on leave.'

In an aside to Hannah, he added, 'Father thinks the aerial bombardment of German cities is wrong.'

His father muttered, 'I'm torn in two. Innocent civilians are suffering.'

'I have to carry out orders, Dad. They're the enemy. What about innocent British civilians? The Luftwaffe are still trying to flatten London.'

'The V2s.' Philomena shuddered. 'I'm so thankful they can't make them come this far north.'

Mr Osborne said, 'You have to do your duty, Rob, I understand that.'

'I'm in a pathfinder squadron. It's the heavies that drop all the bombs, not us.'

'I know. You go in first and drop flares to mark the targets for them.'

'We're very proud of him,' his mother said. 'He did his pathfinder training and then went straight on to operations.'

Robert handed round home-made scones and cups of tea but within the hour he had Hannah back in her coat and outside.

'I drove up,' he said, leading her round the back of the vicarage to where he'd parked his red MG sports car.

Hannah was pleased. 'Such a treat. I was expecting to go over by train.'

'I've been saving my petrol allowance for my leave.'

'A great treat to go to a theatre too,' she said.

From the moment the curtains parted, it was a glittering evening. Out in the dark street afterwards, Rob hurried her round the corner to a small restaurant for a bite to eat. They were offered a special menu with scarce foods and given very generous helpings. Everybody wanted to treat an airman with wings on his uniform. Below his wings, Robert wore his pathfinder badge, which gave him added status.

Hannah was enjoying herself as she tucked into roast pheasant. She knew this was one evening when Aunt Philomena and Mum wouldn't complain she was late home.

'Tell me about your job,' he said.

'It's still the same.' Hannah had told him she was helping to repair Mosquito planes.

'It's coincidence, isn't it, when I fly them? I think of you repairing them when I'm about to set off on a mission. We all like the Mosquito – it's very fast. D'you like your job?'

'I'm knocking nails in all day so it's monotonous. Aunt Philomena disapproves strongly. She's always telling me to keep the crowd I work with at arm's length. But I think they're a great mix and good company, all very friendly. They're the best thing about the job.'

Hannah laid down her knife and fork. 'I'd like a change, all the same. So would many of the girls there, but it isn't allowed. We were directed into the job. It has to be done.'

Rob was thoughtful. 'And what do you do when you aren't at work? I don't suppose you get that much free time, or that it's easy to find boyfriends when so many are away in the Forces.'

Hannah had been wondering how to tell him she had a boyfriend and he'd given her the opportunity.

'They're not all away,' she said. 'I do have a boyfriend.'

'Oh!' His face fell. 'That's one of the problems of working away – all the best girls get snapped up by others.'

She smiled. 'I bet there's plenty of girls around the airfields. Waafs, for instance.'

'Yes, there are but you know what it's like: you set your mind on one and the others don't measure up.'

Hannah wasn't sure whether he was saying he'd set his mind on her. While she was trying to find the words to ask, he said, 'Do I know this boyfriend of yours?'

'His name's Eric Goodwin. He lives at number eight Grasmere.'

'I ought to...' He was frowning.

'He's Arnold Goodwin's son, the church sexton.'
'I can't place him.'
'Eric doesn't come to church.'
'Oh! Does he work in that aircraft repair hangar with you?'
'No, he works in the Co-op shoe shop, but his sister Gina works with me. She's a close friend. That's how I met him.'
She told him about Eric's heart condition and that she thought he was doing something else towards the war effort because he'd gone to a meeting in Preston this afternoon.
'He seems to travel about the country quite a bit and says it's hush-hush and he can't talk about it.'
'Some undercover job? The secret service?'
'Perhaps. I think it gives him a real buzz. He glows with excitement when he knows he's going. I get the feeling he's pleased to do it.'
'Lucky fellow. Are you going to marry him?'
Hannah laughed, feeling shy. 'He hasn't asked me yet.' It brought a moment's awkwardness. To get away from that, she said, 'Tell me about your job. You must find it exciting?'
'It is at times, but at others...' He was pursing his lips. 'Last week I was flying over Berlin when I got trapped in the beam of a searchlight and there was flak flying everywhere. Flak is always bad over Berlin. We fly alone ahead of the heavy bombers and as I'm the only plane in the sky for them to aim at, I get plenty of attention. It's almost impossible to escape the beam because I can't weave and turn like other planes. If we pathfinders are to mark the site for the bombers, our navigation has

to be totally accurate, so we fly on a fixed course, at a fixed height and a fixed airspeed.'

'You must find that terrifying.'

He pulled a face. 'At times it scares me witless, but I try to hide it. We all do. We get back and tell each other it was a piece of cake.'

'You're alone in the plane?'

'No, there's two of us, a rear gunner too.'

Hannah pondered on what he must go through. 'You're very brave to keep doing it.'

'We have to. There's no way out. Pathfinding takes a lot of training.'

'It must take great courage.'

'The thing is, if you do something day in and day out and all your colleagues are doing it, it becomes routine. It can be scary but that gives it an edge, especially when girls like you tell us how brave we are.

'We don't get bored. When the weather's too bad for the heavies, we're often sent out with a four-thousand-pound bomb just to keep the Jerries on their toes.'

'Where do they send you?'

'Sometimes to Berchtesgaden – that's a long way off. Sometimes to Hamburg or the submarine pens on the coast of France. The boys call that "the milk run".'

'It sounds very exciting.'

'It's fun too. When we aren't flying, somebody will suggest a party. They're all very exuberant in the mess.'

Hannah shuddered. 'I'd be terrified. I'd rather be bored than that.'

When he drove home, Rob ran his car straight

up on the vicarage drive and then escorted Hannah next door. She paused, she didn't want to ask him inside the porch. Eric had made it his territory.

She said, 'I'm afraid everybody will be in bed now.'

'Yes, of course. It's late; I can't come in.'

'Thank you,' she said. 'I've had a lovely evening.'

'So have I. I wish we could do it again. What about next Saturday?'

'I'm sorry, Rob ... I'd love to, but I've already said I'd go out with Eric.'

He was biting his lip again; she thought he seemed disappointed. It made her say, 'I could manage a week night as I don't have to work overtime any more.'

'Oh! The thing is, I'm expecting a friend to come up and stay with me for a couple of nights in the middle of next week. Could you meet us for a drink? Say on Wednesday night?'

'Yes, I could do that. Thank you.'

'You know my problem: I don't know any girls. Could you bring a friend along too?'

Hannah smiled. 'I'm sure Gina would love to come. She's up for anything like that. Her boyfriend has been away for years, fighting with the Eighth Army. She likes to go out.'

Eric wasn't pleased when Gina told him about the foursome. 'Shall I come along too?' he suggested.

'No,' Gina said. 'Don't push yourself in. I'm going to round off the numbers; you'd be another spare.'

Eric was frowning.

'On second thoughts,' Gina went on, 'you wouldn't be a spare, you'd hog all Hannah's attention. That's not what these fellows want.'

Gina was really looking forward to the outing and kept asking questions.

'I don't know his friend,' Hannah told her, 'but you'll like Rob. He's good-looking and lots of fun.'

On Wednesday, the men were in high spirits when they met, and kept up a stream of banter all evening. They all laughed a lot and the time went in a flash.

While his friend walked up the road to see Gina to her gate, Rob said goodbye to Hannah.

He took both her hands in his and kissed her on the cheek. She told him to take care of himself. Those words didn't seem enough for a man who was about to report back for further duty from which he might not return. She was choking back emotion as she got ready for bed.

The sixth Christmas of the war came and went. Gina thought they had little with which to celebrate. The aerodrome workers were all back at work after two days' holiday.

Later that week, Gina was pedalling up Grasmere Road with the rain blowing in her face.

Tonight, she'd called in the Grapes again, but Hannah had gone straight home, saying she needed to spend more time with her mother. Gina knew Eric had told Hannah he was taking the afternoon off work to see an old friend living on the outskirts of Liverpool and couldn't see her tonight.

She frowned. Eric had asked her to keep quiet about his little sideline and on no account mention it in front of Hannah.

'The fewer people who know about it, the better.'

'Hannah wouldn't say anything.'

'Safer this way. Besides...'

'What?'

'Hannah wouldn't approve, would she? She doesn't believe in doing things like that. She'd think it wrong.'

'You could stop, but I know you won't.'

Eric had laughed. 'It's a bit of fun, isn't it? Livens things up. The war's nearly over and when it is they won't be calling people up any more. My little sideline will finish soon enough.'

Gina dismounted to open the garden gate, then pushed her bike into the shed. As she opened the back door she could smell the delicious aroma of recently fried liver, but she could hear angry voices. Feeling alarmed, she crept into the dimly lit hall. Her father's police helmet stood on the hall stand and his uniform jacket was on its hook, symbols of authority to which they must all answer. He policed his family with the same rigour he used on his beat. Leslie said he was a despot.

Gina could see her dark eyes reflected in the hall stand mirror. Glistening rain drops stood up on her dark brown hair. She looked flushed and ready to fight. The living-room door was open.

Pa had his back to her and was tucking into a plate of fried liver and mash at the table. Betsy stood facing him and she looked scared stiff. Gina wondered what she'd done. Pa's wrath was mostly directed at herself and Eric.

'Where do you think you've been until now?' Pa's shirtsleeves were rolled up, his arms were like tree trunks. 'Look at the time. Your mother's been frantic with worry.'

'Mam?'

Cicely was sitting by the empty grate. She said apologetically, 'Betsy, you weren't here when I got home from work. You weren't in for your tea–'

Her father's voice broke in, 'How many times do I have to tell you? You must let us know where you are.'

'I did, Pa.'

'You're only nine. I expect you to obey me. I make these rules for your own good. There's a war on, for goodness' sake.'

'I did, Pa. It's not my fault.'

'Of course it's your fault! You should have been here.'

Arnold leaped to his feet and took the birch rod from behind the mirror over the grate. Birch was thought to inflict the most pain with the least amount of bruising and cutting of the flesh. He flipped it, making it whine through the air.

Gina shuddered; she knew only too well what was coming. She wanted to stop this before it went any further, but Eric warned her to stay out of Pa's way when he was in a mood like this.

'No, Pa,' Betsy protested. 'No, please. I did let Mam know.'

'Betsy, how many times do I have to tell you? You must learn to do as you're told.' Pa snatched at her arm and the birch sang down against her bare legs. The shock and the pain of it made her gasp. The shock went through Gina too. She could see the child biting on her lips determined not to cry, just as she herself used to. Betsy wasn't going to give him the satisfaction of knowing how much it stung.

'Arnold, don't hurt her,' her mother said mildly. Gina knew she couldn't stand up to Pa either. 'Please, that's enough.'

'It isn't enough,' Arnold grunted. 'She'll end up like the others if we aren't firm with her. Where've you been until now?'

'To the pictures,' Betsy sobbed. 'Mrs Trevelyan invited me to go with her and Amy to see *Gone With the Wind*. It was a long film and we had to go early, so she said I'd better have something to eat with them first. I didn't think anybody would worry because I was with Mrs Trevelyan and it is the school holidays.'

'You should have let your mother know. Didn't it occur to you she'd be worried?' Pa was on the two-till-ten shift so he'd not been home long.

'I did,' Betsy wailed. 'I left you a note, Mam.'

'I saw no note.'

'I put it on the kitchen table so you wouldn't miss it. Next to the pan of potatoes I peeled ready for your tea.'

Cicely looked blank. 'I didn't see any note.'

'I even stood in a queue to get a pound of liver for you.' Liver was not rationed. 'I thought you'd be pleased.'

'I was pleased with the liver, dear.' Her mother looked uncomfortable. 'I cooked some for our tea, but you didn't come home. I saved some for your father's supper.' She indicated the plate on the table. 'You said it was very nice, Arnold.'

He turned on her. 'If there was a note, why didn't you see it?' he demanded.

'Arnold, I didn't. Somebody must have moved it.'

Betsy was sobbing. 'I did write one. I told Mam I'd be late. I told her the film was going to last three hours and forty-two minutes with an interval in the middle. I could hardly expect Mrs Trevelyan and Amy to come out before the end, could I? I thought it would be all right if you knew.'

'Sweetheart, I didn't know.' Her mother put an arm round her shoulders. 'I told you *Gone With the Wind* was coming round again. You knew I wanted to see it. I said I'd take you, didn't I?'

'You did, but it was a wet day and it was lonely here on my own. It was a lovely film. I'll go to see it again with you.'

Her father thundered, 'You should have waited for your mother to take you. In future, you must have permission before you rush off and do these things. It's the only safe way.'

'How could I do that?' Betsy was almost incoherent. 'You were all out at work when they invited me. They only decided to go because it was a miserable day.'

He looked up, his face black with anger. 'Now you're being cheeky. I'm not having this.'

He lunged at her with his birch but Betsy was already out of his reach. It whacked down on the table, making the cutlery bounce on his plate.

'No, Pa. Please...'

'I'll teach you to obey me, if it's the last thing I do.'

Gina saw him grab at Betsy and spin her round. Pa's arm was rising and falling with all his weight behind it, as he thrashed her already sore legs. Gina knew how much it hurt; she'd received plenty of birching when she'd been young. Betsy's screams of agony were going through her; she could stand no more.

She rushed at him. 'Pa! Stop it! There's no need for this. You're behaving like a savage.'

Gina snatched the rod from him, tried to snap it in two but failed. She flung it across the room. From the corner of her eye she saw his hand coming at her face. It cracked against her cheek; the force sent her staggering back against the wall. She felt half dazed. Betsy had collapsed against the table and was sobbing her eyes out.

Pa was beside himself with rage. 'How dare you interfere when I'm disciplining Betsy?'

'Disciplining? Is that what you call it? If anybody else did it, it would be criminal assault.' Gina's cheek stung but she was defiant.

'If I'd disciplined you older ones more, you might have more respect for your parents now.'

Gina said quietly, 'You made us what we are, Pa.'

Cicely was staring at her. Gina pulled herself upright and said with heartfelt intensity, 'Why do you let him do it? Why don't you protect her, for God's sake? You're her mother. You're too lily-livered to stop Pa doing anything.' Her voice rasped with contempt.

She knew Pa was reaching for the birch again, but she couldn't stop now.

'Most fathers show their children love. All you show is your vicious streak.'

Gina knew she'd gone too far. The birch flailed down across her shoulders with as much force as he could put behind it. She was only half aware of the back door slamming and Eric coming in. He was at the height of his physical powers but he couldn't come to her aid. Eric didn't fight any more because of his dicky heart.

'Father!' He stood facing him, his shoulders back, his voice authoritative. 'Stop this now! I could hear you thrashing the living daylights out of Gina as I came round the house. What are you trying to do, kill her?'

Miraculously, Pa seemed to fold up.

'He's a brute. I hate him,' Gina screamed, and ran for the stairs. She reached her bedroom and threw herself across the bed. Her heart was thudding as she listened. Eric was trying to reason with him. Pa wasn't following her up. She lay still until she'd got her breath back. Her shoulders hurt and her face stung. She got up slowly, feeling stiff, drew the blackout curtains and switched on the light.

Her pride was hurt too. She'd been whipped like a dog. Pa had been doing it all the years of her childhood but not since she'd grown up. He wanted to show the power he had over her and over Betsy and Cicely, but not over Eric. Eric knew how to cope with him.

Gina leaned forward to examine her face in the dressing table mirror. It looked awful. She heard a noise on the landing.

'Gina?' It was Betsy.

'Come in.'

Eric was with her. He said, 'You can't win,

Gina. Not against Pa. Better if you don't try.'

'He half killed me.'

Betsy put her arms round her. 'Thank you for helping me, but it made him turn on you.'

Gina wailed, 'I wish I could get away from him.'

'Don't we all?' Eric said. 'One day we will.'

'I'd hate it if you all went and left me here,' Betsy told them. 'I don't suppose you'd take me with you?'

'We couldn't, Betsy. But there'd be fewer rows. It's not you Pa goes for.'

'It was tonight.'

'I found Betsy's note.' Eric pulled a face. 'It was on the floor under the draining board. The little window in the back kitchen was open and the note must have blown down when Cicely opened the door. She didn't notice it.'

'It's us against them,' Gina said.

'Mam's all right,' Betsy protested.

'All right to you,' Eric pointed out. 'Not to us.'

'She loves you,' Gina told Betsy. 'It's Pa who causes all the ructions. He won't listen; he's unreasonable.'

Betsy said, 'I wish we could all be happy together. I love you all. I try to do what Pa wants to keep the peace. Mam says that, like other families, we're worn out with the bombing, the rationing and war work. It makes us all irritable.'

'Your mam doesn't do much to wear herself out,' Gina said. 'Sits down nursing babies in that creche all day and hardly lifts a finger here. I mean to get away as soon as I can.'

CHAPTER TWELVE

Arnold sank down in front of his half-eaten supper, feeling overwhelmed by what he'd done. The house was suddenly silent. Eric returned to bring in Betsy's note and put it beside him on the table. He seemed quietly controlled, and said nothing. His son's calm demeanour seemed to show up his own excesses.

With a grunt of distress, Cicely heaved herself to her feet to read the note. Then she picked up the birch from the floor and slid it back into its place behind the mirror over the fireplace.

'Really, Arnold, you go too far.' Her tone was mild, her manner self-effacing. It made him realise *she* was frightened of him too! His own wife was frightened of him.

'Burn it,' he shouted. 'Get rid of it.' His face felt hot with guilt, he was so ashamed of what he'd done. It was as though he was possessed by demons and he'd let his family see them raging in his mind.

'How can I? I can't light the fire – we've no coal.' Cicely's plump face was white with misery.

Arnold leaped up to drag the birch out again, trying to snap it so he could never be tempted to use it against his children again. It was springy and wouldn't break however hard he tried. He tossed it into the empty grate in disgust.

The force of his feelings shocked him. He'd

been like a wild animal, wielding that cane against Gina's shoulders. The fact that she'd dared to interfere between him and Betsy had added extra power to his arm. The fact that Gina had felt she had to, now brought added torment.

He wasn't a good husband and father. He was hard and he was cruel to his family. He made them miserable – he made himself even more miserable. How many times had he made up his mind that he'd never lift a finger to any of them again? He'd promised himself that he wouldn't. He'd promised Cicely he wouldn't lay another finger on her, but when the demons got into him he couldn't help himself.

'Finish your supper,' Cicely said. 'You mustn't waste food.' She didn't remind him that Betsy had queued up to buy it and she herself had gone to the trouble of cooking it, but she would have done if she'd dared.

Arnold tried to eat it but it was cold and congealed on his plate and he couldn't get it down. He pushed himself away from the table and stood up.

'I'm going to bed,' he grunted and hauled himself upstairs.

He couldn't get Gina's words out of his mind. She'd screamed, 'He's a brute. I hate him,' and there'd been raw loathing for him on her face. There were other things he was ashamed of. A vision of the cash box that he'd buried sprang into his mind. All that money was a heavy weight on his conscience, but he wasn't going to give that money away – he couldn't afford to. It was his lifeline to a better retirement. Arnold felt tears of anguish scalding his eyes. Why was he so emotional, with tears always so close? Men shouldn't be like this.

He climbed into bed. Cicely had not made it properly – she never did – and he felt wretched as he curled up with his face to the wall. He longed for sleep to come and blot it all out, but it didn't. Half an hour later, Cicely came silently to bed without even switching on the light. She was scared of upsetting him further.

He lay back and felt ridden with fear. Where was all this leading him?

The next morning, when Gina met up with Hannah she asked, 'What's happened to your face? It's all bruised.'

'A bit of a fracas with Betsy. I hoped it wasn't going to show very much.'

Hannah could see she'd tried to cover it with make-up.

'Little sisters can be a bit of a bind sometimes,' she said. 'Too much horseplay in our house.'

When they got to work the other girls were even more pointed. 'Who've you been sparring with, Gina? I hope you gave as good as you got.'

In the middle of that afternoon, Hannah happened to go to the cloakroom and found Monica, the girl who mixed the glue, was also there.

'Look what I've got,' she said, showing Hannah six bars of Hershey's milk chocolate. She peeled off the silver paper and bit off a chunk. 'Mm, smashing.' She rolled it round her mouth. 'Have a bit?'

'No, thanks.' Hannah recognised the packets.

Monica said, 'I'm going to gorge myself on these. Give in to my craving for chocolate.'

'Where d'you get them?'

'Your friend's selling them.'

'Gina?'

'Yes, they're American. Ten bob for six and no sweet coupons. They're going like hot cakes in the doping shop.'

Hannah went back to work deep in thought. Gina had given her two bars of the same chocolate last week. She'd said they were a gift from Spike and he'd wanted Hannah to have some too. She hadn't realized Gina had been given enough to sell. As they were wheeling their cycles out of the shed that evening, she asked Gina about it.

'Spike gets me a few bars from time to time,' she said. 'He buys them from the PX. That's like our NAAFI.'

'More than a few bars? More than you want for yourself?'

'Yes, he can buy as many as he wants.' Gina was pedalling hard as though wanting to get away from her. 'I did swaps for lipstick with Eileen, and Maureen's knitting me a cardigan.'

'Monica bought some from you.'

'Oh, Monica Faraday! They all love chocolate.'

Hannah pedalled hard, determined to keep up. A double-decker bus passed her and made her wobble.

'I love it too,' she assured her. 'So do you. How many bars did Spike give you?'

She thought Gina was going to tell her not to be nosy, but after a moment she smiled and said, 'A whole box, dozens of them.'

Now she thought about it, Hannah was afraid Spike had been bringing her chocolate, perfume and nylons for years.

She said, 'But if you're selling the bars on, that makes them black market goods, doesn't it? It could get you into trouble.'

'It won't,' Gina smiled confidently. 'Why should it? The girls here won't tell on me. They want me to bring more. They're always asking.'

'The police...?'

'Oh, if they were to ask, I'd say it was an unwanted gift.'

'But it's illegal.'

'Three-quarters of the population is swapping things they don't want for things they do, and selling off a bit here and there on the side. It brings in a little more money.'

'But we earn good wages.'

'Never enough, though, is it? Don't you feel starved of decent clothes? I'd love a smart two-piece, some pretty dresses, a fur coat, hats, anything. And a car – don't you dream of owning your own car?'

Hannah smiled. 'You'll have to sell a lot of chocolate before you can buy a car, and it's against the law.'

'The police want the big boys, not girls like me. They want the real black marketeers.'

'It won't make any difference if you're caught, Gina.'

It bothered Hannah, but what more could she say? Gina was charging an exorbitant price for the chocolate. That was profiteering, and there was a law against that too. Hannah wanted her friend to be whiter than white so she'd earn Aunt Philomena's approval.

But selling on a gift, was that so bad? No, but she was almost sure the chocolate wasn't a gift. Gina had known Spike for years, and Hannah and Eric had made up a foursome with them several times. She knew Spike was friendly with Eric too, and that Gina didn't see him as a boyfriend. He was a good bit older and had spoken openly of having a wife and two little boys back in the States. She was afraid Gina had been selling on goods that Spike had obtained for her for that purpose. It was exactly the sort of thing Mum had against the Goodwins.

When Hannah went round that evening, it was Eric who answered her knock. He helped Hannah off with her mackintosh in the back kitchen and gave her a little hug. She could hear family chatter coming from the kitchen. Gina had made a pot of tea in readiness.

Betsy was kneeling up on a stool at the table, a wiry little girl in a gymslip bought two sizes too big to make it last. She was turning over a brown business envelope with stubby fingers, her nails bitten down to the quick.

She said, 'Eric, Leslie won't open it.'

Betsy was not as pretty as Gina, though she had a cheeky grin and the same tip-tilted nose with freckles across its bridge. She was the only Goodwin to have straight hair, neither blonde like her mother's nor dark like her father's; it was a rich nut brown and drawn severely into two thin plaits.

Leslie picked up the envelope and put it down again. His face was white.

'What's the matter?' Eric asked. 'That came this morning.'

'I'm being called up, aren't I? This could be an appointment for my medical. Probably is.'

'Might not be.'

'It's bound to be,' he wailed. 'Didn't I have a notice just after my eighteenth birthday telling me to register for National Service?'

'Well, you might as well find out,' Gina told him, tearing it open. 'You're right. They're telling you to fill up this form and attend for a medical exam. Ten o'clock on Wednesday, the fourth. That's two weeks tomorrow.'

'Oh, gosh!'

'Leslie, you knew it was coming.'

Eric patted him on the shoulder. 'Don't worry, you'll be all right.'

Leslie looked scared. 'But what if I'm not?'

Gina said impatiently, 'We told you to get a job in a reserved occupation, then you wouldn't be called up. But no, you said you were happy at the dry-cleaner's.'

'I wish I had now.'

His father came through the kitchen, and Betsy sang out, 'Pa, Leslie's got an appointment for his medical. He's being called up and doesn't want to be.'

He paused, leaning over Leslie to read his documents. 'Leslie, you've turned into a bit of a sissy, scared of everything. It'll do you good to go in the Forces, put some backbone into you.'

Leslie groaned.

Eric said, 'We don't think he'll pass. After all, he's had rheumatic fever too and he doesn't look robust, does he?'

'I blame your mother for that,' Arnold told Leslie. 'She coddled you. If it was raining even slightly, she wouldn't let you go out. If it was cold, she swathed you in scarves and caps and gloves. She made us all believe you were frail. The only thing wrong with you is that she spoiled you and turned you into a mummy's boy.'

Arnold straightened up, snatched up the sugar bowl from the table and took it to the living room with him.

Leslie wailed, 'Eric, you've got to help me.'

Hannah was listening as she sipped her tea. At home, duty was something you did without question, but she was sympathetic too. She could see Leslie was quaking. She'd noticed he wasn't as self-confident as Eric, and that his older siblings looked after him.

Eric said, 'You'll be found unfit, like I was.' He turned to Hannah. 'He doesn't look strong, does he?'

'Not as strong as you,' she agreed.

'None of us were prepared to hear Eric had failed his medical,' Gina said. 'Came as a shock, but you've had rheumatic fever too, Leslie. You've probably got the same problem. I bet you ten bob you'll be found unfit for active service.'

Leslie looked haunted. 'In a way I hope so. I don't want to fight anybody. But an enlarged heart, that's bad. Something you can die of.'

'Eric hasn't got an enlarged heart,' Gina objected. 'Nothing as bad as that.'

Eric was trying to make a joke of it. 'You'll die a lot sooner if you get a bullet through it,' he said.

'I've had a good time ever since, haven't I? Been paid more than I would in the services and in no danger of being killed. Having a dicky heart can be an advantage in times like these.'

Hannah could feel the tension but couldn't understand what Leslie expected Eric to do. For once they were not in their usual lighthearted mood.

'I'm tired tonight,' she yawned, and got up to leave a little earlier than she'd intended. Gina could see Leslie was beside himself. Having Hannah with them meant they hadn't been able to talk openly. Eric would have to explain properly to Leslie.

'Don't be long,' she hissed at her brother, when she saw him take Hannah's arm to see her home. She didn't want him to spend an hour snogging with her; she wanted to go to bed.

'I'm going up to get undressed,' she told Leslie.

'No,' he protested. 'I want you to get Eric to help me. Wait for him to come back.'

Gina knew well enough why Eric didn't want Hannah to know what he was doing. He didn't want her to turn against him. She could look very strait-laced and disapproving about anything like that, but she'd never tell on him. It wouldn't go any further.

Within minutes, they heard the back door scrape open and knew he was back. As soon as he came into the kitchen, Leslie said again, 'You've got to help me.'

'You know I can't.' Eric was on edge too.

'But you help others.'

'It's too close to home. Look at your appointment. Your medical's being held in St Augustine's church hall. It's just round the corner. There'll be people who know us.'

'You said these things are run by army doctors and they bring their own clerks and everything. How can they know us?'

'But there could be other people there. Pa's the church sexton – how do we know he won't look in to make sure they aren't making a mess? You know how fussy he is. And it's your age group that's being called up. You'll probably meet half your old schoolmates, and some of them will know me. It's too risky.'

'But what if…?'

'You'll be found unfit,' Gina assured him.

Leslie was biting his lip. 'You said some people dodge the call-up by not registering for National Service when their papers come.'

'It's too late for that.' Eric seemed to be losing patience. 'If you'd put your papers behind the fire you might have dodged it, but you didn't.'

'You didn't tell me...'

'I didn't know then. I heard someone talking about it last week. It mightn't be true anyway.'

'I've heard them say doctors will give false certificates for a price,' Gina said. 'But we don't know which ones.'

'Go out and steal something,' Eric advised. 'Get yourself caught. They don't take criminals and bad characters in the Forces.'

'Steal what?'

'Anything. Money, jewellery, food.'

'I couldn't! What would Pa say?'

'What would he say to me, if he knew what I

was doing?'

'Eric only does it when it's safe,' Gina tried to explain. 'No advertising, all done by word of mouth. It would mean prison if he was caught.'

Eric said, 'Your problem, Leslie, is you have no forethought. You knew you'd be called up, you could have avoided this by getting essential war work.'

'Your friend Ben Wilmot wanted you to go with him to that munitions factory, didn't he? Said you'd earn twice as much as in that dry-cleaner's,' said Gina.

'Yes, well...'

Eric sighed. 'Don't you worry, you'll be found unfit like I was. You're always off work with something or other, aren't you?'

Leslie's lip quivered. 'The fumes from the cleaning fluid get on my chest, you know they do.'

Two weeks later, Hannah walked up to Eric's house as usual on the Wednesday evening. It had become a regular fixture. Hannah found Gina and her brothers were usually ready for a laugh, but tonight it seemed they were not.

At work, Gina had been anxious about how Leslie would fare in his medical examination. Now Hannah was struck by the silence when Gina opened the door to her. She thought at first that the others were not in the kitchen, but when she followed her friend in, she found them round the table as usual.

Eric didn't seem himself. He was opening a tin of corned beef while Betsy was spreading margarine on slices of bread. Leslie, sitting with his head in his hands, looked terrified.

'What's the matter?' Hannah asked.

'His medical...'

'Oh, yes, how did you get on?'

Leslie moaned. 'Passed A1. I'm to join Company number five hundred and something in the Royal Army Service Corps. I've got to report to them next Monday. Eric should have done something for me.'

'I was so sure he wouldn't pass.' Eric was upset. 'I'm sorry.'

Hannah asked, 'What could you have done?'

Eric shook his head.

'I'm not the fighting sort,' Leslie told her, lifting eyes that were full of misery.

'We're making him a sandwich,' Betsy said. 'He's eaten nothing since breakfast.'

'I'm not hungry.'

'You'll feel better if you eat something.'

'I wish I didn't have to go.'

Hannah tried to cheer him up. 'Leslie, surely it's better to be found fit and well, and not to have Eric's illness?'

'No!' It was a heartfelt cry.

The door burst open and Cicely came in. 'Betsy, it's time you went to bed.'

'I'm having my cocoa, Mam. I want a sandwich with it.'

Cicely had had her hair permed too often. It was now frizzy and thinning – going grey too, but that didn't show much because she was fair. Her attention switched to Gina, who was laying thick slices of corned beef on the bread.

'Where did you get that?' she demanded, her

whining voice full of suspicion.

'It was in the store cupboard,' Gina said.

'I thought there was only luncheon meat. It's a long time since I've seen a tin of corned beef like that.' She looked nonplussed.

Over recent years, Hannah too had only seen the large tins that were issued to butcher's shops. Generally, a few slices of corned beef were used to make the meat ration up to the amount to which the person was entitled.

Gina said, 'In the store cupboard. That's right, isn't it, Eric?'

'Yes. I saw it in the Co-op on points, so I bought a tin.' They both smiled at Cicely but there was spiked frost in it.

'Leave enough for your father to have a sandwich,' she told them. 'He'll be hungry when he comes home from work.'

When Hannah was offered a sandwich, she said, 'No, thanks. I can't eat your rations. Anyway, Mum made fish pie tonight, and it's barely an hour since I got up from the table.'

'Come on, you're always hungry,' Gina urged.

'Course you can,' Eric added. 'Cicely can open a tin of something else for Pa. I bought this.'

Hannah swallowed hard. It wasn't lack of appetite that made her decline the sandwich but the hunch that the corned beef had come from some black-market source. She told herself she was growing horribly suspicious.

Anyway, Aunt Philomena saw no reason to abstain from sherry and port, and what about the occasional chicken and chocolate biscuits? Hannah loved to help her eat them.

When the day came for Leslie to report to the barracks, Eric tried to comfort him.

'Everybody's saying the war's nearly won. By the time you've done your training it could be over.'

'There's no guarantee of that.'

'You might never see any fighting.'

'I don't want to do this. I'd rather stay at home.'

Eric was sympathetic. 'Don't worry about it, Leslie. You might even enjoy it.' It made him think more about his own plans for the future. The war must be almost over and the time was coming when he'd have to decide where he wanted to open his photography shop. Lots of shops had been boarded up for the duration, because the business carried on in them had become uneconomic in wartime. He began to look at these.

There were several little towns on the Wirral, mostly with busy high streets. The question was, should he choose a shop in one of these, or one near to the centre of Birkenhead? Or should he aim for the sky and look for a shop in the centre of Liverpool?

A lease on a shop in the centre of Liverpool would cost more, so would the rates, but he'd have more customers, and possibly be able to charge more for taking portraits. He was very tempted. To have his own shop in a central position would be a big step up for him.

He discussed it with Gina. 'Go for the city shop,' she advised. 'You'll be able to afford it.'

'Yes, if I get in quick before the Forces are demobbed. But that's a risk too. I have to be able to get the cameras and the film.'

'If you got a shop with living accommodation over it, we could move out of here,' Gina smiled.

Eric pulled a face at her. 'Don't you be getting any ideas about that.'

'I thought it was what you wanted.'

'I'll want to get married, won't I?'

'I haven't heard of any definite plans for that.' Gina looked at him sharply. 'Hannah?'

'Of course.'

'She hasn't said.' Gina was surprised.

'I haven't put it to her yet. But I will.'

It made sense, Eric decided, if he was thinking of his future, to get every part of it settled.

To Hannah, it seemed like any other Friday evening after work. She went up to see Eric after she'd eaten her evening meal with her mother. Gina was there; they drank tea and chatted about nothing in particular, but Hannah could feel a greater intensity in Eric's manner. His eyes wouldn't leave hers, he was radiating love in her direction. She could feel herself opening up to him like a flower in the sun.

Later, in the porch of her home as they said good night, he was raining kisses on her face.

'I love you,' he told her. Hannah clung to him, feeling safe with his arms wrapped round her.

'We're like Romeo and Juliet,' she whispered. Only last night, Aunt Philomena had been singing the praises of Robert Osborne again, to Eric's detriment. 'We're very happy with each other but...' She buried her face on his shoulder.

'That's what counts,' he said, lifting her face to

his. 'I've been thinking a lot about the future. I've told you often enough that I love you and want to spend the rest of my life with you. When this war's over, I want us to be married. Will you, Hannah? Will you marry me?'

Hannah could feel a blissful warmth stealing over her. 'Yes, you know it's what I want. Yes.'

She could see him smiling in the darkness. 'That means we're engaged,' he said. 'Will you tell your family?'

'Yes. I won't let them stop me – stop us. I've never felt like this before.'

His arms tightened round her again, his lips came down on hers, and his kisses had new depth.

'Tell them tomorrow,' he said. 'I want to buy you an engagement ring first. You can show it to your mum and Philomena. It's Saturday. I'll take the afternoon off, we'll choose the ring and celebrate afterwards.'

'Won't you get into trouble? You take a lot of afternoons off.'

'It'll be all right. We'll go across to Liverpool and see what those posh jewellers have.'

Hannah was so thrilled that she went upstairs and chatted to her mother, made hot drinks for them both and all the while her mind was totally engrossed with her engagement to Eric.

Eric had asked her to come up and call for him the following afternoon.

'I want to take a few photos before we go out,' he said. 'You'll be turned out in your best bib and tucker and it'll mark our engagement.'

Hannah made a special effort with her appearance. Eric was waiting for her at his garden gate with his camera in readiness.

'You look lovely,' he told her, as he kissed her cheek. 'It's such a bright day, I thought I'd take one or two here in the garden.' He posed her carefully under a tree. 'I want to avoid getting those cabbages in the background.' He smiled. 'Cabbages don't look romantic.'

He set his camera on a tripod, adjusting the angle of it minutely, and took two. Hannah thought the photographic session was over, but he took her indoors. Gina was ironing in the kitchen. She was all smiles.

'I'm delighted to hear you've agreed to marry Eric,' she said. 'You and I can be friends for life and never lose touch. I hope you'll be happy with my big brother. He's not a bad sort really.'

Eric pretended to cuff her under the chin. Hannah knew they were devoted to each other.

'Come and take a picture of us together,' he told Gina, picking up a vase full of big daisies from the table, before leading the way to a formal sitting room that Hannah had never seen before.

'It's never used,' Gina told her. It smelled fusty and dust motes danced in the rays of sunshine coming between the heavy velvet curtains. Eric placed the flowers in the empty grate and set up his camera again.

'It's a handsome fireplace,' he told Hannah. 'Makes a good background. Come on, Gina, do your stuff.'

He took Hannah's hand and positioned her by his side on the hearth. Even that picture wasn't enough to satisfy him; he took several more of her, standing and sitting in different places.

'I shall blow up the best one into a big portrait to hang on my bedroom wall. With a copy for you, of course.'

'Thank you,' Hannah said. 'I've never had such a photo session. You're making a great fuss of me.'

Eric smiled. 'What better way to mark our engagement? Anyway, it's my hobby.'

They were on the way out when he picked up a photograph that had been mounted in a cover. 'D'you remember that old photo of Uncle Tom?'

'My father, yes.'

'I thought you'd like to have an enlargement. I've blanked off our mothers and blown him up to postcard size. That's the best I can do with it.'

Hannah warmed to him. Eric was very thoughtful of others. Clever too, to do these things.

'I shall treasure it, always. It's all I have of him.'

They walked to Rock Ferry Station and took the train into Liverpool. As they went up in the lift at James Street Station, he asked, 'What sort of a ring would you like? Diamonds?'

Hannah didn't want him to pay more than he felt he could afford.

'It's what an engagement ring means that's important. It means we're promised to each other, that one day we'll be married.'

They walked up to Boodle and Dunthorne's in Tithebarn Street. Hannah was dazzled by the fine display of jewellery sparkling in the window.

Eric studied it. 'Much of it is labelled second-hand.'

'None the worse for that,' Hannah said. 'Some of it is very old. There's a Victorian ring.'

'And there's a nice diamond. Is that what you call a solitaire?'

'Yes. It looks very expensive, Eric.'

'I want you to have a ring you can be proud of. Come on, let's go in.'

Hannah was ushered to a seat at the counter and another was brought for Eric. A black velvet cloth was laid out beside her. When the assistant went to the window, Eric went with him to point out the trays of rings he wanted Hannah to choose from. She heard him ask to have the price tags removed.

'Will you try the solitaire first, miss? This is a very nice ring.' The assistant slid it on her finger.

Hannah stared at it in disbelief. 'It's enormous.'

'Do you like it?' Eric asked.

'How could I not like it?'

'Would you like to try a three-stone ring?' the assistant asked.

Hannah tried on several more, including a sapphire and an emerald. They were all so pretty she felt spoiled for choice.

'I saw a Victorian ring in the window,' she said. 'I rather liked that.'

It was brought out for their inspection. 'The stones are not cut in so many facets as the more modern ones,' the assistant said, and then in an aside to Eric, 'A little cheaper because of that.'

'It doesn't compare with the others, Hannah.' She thought perhaps Eric was right.

'I like this one.' He picked up the solitaire again and slid it on her finger. 'I can see you do too.'

'Yes,' she smiled. 'It's lovely.'

'How does it feel for size?' the assistant asked. 'It's about right?'

'Yes. Yes, thank you.'

A box was produced. 'I'll wear it.' Hannah didn't want to part with it.

Eric smiled. The little box was put in a fancy paper bag and he paid by cheque, while Hannah looked at her ring feeling bemused. She thought, Eric must have been saving up for this for a long time.

'Let's do something to celebrate,' he said as they went out of the shop. 'Tea and cakes first.' He took her left hand in his as they walked to a café and his fingers played with the ring. The best the café could provide was bread and jam or Marie biscuits.

'It doesn't matter,' Hannah smiled. 'There's a war on.'

'Nothing matters now we're engaged,' Eric said. 'George Formby's on at the Empire Theatre. We'll be in time for the early evening performance, shall we go?'

'I'd love to.' It was a variety show with performing acrobats. George Formby and his wife, Beryl, did two acts and he played his ukulele.

'Not very romantic, I'm afraid,' Eric said as they came out.

'It was a good laugh. I enjoyed it.'

'I'm hungry,' he said. 'Let's go to the Bear's Paw and have a dance and something to eat.'

Hannah said, 'I hardly feel dressed for it.'

'Neither do I, but I'm wearing a jacket and tie. Let's go. What does it matter? They can put us in a dark corner.'

'But I mustn't be late. Mum will be anxious.'

'The last train goes at half-past eleven – we can't miss that. Gina says there's a boat at midnight, but that would mean a long walk afterwards. We'll have something to eat and just one dance.'

'It's been a day to remember,' Hannah whispered when they were finally parting that night.

It was late when she let herself into the house and there were no lights on.

She wasn't sorry to find her mother's bedroom door remained closed. Hannah wanted the lovely details of the day to stay undisturbed in her mind. Tomorrow would be soon enough to tell her.

CHAPTER THIRTEEN

Esme drew back the blackout curtains in her daughter's bedroom.

'Hannah, are you awake? I've brought you a cup of tea. It's time to get up for church, dear. Not a very nice morning.'

Hannah had told her she might be late home last night, but as she'd been out all afternoon Esme had expected her back at a more reasonable hour. She blamed Eric Goodwin. He was a bad influence.

Esme had gone to bed early and grown steadily more anxious as she'd listened for the click of the front door and the creak on the stairs. It had settled her mind to know Hannah was safely back and she'd shone her torch at the clock to check the time. She hadn't got up to see her; she didn't want any more arguments.

Hannah sat up and reached for the tea, looking bright-eyed and eager. 'Thanks, Mum.'

Esme couldn't resist a dig. 'Nice to see you so wide awake, even though you were late coming in last night.'

'I'm used to getting up early. Mum…?' She saw Hannah looking at the little leather ring box on her bedside table.

Esme straightened up sharply. She knew what that meant. She felt as though she'd had cold water thrown in her face.

'I don't want you to be upset.' Hannah paused. 'Eric asked me to marry him and I said I would. We're engaged.'

Esme swallowed. Her fingers tugged at her neckline; she didn't know what to say. She'd been hoping Hannah would grow tired of him. She saw this as the worst possible outcome.

'Look, he's given me a ring.'

Not wanting to upset Hannah, Esme said haltingly, 'I do want you to think very carefully about this, dear. I'm not sure he'll make you a good husband.'

'We love each other, Mum.'

'Love can sometimes fade and die.'

'I don't think ours will.' She looked so confident, so happy.

'You'll always be counting the pennies. He won't earn any fortune in that shoe shop.'

Hannah had slipped the ring on her finger and was holding out her hand. 'Isn't it lovely?'

Esme gasped. It was magnificent. 'Yes ... lovely, dear.'

Her head was spinning. She had to go downstairs to help Philomena, and hardly dared to break the news to her. She put it off as long as possible. Esme made her breakfast for her – better if she left her to eat in peace.

When they did tell her, she was so angry she almost made them late for church.

'Engaged to that lad! Hannah, you haven't made it official? Accepted a ring from him? Have you no sense?'

'Eric's given me a very beautiful ring. I'm proud to wear it.' Hannah proffered her hand to show it off.

Esme saw Philomena draw back. 'He must have stolen it. How could he afford a ring like that?'

Hannah was indignant. 'He did not steal it! That's a terrible thing to say. He took me to Boodle and Dunthorne's to choose it.'

'How much did he pay for it?'

'I don't know. He asked the assistant to take the prices off. He wanted me to choose the ring I liked best, regardless of price.'

'Did he indeed? I'd like to know where he got the money from. That must have cost a lot.'

For Hannah, that took some of the shine off her engagement. Where had he acquired that sort of money for her ring? He was full of plans to buy a business, which would cost too. She didn't want to think of Eric in this way. It was taking away the pleasure she felt.

Esme was hovering with Philomena's coat. It was time they were on their way, but she was ranting on.

'After all the trouble your mother had with the Goodwins. You don't understand how she suffered and how much help she needed to get back on her feet, and here you are going down the same path.'

Hannah put Philomena's hat on her head. She pulled it into position herself.

'Bring my coat closer, Esme. I can't get into it from there. That lad will ruin your life, Hannah...'

The congregation was singing the first hymn as they helped Philomena down the aisle to their pew.

On Saturday, the morning post brought Gina a

letter from her fiancé, Jim Latimer. She read it through before she went to work and it left her feeling depressed and let down for the rest of the day.

Jim always ended, 'With all my love', but this was a short and dull note that told her little, and was the first she'd had for several weeks. He was not a good letter writer, but neither was she.

Jim had fought with the Eighth Army through the desert campaign and up the leg of Italy, and Gina wasn't sure where he was now. She knew there were lots of things he hadn't been able to tell her. The censor would have cut them out if he had, but his letters were getting shorter and shorter and she seemed to have less in common with him. She couldn't imagine what his life was like and felt they were drifting apart.

She always answered his letters, but couldn't tell him what was in her heart. She was frightened for him; afraid he'd be killed. He must have used up nine lives already – surely his luck would run out soon. Every so often there was news of a big offensive and the casualty figures horrified Gina. Jim must know what his chances were – he wasn't daft – but it wouldn't help him to know she lived in dread of hearing of his end.

Since that marvellous leave she'd had with him in 1941, he hadn't spent much time on Merseyside. He'd been commissioned last year and had returned to England to spend some time on an officer training course. His family had gone down south to see him.

He'd come up to visit Gina when he'd had a few days' leave later on, but his family had closed round him, and the weather had been so awful, with gales and hailstones, they'd not been able to go back to Thurstaston Common. They'd had very little time alone. It seemed years since they'd got engaged.

When he'd first gone away Gina had been working a lot of overtime and had spent what leisure she had with her family, longing for Jim and feeling lonely, but as time went on she'd felt deadened by her lack of social life.

Many of the men she worked with were too old for military service but some were not. She'd been out with Colin Lewis a few times; he'd taken her to several pubs, to the pictures and to dances. She'd enjoyed getting out and about, but it had made her feel disloyal to Jim, and though she continued to write to him, she didn't mention Colin. That affair had lasted the best part of six months.

There'd been several others, men friends who had come and gone, but when she'd met Doug Sheffield, she'd felt very different. He was one of the managers at the aerodrome and she'd thought she'd found love again. She'd felt even more disloyal to Jim, but though she'd wanted to break off their engagement, she couldn't bring herself to write and tell him so. She didn't know how much he'd care, but in case he still did, she decided not to do it while he was away in the thick of the fighting.

She was glad she hadn't when she discovered Doug Sheffield already had a wife and two children.

That afternoon, Gina and Betsy were almost home, struggling up Grasmere Road with heavy shopping bags. Usually Cicely did the weekend shopping but today she didn't feel well and had asked Gina to do it instead.

They'd been to the Co-op for groceries, the baker's for bread and the pet shop for the twelve pounds of hen food, which they were allowed to buy by trading in their weekly egg ration. Gina felt weighed down, and when she saw Mrs Latimer and her daughter coming towards her, pushing a pram, she put down her bags for a rest and a chat with them.

Gina knew Moira had been married for some time and had a baby, but she hadn't seen her recently.

'Hello, Moira,' she sang out cheerfully. 'How's the baby? Nice to see you, Mrs Latimer.'

Usually they were pleased to stop. His mother always asked, 'Have you heard from our Jim?' and they exchanged news of him.

To Gina's surprise, today his mother pushed the pram past her with a face like thunder.

'What's the matter?' she caught at Moira's sleeve. Jim's sister was not radiating her usual goodwill.

'You'd better ask your dad,' she snapped. 'He says he's going to charge Mam with breaking blackout regulations. She's a widow, she can't afford fines. The Snellgroves next door show much more light but he leaves them alone. Anyway, does it matter any more?' Gina was left speechless. Within moments, they had disappeared round the corner into St Augustine's Road.

Betsy gasped, 'I heard Pa going on about it. He said he'd cautioned her twice this month already.'

It was a moment before Gina could pick up her bags again. 'He might have given some thought to me. How can I get on with her if Pa does this?'

She set off for home at a spanking pace. She had never felt too much at ease with Jim's mother. When he'd first gone away, she'd paid the odd duty visit across the road, taking flowers from their garden or a few eggs as a gift. She'd tried to get on better terms with her, but they had been stiff uncomfortable visits, their only topic of conversation was Jim himself. Moira was all right, but Gina hardly knew her; she'd moved to Liverpool after she was married.

Gina deposited her bags at the back door and shot into the back garden where she could see Pa down at the bottom end, turning over his compost heap.

'What the hell were you thinking of?' she raged at him. 'Charging Mrs Latimer with breaking blackout regulations.'

He was indignant. 'She was showing light through her front window.'

'For heaven's sake, Pa, nobody's being fined for that anymore.'

'She was showing a light...'

'She's going to be my mother-in-law and she's just cut me dead! Why get her back up like this?'

'I'd stay out of her way for a bit, if I were you.'

'You didn't have to do it. Not when we haven't had a raid in years. I know you think a chink of light can be seen from a plane, but there are no Germans up there to see her damned light. So what difference does it make? You're living in the past.'

'It's the law, Georgina.'

'To hell with the law...'

'Come inside. I can't have you screaming like this. The neighbours will hear you.'

'Not her, she's gone out.' Gina turned and ran indoors, wanting to get away from him before she burst into angry tears.

The truth of the matter was she felt torn in two about Jim Latimer. He'd been her first real boyfriend and they'd been head over heels in love. She blamed the war for tearing them apart.

As the months passed, Leslie was writing to Gina telling her about his life in the Army. When Pa saw the letters come with the post, he asked her how he was getting on.

'He says he's unhappy there,' she said, 'but goes on to say he's learning to drive and he quite enjoys that.'

'He'll settle down in his own good time,' Pa said. 'Do him good. He might learn to stand on his own feet and even to fight.'

When she told Eric what Pa had said and gave him the letter to read, he said, 'Not Leslie. It's not in his nature to fight. He just walks away from trouble.'

A week later, it was Eric who received a letter from him. 'Read it,' he said to Gina, pushing it in her hand. 'He's very unhappy down there.'

Not long after Gina had come home from work to find the kitchen deserted and, as Eric was always home before her, she went running up to his bedroom to see if he was there.

Her stomach somersaulted with shock when she saw Leslie sitting next to Eric on his bed, looking very fraught.

'I couldn't stand it any longer,' he moaned. 'I had to come back.'

'You've got a few days' leave?' she asked, knowing as she asked that he had not.

'No,' Eric said, looking grim. 'We've got a bit of a crisis on our hands. Leslie's walked out. What are we going to do?'

Leslie looked scared stiff, even ill. He told them he'd been billeted in a hut with some really tough lads and they'd had it in for him. They'd bashed him about, bullied him, made his life a misery.

They discussed it for hours. Then Gina cooked a meal for them and Eric took Leslie's share upstairs. They all agreed they must make a big effort to find a flat or a room to rent, and get Leslie out from under Pa's nose. Until they did that, he'd have to stay where he was.

March came and winter was over. The days were longer and the gardens bright with daffodils. The news of the war was marvellously good. Cycling to and from work was again a pleasure, but Gina was edgy. How could she not be when she and Eric were trying to keep Leslie's presence in the house a secret?

For once, she was finding it an effort to keep up with Hannah as they cycled to work.

'Have you heard,' Hannah called over her shoulder, 'they've laid off five more carpenters? The war must be nearly over.'

'There's not so much work.' The spring sunshine was making Gina feel hot. 'I need some new sandals and I'd love a new summer dress.'

It soothed her to think of clothes. In recent months, the two friends had taken to going into town together on Saturday afternoons to look round the shops. Gina felt she needed a treat today to take her out of herself, and at the same time she could ask the estate agents if they had anything to rent.

Hannah was keen to go with her. 'Let's see if we can find something really smart to wear this summer.'

Gina sighed as she remembered a chore she must do. 'It's my turn to clean out the hens. I should do that this afternoon.'

'I'll help you with the henhouse when we get back,' Hannah offered. 'All the best things will be sold if we don't go soon.'

They had a half-day on a Saturday, but Eric had to work on until five o'clock when the shop closed. After having a quick bite to eat at home, Hannah called for Gina and they went into Birkenhead on the bus and headed towards the Co-op department store. Outside, Gina pulled Hannah to a halt so they could study a display of shoes in the windows.

'They're not all that wonderful,' she grumbled. 'Nothing to get excited about. They're utility.'

'I don't know,' Hannah sounded quite keen. 'They're not bad. I'll have to get a pair – I've nothing to wear in hot weather.'

'I'm going to get a pair too.'

'Those brown ones, I think.'

They went in and sat down. A girl came over to

serve them.

'We'll wait for Eric,' Gina told her. He was fitting two little girls with sandals exactly like those Gina had worn as a child.

'Oh, right. You're his sister, aren't you?'

Gina could see Hannah was watching Eric. He'd seen them and kept darting little smiles at her. At last he was free and came over.

'There are three styles this year in both black and brown,' he told them.

'I'd love a pair of white sandals,' Gina sighed.

'Not a hope.'

'What about beige?'

'Nope. We've only got black or brown.'

'Brown ones for me, please,' Hannah said.

Gina watched her brother handle Hannah's foot as the Prince would have handled Cinderella's, easing it into the sandal, fondling it between his hands. An array of shoes spread round them on the floor. Hannah made her choice.

Eric said, 'We have that style made by two different firms, which means the last they're made on may be different. You'd better try them both and see which is the more comfortable.'

Eric was pleased to show how knowledgeable he was, and he had infinite patience with Hannah. He didn't appear to have a care in the world. Gina was getting impatient. She'd decided on a different style but he was continuing to fuss over Hannah. There was much discussion about where they would go tonight. Gina had arranged to see Spike O'Hanlon.

At last they were following Eric to the till. Gina paid for her purchases. The sandals were put into bags. Hannah handed over payment with her sheet of clothing coupons. Eric handed over her change with a flourish, and returned her sheet of coupons.

Hannah said, 'You've forgotten to cut the coupons off.'

Gina closed her eyes. Oh Lord, she should have said something to Hannah about this. She'd been so keen to come, she thought Eric already had.

'Shush,' she said. 'Not so loud.'

A large pair of scissors was attached to the counter by a chain. Eric picked them up and went through a mime, pretending to cut the coupons off. 'I can fiddle them,' he whispered to Hannah.

Gina moved closer to her friend. 'That's why I always come here for my shoes.'

'No,' Hannah protested. 'I'd rather you took them, Eric.'

'Why?' Gina said under her breath. 'You can use them to get a dress.' She picked up the coupons and bundled Hannah out of the shop as quickly as she could.

'What did you do that for?' she demanded as soon as they were safely outside. 'Making a fuss like that – you could have got Eric into trouble. Luckily there was nobody standing near us.'

Hannah looked embarrassed. 'I thought he'd forgotten to take them.'

'Eric thought he was doing you a favour.'

'It's dishonest.' Hannah's face was white and determined.

'No, it isn't. You paid the money.'

'I'll be getting more than my fair share of clothes.'

'I thought you wanted lots of clothes and all the

other luxuries that are going.' For once Gina was losing patience with Hannah. 'You're always going on about having a whole new wardrobe and perfume and all the rest of it.'

'Gina, I thought we were just longing for those things in the way we long for the end of the war. I didn't think you'd do anything about it.'

'Eric says, "If you want something in this world you'd better do all you can to get it. Nobody else will help you."'

They were outside an estate agent's office. 'Wait here a sec,' Gina said. 'I want to pop inside.'

The man there shook his head when she asked for property to rent.

'Not even a room?'

'Nothing.' It was the same old story.

When she came out Hannah was still going on about the coupons. 'You know right from wrong, Gina. I don't think you should do it.'

'Everybody's at it.'

'Not everybody. My mother and Aunt Philomena...'

'You're wrong there. Your aunt isn't above paying over the odds for a little extra coal. Eric went to school with the lad who used to work for that coal merchant on Price Street. He said so, and he used to hump it into her coal hole.' Gina thought that would shut Hannah up. She certainly flinched. 'And she'll pay extra for sherry.'

'Those things aren't rationed.'

'We're talking about the black market. There's all sorts of lovely things to be had there, at a price. Luxuries that aren't rationed. You either get what you can or you do without. We've had five years of shortages. Most of us think that's enough.'

That did shut Hannah up. She was quiet and withdrawn. Gina made enquiries at two more estate agents with the same result before giving up.

'Have you thought about lodgings?' Hannah suggested. 'I saw a notice in the newsagent's, offering weekly board.'

'We don't want lodgings,' Gina said shortly. The first thing any landlady would want would be a ration book, and Leslie no longer had one.

'I don't want you to move anyway,' Hannah said. 'I like having you and Eric just up the road.'

'I'd better go home and clean out the hens. Spike's calling round for me at half-six, and I want to have a bath before I go out. D'you still want to come and help?'

'Yes, I'll come.'

Clearly Hannah thought it might cause something of a rift if she went home in a huff without giving her a hand. Gina told herself she had to relax and throw off this feeling of doom.

'There won't be anybody at home,' she said. 'Pa's at work and Betsy will have gone shopping with Cicely.'

She unlocked the back door. There were several pairs of Wellingtons in the back kitchen.

'Better put a pair on,' she said. 'And a pinny over that dress.' She did the same herself and then fetched the wheelbarrow from the shed and put in it the spades they'd need.

'I love the hens, but this isn't my favourite job.' She opened the main door of the henhouse. There were two hens inside but they immediately fluttered through the small opening cut in the side to join the others in their outside pen. This was a few yards of bare earth behind a seven-foot fence Gina's brothers had made from chicken wire. The henhouse had once housed garden implements, and both that and the pen ran alongside the house.

'Look, they've laid two more eggs. Now spring has come they're laying more.'

'What d'you want me to do?' Hannah asked.

Gina was pushing fresh straw in the nesting boxes. 'Take one of those spades and scrape the bird droppings off the floor.'

She watched her friend scrape very gingerly. 'This stuff smells.'

'It stinks, it's manure. It's worse because it's a warm day, but I've got used to it. Pa says it's marvellous on the garden. It grows the best potatoes. You do it like this.'

Two perches made from broom handles crossed the shed three feet from the ground. Gina bent double to work under them.

'Do the hens sleep on those perches? You'd think they'd fall off, wouldn't you?'

Outside, the hens clucked excitedly. 'They don't like us here in their house,' Gina said.

They were both outside, dropping spadefuls of manure into the wheelbarrow when one of the cockerels put his head back and crowed.

'Sounds like early morning on a farm,' Hannah smiled. 'We can hear them from our house sometimes – makes us think we're out in the country.'

'That's Joey. He's only a few months old.'

Hannah went closer to the wire for a better

look. It made the fowls stampede to the far side of the pen. Joey opened his wings and flew up to the hall windowsill, six or seven feet above them.

'Gosh, look at that!' Gina was surprised. 'None of them has ever done that before.' Joey had perched on the windowsill, looking down at them but the window was open.

'Oh! Pa said I must clip his wing feathers to stop him flying and I forgot.' As she watched, Joey turned to look inside and then fluttered down out of sight.

'Oh, heavens! We'd better get him out of there.' They were both rushing towards the back door, but their sudden movement made the hens cackle noisily and scurry into their house. Too late, Gina saw they'd left the main henhouse door open and within seconds, the birds were streaming out into the garden.

'Oh, no!' She swung Hannah round. 'We've got to get this lot back first. Pa will have a fit if they scratch in his vegetable plot.'

Laughing and shouting they tried to round them up. 'Watch where you put your feet, Hannah. Mind that row of lettuce – Pa only planted them out yesterday. Betsy let the hens out once and he went mad.'

Gina was hot and sticky before she'd got the door closed on them all.

'Fourteen, I counted.' They collapsed on what little lawn remained in a fit of laughter. 'I'll have to hoe round his seed beds or Pa will know.' It had taken nearly fifteen minutes.

'Joey's still in the house,' Gina remembered and jumped to her feet. 'I hope he's not making any mess or I'll have Cicely on my back too.' She ran to the back door and pulled off her wellies against the step. 'We've got to get him back in the pen too.'

She led the way barefoot into the hall, and had a quick look in the rooms where the doors had been left open, but there was no sign of him. The window he'd come through was on the landing halfway up the stairs. She slammed it shut. They didn't need to have this happen again.

'He must have gone up.' As she raced up, Gina could hear Hannah padding behind her and that brought the other problem crashing back into her mind. She shouldn't let Hannah come up here.

The bathroom door was open; there was no sign of Joey in there. Gina could feel her heart thudding as she closed the door carefully. Pa and Cicely had a room on this floor and she and Betsy each had one. Both their doors were open. Gina crept to her own room. It would be safe enough for Hannah to see in here.

'Joey's here,' she said, flooded with relief. The young cockerel was on her dressing table, strutting back and forth between her alarm clock and her jar of face cream, clucking with consternation as he caught sight of himself in the mirror.

Hannah chuckled and Gina couldn't help but do the same. She'd never seen anything quite so funny. Joey was turning to look from them to his own reflection, not knowing what to make of it. He'd never been near a mirror before and clearly didn't know whether he was seeing another bird or himself. He pecked at the glass and his reflection pecked at him. The sun shone through the window, putting a dark green gloss on his tail feathers. He tossed his head and crowed again, his scarlet comb standing up straight.

'You're all right, Joey.' Gina tried to soothe him, as she shook with merriment. 'We'll have you back with the others in two ticks. Just stay still.' She closed her window and crept closer to catch him.

He was agitated now and as he strutted along the dressing table he tripped over her hairbrush. It made him cackle in surprise. They both collapsed on the bed in a fit of giggles. Hannah had tears of laughter running down her face.

'We've frightened poor Joey. He knows we're chasing him,' Hannah said. 'Oh, look what he's doing!'

'Thank goodness he's missed my duchess set.'

'At least he's not made his mess on your bed. It'll wipe up from there.'

Gina closed her bedroom door. 'We've got him cornered now, we've got to catch him.' She advanced purposefully towards him but he backed away.

'You go over there, Hannah, and keep still. Be ready to grab him if he comes close enough. A hand over each wing is what's needed. Quiet now, let's cut out the giggles.'

As Gina advanced on him, Joey was backing slowly towards Hannah. Suddenly she pounced.

'Marvellous,' Gina said, 'you've got him.' He was struggling and crowing. 'Are you all right? Can you manage?'

She opened her bedroom door, meaning to lead the way down. On the landing, Hannah gave a cry of distress as Joey flapped free and fluttered up another flight of stairs leading to the second floor.

'I'm sorry,' Hannah wailed. 'I couldn't hold him.'

Gina felt the blood drain from her knees as a small brown feather floated down to her. Surely Leslie must have heard them? They'd made plenty of noise giggling and laughing. He'd have hidden himself in the wardrobe – that was what they'd agreed he must do.

To be on the safe side, she said loudly, 'Don't worry, Hannah. You stay here, I'll be able to catch Joey now.'

She sped up the flight of stairs. Eric's door was closed but Leslie's was open. Good, he'd have heard Hannah's voice. The cockerel would be in his room.

It shocked her to find Leslie by his bed, holding Joey in a firm grasp. They were all used to handling the birds. Before taking him, Gina put a finger to her lips to warn him to be quiet.

Behind her, Hannah sounded astonished. 'Gosh, Leslie, I didn't know you'd come home. Have you got leave?'

Gina gasped with horror. Hannah had followed her up after all!

Leslie was folding up before her eyes. His secret was out. Poor kid, she thought, he looks scared stiff.

'Oh Lord!' Gina had come out in a lather of sweat. 'Hang on while I put this blasted cockerel back in the pen.'

CHAPTER FOURTEEN

Hannah stood stock-still; she could see the consternation on Leslie's face. She asked, 'What's the matter? Is something wrong?'

He sank back on his bed without a word. His room looked bare and unused. There were no clothes or possessions to be seen, except for a bundle of newspapers and a large pile of glossy American magazines. An ashtray full of butts was pushed half out of sight under the bed.

She could hear Gina running back up. She was puffed when she reached them.

'Leslie's gone AWOL,' she said, closing the door and throwing open the window. 'I can smell your fags down on the landing. You don't want Pa to get a sniff.'

'He'll think it's Eric.'

'Not when Eric's been at work since early morning.'

'Don't open my window. Pa might see it from the road and come up to close it.'

'I hadn't thought of that.' Gina closed it to, so it wouldn't be noticeable.

'What's AWOL?' Hannah asked. She could sense Gina's panic.

'Absent without leave. You mustn't tell anybody you've seen Leslie.'

'No, of course not.'

'Nobody must know he is here. He will get

into trouble.'

'I won't say a word.' Hannah's mouth went dry. What had she promised? 'Is that why you're looking for a room to rent?'

'It's not safe for him to stay here. Betsy's running about everywhere. She's only a kid. We daren't let her know, it wouldn't be fair. If she let on to her mother or Pa, all hell would break loose.'

Leslie sounded scared. 'Pa knows I've gone AWOL, but not that I'm back here.'

'The military police came round.' Gina rolled her eyes to the ceiling. 'They spoke to Pa. He'd just come off duty and was still in his uniform.'

'They came up here and poked round.' Leslie looked pale and drawn, 'but they didn't find me. I hid in the wardrobe.'

Hannah looked at the huge piece of Victorian furniture and shuddered. She knew how seriously the Army regarded those who deserted.

There was a key protruding from the lock. She asked, 'Can you open it from the inside?'

Leslie shook his head.

'Aren't you afraid of being trapped? Suffocated?'

'I was,' he admitted. 'The key's just for show now; it doesn't work. Eric fixed the lock so it wouldn't. I push myself behind all these clothes on this side and leave the door open.'

'Golly, they didn't look closely enough?'

'No, I borrowed a lot of Eric's old coats and things to hang here and I stand with my back against the front of it so if someone pokes a stick in, it would go right to the end. It's dark inside even if they look.'

'Anyway,' Gina said, 'he got away with it. Once the redcaps went, Pa went berserk. He didn't stop sounding off about Leslie all night.'

'I could hear him from up here,' Leslie said. 'He was being horrible about me.'

'I don't understand why you didn't hide today.' Gina was exasperated. She threw herself on the bed and started leafing through one of the American magazines. 'The fewer people who know you're here, the better.'

He shook his head in despair. 'I was listening to you laughing your heads off. You sounded as though you were having fun, but I didn't understand what was happening. I was getting ready to hide but Joey came flying in, and I heard you tell Hannah not to come up, so I thought it would be all right.'

'Well, it wasn't,' Gina said shortly. 'I wish you'd keep your wits about you. So now it's not just me and Eric who know, it's Hannah too.'

'Hannah's promised not to tell, haven't you?'

Hannah caught her breath. Of course she wouldn't tell anybody if it would get Leslie into trouble, but she'd much rather have remained in ignorance.

It was not only Aunt Philomena who viewed deserters as criminals. Many thought them cowards, unwilling to do their duty and serve their country.

Hannah had never seen Leslie as a coward. He was just a frightened, mixed-up lad. 'Why did you run away, Leslie?'

'I didn't like it in the Army. I was put in with a

really rough crowd and they were always sniping at me.'

That shocked Hannah again. 'I thought Gina said they were teaching you to drive?'

'They were, on big trucks.'

'You said you enjoyed that,' Gina put in.

'Yes, but it was a roughhouse. The other lads were thugs and bullies.'

Hannah said haltingly, 'But the driving – wouldn't you like a job driving after the war? You could drive a bus or a lorry or something.'

'I wouldn't get a civilian driving licence. Not from the Army.'

'But if you can drive a big truck you can drive almost anything. You'd only have to take the test.'

Leslie was shaking his head.

'What would happen if you went back?' Hannah persisted.

'I'd be in big trouble.'

'But less trouble surely, than if you're found and taken back?'

'I'm not going back,' he burst out.

'But you'll get Gina and Eric into trouble if they're found to be hiding you. And what about your father?'

'Pa would half kill me.'

'Me and Eric too,' Gina said. 'But being a copper's house, I don't think the redcaps will come back.'

Leslie said, 'Even if they do catch me, they don't do much to relatives, just a small fine. Here, it says so in this newspaper.'

He pulled a bundle out from under his bed and flicked through them. 'Read this.'

Hannah did.

Leslie said, 'It's a report of court proceedings. A wife and mother were each fined five pounds for harbouring their son, a naval deserter who went absent in July 1942.'

'He's been free for a long time.' Gina was reading over her shoulder.

'Could you keep it up?' Hannah asked. 'How long is it since...?'

'Six days,' Leslie gulped. 'It also says there's up to twenty thousand deserters on the run now. I'm not the only one who can't stand the Forces.'

'I still think it would be better if you gave yourself up,' Hannah insisted.

That made him draw back from her. 'I thought you'd want to help. I didn't think you'd be like this.'

'Of course I want to help. What d'you want me to do?'

Gina sighed. 'You could bring him some books or old magazines to pass the time. He's bored out of his mind.' She went back to the American glossy again. 'Spike gave me these but I haven't had time to read them yet. Just look at these blueberry muffins – all this lovely food in coloured pictures. Makes my mouth water to look at them.'

'See the size of the refrigerators, and the cars.'

'Beautiful clothes too, very different. A lifestyle to drool over. If only we could have all this now.'

Hannah went home to have high tea and get ready to go out with Eric. Niggling at the back of her mind was the understanding that her mother and Aunt Philomena would regard a deserter as a criminal who ought to be brought to justice.

But Hannah knew it was the tug of loyalty and affection for Leslie that forced Gina and Eric to help him evade capture. She felt torn both ways.

Later that afternoon, Gina was whipping eggs together preparing to make scrambled eggs on toast, when Cicely came tapping through to the back kitchen without saying a word. Gina heard her light the gas cooker there.

Cicely had just returned home from a shopping expedition and was wearing high-heeled court shoes, over which her weight seemed precariously balanced. Betsy came with her, running from the kitchen to the back kitchen.

'We're going to have fried egg and chips,' she told Gina. 'Lovely.'

When Pa was out, Cicely cooked only for herself and Betsy. It made managing the rations doubly difficult. Gina went into the back kitchen and picked up a packet of butter.

Cicely snatched it from her hand. 'Here, you use this margarine. Leave a little butter for me and your father for once.'

'We're entitled to three ounces of butter each,' Gina said.

'Be grateful for a bit of marge. You take our rations as well as your own.'

Cicely had now fastened an old cardigan over her dress and a dirty apron over that. She was kicking off her court shoes and feeling for the carpet slippers she'd left in the kitchen.

Cicely was usually short-tempered with Gina; she'd fought her too often to like her. Gina knew she resented her and her brothers as much as they resented her. 'Rowena's children', she called them, and blamed the failure of her marriage on them.

For Gina, having to provide a clandestine meal for Leslie meant that everything had to be timed to the second. She had to wait until Cicely and Betsy were occupied elsewhere and would not notice what she was doing. At half-past five Eric came home from work. He understood the situation and sat down to drink a cup of tea with Gina.

When she judged Cicely's meal to be nearly ready, Gina started her own cooking on the old stove in the main kitchen. It was ready shortly after Cicely and Betsy had taken their meal to the living room and closed the door. She dished up three helpings, while Eric poured a large mug of tea and sped quietly upstairs to Leslie with the tray. He was down to eat his own meal within moments.

'It's a miracle that we're getting away with this,' he said between mouthfuls.

'Hannah knows.'

'What?'

She told him what had happened that afternoon. 'Leslie had plenty of time to hide,' Gina complained. 'He heard me say Hannah's name. Either he thought it didn't matter if she knew, or he just couldn't be bothered getting himself out of sight.'

'We've got to find somewhere else for him.'

Gina bit angrily into her toast. 'We've been saying that since you came home and found him asleep on your bed. Perhaps we've all petted him too much.'

'We can hardly tell Pa he's here now,' Eric said. 'We're involved in this up to our necks.'

'Well, if you'd done what he wanted in the first place we none of us would be in this position.'

'I expected him to fail his medical,' Eric hissed. 'We all did.'

Leslie's predicament was constantly on Hannah's mind. She'd promised to help him, and she certainly wouldn't breathe a word to anyone of his whereabouts. All the same, she was beginning to see her mother's point of view. Gina and Leslie did sail close to the wind. Not Eric so much – he was lovely – and it was Eric she was going to marry.

He was doing important war work: something he couldn't talk about, something secret, possibly for the secret service. It took personal courage to do what Eric and Gina were doing. Leslie should not have put them in this position.

She was ready when Eric rang the doorbell and ran down to meet him. He pulled her arm through his as soon as the garden gate clanged behind them, and said, 'You've found out about Leslie. I'm sorry. It puts pressure on you too now.'

'You and Gina have been on edge these last few days. I could feel you both seething away inside. Now I understand why.'

'We've got to find somewhere else for him to live. We can't keep him in the same house as Pa.'

Hannah said, 'I still think the best plan would be for Leslie to return to his unit before he's caught. I didn't like working in the hangar when

I first started, but I gritted my teeth and carried on. I said something along those lines to him.'

She was aware she sounded like a self-righteous prig, as though she was against him and didn't want to help.

'He won't go back,' Eric said. 'We tried to persuade him. He was put in with a rough crowd. They knocked him about. You know what Leslie's like. He's frightened.'

'Can't he explain the problem to whoever is in charge?'

'He says he's tried talking to his sergeant about it. He jeered at him, did nothing to help.'

Earlier in the week, Eric had suggested they go to the pictures, but now he said, 'Do you mind if we don't? There's such a lot on my mind. A drink perhaps in the Grapes?'

Hannah said, 'You know I don't mind where we go. I just want to have you to myself.'

He took her into the lounge bar. It wasn't yet crowded and they found a quiet table. He brought her a glass of sherry from the bar.

'Leslie's like a hot potato.' She could see he was fraught. 'For any long-term solution, we've got to get him out of Rock Ferry. He worked in that dry-cleaner's in Bedford Road for years, so lots of people know him. He'd be recognised if he left the house, and if the military police came asking for him again.'

He took a long pull on his beer and groaned. 'The trouble is, as soon as a man deserts, he's without a legal form of identity or any means of buying food. We can just about manage to feed him at home, but it's a struggle to do it without

Pa or Cicely noticing. Luckily, Spike gave Gina some big tins of peaches. They're smashing, haven't had anything like them for years. Gina's livid she can't gorge on them herself. Leslie's got them up in his room with an old tin opener. The only other thing is eggs – it's a good job he likes them. Eggs and peaches are what he's living on.

'Pa and Cicely don't know how many eggs are laid, but Betsy does. She collects them when she comes home from school. It would be better if she didn't find out. I'm sorry you have.'

'Eric, there's no way you can go on keeping him hidden at home.'

'I know, but if Leslie is to move somewhere else, we've got to find an identity card and ration book for him.'

'There's no way you can do that either.'

'If he had those, at least he'd be able to look for work. He needs a job, and not just for the money. He'd feel better if he had something to do. Just hiding up there in his room and never going out, it's driving him up the wall.'

Eric's dark eyes were searching hers. 'Will you do a great favour for us?'

'You know I will.'

'I hardly like to ask...' He was hesitating, undecided. 'No, better if I don't.'

'What is it?'

Eric shook his head and sighed. Then he made up his mind. 'Look, your mother works in the Food Office, she's handing out new ration books to people who've lost theirs for one reason or another. She's doing it all the time, isn't she?' He was pleading now, deadly serious, 'I mean, couldn't she help? Would you ask her? Without a ration book, Leslie can't go anywhere else.'

Hannah felt her heart bounce like a tennis ball. She was astounded. 'No,' she protested. 'No, absolutely not.' Then more calmly she added, 'Mum would refuse, anyway.'

'Yes, I suppose she would.' Eric covered his face with his hands. 'Pa calls her Goody Two-Shoes.'

Hannah was upset; she was sure Arnold saw her in much the same light. But what was much worse was that Eric had suggested she ask her mother to steal a ration book. That had shaken her to the core.

She said, 'If she knew about Leslie, she'd feel it was a secret she couldn't keep.'

'Would she?'

'Mum believes in being honest. She doesn't steal, not even to help people in trouble.'

Mum would be a nervous wreck if she knew what they were up to, and be very cross with her for getting involved like this.

'She's not whiter than white, Hannah. She told you lies about your father.'

After a long-drawn-out pause, she had to say, 'You're right about that, of course.' Hannah was upset too.

Eric apologised when he kissed her good night. Once in the porch, he put his arms inside her coat and hugged her close to him.

'I'm feeling desperate about this,' he whispered. 'I've got to find a safer place for Leslie.'

Hannah could sympathise with Leslie – he'd been given a hard time in the Army – and she knew Eric just wanted to protect his brother, but she felt she was seeing a side to the Goodwins that she hadn't known existed. No, that wasn't entirely true – she'd begun to suspect it did. They were daring, real risk-takers, quite the opposite of herself and Mum. They sought pleasure and fun, and if the law didn't allow what they wanted, they ignored the law, which is surely what had turned her mother and Aunt Philomena against them. That scared her.

Yet she loved Eric, and Gina was her best friend. She couldn't cut herself off from them. She told herself there was a war on and that changed everything. Things would get back to normal once it was over.

When she let herself in to Highfield House and went upstairs, she felt disappointed and a little sick.

Her mother had some more bad news for her.

'Robert Osborne is in hospital near Portsmouth. Flak damaged the undercarriage of his plane, and he couldn't get it down when he returned to base.'

Hannah's heart skipped a beat. 'Is he all right?'

'He did a belly landing on grass. He and his gunner got out but Robert's leg is badly broken.'

Hannah sighed. 'At least he made it back to England. It could be worse. I've been dreading to hear he'd been shot down over enemy territory.'

'Yes, there's always those missing or killed. He'll be safe from that now he's in hospital. Mrs Osborne is going to go down to see him.'

'All the same,' Hannah said, 'he's probably feeling rotten.'

'Write to him,' Esme suggested. 'Give her the

letter to take. It might cheer him up.'

Arnold Goodwin cycled home to an empty house after a busy night on duty. He was later than usual and it irked him to find Cicely had already left for work, which meant he'd have to cook for himself. But at least the rest of the family had gone too. He didn't find sleeping during the day easy and an empty house gave him peace and quiet.

He was tired; he'd had difficulty sleeping since the redcaps had been to tell him Leslie had gone AWOL. He'd seen it as a great indignity to have them search his house as though they suspected him of harbouring a criminal. As a police officer, one of his duties was to arrest deserters. Leslie might be his son but he knew better than to come home. He'd know what would happen if he dared to turn up here.

Of course, deserters weren't criminals in the true sense of the word, but they were a shirking cowardly lot. He was ashamed of what Leslie had done. To have a son on the run belittled him and the whole family.

Arnold stifled a yawn as he set about frying himself a supper of egg and bacon. His anger bubbled up every time he thought of Leslie.

Of course, he'd been very ill with rheumatic fever as a child. He looked frail, and none of them had expected him to pass his medical for the Forces. Eric hadn't passed and he looked far more robust. He was more prepared to fight his own battles too. Perhaps they'd mollycoddled Leslie too much. He was weak, quite girlish – all he wanted from life was an easy time. No, that wasn't quite true. Like his siblings he wanted a good time, with plenty of money, girls and fun. Arnold doubted he'd be having much fun now he was on the run.

It very much worried him. Even if he despised the lad, he was his son. Arnold finished eating and was glad to go upstairs to bed. As usual, Cicely had done the absolute minimum to make it – just tossed the bedding roughly back. He drew the blackout curtains. At least they had the advantage of shutting the daylight out.

He felt exhausted. His body just couldn't adjust to night duty. He settled down, still thinking of Leslie, wondering where he could be hiding now. The redcaps had asked him for a list of possibilities, but he honestly could think of none. Leslie was a homebody.

Arnold had drifted off and was in that state halfway between sleep and wakefulness when a new sound made him lift his head from his pillow. Could it be water running in the bathroom pipes across the landing? He listened for a moment or two, but now there was silence but for the fussy tick of his alarm clock. It was a quarter-past two; there could be nobody else in the house at this time.

He relaxed into his pillow, wanting to go back to sleep, but it was slow to come. He was dozing when a soft creak from above brought him back to wakefulness. Arnold had done his share of night duty and he knew the sounds of this house when he was alone in it. The ceiling shouldn't creak like that.

The thought when it came, knocked the wind out of him. Was Leslie here? Was he hiding upstairs in his bedroom? It was just the thing Leslie would do, hide in his own home! Why hadn't he thought of this before? It was the most obvious thing for him to do. Gina and Eric would be feeding him. He'd be living the life of Riley up there, lolling on his bed, not having to work at all.

His heart pounding, he pushed his feet out of bed, found his slippers and raced up to face him. He went bursting into Leslie's bedroom, fully expecting to find him stretched out on his bed. He was ready to give his son a real piece of his mind.

Arnold was surprised to find the room had a deserted look. There wasn't a crease in the counterpane. He turned back one corner, to find the blankets neatly folded beneath it. The bed wasn't made up.

He straightened up, breathing heavily. The room had been tidied up, nothing was out of place. It would never be like this if Leslie were here. The window was open a little at the top, the curtains were moving slightly in the breeze. The big Victorian wardrobe was large enough for Leslie to hide in but the door was wide open. He pushed at the thick welt of clothes hanging inside, they swung on their hangers. The boy wasn't here.

Arnold threw open the door to Eric's room and grunted with distaste. Here, it was only too obvious that the bed had been slept in recently, the bedding had been roughly thrown back. Half the drawers and cupboard doors had been left open, with belongings hanging out. There were books, clothes and photographs piled on every flat surface, it was an untidy mess.

He paused, listening; the utter silence seemed heavy. He'd been wrong; Leslie wasn't here. There were two more bedrooms on the attic floor that had always been used to store family belongings that were no longer needed.

Arnold opened the first door and recoiled at the mess. Open boxes and crates with old clothes, curtains and papers spilling out of them. The children had been rummaging round in here, spreading things about, but not necessarily Leslie.

In the fourth room there was hardly any floor space left with old and battered furniture and other odds and ends piled high. Leslie might have made a den under that old table and be hiding amongst the junk. Arnold dragged an old chest of drawers out of the way, heaved chairs and suitcases aside, but there was nothing but boxes of papers under the table.

Arnold paused again to get his breath back. The air smelled stale and dust-laden. Feeling cold and irritable, he went back to his own bed and pulled the sheet up under his chin. He was being silly. It was all in his sleep-fuddled brain. He was imagining Leslie to be here. That his own son had gone AWOL was preying on his mind; he had to forget about him.

It was only after coming to that conclusion that Arnold was able to go back to sleep.

CHAPTER FIFTEEN

After six more difficult days, Eric came home from work and found the back door locked, which meant Betsy must have gone to her friend Amy's house when they came out of school. He hoped she'd stay there a bit longer. He retrieved the key that they kept hanging just inside the henhouse door and let himself in.

He lit the gas under the kettle as he went through the kitchen then ran upstairs to talk to Leslie. They'd have the house to themselves for about twenty minutes, after which Cicely would be due home. Leslie came to meet him out of one of the top-floor bedrooms at the back of the house, which was used only for storage.

'What are you doing in there?' Eric asked.

'Sorting out some stuff to sell. Come and have a look.'

He put his head round the door. A pile of bric-a-brac was building up in one corner. 'That's Betsy's old teddy bear.'

'She's too old for teddy bears and it's in good condition. If you put these things in Dobb's Auction Rooms, they'll bring more than they cost when they were new.'

'Where did that tennis racquet come from?'

'It was our mother's. There are dance dresses here that must have belonged to her too, and handbags.'

'Leslie, you'll have to clear those with Gina. She may want them. I mean, if they were Mother's... What are all those letters?'

'They're all addressed to Mam. They're interesting.'

'You've been reading them?'

'I've nothing else to do, have I? Did you get to see Harry?'

'Yes. I had to go round to his mother's house to find him. He's not working at the dry-cleaner's any more.'

'Why not?'

'He said he was given the sack. They accused him of taking money from the till, but he said he didn't and it was all a mistake.'

'Has he got another job?'

'Yes, he's working in the munitions factory. He says he can get you a blank identity card for five quid, two for seven. It's better to have two.'

'What about a ration book?'

'He thinks they're easy enough to pinch. Easier than trying to forge all those coupons. He says he'll give us a hand, show us how. He reckons the thing to do is to take a lot and sell some of them on.'

'You mean steal them?' Leslie looked shocked. 'You're going to do that?'

'You've got to have one or starve. It'll be a lark. I think we might try.'

'Oh God!'

'You should have thought of all this before you nipped out of camp and came home.'

Two floors below, the front door creaked open. Only Cicely had a key to the front door.

'She's home.'

Eric had wiped the oil off the front door's hinges and put bits of grit in them, so the noise would warn Leslie that she was home.

'I'm going down to make something to eat,' Eric whispered.

'Don't forget me, I'm starving.'

'As usual,' Eric sighed.

When he went down, the kitchen was full of steam and the kettle almost boiled dry. Cicely gave him a ticking-off for wasting gas. When Gina came home, he sat close beside her at the table and told her the news.

'Steal a whole lot of ration books?' She looked shocked. 'Will we get away with it?'

'Of course. It'll be fun,' he said. 'I can feel a stirring in my gut just thinking about it.'

'I don't know...' Gina looked nervous at the prospect.

'We'll be fine with Harry. He knows what he's doing.'

'You, me, and Leslie too?'

'Not Leslie.'

'Why not? The ration book's for him, isn't it?'

'He's scared stiff at the thought – he doesn't want to – and we'd have to get him out of the house then back in again.'

'Hardly a problem at three in the morning. We'll have to do it ourselves.'

'He's afraid somebody will see him.'

Gina said, 'I'm afraid somebody will see me.'

'You know what I mean. If Leslie was caught, being a deserter would mean a heavier sentence. Anyway, I'd feel safer without him. He'd be a bag of nerves.'

'You're right, he'd make the rest of us nervy. You, me and Harry then?'

'Yes. Harry says it'll take a few days to set the job up.'

A day or two later, Eric took Gina to meet Harry in the Coach and Horses over a drink. Harry came swaggering up the pavement as they reached the door; a sharp dresser in a belted mackintosh and a wide-brimmed trilby. He was small in stature like Leslie, and sharp-featured. Gina said he was ferret-faced.

'I'll get the drinks,' Eric said. 'You find a quiet spot.'

Gina led Harry to a table in the corner. He said, 'How did Leslie get himself in this mess? When he moaned about being called up, I told him he needn't go.'

'How would you have got him out of it?' Gina asked.

'I know a doctor who gives false medical certificates.'

'What does he charge?' Eric was back and heard that. He was keen to find out what a service run in competition to his own would cost.

'Whatever he thinks his customers can afford. He's good, though. He teaches people to feign epilepsy in case they're called before a medical board. In fact, I've heard of men who are given a discharge on medical grounds after they've been conscripted. For how long was Leslie in?'

Gina said, 'Six months, and no sign of a fit in that time. And he's been AWOL for nearly three weeks. It'd look suspicious, wouldn't it, for him?'

'Army life might be said to have brought it on.'

Eric persisted, 'How much does your doctor charge?'

'Sometimes as much as three hundred and fifty pounds.'

'What?' he was aghast. He made up his mind to ask for more from those he impersonated. 'Did you tell Leslie that?'

'He asked, but I'd have got it down for him,' Harry smiled. 'Maybe as little as fifty.'

'That's still outrageous. Where would Leslie have got all that?'

Harry shrugged. 'Did you read in the paper last week about a doctor who was caught with seven hundred medical certificates he'd had specially printed for him? They gave his address as the Forest Hill Hospital, though no such place exists. He said they appeared more genuine if they came from a hospital rather than a private address.'

Eric took a deep breath and let it out slowly. It seemed the doctors were creaming off the men who could afford to pay well. Still, thc war was almost over and that would kill the business for them all. Some were saying conscription would go on, but lads wouldn't mind so much if they didn't have to face enemy guns.

Gina was telling Harry why they'd expected Leslie to fail his medical.

'It looks like the best we can do for him now is to get him a ration book,' Harry said.

'What about an identity card?' Gina asked. 'He'll need one of those too.'

Harry smirked, 'I know somebody who sells those. They're forged, but pretty good. They pass muster.'

As they made their plans to break into the Food Office, Eric felt his excitement growing. It was lifting him out of the daily monotony of the shoe shop. It wasn't just the money, though he liked that too; he needed the thrill of doing these things.

When Harry suggested a date, he said, 'Soon, the sooner the better.'

'I think we should wait another week for the moon to wane,' Harry told him. 'We want a dark night so we can't be seen.'

'We need to get Leslie out of our place as soon as possible. It's dicey, having him there.'

'Properly thought-out plans can make all the difference between success and failure,' Harry said firmly. 'Trust me, I've done a job or two in my time.'

'Right,' Gina said. 'We do it your way. You're in charge. What do we do?'

'Start collecting plain brown-paper carrier bags to carry the ration books in. No shopping bags from home, nothing that could be traced back to you.'

'We need only one or two,' Gina protested.

'Don't be daft,' Harry told her. 'How much would you have paid if I knew of a ration book for sale? If we're breaking in, we might as well make it worthwhile, and we'll need somewhere to stash the haul until I can sell them on. I've had ration books before, they're quite bulky.'

'We can't have them in our house,' Gina said firmly. 'Think of Pa.'

'OK,' Harry agreed. 'My grandpa's got a little shed on his allotment. He's in hospital at the moment, so it's fairly safe to hide things there. The problem is, right now, I've got it stacked with other stuff.'

'You're into the black market then?' Gina asked.

'You know I am.'

'Have you got any nylons? Lots of people want them. I could sell loads.'

'Come and keep watch for us and I'll get you some.'

Eric said nothing. Nobody went in the attic rooms next to his bedroom. If need be, he could hide a few ration books in the rubbish that was already stacked in there.

'You must wear dark clothes and soft-soled shoes on the night. Shoes you can run in, Gina.'

'Will we have to? Run?'

Eric was afraid Harry was making her nervous.

'I hope not, but you never know. Gloves – don't forget you must wear gloves all the time we are anywhere near that Food Office. We don't want to leave fingerprints and, each of you, bring a small torch.

'We'll do it early on the Sunday morning,' he decided. 'The bobbies will have their busiest night on Saturday. Let's hope they're tired by three o'clock and taking it easy.'

'Pa should be on nights by then,' Gina said. 'That's fine at home, but I'd hate to come face to face with him while we're doing this.'

'Unlikely,' Eric said. 'The Food Office is in New Ferry, not on his beat.'

Harry said, 'We wait quietly out of sight, watch the bobby doing his round and start as soon as the coast's clear. I went to look at the place this afternoon. Before the war, a firm of solicitors used that building as offices. I went in and told them I'd lost my clothing coupons and was given a form to apply for more. There was a queue and I had to wait ten minutes or so. It gave me a chance to look round.'

'So how do we get in?' Eric asked.

'Not the front door. It's solid and strong and can be seen for some distance along the street. There's a back door but it's got two good bolts on it – we'd never get in that way. I'll have to break a window. The best one is round the back, but there's a wall to climb first.'

'It's all commercial property round there?'

'Sort of. There's a side street on one side – that's fine – but there's a newsagent's on the other side and it looks as though he lives over the shop. We'd have to be quiet.'

Eric took a gulp of his beer. He could feel himself tingling with anticipation. 'But it's a possibility?'

'It's a sure thing. Once inside it should be a piece of cake,' Harry assured them. 'I'll have to come on my bike. It's too far for me to walk.'

Eric nodded. 'No public transport at that time of night, and you wouldn't want to use it if there was. I think bikes for us too.'

'There's some waste ground behind Marquise Street. Do you know it?'

'Yes,' Gina said. 'Quite a big field.'

'A good place to leave our bikes, only a couple of hundred yards away. We'll meet there at three o'clock.'

Eric was looking forward to it. He spent the next few days putting together the things he'd need, and making sure Gina had them too. He checked over their bikes, oiled them; they both had to be in good working order. He was itching to get on with it, though Gina was full of foreboding.

'We'll be all right,' he assured her, and felt in his bones that they would.

On Saturday night, Eric put his alarm clock under his pillow so nobody else in the house would hear it when it went off. When the muffled ring sounded at two o'clock in the morning, it took him a moment to clear his head of sleep. He was surprised to hear Leslie hiss from the doorway.

'Are you awake, Eric?'

It seemed Leslie had been awake in the next room and had heard it. His face was ghostly white in the gloom. He looked fraught. Eric was glad he wasn't coming.

'Go back to bed,' he whispered. 'Go to sleep.'

'I can't sleep.'

Eric got out of bed and tiptoed down to Gina's room to shake her awake.

'Five minutes to get dressed,' he whispered. 'I'll see you in the kitchen.' Cicely slept on the same floor as Gina – Betsy too, and her bedroom door was open. They must not be woken up.

Already Eric felt quite heady, intoxicated with the thrill of doing something out of the ordinary. He thrived on excitement like this. It was too bad he hadn't been allowed a more active part in the war. During the Blitz he'd done fire-watching on four nights a week. Most of the time it had been deadly dull, but he'd had a few exciting nights, but the need for that had gone now. This last year, London had been getting the buzz bombs but nothing had come up here.

Eric had had dreams of being a spy. He reckoned he'd have made a good one. It would have given him the kicks he craved.

Gina came down with her shoes in her hand. She and Eric put coats and gloves on and went out to get their bikes. It was a dark night and they pedalled together into New Ferry without seeing anybody.

They went down a side street to the waste ground and dismounted. Eric could see Harry following them down from the main road. He was minus his bike, but carrying a strong galvanised bucket. The site had a thick covering of rosebay willowherb, nettles and rough grass.

'I've hidden my bike,' he said softly. 'Lie yours flat so they won't be seen in the dark. But count so many paces in from this corner, so you know where to look. When we come back, you might want them in a hurry.'

Harry led the way back to the main road. Behind the buildings fronting it was a back entry. 'We'll wait here,' he told them.

'Aren't we going now?' Gina asked.

'Hang on a bit. I got here early and the bobby hasn't done his round yet. Generally you can set your watch by him. When we go, let's make it single file with plenty of space between us. If we march up the pavement three abreast, we'd be noticed if someone happened to be looking out of a window. It might be important – you never know at this game. I'll go first.'

'I'll be last then,' Eric said with a shiver.

One car drove past on dipped headlights at the wartime speed limit of twenty miles an hour. There was utter silence when the engine noise died away.

'Listen,' Harry said. 'Can you hear anything?'

Erie almost said no, but then it came, footsteps, the odd rattle of a letter box. A pause, then more footsteps.

'It's the bobby.'

He was passing on the other side of the road, trying doors, making sure premises were securely locked.

'Right,' Harry whispered, 'let's move up to the main road but stay out of sight in the shadows. We'll give him a moment to turn the corner and I'll get started.'

Eric waited and watched. He couldn't always see Harry as he went silently up the road, keeping to the shadows. He dug Gina in the ribs when Harry had gone twenty yards or so.

The Food Office was faced with light-coloured stone and stood out, but the door was recessed into an open porch. Eric joined the other two there.

'You stay here and keep watch, Gina,' Harry told her. 'If you see someone coming, keep out of sight until they've gone. If it's a bobby or you think we're in danger of being caught, ring the doorbell – just once, but make sure it sounds. I tried it the other day; it does work. Then skedaddle and get yourself home.'

'Right,' she said. Harry and Eric turned to go.

'Hang on,' Harry hissed urgently, catching at Eric's arm and flattening him and Gina back against the door. A motor bike came slowly down the street. Eric held his breath until it chugged past.

Harry was suddenly more tense. 'Gina, only ring the bell if we need to get out in a hurry, OK?'

Eric could feel his heart thudding.

'Come on, Eric, let's get going. Round the back.'

To Eric, the wall he'd have to climb looked dauntingly high. Harry placed his bucket upside down against it, then crossed to the other side of the entry and indicated a dustbin. Eric helped him carry it over and place it against the wall and the bucket.

'OK, this is to give us a leg up. You first, and don't make any noise. See if there's another bin on the other side.'

Eric didn't find it hard after all. He dropped down, it was even darker in the small yard on the other side, but a dustbin showed up in the thin beam of his torch.

'Here,' Harry hissed from the top of the wall, and handed the bucket down to him. With a soft thud he landed beside him.

'Let's organise our getaway route first.' They carried the other bin into position against the wall.

'The window next.' It was of Georgian type with twelve small panes. Eric wondered how they'd get through that. He watched as Harry pulled a rolled-up hessian sack from under his coat, put it against the lower central pane and give it a sharp tap. The tinkle of falling glass made them both freeze and listen.

A dog barked in the distance, otherwise there was silence. Harry stood on the bucket and put his hand inside to release the catch. Then he was able to lift the sash window high enough for them to get in.

'There's a sink and draining board on the other side,' he whispered. 'This must be where they make the tea.'

Placing the sack across the sill to cover the shards of glass, he scrambled in.

Eric followed. 'You've done this before,' he whispered.

'Once or twice.'

Harry was calm and collected, and seemed very much in control. He pulled the sack inside and shone his torch on it, then picked off two large pieces of glass and shook off the bits.

There was one chair in the narrow room; he put it in the best position to climb quickly back onto the draining board. The door was open and they went out into a passage way.

Eric was all keyed up. He felt on top form, like a tiger ready to spring. He followed Harry to some stairs. They went quietly up.

'I think this is where they store the ration books.' Harry tried the door. 'Locked.'

Eric felt a searing disappointment but Harry brought a Swiss knife out of his pocket and set to work. 'This wouldn't keep a boy scout out,' he whispered. 'Very old lock. The housing is loose.' Two minutes later there was a click. 'Got it.'

Eric heard the note of triumph in his voice. He'd never felt more alive. 'Get your carrier bags out and get ready to grab all you can.'

Harry pushed the door open and the sudden ear-splitting clang of an alarm blasted into the silence, making Eric jerk with shock. He saw Harry turn ready to run, but he caught him by the wrist.

'Grab what you can, first,' he shouted above the racket.

He switched on the light. On both sides of a narrow room there were shelves stacked high with countless ration books, some loose but most done up in bundles. Eric started to fill his carrier bags while Harry was filling his sack. They were snatching at the bundles, sending many to the floor in their haste.

'That'll do. Come on, let's get out of here.' Harry was racing back to the stairs. Eric followed. The clangour seemed to reverberate through the building. The window was still open, Harry threw his sack through, took two of the carrier bags and was gone. The bucket scraped on the concrete yard as he landed on it. Eric handed out the remaining two bulging carrier bags; he heard Harry push the bucket back in position for him as he dangled his feet, feeling for it. He felt a sharp jab on his knee and let out an audible gasp of pain. He must have cut himself on a piece of glass.

Harry had moved the bucket back in place to help them over the wall. Eric tried to scoop up the four carrier bags that Harry pushed at him.

He missed one but saw Harry swing the sack over his shoulder and grab for the bag. Eric was relieved to be safely out, but he could hear shouts and nearby windows being raised.

'Stop,' a voice commanded. A cyclist was drawing to the kerb just ahead of them. 'Stop, I say.'

Harry swung his sack at him just as he was trying to dismount and the man collapsed on the road amidst spinning wheels.

'Come on,' Harry urged. 'Hurry up.'

Eric could no longer keep up with him. His heart was pounding and felt as though his chest would burst. His bags felt weighted with lead.

'Come on.' It was Gina's voice. She was taking two of the carrier bags from him, swinging them easily in one hand. Her arm slid through his to tow him along.

A car was coming. Was it the police? Eric couldn't turn to look and had no breath to ask. Down the side street at last and they were back at the waste ground. A few steps in and Gina was pushing him to the ground. He collapsed on the cold damp earth, feeling the sharp sting of a nettle against his cheek. He was struggling to get his breath.

'We've got to get out of here,' Harry was kneeling over him. 'The police have gone in. They'll know what we've taken. They'll come looking for us in a minute.'

'You get going,' Gina was saying. 'Eric will have to rest for a few minutes.'

Harry got up and started looking for his bike. 'Is he all right?'

'He will be. What am I to do with all these ration books?'

Harry was taking some from a carrier bag and pushing them into his sack. Another few bundles went into the saddlebag of his bike.

'Yes, the saddlebags,' Gina said. 'We emptied them before setting out. You go, don't wait for us.'

'Will you be all right?'

'Yes. Go while you can.'

'Right – I will.'

Eric lifted his head. Gina was hastily stuffing their saddlebags. She screwed up the last few in the carrier bag and pushed it into the basket on her handle bars.

'Come on, Eric. We've got to move. Here's your bike.' He stood up unsteadily, and Gina thrust the handle bars against him. 'Harry went along the main road, we'll go down towards the river. Get going.'

He wheeled his bike to the rough track crossing the waste ground, got on, wobbled a little and started to pedal. It was easier going when he reached the Tarmacadamed road on the other side. Then it was downhill, thank goodness, the wind clearing his head.

Gina caught him up, 'Switch your light on,' she hissed.

He leaned over and did it. Gina had a dynamo on her bike but he'd never bothered. He wasn't much of a cyclist, but it was almost the only alternative to shanks's pony.

'Better if we separate. You go back along the Esplanade – that's the shortest route. I'll take to the backstreets.'

'OK.' They'd agreed they would if there was any trouble. Gina was a more practised cyclist and she knew her way round.

He'd only gone a few yards when a police car came racing towards him on the opposite side of the road. He held his breath until it was safely past. If the police did stop them they'd be in trouble with all these ration books on them.

He was relieved to reach the Esplanade, which was deserted, and even more relieved to reach Grasmere Road. Their front gate was open and Eric cycled up the path. He was safely home and Gina's bike was in the shed, its saddlebag still plumped out. The basket on the handlebars was empty. Pa's bike wasn't here but he'd finish his shift at six and Gina had left wet tyre marks on the wooden floor. Eric lifted his own bike in, found an oily duster and wiped both their tyres dry before attending to the floor.

He let himself into the back kitchen, turned the key in the lock and kicked off his shoes. Gina's bedroom showed a dim glow. She was in bed and had switched her torch on.

'Am I glad to see you,' she whispered, sitting up. 'We've got away with it, d'you think?'

'Looks like it. What did you do with the rest of the ration books?'

'They're under my bed. They'll be safe enough there till tomorrow.'

Eric shivered. 'That alarm...'

'When I heard it I was terrified. Didn't know whether to run for it or not.'

'I'm glad you didn't. I needed a hand with

those bags.'

'I decided you must have set it off and no point in ringing the bell, it would make you think somebody was coming and panic you more.'

'You did right.'

'And when Harry knocked that ARP warden off his bike, I could have died.'

'*Was* it an ARP warden?'

'Yes. I was afraid he'd seen me. Are you all right?'

'Fine. Glad it's Sunday, though. I could do with a lie-in.'

'Me too, good night.'

Eric climbed the last flight of stairs to his room. He was shattered, but the blood was still coursing through him. That night's work had been marvellous. They made a good team. He'd do it again just for the kicks.

CHAPTER SIXTEEN

Eric was still half asleep when he heard Gina say, 'Come on, wake up. It's nearly half-eleven.'

His bed sank under her weight as she sat on it. 'I've just taken a cup of tea to Leslie. I told Cicely it was for you. She's cooking dinner and hovering too close for comfort.'

Eric heaved himself up on his elbow. Feeding Leslie on Sundays was more difficult than weekdays. 'I could do with a cup myself.'

'If you get up you can have all the tea you want.' She was smiling at him.

'You're heartless.'

'Look, Leslie's found these two letters.' Gina put them on the counterpane in front of him.

'There's hundreds of letters in the spare rooms. I thought he was supposed to be looking for things to put in the auction?' Eric picked them up. 'What are these letters about?'

'They were written to our mam. They're from Uncle Tom.'

He stifled a yawn and lay back against his pillows. 'It's all right for Leslie. He can get all the sleep he wants. He has plenty of time to read old letters.'

'Too much time, but not for much longer. Now we've got a ration book for him, he can live somewhere else.'

'Yes, there's that, but I wish now I hadn't asked

Hannah to help. She was shocked at the thought of her mother purloining one.'

'I could have told you she would be. She'd never ask her mother to steal.'

'I couldn't see any other way. I was feeling desperate.'

'Read those letters, Eric.'

He sighed. 'They'll be ancient history.'

'Isn't that what Hannah wants to know about? They'll put you back in her good books. They're about her mother. Anyway, you'll be riveted.'

His bedroom door slammed behind her. Eric didn't want to read his mother's correspondence. It would feel like prying and probably rake up childhood grief, but for Hannah, he should. Stifling yet another yawn he opened the first letter and made himself concentrate.

After the first few lines he was reading with rapt attention. Who could fail to be moved by letters such as these?

They'd been written by the man he'd called Uncle Tom, who had died when Eric was very young; he had no real memory of him. Hannah thought the fault lay with Eric's family, but from these letters, which seemed so alive, so genuine, it appeared it lay as much with her own. Hannah had said she wanted to know more, but she didn't know where to start looking. He'd take these letters to her this afternoon. They'd open her eyes and she ought to know the truth.

Eric got dressed and went down to the kitchen to make tea and toast. He couldn't get the letters out of his mind. He wanted to know if there were any more like them. He had a couple of hours to spare before the Sunday dinner would be ready, so he made two more slices of toast, buttered them, and, keeping them hidden in his hand, went back upstairs.

Leslie wolfed down the toast, and as always was pleased to have company. 'More letters? Yes, loads of them. Come and see.'

Eric remembered playing in the two spare attic rooms as a child on wet days. He'd seen Gina dress up in clothes of an earlier era that smelled of mildew. Now he looked round at the open boxes and crates. There was a whole tea chest full of shoe boxes and packets all stuffed with letters and other papers, and many more strewn round the room.

Leslie said, 'I found this set of old golf clubs – could we put them in the auction?'

Eric eyed the half-rotted leather bag. 'They're ancient. Nobody would want them.'

'And a tennis racquet. It's been kept in its own press so the frame won't have distorted.'

Eric shook his head. 'It's a funny shape, old-fashioned, and the strings are like limp elastic. It's useless. You couldn't hit a ball more than a yard or two with that. What a mess this place is in.'

Leslie shrugged. 'I can amuse myself scratching through the stuff, can't I?'

'If Pa came up, he'd know somebody had been here recently.'

'He'd think it was Gina or you. Anyway, he never comes up.'

'You should put things back where you find them.'

Eric picked up a flowered dress. He thought it could have been his mother's. From somewhere at the back of his mind, he could see her wearing it. He shivered. 'This place is full of ghosts. Do you feel that?'

'No, I don't believe in ghosts. I saw something you might be interested in.' Leslie was off at a tangent. 'Now where is it?' He shifted a sea chest a few feet to reveal a large cardboard box.

'Don't drag things,' Eric hissed. 'Anyone in the room below would hear that.'

'Is it Betsy's room or the bathroom below here?'

'It doesn't matter, don't do it. You must be quiet.' He thought Leslie wasn't half careful enough.

'Here, take a look at these. Old copies of the *British Journal of Photography*. Do you want them?'

'Wow, yes. This one dates from 1919. I'll take a few to my room.'

'There's loads of them here.'

'Loads of letters too, Leslie. Why don't you read them? See if you can find out any more about Hannah's mother. You're the only one who has the time to do it.'

'They're beginning to bore me. The writing's not easy to make out and I've never heard of most of the people who wrote them.'

Eric sighed. 'Look at the end first – that'll tell you. See if you can find any more written by Tom or people you do know.'

On the previous Friday, Hannah had looked in the evening paper and seen there was a film showing at the Lyceum in New Ferry that she'd very much like to see. She'd taken the paper and gone round to see Eric.

'Let's go tomorrow night,' she suggested. 'It's Ingrid Bergman in *For Whom the Bell Tolls*. It's doing the rounds again.'

'Sorry, I won't be able to,' he said. 'There's something else...'

'Your special job?'

'That's right.' He looked a bit self-conscious.

Hannah said, 'Now I have every evening off, it doesn't really matter, does it? I'll see if Mum will come with me instead.'

Her mother seemed pleased when she suggested it. They both thought it was a marvellous film. Hannah felt closer to her mother when they did things together. She felt sorry for her. She'd had a hard life, and she wanted to spend more time with her.

Over the last few days, Hannah had been thinking even more about Eric. She loved him, and the diamond sparkling on her left hand reminded her how much he loved her. She would have been happier, however, if he hadn't talked of needing a ration book for Leslie and tried to persuade her to get her mother to help.

Hannah had told herself half a dozen times that they only did these things because there was a war on, that it was Leslie's fault, and that Eric and Gina had to help him, but she wished he hadn't asked. It gave her mother's opinion of them a foundation of fact.

Hannah asked herself what she was going to do about it but she didn't know. She thought the world of Eric and couldn't even think of breaking off her engagement. Eric had said he'd call round for her at four o'clock on Sunday so they could spend the afternoon and evening together. She must try to talk to him about it then.

Sunday morning was damp and drizzly, but it brightened up. The afternoon was sunny, but there was a cool blustery wind. Eric seemed in rather a dreamy state when he came for her, she was glad when he suggested a walk along the Esplanade towards New Ferry.

It was high tide and a spring tide at that. The blustery wind meant the Mersey was hurling itself at the sandstone wall of the promenade. Every so often, with a noise like the crack of doom, a larger than average wave sprayed great fountains of spume into the air, which then rained down on the prom. The sun sparkled through it and Eric, like everybody else, kept as far from the edge as possible to avoid them being drenched. He strode along with her hand in his, his fingers turning her ring round and round.

The promenade was a mile long and at the end was a little beach called the Gap, where it was possible to get down to the river. There were one or two families there already, with small children making sand castles. It wasn't warm enough for bathing suits and the river was too rough for paddling.

Eric spread his gaberdine on the yellow sand and they sat down with their backs against the wall of the prom. Hannah didn't want to offend him, and she was searching for the words to talk to Eric on this difficult subject when she saw him take two letters from his pocket.

'I'd like you to read these,' he said, putting them in her hand. She could see by his face that he thought them important. 'You said you wanted to know more about your father. He wrote these to my mother.'

Hannah's heart turned over. 'To your mother, not mine?'

'To my mother, his sister.'

She opened the first and read it with the wind and tide roaring in her ears. It was dated 18 March 1923.

Dear Rowena,

Please, please help me. I am desperate for news of Esme. Her baby was due to be born a week ago, but I've heard nothing.

I know she's at the vicarage. I've called there twice but she's being guarded by that dragon of a sister-in-law. She tells me to go about my own business when I knock on the door.

I've pleaded with her to let me speak to Esme, but she says Esme refuses to do so, and that the kindest thing I can do now is to leave them in peace.

I've asked about the baby, but she won't tell me anything. I don't even know if it was a boy or a girl, only that it was born safely, that they are both well and want to start a new life in which I'm to have no part.

I have rented three rooms in a decent house. You'll see from the address at the top that it's in Bromborough, a nice area. I've found a job as a clerk in Lever Brothers soap factory in Port Sunlight, and I've now got prospects. The pay isn't wonderful but it's enough for me to keep them and possibly put a bit by to pay off my debts.

Please tell Esme that I love her and want to marry her. If she'll come with the baby, I promise I'll play it straight in future. I've got the chance to do that now, and I'll not let it slip through my fingers.

I know you've been friendly with Esme for years. Please talk to her, tell her all this and plead my case for me. I swear I'll stand by them and stay out of trouble. They'd be my lifeline.

Please write and let me know what she says as soon as you can. I pray that she'll agree.

I hope all is well with you and yours.

As ever,

Tom

Hannah could feel a lump growing in her throat as she turned to the other letter. This was dated a few days later.

Dear Rowena,

Thank you for your letter. Yes, I feel very cast down, deeply depressed because I can't have what I so much want. My life won't be worth living if the answer really is to be no. I won't even want to go on.

I know, if only Esme would come, I could make her happy. Could I ask you to try again? It's the only hope I have. I've written to her several times but I get no reply. Esme isn't hard like this – she's generous and loving. Tell her I'll never stop loving her. I'm sure it's the vicar's wife who's turned her against me.

At least I know I have a daughter who weighed seven pounds at birth and she's to be called Hannah. I would give anything to see her. See them both, I mean. Do please try again for me. Do your best.

With love from your brother,

Tom

When Hannah let the letters fall into her lap, the Liverpool waterfront shimmered through her tears.

'I wanted you to see that it wasn't all the fault of my family,' Eric said gently. He put an arm round her shoulder and pulled her close. Hannah buried her face in his rough tweed jacket and wept.

She felt sick. Until now, her sympathy had gone to her mother. She'd always seen her fatherless state as first and foremost a hardship for her mother to endure. Yes, of course, she'd have liked to have a father, but since she'd never known one, and her mother had done all she could to compensate, she hadn't missed his presence.

Now, reading her father's letters, so full of raw longing, changed that. He would have loved them both, given them a very different life. Hannah lifted a tear-stained face from Eric's shoulder. 'It's as though Mum was made of stone.'

'Uncle Tom sounds absolutely heart-broken.'

She said, 'It was cruel not to let him know what was happening, not even to let him see Mum and me. What exactly did he do to deserve this? Aunt Philomena speaks of criminal acts, but surely she doesn't mean starting a pub fight? We could all have had a much happier life, if only she'd given him a second chance?'

'Perhaps she did,' Eric said softly.

'No, she didn't. He wrote this second letter only a few days later.'

'I meant in the weeks that followed. Tom was asking my mother to try again. Your mum may have agreed. Perhaps he failed to keep those promises.'

Hannah shook her head. 'I don't think they got together again. Mum said she was never married.'

She felt a ripple of anger that her mother hadn't tried harder. 'I want to go home. I want to show her these letters. This isn't the story she's been telling me. Come with me. I think we should have this out with her.'

They walked the mile back along the prom at twice the speed they'd sauntered down. The tide had turned, the water was no longer splashing over, but the sun had gone and it was chilly.

'Do you really think I should come in to talk to your mum?' Eric was having misgivings before they reached Grasmere Road. 'I mean, she doesn't even like me calling for you when we're going out. This is very personal. She'll think this is none of my business.'

'I need you,' Hannah told him.

When she used her latchkey to let them into the hall, her mother put her head out of Philomena's sitting room.

'Hello, dear, you're back early.' It was only then that she saw Eric behind her. 'Oh!'

'Will you come upstairs, Mum? We've something we want to show you.'

'I'm having my tea with Philomena. Just a meat

sandwich and a piece of cake.'

'This won't take long.'

Philomena's voice was loud and irritated. 'What is it, Esme? Is that Hannah?'

'Please, Mum.' Hannah felt she couldn't wait. She wanted this sorted out now.

'Come and finish your tea, Esme,' Philomena commanded. 'It's bad for your digestion to leap up and down like this in the middle of a meal.'

Hannah put her head round the door. 'Sorry, Aunt Philomena. I want a word with Mum. It's important. She'll come back soon.'

Mum was looking askance at Eric. 'What is it?'

Hannah took her arm; she could feel her trembling as she led her to the stairs.

'Let's sit down first.' Hannah poked their fire into a blaze and threw on more coal. 'Now, Mum, Eric brought me two letters. I want you to read them.'

'What sort of letters?' Esme's eyes were wide with apprehension.

Eric said, 'We were looking through some old things in our attic, and came across a lot of letters that had been written to my mother.'

'To Rowena?'

'Yes, a very long time ago. These two were written by my Uncle Tom.'

Her mother's face showed acute anxiety. Hannah took the first letter out of its envelope and handed it to her. 'Read it.'

Hannah was watching her as she slowly scanned the page. Her expression changed to one of astonishment; her eyes were wet when she looked up.

'Didn't you know about this, Mum? Didn't you

know my father was pleading for a second chance?'

'No.' It was a barely audible whisper.

'So what did you believe happened?'

Esme shook her head, looking dumbfounded.

'You thought Tom had abandoned you?' Eric asked softly.

'Yes. Rowena said nothing about this to me. I didn't see her. I thought she'd forsaken me too. She and Tom had always been good friends.'

Hannah said, 'I'd be only three days old when that first letter was written. You wouldn't have been out and about, doing things, like going to church where Rowena could have spoken to you?'

'No. I was lying in. Philomena was very good. She provided a nurse for the first month, and she kept me indoors for weeks after that. The weather was bad, you see, not fit to take a new baby out. I was a bit depressed too and I didn't want to go out.'

'Rowena might have come to the vicarage and been turned away?'

'Philomena wouldn't had done that!'

Eric said, 'Somebody did. Rowena was able to let Uncle Tom know about the birth, Hannah's name and weight and that you were both well. She certainly spoke to somebody.'

'In the letter, Tom says he called at the vicarage twice and that "dragon of a sister-in-law" wouldn't let him near you.'

Her mother was no longer able to hold back her tears. 'Afterwards, I did see Rowena in church, but she always seemed to be in a rush. One Sunday, I made a point of catching her, meaning to ask how Tom was, but she said a cold hello and turned away. I knew then she'd taken his part, that I'd lost my friend as well as Tom himself. They were both dead within the year.' She picked up the letters. 'I never knew he felt like this.'

Hannah went to perch on the edge of her mother's chair and wrapped her arms round her. She said, 'The Goodwin family isn't all bad, you see, and our relatives aren't all good.'

Anger was welling up inside Hannah for what Philomena had done. 'I'm going down to let her know what I think of her. What she did was–'

'No,' Esme caught at her sleeve. 'No, Hannah. I don't want you to.'

'You're going to let this pass? Say nothing to her? Let her get away with it?'

Esme was biting her lip.

'Mum, what she did was despicable. She was pretending to help you, yet she kept you and Tom apart.'

Her mother shook her head. 'I want to do it myself,' she said with a firmness Hannah rarely saw, 'but I need to get over the shock of it; cool down first.'

Hannah stared at her, not sure that she meant it.

'I can't go near her again tonight, I'm too upset. I want you to help her into bed. Will you do that?'

'And not mention these letters?'

'I want you to say nothing. Absolutely nothing. I don't want her to prepare her excuses.'

Hannah nodded. 'If that's what you want. It's a bit early yet. I'll get us all something to eat before

I do that.'

Eric stood up, looking uncomfortable. 'I'd better go home.'

Hannah was afraid Mum wouldn't be able to cope with having him here tonight. She'd never seen her looking like this before, half dazed with shock. 'Perhaps you had,' she agreed.

Hannah saw Eric down to the porch, shut the door behind her and clung to him.

'Poor Mum,' she sighed. 'That cut her to ribbons.' It had proved an emotional onslaught for them both.

Eric felt quite emotional himself as he came out of Highfield House. The evening he'd planned was not to be, but he didn't feel like going home yet. Instead, he set off to the Coach and Horses in Bedford Road. He hoped to find some company, but though he passed the time of day with an acquaintance, there was nobody he really knew in tonight.

He thought about the letters. They'd gone some way to revealing the truth and, he hoped, heal the breech between the two families. But Hannah needed to know the whole story before she'd let this rest.

Hunger drove him home. He knew Gina would be out and Leslie would be hungry too.

When he let himself in, his father was in the back kitchen polishing his shoes and whistling softly through his teeth. Pa was never satisfied unless he could see his face reflected in his toecaps. He was preparing to go to work on what he called the graveyard shift, ten at night until six in the morning, and seemed in a reasonably good mood.

'Pa,' Eric said, 'what's all this bad feeling between us and Hannah's family?'

Arnold looked up and smirked. 'Don't they think you're good enough for her? I'm not surprised. They're a snobby lot.'

'It's more than that.'

'They look down on me too, though I work for the Church. I had a run-in with Philomena Wells not long ago.'

'On Church business?'

'She's never forgiven me for getting the better of her.'

'What happened?'

'She said the churchyard was a disgrace. The grass wasn't kept short enough, and mud and soil was being tramped along the paths. She had the nerve to say that I must lay the law down to the men doing it. That instead of working, they were sitting around on the gravestones smoking. They were just having a short break. She doesn't seem to realise that, like me, they're all volunteers and doing it for nothing.'

Eric knew his father would resent anything like that.

'She even said the churchyard looked better when Mr Dovedale had been in charge. I told her that unfortunately, Mr Dovedale had gone to meet his maker and could no longer attend to our churchyard, and that she'd have to be satisfied with my efforts.'

'It's got to be more than that, Pa. Mrs Wells has real hard feelings against us.'

'Mrs Wells thinks she sits at God's right hand.

She even tries to make the vicar do things her way. She's bossy...'

Eric felt this was not getting him anywhere. To get his father on course, he said, 'I think it has to do with Uncle Tom.'

'Tom Caxton?'

'Was that his name?'

'Yes, he was sweet on Esme Wells.'

'Sweet on her?' Eric thought that the understatement of the year. 'Pa, you said he was Hannah's father.'

'So he was. You can't expect them to like us when Tom gets her in the family way and doesn't marry her.'

Pa was in an unusually expansive mood. Eric knew he'd picked a good moment for this. 'Tell me about him. He was my mother's brother?'

'Yes, they were close.'

'Why didn't he marry Hannah's mother? Mrs Wells tells Hannah he committed criminal acts but not what they were.'

Arnold decided his shoes would pass muster. He sat down and started to put them on.

'Oh, that! Tom went off the rails. It was not only embarrassing, but it put me in a difficult position. I was a policeman and my brother-in-law was being investigated. It was all over the papers.'

'What was? I know he started a fight in a pub, but it wasn't just that, surely?'

'No, it was theft.'

Eric was shocked. 'What did he steal?'

'It was a long time ago.' His father was frowning.

'Pa, you can't have forgotten! You were a

policeman – you must have known every detail.'

'Tom was caught in a bakery helping himself to bread and meat pies. He said he'd run out of money and had had nothing to eat that day. He was let off with a caution for that.'

Eric tried to think. 'Tom had lost his job so he had no money – wouldn't my mother have given him food?'

His father gave a snort of contempt. 'If you must know, I'd warned him to stay away from us, not come begging from Rowena.'

Eric was frowning, 'And she agreed with you? Mam was full of compassion – she'd help anyone.' He remembered that much.

'Rowena persuaded a friend of my father's to give Tom a job in his jeweller's shop. Jobs were hard to get at that time, and without one Tom didn't stand a chance. We thought the problem was solved. He rented some rooms and was making plans to get married, a quiet wedding. We thought it would settle him down.

'But within a week or so of Tom starting work, there was a break-in at the shop and thieves got away with some valuable jewellery.'

'And Tom had something to do with it?'

'I found it hard to believe at first, but yes. He'd got into bad company, a gang. Tom was persuaded by them that one job from the jeweller's shop and he'd be able to pay off his debt and live an honest life afterwards. Well, quite apart from trouble at work, it caused a family row. I couldn't allow Rowena to have anything to do with Tom Caxton after that.'

'He was charged with theft?'

'Found guilty, he got sent down for three months. Anyway, it's time I was off.' Arnold went into the hall and put on his jacket and helmet. Then put his head round the living-room door to say good night to Cicely.

As he came back through the kitchen, Eric said, 'What became of Tom? When he came out?'

Pa paused at the table. 'He was upset at being shut out of Rowena's life, and Esme's, of course. He went to pieces.'

Arnold went to the back door to struggle into his cycle cape.

Eric followed. 'Don't go without telling me how it ended,' he implored.

'Tom found some rooms in Bromborough, lived there alone for a few months but his health wasn't good. He found another job at the soap factory, but he wasn't able to hold it down. He was persuaded to take part in a raid on a bank.'

'Without a wage, he'd have had to steal.' Eric could feel himself sweating. 'The raid went wrong?'

'Yes. We were after them. I didn't know Tom was involved to start with. He had to lie low with the gang in a semi-derelict farmhouse. He caught pneumonia and, of course, for obvious reasons they delayed calling a doctor until it was too late.'

Pa was very hard. Perhaps his job had made him so, for he certainly had no sympathy for people who broke the law.

His face was twisting. 'I've never had any promotion. I blame Tom Caxton for that.'

Eric shivered at the resentment in his voice.

CHAPTER SEVENTEEN

Esme slept little. She'd read the letters through umpteen times and wept for Tom until her eyes were puffy and red. That he'd tried so hard to reach her and been capable of expressing such tender feelings altered the perception of him she'd built up. She'd thought Tom hard and callous, but he'd served his three-month prison sentence and come out determined to make good. He'd found somewhere for them to live and a job to support them. It seemed he'd never intended to abandon her. He'd written that he loved her and wanted to marry her. For Esme that changed everything.

Believing Tom had let her down had robbed her of confidence and self-esteem. Her life could have been very different, much happier, more normal, if it hadn't been for Philomena's interference. Esme was still trying to come to terms with that. She'd lain in her bed for what seemed hours, feeling sick and aching all over.

When she was going to work, Hannah always got up before she did. She came in looking concerned, bringing the usual cup of tea.

'Are you all right, Mum?'

'Yes, not too bad, dear.' Actually, she felt quite shaky. 'I'll be fine when I've had this.'

Before getting dressed, Esme normally allowed herself a scant five minutes to drink her tea, but today she just couldn't get going.

She found it hard to believe Philomena would take the decision not to allow Tom to see her and his new-born daughter. But the letters were proof that she had. It was an outrageous thing to do, and she hadn't even mentioned Tom to her. She must have known it would change Esme's life – change Tom's life too – and leave Hannah without a father.

Before she went to work, Esme saw it as part of her morning routine to take Philomena some breakfast and help her get up. Today, she felt shattered and just couldn't face her. She pulled the sheets up round her neck and continued to agonise.

How many times had she told Philomena she was grateful for what she'd done for her and Hannah? She'd put a roof over their heads and food in their stomachs, but now Esme realised that might not have been necessary if she hadn't prised her away from Tom.

She knew Philomena was manipulative. She still did as much work for St Augustine's church as she had when she'd been the vicar's wife. She had a finger in everything: she was the driving force when it came to raising money for church funds, she still chaired most of the committees set up to organise fêtes, hotpot suppers, bazaars or flower shows.

She put herself in charge of drawing up a rota of willing ladies to clean the church and the church hall, and another to provide flower decorations. She always let them know if their efforts didn't meet with her approval.

She'd tried to push Mr Goodwin aside and tell

the men he organised to keep the churchyard tidy, that their efforts were not good enough, but he was having none of that. Philomena had been most offended when he'd told her plainly that if she had a problem with the churchyard he'd prefer her to discuss it directly with the vicar. It seemed Mr Osborne thought highly of what Mr Goodwin did.

Recently, after many years, Philomena had relinquished the role as church treasurer but the figures were shown to her before they were written in the official ledger, and no money collected was ever spent without her approval.

At one time she'd edited the church magazine, but the present paper shortage had brought that publication to a halt. Philomena's opinion was still regularly sought on many subjects. She wanted to be at the centre of things.

Esme had, for a long time, suspected Philomena's rheumatoid arthritis was not as bad as she made out. Ten or twelve years ago, she'd fallen down the steps of the church tower after going up to make sure the bell-ringers had not left sweet papers in the belfry again. She'd broken one ankle and twisted the other and had to use a wheelchair for a time. She'd found it brought her sympathy and offers of help from the congregation, and as a result, she'd never really given it up.

Philomena was a strong-willed woman who directed not only Esme's life, but the lives of many others in the parish. For the first time, Esme realised she'd become a marionette, with Philomena pulling all her strings. Her sister-in-law had absolute power over her. Esme wheeled her round, looked after her, and did as she was bid. Philomena wanted that sort of power over Hannah too. Esme knew it was time she made a stand against her.

She sighed, and struggled out from under the bedclothes. She really must get up and go to work. That would keep her away from Philomena for a few hours, give her time to think about what must be done. She was used to the Food Office and the people who worked there. It would feel normal and steady her up.

Esme felt better when she was up and dressed. Another cup of hot tea and some toast helped. She felt she had to make the same for Philomena and took it down with her on her way out.

'I'm a little late this morning,' she told her, putting the teacup down on her bedside cabinet in order to open the curtains.

'More than a little late,' Philomena said tartly. 'I've been waiting for my early morning tea.'

'I'm sorry.'

'And what about my egg? You know a good breakfast makes all the difference to me.'

'Terribly sorry. At least it's Monday and Brenda will be coming. She'll be happy to boil you an egg.'

Philomena was petulant. 'I like her to start by lighting my fire and dusting the sitting room.'

'I'll have to rush,' Esme said. 'Bye-bye.'

She ran out to the road, relieved that she could put off having things out with Philomena until this evening. She was sure she'd feel better once she was inside the doors of the Food Office. To chat with her colleagues, to sit down at her desk and deal with routine enquiries would bring her back to normality.

Earlier in the war, the Food Office had been a busy place, with queues of people applying to replace ration books and coupons lost in air raids. Now, generally speaking, they were less busy, but the period covered by the present ration books was coming to an end, and everybody would have to be issued with another. Esme expected to be busier than usual today.

She was late and by the time she arrived, the police were already there. She was shocked to find the Food Office had been broken into over the weekend and thieves had got away with a lot of blank ration books. It was the third break-in they'd had in a year.

Nothing seemed normal after that, as they tried to work out exactly how many books had been taken. They were all kept desperately busy. The place teemed with police for most of the day. Esme had a headache and felt harassed.

By late afternoon, she'd taken some aspirin and was telling herself to calm down. She made up her mind that in future she wouldn't allow Philomena to take up all her spare time or dictate exactly how she would live her life. Hannah had been right when she called her Philomena's doormat. Hannah had had the guts to stand up to her and Esme decided she would do the same. Philomena would have to do more for herself or find another slave.

As Esme let herself into the house, her sister-in-law's querulous voice called, 'Is that you, Esme?'

She flung open her sitting-room door. 'Yes, it's me.'

‘I need another scuttle of coal bringing in. My fire’s gone quite low.’

In a rush of impatience, Esme retorted, ‘It’s stuffy in here and hot. I’m sure this can’t be healthy. It’s a lovely sunny day and quite warm. Are you sure you need a fire?’

‘That’s for me to decide. You don’t realise that sitting still as I have to, I soon feel cold without a fire. Another scuttle of coal, if you please.’

Esme poked the fire into a blaze, then sat down in an armchair and removed her hat.

‘Esme! What’s come over you? You rushed off yesterday in the middle of your tea and you’ve hardly spoken to me since.’

‘I was too upset to come near you.’

Philomena sounded irritable. ‘What happened?’

‘Eric Goodwin brought me two letters to read.’ Esme took them from her handbag and held them out. ‘Tom wrote them to Rowena. You didn’t tell me that when Hannah was born he’d called to see me several times and you wouldn’t let him in. You didn’t tell me Rowena came to plead on his behalf and you wouldn’t let her see me either.’

Philomena drew herself up straight in her chair. ‘I don’t recall anyone coming to see you.’

Esme closed her eyes and tried to shut out all those nights when she’d felt alone and abandoned by those she’d loved. That awful feeling of not being wanted, of being rejected, jabbed through her again. Having a new-born daughter had not eased that. Rather it had spoiled the joy she should have felt in Hannah.

‘Read them, please.’

‘Read other people’s letters? No, thank you, Esme. I was hoping you’d put all that behind you. It was all a very long time ago.’

‘Read them,’ Esme insisted. ‘It’s proof they came, asking to see me. You knew I was longing to see Tom. And what about the letters I wrote to him and asked you to post for me? He doesn’t seem to have received them. I suppose you put them behind the fire.’

Philomena’s aura of power suddenly collapsed. ‘What if I did? I went to a lot of trouble for you. I had to protect you from yourself. You’d have gone running back to him.’

‘Yes, I probably would. Tom wasn’t as bad as you painted him.’ Esme knew things could have been different if she’d been able to talk to him, if she’d had faith in him.

Philomena was defiant. ‘You wouldn’t have cared what that did to Fred’s position or mine. Our help was given on the understanding that you had no more to do with Tom Caxton. He was no good to you and never would be. Fred did his duty, he looked after you, and since his death I have done my best to follow his wishes.’

Esme swallowed hard. They’d told her that because of her brother’s position as vicar of St Augustine’s, she must hide the fact that she was a spinster and her child illegitimate, and she could have no connection with a man just out of prison. Philomena had bought her a wedding ring and Fred had helped her change her name by deed poll.

‘We saved your reputation for you. Nobody knows you’re a fallen woman. You’d have thrown all that over and gone off with Tom Caxton again. You'd have been back, believe me. I know that type – he couldn't stop thieving. We couldn't have helped you a second time. It's impossible to keep covering things up.'

Esme felt a hot flush run up her cheeks. 'You kept me away from him, and broke my friendship with Rowena. What did you tell her? You had no business to take decisions like that without even telling me.'

'Fred thought it the best way.'

Esme didn't think it could have been Fred's idea. He'd been full of compassion for other people. Philomena could have done that without him knowing.

'We had only your welfare at heart, yours and Hannah's. We did it for you.'

She'd never be able to look at Philomena's hard eyes glinting behind their rimless spectacles again without remembering what she'd done. Philomena didn't deserve to be fussed and coddled and Esme wasn't going to run round after her as she had. She stood up.

'Coal, Esme, I must have more coal for the fire.'

That brought her to a halt before she reached the door. There were some things Philomena couldn't do for herself, and one of them was to carry in a scuttle full of coal.

'Yes, I need coal for my own fire too.' Esme picked up the scuttle and went to fill it. She couldn't just withdraw her help. Philomena wouldn't be able to manage without it. She was trapped into doing the essentials, but she promised herself she'd do less, and she'd make sure

Hannah did less too.

When Hannah got home, she found her mother was more worked up than she'd been in the morning.

'What a day we've had,' her mother told her. 'The Food Office was broken into on Saturday night and a huge number of ration books were taken.'

That made Hannah think of Leslie's need for a ration book. Even though she'd refused to ask her mother to steal one, it seemed others would. What made her doubly uneasy was that Eric had not wanted to take her out on Saturday night. He'd said he had work to do. She told herself she was letting her imagination run away with her. The break-in could have nothing to do with Eric.

Esme's face was flushed. 'Blank ration books are like gold dust on the black market. I believe people pay a high price for them.'

'Where would you go to buy one?' Hannah couldn't stop thinking of what Eric had said.

'How would I know? But there are people who deal in anything that's scarce in order to make money for themselves. If you know somebody who's selling extra meat, they probably have the contacts and can get you extra petrol or whatever. An extra ration book is a huge advantage.'

Hannah nodded. 'Double rations of everything.' Or in Leslie's case, the possibility of being able to buy enough food to keep body and soul together.

Esme was incensed. 'Everybody is to be issued with a new ration book soon, our present ones are almost used up. Every year, it's a race to get it done in time. They're all printed well beforehand and we build up our stock. This last few days, I've been filling in the names and addresses of local people and posting the replacements out. Now, we've got to get more.'

Hannah said, 'Didn't you say you had a safe there? Can't you lock them away where thieves can't get them?'

'No. No Food Office has a safe large enough to hold new ration books plus the millions of sheets of coupons. It's a nightmare.'

Eric was itching to tell Hannah all Pa had told him about his Uncle Tom. She'd said she'd come up tonight. He was ready and waiting to take her out as soon as she knocked on his door.

He wrapped her arm through his and they sauntered down to the river. Hannah's mind was on other things. She told him about the Food Office being burgled. Eric had expected she would, and had rehearsed some suitable comments. Then he relayed what Pa had told him about Uncle Tom. She was thrilled that he'd found out what had happened to him.

'It makes a huge difference to Mum, to know all this,' Hannah said as she thanked him.

Eric tried to persuade her to go for a drink, but he could see she wasn't in the mood. She wanted to go home and tell her mum the new facts.

'Come with me,' she urged. 'Mum will be grateful for all you're doing.'

He shook his head, remembering the embarrassment he'd felt when her mother burst into tears.

'Better if I leave you to get on with it,' he told her.

It was quite early when he got home. Gina was out. Eric made himself a sandwich, and since Cicely and Betsy were in the living room, he made one for Leslie too, and took them all upstairs.

Leslie was lying on his bed surrounded with letters and other papers. 'I'm mostly drawing blanks but there's this note here from Hannah's mother. It was in four pieces, as though Mam meant to dispose of it but forgot.'

Eric pieced it together and read the scribbled pencilled note.

Dear Rowena,

I beg you not to do anything in haste. If Arnold is on two to ten this week, I'll be in any evening but Friday. Come and see me and we'll talk it over. We must try to come up with a plan.

I'm worried that if you leave him, you'll put yourself in a difficult position. You will not find it easy to support yourself and a child. I'll willingly help, and I'm sure Tom will, but you need to think this through before you do anything.

Be sure to come and see me. I can't stop thinking about your plight, all my sympathy.

Love from Esme

Leslie said, 'What d'you make of that? Mam was thinking of leaving Pa? I didn't know that, did you?'

Eric shook his head.

'You said he used to hit her,' Leslie went on. 'Would that be why she wanted to leave him, d'you think?'

'I don't know of any other. He was always laying into us when we were kids. Probably he was always laying into her.'

'He's still knocking Gina about, and Betsy.'

'He doesn't hit Betsy all that much – she's his favourite. He didn't hit you as much as me and Gina.'

'I got quite enough, thanks.'

Eric sighed. 'There's no date and no address on this note, I wonder when it was written?'

'Hannah's mam must have been in lodgings with her own room.'

'She was working, because she says come in the evening. Probably dates from before her difficulties started and before you and Gina were born. Why did Mam keep it?' Eric wondered. 'Pa would have gone for her if he'd seen this.'

'Perhaps he was at home when it arrived. Perhaps she had no fire lit. Whatever she did with it, he didn't find it.'

'We aren't the only ones with problems, are we?'

'By the way,' Leslie said. 'I found something else you might be interested in. A whole box of stuff to do with photography and it's all very old. Come and see.'

Eric followed him. Out on the landing he listened. 'It's about time for Betsy to come up to bed,' he whispered. 'Better be quiet.'

The light bulbs had been removed from their sockets in here to replace those in their bedrooms when they had burned out. Leslie had brought a torch and shone it round the attic. 'What are these?'

Eric bent over and whistled through his teeth.

'Old glass photographic negatives.' He lifted one out. 'I wonder who took these?'

'You aren't the first in the family to be interested in photography then.'

'So it seems.'

'I found an old camera too.'

'Where is it?' Eric was riveted now. 'Gosh! That's marvellous. Shine the torch this way. It's a Pearson and Denham full plate camera. That's its tripod over there.'

'Could you still use it?'

'Not with modern film. It uses those glass plates and I don't think they make them any more.'

'It's no good then. It's an antique?'

'I can't see a date on it but I think it's about forty or fifty years old. I could make prints from these negatives, though. In fact, I might go down and try a few now; see who is on them.'

Eric took an armful of glass negatives to his own bedroom and held them up against the electric light. It was still difficult to see what was on them but he could pick out those that showed people rather than views. He was curious to see what his forebears had been really like, and took several down to his cellar darkroom.

Gina was in the kitchen drinking tea. 'Feel like giving me a hand?' he asked. She was just as curious when he told her what he'd found.

'Will you be able to print from these old negatives?'

'Contact prints will be no problem. Just put the negative directly down on the printing paper like this and expose to light, then develop and fix as usual.'

'They're huge, aren't they?'

'About six and a half inches by nearly five. I won't need to enlarge them. I think this size was known as half plate.'

Half an hour later Eric had hung the pictures up to dry. He had two portraits: one of his mother and one of Hannah's mother.

He'd have more to tell Hannah when he saw her tomorrow, and he'd give her the picture of her mother. It was a much clearer photograph than the ones he'd been able to give her up to now.

The following Monday, Hannah saw Gina go to a public phone box to make a call in their dinner hour.

'To Spike,' she told her when she came back to the table in the canteen. 'I wanted to confirm a date. He's going to meet me at Reece's on Saturday night. Eric said last night that you might like to make up a foursome. Spike will run us home afterwards.'

Hannah didn't like Spike very much; he was a bit flash, and now she was afraid he was a black marketeer who was using Gina to sell on his wares. But Gina wasn't willing to give that up, and Eric would say it was better that she didn't meet Spike on her own. Hannah knew she and Eric would spend most of the time dancing together.

'Yes,' she agreed. 'I'll come.'

Dances were held regularly in a hall over Reece's Restaurant in Liverpool. Reece's was one of the city's premier dance halls and was considered quite sophisticated.

'It's a smashing place,' Gina said. 'Spike's not all that keen, though.'

'I thought you said he liked dancing?'

'He loves it. You've seen him jitterbug? No, it's because he can't get beer there. Alcohol isn't allowed inside.'

'Most dance halls are like that.'

'That's what I told him. Reece's is handy for both of us. Easy to get to from both Birkenhead and Burtonwood.'

That evening, Hannah ran up to see Eric. He was in the kitchen with Gina and Betsy, and immediately confirmed they'd both go dancing on Saturday night. Hannah knew both Gina and Eric were getting very fraught because they were hiding Leslie upstairs. Both had warned her to be on her guard if Betsy was within hearing. She must be careful not to mention Leslie's name.

She hadn't seen him since the day Joey the cockerel had flown indoors. Gina said he was fed up at having to keep to his room if the rest of the family were at home, and he desperately wanted to be out and about. At the same time he was frightened he'd be recognised if he did go out and that he'd be reported to the police.

It was only when Cicely called Betsy into the living room that Eric said, 'I saw Harry Oldshaw today. He's willing to let Leslie move in with him. They were always very friendly.'

Gina's mouth dropped open. 'But Harry lives near the dry-cleaner's and he used to take Leslie home with him sometimes. Harry's mother will know Leslie joined up.'

'Ah, but Harry isn't living at home any more. He's moved to a rented two-up-and-two-down in Price Street, and he's got it to himself.'

'What luck! Just the thing for our Leslie – living with his friend and out of Pa's reach. Harry's fallen in the gravy, hasn't he? How did he manage to get a house like that?'

'It was his grandfather's. He's eighty-three and was living there alone until he fell and broke his leg. He was in hospital for weeks and when he was ready to be discharged, they thought he wouldn't be able to manage on his own. Harry's mother wanted to take him in to look after him, but there were only two bedrooms in her house. So she suggested Harry move into his grandpa's house so he could use Harry's room.'

'The lucky thing!'

'Isn't he just?' Gina's eyes lit up. 'It'll be a relief to get Leslie out from under Pa's nose. Cicely keeps saying we're eating like horses.'

'It might only be temporary,' Eric warned. 'Depends how well Grandpa recovers, and whether he wants to go back to his own house.'

'If he fell once, he's likely to do it again, isn't he? They won't want him to live on his own.'

Eric grinned at her. 'That's what Harry said.'

'Even if it's only for a week or two, Leslie had better go. Have you told him? What does he think?'

'You know Leslie. He's a bit anxious that if Harry wants him to do something dodgy, he won't be able to cope. But he can't wait to get out of here.'

'So what are we waiting for?'

'We have to fix up ... you know, the things Leslie needs to take with him. Harry said he'd pop into the shop tomorrow to talk about it. He's off work; says he's hurt his back.'

To see Eric's eyes flashing some sort of a warning at Gina surprised Hannah. She thought they were very open about their plans for Leslie. She wondered if they were keeping anything from her.

Gina was shaking her head. 'We talked of taking Leslie with us to Reece's on Saturday, didn't we? He's desperate to get out and have a bit of fun. He's scared to go out in daylight as all the neighbours know him.'

'It should be all right. Liverpool's far enough away, so he isn't likely to come face to face with anyone he knows that well. I think I'll arrange with Harry to meet us there, and he can take Leslie home with him.'

'That should be OK,' Gina said. 'Pa's on two-till-ten this week. He won't be here when we leave.'

'I'll go up and see what Leslie thinks after I've seen Hannah home,' Eric said.

They left Gina putting together a bit of supper for him. Hannah could see brother and sister were fizzing with vigour now they had a plan to get Leslie moved to somewhere safer.

Saturday night came. Hannah got herself changed and ready for the dance and, because Gina had insisted on it, went up to the Goodwins' house to join them.

'We want you to pin Betsy down so she doesn't

see Leslie,' Gina explained.

Hannah hadn't foreseen the difficulty in getting him out of the house.

'Pa's had to change his shift because someone's off sick. He's now on nights and doesn't go on duty until ten. Just our luck.'

Eric was waiting for her in the kitchen when she arrived.

'We have to make sure the coast is clear when Leslie comes down. I'm going to keep watch from the top of the attic stairs. Gina's getting changed, she wants you to go up to her bedroom.'

'Right.' It wasn't what Hannah usually did.

'Betsy's with her, watching her put on her lipstick and all that. When she's ready, Gina will go to the living room and make sure the door's shut. She'll stay talking to Pa and Cicely while I bring Leslie down and get him out.

'If Betsy doesn't go to the living room too, then we want you to stay with her and distract her. Make sure she's in a room with the door shut so we can get down without her seeing us.'

Eric took her upstairs to the first landing and nudged her towards Gina's room. 'She's expecting you.'

When she went in, Hannah could see the frown of tension on Gina's face. Betsy was having a fine time inspecting Gina's cosmetics.

'No, you can't try that face cream. It's almost impossible to buy it, I won't be able to get any more.'

'Don't be mean. It's nearly full. Is it American?'

'Spike gave it to me.'

'Would he give me some?' Betsy asked.

'No.' Gina reached into her wardrobe for her best coat.

Betsy said, 'Come and let Mam see you all dressed up. You look smashing, even your face. It must be that cream.'

Hannah was glad to see Betsy leading the way downstairs. It meant she wouldn't have to distract her. Gina raised an eyebrow to signal her satisfaction. Hannah followed them to the living room, and once inside, carefully shut the door behind them.

'Gina's got a new dress,' Betsy told her mother. 'Doesn't she look nice?'

Cicely was interested. 'Where d'you get that?'

'The Co-op. It's nothing extra. Utility – they all are.'

Her father eyed it up and down. 'You're not going out like that, are you? It's too short,' he said. 'It shows your knees.'

Gina ignored that. 'It's not dressy enough for a dance, but I couldn't find anything better.' It was green cotton, cut on plain, rather military lines and fastened all down the front.

Pa said, 'Where are you going?'

'To Reece's.'

'All the way over to Liverpool at this time of night?'

'It's not seven o'clock yet, Pa.'

'Are you going too, Hannah?'

'Yes,' Hannah said, 'and Eric.'

'Don't be late. Don't forget the trains and buses stop before midnight.'

'No, Pa, we won't.'

Eric's voice shouted from the kitchen, 'Come

on, Gina, I'm waiting.'

Hannah said, 'Good night, Mr Goodwin, Mrs Goodwin.'

Eric was at the back door, Leslie was already outside and carrying an overnight bag.

'Well, we managed that all right,' he said with a wide smile at Hannah.

CHAPTER EIGHTEEN

When they reached Reece's dance hall, Hannah followed Gina upstairs to the cloakroom. There was quite a queue to leave their coats. She could hear the band playing in the distance and tapped her foot to it. Afterwards, Hannah combed her hair and watched Gina arrange her dark curls into bangs round her face, repowder her nose and apply more lipstick. There was a sparkle about Gina tonight.

'It's the relief of getting Leslie safely out,' she smiled.

He and Eric were waiting outside the big double doors to the dance floor. Leslie was wearing civvies: a Harris tweed jacket and grey slacks. Spike arrived at that moment, smartly uniformed as a sergeant in the American Air Force.

'Hey, honey, you look swell,' he told Gina, clasping her enthusiastically in a bear hug.

'Let's go in.' Eric swept Hannah and Leslie through the doors. A glittering sphere revolved above the dancers' heads; the ten-piece band wore crimson jackets decorated with gold braid. Compared to the outside world, here was glamour.

'A slow foxtrot,' Eric said, 'let's dance.' And Hannah found herself skimming round the floor in his arms. She thought him a better dancer than she was. She could see he was watching Leslie, who was still standing near the door.

'Harry's just come in,' he said into her hair. 'Leslie's seen him.'

Hannah turned to look. She wasn't sure she liked Eric's friends. Harry looked a bit of a spiv.

'He's a great guy.' Eric was smiling. 'If there's anything you want, he'll get it for you – at a price.'

'There isn't,' Hannah said. 'Is he another black marketeer?'

Eric laughed. 'I wouldn't go that far. No, not really. I'm very grateful he's taking Leslie in.'

'Is it a good thing for Leslie to live in his house?'

'He couldn't stay at home, could he? It's wearing me and Gina out. He'll be all right now. They get on well together, and nobody will know him down in Price Street.'

'But he can't get a job, can he? Not without an identity card. So he'll have no money.'

Eric was pulling a face. 'We raised a bit by putting some old stuff Leslie found in our attic into an auction sale, and Gina and I will chip in and see he's all right.'

Hannah didn't think it was wise – not for Leslie, who was the sort of person who could be easily led. She was afraid almost everybody was engaged in unlawful dealings these days.

But it was fun dancing with Eric and she was enjoying the evening. There was a sprinkling of American servicemen in the crowd. Despite the large notices saying jitterbugging wasn't allowed because high heels and army boots cut the floor to pieces, several couples were hard at it in one corner of the ballroom. Spike and Gina were among them. She'd hitched up her rather tight skirt and her heels were kicking up with great verve. All the Goodwins were good dancers and seemed in top form. Even Leslie had found a girl to dance with.

The band retired for a break halfway through the evening and records of famous bands were played instead. Eric bought glasses of lemonade, but they barely stopped dancing long enough to drink it. For Hannah, the evening was going by in a flash. There were more dancers on the floor now it was getting late and the jollity was at its height.

The band was playing another quickstep, a Glenn Miller tune, 'In the Mood'. Eric was whirling her faster and faster. Hannah was dazzled by the shards of light reflecting off the silver ball turning slowly above them. Suddenly she realised Eric was slowing down, though the music was blasting out faster than ever.

'What's the matter?'

His face had gone deathly pale and he was leading her off the floor.

'I'll have to sit down.' He was breathless. Hannah was concerned.

'It's my dicky heart,' he gasped. 'Gets me like this sometimes.'

'You haven't stopped dancing since we came in. You should take it easier.'

'I know ... I know.'

Gina had noticed Eric's distress and brought Spike over to join them.

'You've overdone it again,' she told him. 'I thought you were going at it too hard.'

'I'll be all right in a minute. Leave us alone.'

Hannah sat beside him. She couldn't help but

admire Eric for not allowing his disability to stop him enjoying life. 'But you should be more careful.'

Leslie came over. 'Don't worry about our Eric,' he told her. 'A short rest and he'll be as good as new. How about a dance with me?'

It was a waltz, a slow one. He said, 'This is more suited to Eric. Gina's told him to sit quicksteps out but he won't.'

Hannah asked, 'How long has he been like this?'

'Hard to say,' Leslie shrugged. 'He gets over it quite quickly.'

'He won't be dancing any more quicksteps with me.'

'Mustn't let it spoil the evening. Bit of a celebration for me. First night out in ages.'

Harry danced past them with a redhead in his arms.

'I'll be able to live again. I was a prisoner in my bedroom at home.'

That dance over, Hannah went back to Eric. The colour had come back to his cheeks. A slow foxtrot was being played. 'Let's have this dance,' he said, getting to his feet.

'Should you?'

'Yes, I'm fine. Look at the time. It'll be the last waltz next.' Hannah felt his arm go round her. Eric was dancing with all his old spirit.

Suddenly, the commanding figure of a civilian police inspector strode on to the dais in front of the band and signalled to it to stop playing. The music fell away in mid-bar, the dancers came to an uneasy stop, still holding on to their partners.

The policeman's voice broke across the sudden silence. 'Ladies and gentlemen, may I have your attention?'

'He's already got it.' Eric was tense and breathing heavily again. A pin could have been heard to drop in the large ballroom.

'A search is being made for absentees from the Forces,' he announced. 'The military police are manning all exits. All service personnel will be required to have their pay books or leave passes inspected.'

Hannah shivered. Was Leslie going to be caught? She whispered, 'Leslie still has his pay book, hasn't he?'

'He can't show them that. It's a dead giveaway. They'll see he's not drawn pay at his unit for a while,' Eric said.

The police inspector went on: 'All civilians must show their identity cards. Those unable to do so will be detained.'

A ripple of unrest ran through his audience. They were no longer silent.

His voice rose an octave. 'Will everybody please collect their coats and belongings and proceed in an orderly manner to the doors?'

As the band played a hurried 'God Save the King', Eric's arm tightened round Hannah till it felt like an iron band.

'Oh my God!' he gasped. 'I'd heard they were doing this at football matches and race meetings.'

Gina and Spike joined them. 'The US military police are here too,' Spike said. 'Naval pickets and RAF special police as well. They're going after deserters like dogs chasing rats.'

The crowd was milling round, pushing past them to the doors; there was a sense of panic. Hannah steered Eric to a seat. He was deathly white again; she could see he was worried.

'I'd better give Leslie my identity card.' He sounded desperate. 'Where is he?' He and Harry were pushing their way through to them. The sweat was standing out in beads across Leslie's nose.

'They can detain me as long as they like,' Eric said, pushing his identity card on him. 'They'll find me in the clear. That's the best way round this.'

'No panic,' Harry said smoothly, pushing the card back to him. 'I told you I'd fix it and I have.'

'Gee whiz,' Spike clapped Harry on the back, 'isn't he the bee's knees?'

'I've got an identity card now.' Leslie flashed it in front of them. Gina snatched at it, comparing it with her own.

'Is it a forgery?' Hannah was shocked.

'It's all right, a lovely job,' Harry said. 'But we'll get going. Better if we go through in the thick of the crowd.'

'So long, thanks for everything you've done,' Leslie said to Eric. 'And you, sis. Come and see me. I won't be able to come home.'

The four of them were silent as the floor cleared.

'You look all washed up,' Spike said to Eric.

'He'll be all right in a minute,' Gina assured him. 'He always is.'

'It was a bit of a shock.'

Spike said, 'Come on, let's get out of here. I'll give Eric a hand. You girls get your coats and fight your way through. I'm parked on the other side of Clayton Square.'

'Did Harry get him a forged identity card?' Hannah asked Gina as soon as they were alone.

'He said he had, didn't he?' Gina was short with her.

He'd certainly implied it, but that must mean...? 'What about a ration book? I told you Mum said they'd had a lot stolen from the Food Office...'

'Give over, I'm tired. Harry's seen to everything.' Gina sounded irritable, but she took hold of Hannah's arm and led her across Clayton Square to the large American sedan. Hannah got in the back, Eric was slumped in the far corner of the seat. He was breathing normally, but didn't speak. They were all tired now and said little on the journey home. Hannah was surprised to find Spike stopping his car at her gate.

'OK, kid, this one's your home?'

Eric made a move to get out too. 'You stay with us, Eric,' Gina said.

'I always see Hannah in. I'm quite all right.'

'Yep, we know, sonny. Tonight, we'll need a hand. You know, with the chores.' Spike sounded firm.

'Oh! OK. I'll see you tomorrow, Hannah. I'll come down about four.'

The car waited until the porch door closed behind her. Hannah leaned back against it and closed her eyes. The events of the evening had unnerved her.

After reading those letters her father had written, Hannah had felt able to blame their problems on Aunt Philomena. She'd been quite sure the

Goodwins were not as black as Philomena was painting them. That had made her feel better, but now she thought about 'the chores' Spike wanted Eric to help with.

She was afraid the boot of his enormous car was filled with nylons, chocolate, tinned fruit and cigarettes for Gina to sell on, and Eric's help was needed to empty it and carry the goods upstairs where they could be hidden.

She could no longer turn a blind eye to what they were doing. This could be what had happened to her father. He'd seen his friends doing things that broke the law, and gradually he'd been drawn in deeper, just as she had. This was what Aunt Philomena had wanted to protect her from. Hannah felt poised on the brink of disaster.

She went to bed, glad she didn't have to speak to her mother, but she couldn't sleep. Her worries went round and round in her mind. It was the first time she'd seen Eric feeling the effects of his heart problem, and her sympathy made her want to comfort him. But it seemed he'd asked Harry to provide an identity card for Leslie, possibly a ration book too, and she could only see that as very wrong. Dangerous as well. She'd seen how stressed and breathless he'd been when the police started checking for deserters.

Then on top of that, Gina was involved with Spike's black market. They were breaking the law and all three of them could end up in big trouble.

Usually Hannah enjoyed Sundays. It was the one day of the week she didn't go to work. Today she felt miserable. Mum and Philomena were not on good terms, and she wondered whether she'd be able to change Eric once they were married. Would she be able to persuade him to give up all his money-making activities? She felt helpless when she thought about changing Gina.

When four o'clock came, she was ready to go out and listening for the doorbell. When it rang, she ran downstairs and was surprised to find Gina on the doorstep instead of Eric.

'I bet you weren't expecting me,' Gina said, looking through her mass of dark curls. 'Eric isn't very well. He's been in bed all day. He wants you to come up and see him.'

'Of course.' Hannah pulled the front door shut behind her. 'Poor Eric, what's the matter?'

'He says he's just tired.'

'I thought he was overdoing things last night.' Hannah remembered how he'd struggled for breath.

Gina tossed her head. 'I told him he was, but he doesn't listen. It got a bit hectic. Are you all right?'

'I'm fine. Except things are a bit awkward at home at the moment. Those letters written to your mother...'

'I told Eric he must show them to you.'

Hannah nodded. 'I'm glad you did. They put a very different slant on what happened. Mum thought she'd been abandoned when she hadn't. She's at sixes and sevens as a result and Aunt Philomena is decidedly shirty.'

'What's she got to be shirty about? It was her fault. She caused the trouble.'

'She thinks Mum doesn't want to look after her any more. Well, she's right about that, but what can we do? We can't just leave her to stew in her own juice. Mum keeps sending me to do things for her, but Philomena finds fault with everything I do, there's no pleasing her.'

'She's an ungrateful old woman.'

'We ate our Sunday dinner in dead silence. Not that it's ever a load of laughs, but today the atmosphere was icy, to say the least.'

They'd reached Gina's home. 'Come on upstairs,' she said. 'Eric's still in bed.'

Hannah followed her up to the second floor. She hadn't been inside Eric's bedroom before. He was sitting up playing cards with Betsy. It seemed strange to see him wearing striped pyjamas, but he was all smiles for her.

'Sorry about this, Hannah. I feel a bit of a fraud, lying here in bed.'

'It's your turn,' Betsy prompted.

'Can't we leave it now?'

'No,' she wailed. 'I'm winning, come on.'

Hannah sat down and watched them both flashing cards down on the counterpane in quick succession. There was a whoop of joy from Betsy.

'I've won. Beaten you again. Let's have another game.'

Eric protested, 'No, not now. I want to talk to Hannah.'

'Go on,' she nudged his arm.

'Push off now, Betsy. Leave me alone.'

'Just one more game.'

He laughed. 'Get lost. Go on, scram. Perhaps your mum will play with you.'

'Perhaps.' Betsy picked up her cards and ran downstairs.

Hannah smiled at him. 'I was worried when I heard you weren't feeling well. It's a relief to see you like this.'

Gina was biting her lip. 'Before he went to bed last night, he was doubling up with pains in his chest. It put the fear of God into me.'

'I'm all right, Gina, honest. No pains today. I just feel weary. Nothing a day in bed won't cure.'

'I think we should send for the doctor tomorrow.' His sister was frowning. 'He'd probably give you a week on the sick. You'd like that, wouldn't you?'

'I'll be all right for work tomorrow.'

'Eric! You've been told to take things easy. You're doing too much.'

She turned to Hannah. 'He's booked to go to Manchester tomorrow. I don't think he should go.'

'Give over.' Eric was giving Gina knowing looks. 'I'll be perfectly all right.'

Hannah couldn't help but pick up on that. 'Manchester? You shouldn't travel tomorrow, you aren't well enough. Is it for your secret war job?'

'That's right,' Gina said. 'Going for an army medical on behalf of someone else.'

Hannah felt the blood drain from face. 'Why?' But she didn't need to ask, she'd heard about people who did that. Was this what Eric had meant when he spoke of war work? Had he deliberately misled her?

'Why?' she demanded more forcefully.

They didn't answer. Gina was embarrassed; Eric looked mortified.

Hannah answered for them. 'So they won't be called up? To avoid conscription?'

'Yes,' Gina shrugged. 'They always find Eric unfit for military service.'

'Oh, my goodness!' She was watching Eric's face. He looked ashamed and she guessed he hadn't wanted her to know.

He muttered, 'I knew you wouldn't like it.'

Gina was looking guiltily from her brother to Hannah. 'I told him years ago he shouldn't keep it from you. Don't tell me you really didn't know?'

Hannah shook her head. She was taken aback. 'I do now.' It was a terrible thing he was doing. Hannah shivered. She felt let down, disappointed in him. For years she'd been telling her mother and her aunt that he was a lovely person.

'It started as a little ruse to make some extra cash,' Gina explained. 'but the business built up.'

'I tried to tell you,' Eric choked.

Last night, for the first time, she'd seen enough to know without a doubt that he and Gina were breaking the law. She'd half suspected it many times but told herself she was imagining it, and really it was just a bit of fun, a lark. But it wasn't just dabbling in the black market – it was so many things. Worse things. Mum and Aunt Philomena were right to be scared of them.

Hannah turned on him. 'I knew you travelled to different places, from time to time – you told me that.' She was indignant. 'But you gave me the impression you were engaged in some secret business to help the war effort. I imagined it to be something important, like intelligence gathering.' She heard the note of scorn coming into her voice, but she couldn't stop. 'You said you couldn't tell me, couldn't talk about it. You seemed to be proud of what you were doing.'

Gina was shocked to silence. Eric looked as though he'd like to pull the sheet over his face.

Hannah said, 'Please don't go tomorrow, Eric. Please don't do it ever again.' He covered his face with his hands.

'Only last week, I read in the paper that somebody had been caught in Caterham doing the same thing. He was sent to prison. Please stop before you're caught. Don't take that risk again.'

There was a long silence.

'I was going to stop when the war was over anyway.' Eric looked contrite. 'I wanted the money to set myself up in a business, to get married, to have a decent life...'

'He's saved all he's earned,' Gina added. 'It'll make all the difference to you when you're married.'

Hannah felt tears pricking her eyes. 'It's dishonest money. I wouldn't want it.'

Gina's laugh was cynical. 'All money is the same. We have to have it or be deprived of the things we need.'

'How d'you think I'd feel if Eric ended up in prison? It would be a terrible disaster. Think of my mother and your Uncle Tom. Was he trying to do something like this? Stop now, Eric, please.'

'Everybody does a bit on the side,' Gina said. 'I know lots of people who do, but none of them has ever been caught.'

Hannah shook her head. She felt frustrated because she couldn't make them see how wrong it was. Anger made her raise her voice.

'Last night I realised Harry had provided an

identity card for Leslie, and I've long since suspected that Spike is providing nylons and chocolate for you, Gina, to sell on the black market – and now this. I'm frightened for you both. Frightened you'll get caught. What else are you doing that's against the law?'

Her cheeks were burning now. They thought they were being clever; she had to make them change their ways.

'If your father knew, what would it do to him? He's a policeman, for goodness' sake. Think how he'd feel if either of you was charged with offences like these. Think of me. Aunt Philomena would go spare and say she'd told me so. Yes she has, but I didn't believe you two could do bad things like this.

'Think of my mother – she's had a very unhappy life. Happiness is what you should be aiming for, not money.'

'It's not just the money,' Gina mumbled. 'It's the only way I can get the things I want. Nice clothes, nylons and chocolate and that.'

'You won't get them in prison, and they won't seem important once you're caught.'

Eric said, 'It's been a bit of fun as well. Breaks the monotony of that shoe shop.'

'Eric! If you're caught, you won't find it fun. If you're not well, you won't be thinking quickly. You could make a mistake. Promise you won't go to Manchester tomorrow. It could be the time something goes wrong, and you aren't well enough to travel anyway. What's more exhausting than travelling by train? They're packed, never on time and you probably won't get a seat.

'I'm going home. I can't stand arguing with you two.' Hannah got to her feet, feeling drained.

'No,' Gina caught at her arm. 'Not now, not like this.'

Eric's dark eyes implored hers. 'You won't let this change anything? Between you and me?'

'I don't want it to. I love you,' Hannah said. 'And, Gina, you're my best friend, but none of us can be happy if you carry on like this. You'll ruin your own lives and mine.'

She rushed downstairs and out into the road, taking deep breaths of the cool damp air. She felt sick. She'd thought it was just a matter of a family feud. Blame for that had swung backwards and forwards from her family to Eric's, but this was worse than she'd ever imagined it could be.

She was back home with her mother much earlier than either of them had expected. She couldn't conceal her anger and agitation.

Mum asked, 'Have you quarrelled with Eric?'

Hannah was breathing heavily. 'Let's say we've had a difference of opinion.'

She couldn't possibly tell Mum what their differences were about. She'd say, 'I told you so. Be thankful you've found out now before you married him. Everything would be twice as difficult if you had.'

Hannah had another restless night. She knew she had to decide what she was going to do about Eric. She'd be fearful of what the future would bring, knowing that sooner or later he'd surely be caught. Yet she couldn't even think of returning his ring. She loved him.

CHAPTER NINETEEN

When Gina came cycling down the next morning, Hannah thought she seemed subdued.

'Eric's in a terrible state,' she said. 'He's terrified you're going to throw his ring back in his face.'

Hannah hadn't been able to calm down either. 'I told him I still loved him, didn't I?'

'He's decided not to go to Manchester. He said he'll go to the doctor's instead. He wants you to come up and see him tonight.'

All day, Hannah turned over in her mind what she could do. It ought to have been soothing to knock tiny nails into wood all day, but now there wasn't enough work to keep her occupied and she was agitated and impatient.

When she went up to see Eric that evening, Gina let her in. He was sitting at the kitchen table with Betsy. They all looked rather down in the mouth.

'How are you, Eric?' Hannah asked.

'I'm all right. I've been given a week on the sick and told to rest. Shall we go for a walk?'

'That's not resting. Also it's raining.'

'Not very much. I want to go out. We can't talk freely here,' he told her. He took a large umbrella with him, and put it up over them both as they sauntered towards the promenade.

Hannah didn't feel as close to him in mind as

she had, but in order to keep dry she had to hold on to his arm, so they were close in body.

'I'm sorry,' he said. 'Will you forgive me?'

'It's not as simple as that,' Hannah said. 'It isn't a little tiff we've had. It's a fundamental difference about the way we'll live our lives.'

'Yes, I see that. I couldn't bear it if you changed your mind about marrying me.'

'I haven't done that. I still want to, but only if you promise to give up all these wild money-making schemes.'

'Yes, I will,' he agreed.

'And not just you. I want Gina and Leslie to give them up too.'

'I can't speak for them.'

'Yes you can. They go where you lead them. If it's the safest thing for you, it's the safest thing for them too.'

'Leslie won't agree to go back to his unit. Not now, when we've just got him sorted out with somewhere to live. The war's nearly over, Hannah. They won't be hounding deserters for much longer. He can get a job now, live quietly, he'll come to no harm.'

Hannah was frowning. 'It's the wild schemes you all get up to. The three of you must promise to give up all that kind of thing.'

Eric sneezed, and Hannah said, 'You aren't well. You really shouldn't be walking around in the wet like this.'

'Let's go and have a drink in the Royal Rock Hotel.'

Hannah hesitated but decided she and Eric had to talk somewhere where they wouldn't be disturbed. The bar was almost empty and, with a glass of sherry on the table in front of her, Hannah said, 'Those are my conditions, Eric. I won't marry you unless you go straight. I want you to take a few days to think over what I'm asking you to do. Talk it over with Gina and Leslie and then make a solemn promise never to break the law again.'

'Hannah, I'd do anything for you, but I don't know whether I can persuade Gina and Leslie. I'll try, but I can't promise for them, can I?'

'You could persuade them.'

'I wish I was as strong as you.'

Hannah didn't feel strong. 'I'm not strong enough to live with you if you carry on like this. I'd be in dread of finding a policeman on the doorstep and of you being sent to prison.'

When Eric returned home, he found the kitchen light off and the rest of the family in bed. As he crept upstairs he saw the light showing under Gina's bedroom door and heard her call softly, 'How did you get on, Eric?'

He went in to sit on her bed and tell her about Hannah's ultimatum.

She was indignant. 'It's one thing to ask you to give up all your fun, but I can't see why I should. I mean, what's in it for me?'

'I'm asking you to. Hannah's got such strong ideas about right and wrong. I don't want her to throw me over.'

'She won't. She thinks the sun shines out of you.'

'She wants me to promise to go straight.'

'Well, if you want to keep her happy, do that.'
'But she wants you and Leslie to promise too.'
'She isn't going to marry us. Why should she dictate what we do?'
'She's afraid you'll be caught.'
'We won't be. We're all very careful. Leslie will have to carry on. Doesn't she understand that he's put himself beyond the law by deserting? He's still got to live.'
'I've told her it could be difficult for Leslie, but you could promise.'
'I will if that's what you want. I mean, so what if it makes her feel better? We don't have to keep our promises.'
'Yes we do. I've already promised not to stand in at any more medical exams. I'm giving that up.'
'What about the rest of it?'
'Ye-es, I think so.' Eric knew he'd built up enough capital to provide very well for himself and Hannah. He could set himself up in business without borrowing any money. He could buy a house too, if they wanted it. He felt rich when he contemplated his savings. 'You're not going to stop?' he asked Gina.
'No. It's all right for you – you've got lots of ways of picking up a bit of extra cash. I have only Spike.'
'You get your cut from Harry as he sells off those ration books.'
'He'll probably have more for us now. We should go down and see him. How about Sunday?'
'You know I usually take Hannah out on Sunday afternoons.'

'You don't have to come. I can go by myself.'

'No, I want to. Now Leslie's with him, we'll be able to find out how he's getting on.'

'Why don't we go on Sunday morning? Then you'd be back in time to take Hannah out.'

Sunday came and was very wet. The rain was swishing against the bus, and Gina had to rub condensation from the window before she could see out.

She said, 'You're too secretive with Hannah. Once you're married, you won't be able to hide anything from her.'

'I'll have everything sorted by then.'

'You won't sort out Leslie and Harry. Harry's in too deep. He's playing with the big boys now.'

'Hannah wouldn't approve of Harry. I'm glad she doesn't know too much about him.'

Gina smiled. 'Eric! You know she does. She knows Harry's fixed Leslie up with an identity card and he must have got a ration book from somewhere.'

'She doesn't know half of it. She'd be horrified if she knew we'd raided the Food Office ourselves.'

'She's too honest. We did a good night's work there, and we're still reaping a good profit from it.'

'An enormous profit. It's keeping us going. We get off here, come on.'

Leslie was glad to see them and welcomed them warmly. He led them to the bright fire in the living room. Their little house seemed cosy on this miserable morning.

'Are you all right?' Eric asked him.

'I'm fine,' Leslie beamed at him. 'Harry's fixed me up with a job. I started on Thursday.'

Gina squealed with delight. 'What are you doing?'

'Driving a lorry. Harry got me fixed up with a firm of hauliers called Fanstones. I was a bit worried about doing it the first day, but...'

'You coped,' Harry said. 'He's much better off here with me.'

'I am,' Leslie agreed. 'Much better than having Pa downstairs. I hardly dared to move.'

'It's not just plain driving,' Harry said. 'We've got a few plans worked out.'

'Nothing to get our Leslie in trouble, I hope.' Eric sounded nervous.

'It's safe enough. He's got a forged driving licence in a false name with a false address. We had some references forged for him too. It'll be impossible to trace him back here.'

'I'm clean,' Leslie said.

Harry explained, 'In civilian life, Leslie has no criminal record and therefore no files in the Criminal Records Office. The police won't be able to identify him readily, even if he gets stopped.'

Gina could see Eric stiffening up. He didn't trust Leslie to cope with jobs like that, and she knew he'd be glad Hannah was not hearing this.

Hannah felt fraught all week. She'd had to screw up her courage to spell out her ultimatum to Eric. She was half afraid he'd refuse, and then she'd have to decide finally whether to do as she'd threatened. She didn't want to break off her engagement.

She and Gina cycled to work as usual, but Gina was a bit frosty, and the atmosphere even spilled out over the canteen table at dinner time.

Gina told her, 'Eric wants to do what you ask, but I don't like him battening on me to give Spike the push. I don't really see why I should.'

'Sooner or later you'll get caught, and it's black marketeering and profiteering.'

'What I do is my business, Hannah, not yours.'

On Saturday night, Eric took Hannah to the pictures. On the bus going into town, he said, 'I give you my promise, Hannah. I'll do what you ask, but it's not in my power to guarantee that Gina and Leslie will.'

'Gina's already told me it's none of my business,' Hannah said.

'I'll do my best, but they have their own ideas about what they want to do.'

'I know,' Hannah said. 'I bargained for too much, didn't I? I wanted to keep them out of trouble too.'

'Will you settle for what I can promise?' Eric's eyes were pleading with her.

'You know I will.'

He gave a sigh of satisfaction. 'I couldn't contemplate the future without you,' he told her. 'I do love you.'

Hannah felt reassured that Eric had promised to call a halt to his law-breaking schemes, but she'd been thoroughly unsettled by the whole business. She'd seen her mother's distress when she'd spoken of similar misgivings and had the example of what she'd endured.

In her heart Hannah was still looking forward

to being Eric's wife; but her head was telling her she could be caught up in trouble. If Leslie and Gina were found out, Eric would not remain aloof.

On Sunday morning, she went to church with Aunt Philomena and her mother as usual, her mind still churning on her own problems.

Mrs Osborne made a point of coming over to speak to them. Hannah always asked how Robert was when they came face to face.

'Such good news, dear. He was moved to a hospital in Liverpool last Wednesday. I've been to see him and he's much better. I'll be able to see so much more of him now he's nearer. He asked to be remembered to you, Hannah.'

'You must go and see him, Hannah.' Aunt Philomena's voice was loud and insistent. 'He won't have had many visitors down in Portsmouth.'

'Of course I'll go.' Hannah asked for details of how to get there.

His mother said, 'I'm going to visit him this afternoon – would you like to come with me?'

'It'll be better for Rob if we go separately. Tell him I'll come tomorrow evening.'

Hannah cycled home from work as quickly as she could on Monday evening, had a quick meal and caught the train over to Liverpool. She wanted to take him a little gift, but there was so little available that she'd accepted Philomena's offer of books from her bookcase. She chose two she thought he might enjoy; reading was surely something he'd want to do to pass the time.

He was pleased to see her, and Hannah could see smiles of welcome lighting up his face as she went down the ward. With Rob, he could be gone from her life for months, even years at a time, but when she saw him again it was as though she'd spent time in his company only yesterday. They took up instantly where they'd left off. He didn't seem much changed.

'I'm doing fine, learning to dance again.' He was lying on his bed but a pair of crutches propped against the wall told their own story.

'I'm hoping to be allowed home before much longer. I'm fed up with being cooped up in hospital.'

Hannah was wearing her engagement ring. He noticed it almost immediately and caught at her fingers to look more closely.

'He did ask you to marry him then?' His smile had faded. 'He's given you a fine ring.'

Hannah nodded.

'When's the wedding to be?'

'When this war's over.'

'Very sensible. He's a lucky fellow, very lucky. Tell him I ... I envy him.'

He wanted to hear all her news. She told him that more of her colleagues repairing Mosquito planes were being laid off. The work-force was being much reduced, and that there was talk of the hangar closing down altogether as soon as peace was declared.

But it was her friends Robert really wanted to hear about, especially Eric. Hannah couldn't talk about her concerns about the Goodwins to anybody, though they were rarely out of her mind.

When she was leaving, she bent to kiss his cheek, and he pulled her closer and planted a return kiss on hers.

'Will you come again?' he asked.

'If you want me to.'

'You know I do.'

'All right, this time next week?'

He sighed. 'That's a long way off. Not sooner?'

Hannah was tired. She felt emotionally drained by the problem with Eric. It had been a rush to come over to Liverpool after work. 'Be a sport,' he said.

'Friday night then?'

'That's better, I'll look forward to it.'

'So will I,' she said. She always enjoyed Rob's company.

But when she got home from work the following night, Aunt Philomena told her that Mrs Osborne had been round to let her know Robert would be discharged from hospital on Thursday afternoon, and would Hannah come to see him at home?

On Friday Hannah did, and his mother made tea for them and pressed fairy cakes on her. Rob suggested a turn round the garden. He'd really mastered the art of using crutches; he could swing himself about quite gracefully.

'It's marvellous to be home again, but I'm afraid my flying days are over. Anyway, I think the war could be over before I'm well enough again. I'm trying to make up my mind what I'll do when peace comes.'

'We're all racking our brains about that,' Hannah said. 'What are you thinking of?'

'Dad's always wanted me to follow in his footsteps, but I don't think I'm cut out for that. I started reading law before joining the RAF. I suppose the sensible thing is to carry on and be a solicitor.'

'Why not?'

Rob shrugged. 'I've developed a taste for flying aircraft. I'd like to be a commercial pilot, but I know a hundred others with the same thing in mind. There'll be a scramble for the few jobs available. It might be wiser not to set my sights in that direction. I have to make up my mind.'

'So do I,' Hannah frowned. 'I rather fancy teaching.'

'I thought you were planning to get married?'

'I am, but not immediately. Eric has to make his plans for peace too, and get them up and running so he can support a wife.'

'Of course. I'd like to meet your Eric. Would you both come out with me for a drink somewhere?'

Hannah hesitated for a moment, but felt sorry for him. 'Yes, why not? I could ask his sister Gina too. You remember her?'

'Of course I remember her,' Rob said, brightening up. 'A very pretty girl. I don't know many people here, and I'm not finding it easy to get out.'

When Hannah went up to the Goodwins' house that evening and put it to Eric, he was reluctant. She had to persuade him to make up a foursome. 'Don't you like Rob?' she asked.

'I hardly know him. I'd rather have you to myself. I suppose I think of the vicarage crowd as being Pa's friends.'

'Rob's all right,' Gina told him. 'But I suppose

he's more Hannah's type than yours.'

When Hannah went to talk to Rob about the arrangements, he said, 'I'll order a taxi to take us all. I can't walk far and I haven't driven yet. I hear there's a good pub on the road to Bromborough. Shall we go there?'

On the night they went, Rob was using two walking sticks to get about, and he looked none too secure with them.

'I'll be fine,' he assured Gina. 'It's just a question of time and practice.'

The evening went well. Gina and Eric chattered on and were their old selves. Hannah enjoyed it and felt she was back on good terms with them.

BOOK THREE

CHAPTER TWENTY

May 1945

In the first days of May, the news programmes Hannah heard on the wireless kept repeating that Hitler was dead and Germany in chaos. Everybody began to think the war must be over. At work, people were standing around in groups, talking about it, though there were two planes in to be repaired. The days seemed to crawl as they waited for an official announcement.

Hannah was at home eating high tea with her mother on the evening of the seventh when Churchill was heard to announce that all German forces had surrendered unconditionally to the Allies, and the following day was declared a holiday to celebrate Victory in Europe. Hannah leaped up from the table with a shout of triumph.

'It's over at last! Can you believe it?' She hugged her mother and waltzed her round, both shrieking with joy. The familiar thump, thump, thump sounded beneath their feet and brought them to a sudden stop.

There was a moment's silence, but Hannah felt all her pleasure in the news bubbling up again. 'I wonder if Philomena's heard the news?' she said.

Esme smiled. 'She probably has. We'd better go down and talk to her. This is no time to bear a grudge.'

Hannah abandoned her half-eaten Finnan haddock and ran for the stairs.

'It's over, Aunt Philomena.' She kissed the soft lined cheek. They were all laughing and crying at once.

Philomena recovered first. She too seemed to have forgotten their differences.

'A glass of sherry, Esme,' she said. 'We must have a drink to celebrate. What a shame I finished the port. I prefer that after my supper. But there's a special bottle of sherry in that cupboard I've been saving for this. Such a relief to have the war over.'

After two glasses of her aunt's sherry, Hannah went back upstairs and finished off all the cold Finnan haddock before washing up. Then she pulled on a coat and ran up the road to the Goodwins' house. The long-awaited end to the war had banished all her worries about them from her mind. In peacetime conditions, there would be no need for a black market, they'd have no customers.

She could hear them laughing and shrieking with pleasure as she knocked on the back door. Eric let her in and kissed her before whirling her round. She hugged Gina and finally Betsy. For the first time Hannah found the older members of the family had come to the kitchen to share in the pleasure of the moment. They were all sparkling with excitement and trying to talk at once. All had pink cheeks and bright eyes.

'Come and join the feast.' Betsy pulled her to the kitchen table. Bottles of whisky, gin, orange cordial and sarsaparilla were laid out. 'Mam has been hoarding all this.'

'To celebrate the peace,' Cicely smiled. She was slicing up the contents of a tin of ham. 'Come on, you can make sandwiches for yourselves.'

A huge tin of peaches had been opened on the draining board. Eric was ladling them directly from the tin into bowls. He handed one to Hannah. 'It's all over! Finished, no more war. Marvellous, isn't it?'

'I'm having a lie-in tomorrow,' Gina said. 'Just think of it – no more making do ever again. Lives of bliss for all of us from now on.'

'I'd better go back to Mum,' Hannah said. 'I can't leave her on her own tonight.'

'I'll walk you back.' Eric found her coat amongst the kitchen clutter and helped her into it.

Once outside, he said, 'Everybody will be out on the town tomorrow. Gina and I thought we'd have an early lunch, then go out and join in the fun. Shall I pick you up about one?'

'Yes, please. Tomorrow's going to be a big day.'

The bells of St Augustine's church began to peal out.

'A lovely sound,' Eric said. 'We've not heard that since the war started.'

Hannah smiled. 'Haven't wanted to. It was supposed to be a warning we were being invaded.'

'The bell-ringers are out of practice.'

'A marvellous sound, all the same.' Other more distant churches were ringing their bells. The long summer evenings had come, but now it was dusk and already lights were coming on in the houses all round them. Hannah and Eric reached the gate of Hannah's home, and there too, lights were showing at several of the windows.

'Mum's torn down the blackout curtains. There's lights everywhere – don't they look wonderful? It seems a different place.'

Eric pulled a face. 'Too much light for the porch. We won't get the privacy we've been used to.'

Hannah laughed. 'You're right. Mum and Aunt Philomena are all excited tonight. They'd know we were there.'

'Don't go in yet,' Eric pleaded. 'Just another half-hour. Let's walk on a bit, see what's happening in New Ferry.'

Hannah didn't want to go in either. She strolled on with Eric's arm round her waist. There were more people than usual out in the streets. The public houses were full and noisy. They could see the lights of Liverpool glinting on the other side of the river. The ships in the Mersey were letting their fog horns rip. The breeze carried the sound of bells from near and distant church towers. Everywhere, lights were streaming into the street. There was a carnival atmosphere that drove home the message that peace had come at last.

'Magical,' Hannah breathed.

'Marvellous. I can't believe it's all over.'

When they returned to Grasmere Road, the blackout curtains were now drawn in Aunt Philomena's ground-floor bedroom.

'She's gone to bed,' Hannah whispered.

Upstairs, Mum still had the lights shining out from their living room. Hannah clung to Eric for a good night kiss and then ran in to see her. The wireless was playing triumphant music. Mum had lit the fire and looked relaxed and happy.

'The end of an era,' she said. 'Life is going to be very different from now on. So much better for us all.'

The following afternoon, Hannah walked up to meet Eric and Gina. Eric had two cameras: his box Brownie, which had been a twenty-first birthday present from his father, and a Leica, which he'd managed to pick up second-hand more recently.

'I've got film in both,' he said. 'Should get some good pictures today.'

As they sat upstairs on the bus going along the New Chester Road into Birkenhead, Eric took his first picture of the jostling crowd in a side street. It had red, white and blue streamers crisscrossing it from one side to the other. There were Union Jacks to be seen everywhere: large ones hanging out of upstairs windows; smaller ones pinned to front doors. Bonfires were being laid on almost every bomb site.

They got off opposite Birkenhead Park. A military band was playing in the entrance and already a crowd was gathering. Almost immediately they came face to face with Leslie and Harry.

'I'm so glad we've met,' Leslie was beaming. 'A miracle in this crowd. I wanted to get in touch but didn't know how.'

Hannah and Gina were hugged and kissed by both. Eric was slapping them on their backs.

'We were going to come up to your house to see you,' Eric said to Leslie. It was the first Hannah had heard of that, but perhaps she should have expected it. Both Eric and Gina were fond of their brother.

Harry said, 'I told Leslie he should go home as your father might be pleased to see him today.'

'I told him no,' Leslie laughed. 'It would take more than winning the war to do that.'

'But the Army won't want you any more, will they?' Gina said.

Leslie was laughing. 'The Army won't want any of the thousands they've called up.'

'They won't want Jim! How long will it be before he comes home, do you think?'

'Shouldn't be long.' Leslie was in high spirits. 'They'll want to cut the Forces down in size, won't they?'

'Does that mean they'll just forget about you?' Hannah asked. 'You're free to do what you like?'

'We don't know,' Harry said. 'They'll be demobbing all those they called up, but it remains to be seen what they'll do about those who deserted.'

'I don't want to throw a damper on things,' Eric said, taking a photograph of the group, 'but I can't believe you'll all be pardoned, just like that. They made such a song and dance about deserters, with redcaps and naval pickets rushing about trying to round you up.'

'They won't want us now, stands to reason.' Leslie could not be persuaded otherwise.

The military band struck up a Sousa march and moved off down Conway Street into town. A procession was forming behind it.

'Come on,' Harry urged, turning in the opposite direction. 'Let's start walking home. There's something going on in every street.'

Harry's house was in the north end, which Aunt Philomena considered to be a rough part of the town. As Hannah walked along the pavements, she could see almost every living-room windowsill had a patriotic display. There were blue vases filled with red and white flowers, pieces of ruby glass arranged with photographs of Winston Churchill, ribbons and streamers of the right shade pinned to curtains.

Harry's house was in the middle of a terrace of small houses that opened directly onto the pavement. Once inside he offered glasses of gin and orange to Hannah and Gina.

'I'd rather have tea now,' Gina said, 'and leave the gin till later.'

Leslie went to put the kettle on. He seemed very much at home and on good terms with Harry.

'I'm going to cook a big dinner tonight, to thank you for helping me,' Leslie chortled. 'Harry's got a big piece of pork for us.'

'How's the job going?' Eric asked him.

'You've got a job already?' Hannah asked. They hadn't told her. 'What are you doing?'

'Driving a lorry.'

'But I thought you said you had no driving licence?' Hannah was shocked.

'He can drive, can't he?' Harry said out of the corner of his mouth. 'The bits of paper can always be fixed.'

Hannah flinched. This was one more instance of flagrant lawbreaking, but today, in this atmosphere of universal rejoicing, she couldn't bring herself to speak out against it. It made her feel a prig to keep carping, and today she'd be a spoil-sport too.

'I really love it.' Leslie was enthusiastic. 'It's been great driving round all day, seeing the outside world, talking to people. Much more interesting than staying at home by myself.'

'You're coping all right, then?' Eric asked.

'More than all right,' Harry laughed. 'Leslie's excelled himself. I'm right proud of him.'

Leslie was pouring tea. He handed Gina a cup. 'Chocolate biscuit with it?'

'Yes, please. You're driving for that big national firm, Fanstones, isn't it?'

It was Harry who answered. 'Not for them any more.'

'Why not?' Eric asked.

'It's a bit of a ruse, you see,' Harry chuckled. 'Fanstones were despatching loads of cigarettes from Ogden's factory in Liverpool. Leslie was sent with a load to a NAAFI store down near London, but he made the load and the lorry disappear.'

Gina giggled. 'That's a good one.'

Leslie was handing round the biscuits again. 'Harry knows all the angles. He's in with a crowd who gets things organised.'

Harry went on, 'We fixed the lorry up with a respray and new number plates and sold it on. There's no problem selling fags on. Do you want some? We've got plenty here.'

'I wouldn't mind some to sell,' Gina said.

'No,' Eric protested. Hannah saw him cast an anxious glance in her direction. 'If you're going to lose your job, you'll lose your customers.'

'Then we found another job for Leslie. With Lamberts this time. He was carrying loads of women's clothes to the major retailers. The new autumn fashion range.' Harry's sharp eyes were assessing Eric. 'It was heading for Debenhams, but that got diverted too.'

'I'd love to get my hands on some decent clothes,' Gina sighed, reaching for another chocolate biscuit.

'Too bad. It's all out of reach now.' Leslie was smiling at her, 'I'm working for yet another firm now. I do it for a week or so until I can figure out where the best loads are going. Then Harry fixes it up.'

'It sounds chancy.' Eric was frowning. 'Won't Leslie be picked up? I mean, the police will be mustard on big thefts like that, especially when they're taking place again and again.'

'I have a different name and address for each job,' Leslie explained. 'I'm Leslie Miles Morgan now. I tell everybody to call me Les. I'm scared that if I suddenly became Bill or something, I might not answer when I'm spoken to.' He was laughing.

'Different driving licence and references,' Harry smirked. 'We've got half a dozen fellas working the same racket.'

'Leslie, it sounds dangerous,' Eric said.

'No it isn't. We've got half the haulage firms in the country sewn up,' Harry boasted.

Hannah was so appalled she couldn't speak. She'd thought Eric was the ringleader but she'd been wrong, it was Harry Oldshaw, and the schemes he was perpetrating were of blatant theft and of far larger amounts than she'd imagined. Eric wouldn't look at her; he'd know what she was thinking.

Leslie turned to Gina and asked, 'What will happen to your job now?' Hannah guessed he was trying to change the subject.

'We've heard rumours that they'll close the place down and we'll all get the sack. If there's no war and no fighting, there'll be far fewer planes to repair. We'll have to find new jobs, won't we, Hannah?'

Hannah couldn't get any words out.

Gina went on, 'Well, we've been saying for some time we'd like a change. Is that music I hear out in the street?'

'Yes.' Leslie opened the front door. 'A pity to miss any of this. Let's have a walk round to see what's going on. I'll put the joint on a low heat so we'll not have to wait long when we come back.'

'Leslie likes to get out,' Harry smiled. 'I reckon the real fun won't start until tonight.'

Hannah's high spirits had evaporated. She felt heavy with foreboding. The fun and merriment all round her seemed false.

Further down the street, a loudspeaker had been attached to a wireless, and a small crowd was watching as children played a game of musical chairs. A gramophone was being wound up in readiness, in case the programme being broadcast was no longer suitable.

In the next street, a children's tea party was in full swing and a piano had been dragged out of one of the houses. A young man was bashing out 'Lilli Marlene'.

There was an accordion playing 'The Lambeth Walk' not far away and the sound of various instruments playing different tunes mingled on the breeze. They walked down to the docks because every so often the ships on the Mersey started sounding their fog horns again, each trying to outdo the last with longer joyous whoops. They reached a point where they could see that the ferry boats and many of the ships were dressed over all.

When they retraced their steps, the children's tea party was over. Mothers were tidying up, fathers were removing the tables, but Henry Hall's dance band was blaring out. When they returned to Harry's street, the children were playing pass the parcel.

Gina and Hannah helped Leslie to get their celebration dinner to the table.

'Lovely tender pork.' Harry rolled it round his mouth. 'With crisp crackling. As of now, no more whale meat and offal.'

Hannah couldn't remember seeing so much luxury food before and in such large quantities. She knew it must have come from the black market. They went out again later in the evening. By then people were dancing in the streets. Crates of beer were out on the pavement, and the rival sources of music louder than ever. Outside Harry's door two circles of neighbours were doing the hokey cokey.

An accordion player led in two chains of conga dancers from the next street to weave round them. The fog horns could still be heard from the river and the bonfires had been lit. The streets were lit up like day and everybody seemed infused with tremendous energy.

Hannah hung on to Eric's arm as they watched. 'It's unbelievable,' he said. 'Everybody's hellbent on enjoying themselves.'

'So they should be,' Gina retorted. 'We've had six long years of blackouts and shortages.'

'Slaughter and grief,' Eric said.

'Frustration and boredom,' Leslie added.

Hannah thought of Rob Osborne, still recovering from his injuries. Harry had the last word. 'The war had its moments. I've had some good times.'

'You've earned yourself a pretty penny,' Gina said.

'Yes, people like us have to grab the chance when we can,' Harry said. 'In the depression, before the war, my dad was out of work and we all went hungry. Only a fool would let chances like we've had pass them by.'

'But now we'll be back to normal,' Gina said. 'Peace and plenty at last.'

'I'll have some good pictures to remember this by.' Eric patted his Leica.

Hannah remained silent. What she'd learned today had made her realise that Harry Oldshaw was a much bigger operator than she'd imagined. Leslie was in need of protection – why couldn't Eric see that?

Late that night, when he was saying good night to her in the porch and they were at last alone, Hannah tried to tell him how she felt.

'You promised me you wouldn't do anything illegal again,' she said, 'and now I find out what Leslie's getting up to. Harry's a dangerous person for him to live with. You didn't tell me half of what was going on. This won't do, Eric.'

But Hannah was tired, she couldn't make herself keep on at Eric. She went in feeling disappointed in him.

Hannah found it difficult to get up the next morning. She was a little late for work, but so was Gina.

'One day's holiday to celebrate the end of the war in Europe,' Gina scoffed. 'With Churchill urging us to put our shoulders to the wheel again until we've won the war with Japan. We didn't get long to celebrate, did we?'

Hannah couldn't help herself. 'If it had been any longer I wouldn't have been able to keep my mouth shut. I had my eyes opened by Harry Oldshaw yesterday. You're all going to end up in prison if you don't stop.'

'Don't be daft,' Gina told her. 'Harry's very careful. They won't catch him.'

Everything seemed at sixes and sevens at work with nobody getting down to it. Hannah was glad; her head was whirling. She could see her friends heading for real trouble if she couldn't persuade them to stop. They were already in more deeply than she'd imagined.

After tea that evening she went up to see Eric. He seemed reluctant to go out for a walk with her, but she insisted. 'I want us to have a talk,' she said, 'on our own.'

'I know what you want.' Eric was agonised. 'I've done my best. I've kept my promise...'

'But you haven't been honest. Harry Oldshaw

is an out-and-out crook. You knew what he was doing and Leslie's in it with him up to his neck.'

'I told you I couldn't speak for Leslie.'

'But you say you feel responsible for him.'

'Yes, I do.'

'Then you've got to get him away from Harry. Find somewhere else for him to live. I want you to promise that none of you will have any more to do with him.'

Hannah felt him stiffen. 'How can I promise that? Harry's our friend, for heaven's sake.'

'More's the pity. He's dragging you all deeper into crime. You should have been tougher with Leslie at the beginning.'

He burst out petulantly, 'You sound like Pa.'

'And Aunt Philomena,' Hannah tried to smile. 'I hate having to carp on at you like this. It makes me feel a prude, but what else can I do to stop you? I can see you all heading for big trouble. Why can't you see it?'

'Hannah, I'd do anything for you, but I've tried talking to Leslie and Gina too. They won't listen.'

'You'll have to find Leslie somewhere else to live. All the time he's there...'

'I'll try, but it's easier said than done. There are no flats to rent anywhere.'

'There are lodgings to be had,' she said. 'I've seen them advertised, and lodgings, all found would suit Leslie better than a flat.'

'I'll try,' he said.

On pay day the following week, Hannah, and all the other workers at Hooton, received a letter with their wages giving them one week's notice and telling them the hangar was closing down.

Few said they were sorry. Most felt ready for a change. It was war work and most were looking forward to getting a peacetime job now.

'Shall we go down to the Labour Exchange together, and see what jobs they have?' Gina suggested. 'Though I wouldn't mind a bit of time off before I start somewhere else.'

Hannah said, 'Mum thinks I should learn a skill. She says I'd get a more interesting job and earn more. You should think about that too. There's no reason to take unskilled work now the war's over.'

'What sort of a skill?'

'I thought of being a teacher when I was leaving school. It seems they're desperate to get more teachers now and there's to be a new shortened training course. I could do that.'

'Do you still fancy it?'

'Not so much. Do you?'

'No. I didn't like school.'

'What about secretarial work? Mum suggested that too.'

'I wouldn't mind working in an office,' Gina said. 'That'd be more like it. What would I need to learn to do that?'

'Typing, shorthand or bookkeeping.'

'What are you going to do?'

Hannah shook her head. 'I haven't quite decided.'

'I thought you were going to marry Eric and help him in his photography shop?'

'That's what I told Mum, but she's pressing for one of the other options as well.'

Eric had developed his pictures, and after work he and Gina took Hannah down to his cellar darkroom to see them.

'They're full of exuberance and jollity. Marvellous mementos of the day,' Hannah said.

'Everybody was so happy.' Gina sighed. 'Everything's fallen a little flat since, hasn't it?'

'At least the fighting's over.'

'Yes, and Jim has survived four long years of it. I'm thankful for that.'

'Does he know when he'll be coming home?'

'No, not a clue. He says they're all getting restive.'

'It'll take a little time to sort things out.'

'A lot of time, more like. They were quick to call them up, but they're tardy at letting them go.'

Hannah went home and thought hard about her own future. She rejected teaching, because before the war teachers had to leave the profession if they married, and she meant to marry Eric. They were saying that wouldn't happen in future, but who could bank on what the Government told them? It might not fit in with her plans.

'I'm going to start looking round for a shop,' Eric said, 'and think about setting up a business.'

Hannah smiled. 'We said we'd get married when the war was over, didn't we?'

'If not this year, definitely next. Really, we've waited long enough.'

Hannah knew Eric wanted to get his shop up and running before they were married, so she needed to do some kind of work in the meantime.

Aunt Philomena was trying to get back on the

old comfortable terms with her and Mum, and had offered to pay for Hannah to take some sort of training.

She said, 'I don't want to tell people you're working in a factory. There are more suitable positions for a young lady like you. The war dragged us all down.'

Hannah knew the photography business Eric wanted would need a bookkeeper, and no doubt he'd have letters to write. So why not a commercial course? If they were unable to marry right away, she'd have the means of earning a living in the meantime.

She slept on her decision, and when she took in her mother's early cup of tea the next morning, she told her. Mum favoured teaching for her and urged her to think again, but Hannah's mind was made up. She discussed it with Gina as they cycled to work.

'I've been thinking about it too. I might do the same. I've saved a bit of money, so I could. Wouldn't it be great if we could go to commercial college together?'

It was Saturday. Hannah went home to eat lunch with her mother and talk about her plans. Afterwards, Esme sent her downstairs to discuss them with Aunt Philomena.

'If you've decided on an office job–'

'I have, Aunt Philomena.'

'Then I'll pay for your training.'

'That's very kind of you, very generous too, but Mum and I can manage.'

'I said I would and I will. You must get a more respectable position next time.'

'Thank you then. I do appreciate what you're doing for me.'

'Skerries Commercial College in Liverpool, that's the place to go. It's got a good reputation. Always good policy to have the best training. Pass me the phone book, dear.'

'It's Saturday – will there be anyone there?'

'Probably not, but you can ring them on Monday morning on my phone. Find out what the course consists of and how much it costs.'

'I'll write to them,' Hannah decided. 'I'll do that now. I have to be at work on Monday, to work out my week's notice.'

'Take the book; it gives their address. I expect their school year starts in September. Ask them to send you a prospectus,' Aunt Philomena ordered.

Hannah wrote her letter and then ran up the road to see Gina. She was cleaning out the hen-house.

'You don't hang about,' she said. 'I was going to wait until after next week, when I'll be having a bit of a holiday from work. It's a big decision, isn't it? I think I'd like to come with you and learn to type. If I don't, the best I'll be offered is shop work. I'm not going in a factory.'

'Smashing,' Hannah said. 'I hoped you were going to say that. As soon as they send their prospectus, we can both apply together for the course. Why don't you learn shorthand too and be a proper secretary?'

Now that the war in Europe was over, everybody began asking how long it would take to end the war in the Far East. Several newspapers estimated another eighteen months, but it followed more quickly than expected because the new atomic bombs were dropped on Japan, and the devastation brought instant surrender. By 6 August the same year, the world was at peace.

Hannah was really enjoying having time to herself. After having so little leisure, it now seemed unlimited. She spent a lot of it with Eric, going round estate agents. They'd enquired about lodgings for Leslie, but he'd refused to move away from Harry. He said he was happy where he was.

Eric took her to see a lot of shops, and she found he had very clear ideas about what he wanted. She was able to do more about the house and inevitably more for Aunt Philomena.

Mrs Osborne was invited round to have afternoon tea with Philomena quite often and her invitations were returned, so Hannah saw something of Rob. He would take her off to sit in the garden or the conservatory with him and they'd talk over their plans for the future. His leg was getting stronger. He'd arranged to return to Liverpool University to complete the course he'd abandoned in 1940.

'I've decided to carry on and train to be a solicitor. It was what I originally intended to do and I've done two years of law already. It means I can continue to live at home, which pleases my parents.'

'It pleases me too.' Hannah smiled. 'I hated to think of you flying over enemy territory on moonlit nights, putting your life at risk.'

Rob sighed. 'I think we all got high on the thrill of it. It's hard to settle down to ordinary life after that, especially with a gammy leg like this.'

CHAPTER TWENTY-ONE

Gina was glad to have her future settled. She and Hannah both had places in college and would be starting in the middle of September. In the meantime, she would have loved to be like Hannah and have the rest of the summer off, but she had only limited savings. She'd been too free with her money and not saved as Eric had.

He told her he'd heard they were looking for a temporary part-time filing clerk in the Co-op office in Birkenhead. She applied for the job and got it. She was pleased she'd have a little income coming in over the summer and hoped it would be good experience.

The weeks of peace began to pass. Gina had a letter from her fiancé, Jim Latimer, telling her he'd soon be back in England, though as yet he had no date for his demob.

He'd written to her all the time he'd been away, but his letters no longer conveyed the warmth and intimacy they once had. She felt the ties that had bound them had loosened, that his life and hers had diverged.

She had loved him. The first months of separation had been almost impossible to bear, but they'd grown apart. She didn't know how she'd feel when she saw him again. She hoped they'd find their love again, but there had been a number of articles in newspapers and magazines about the difficulties men were facing when they returned home to their loved ones.

Even those who'd been married were finding it difficult to settle down again. Women had grown used to fending for themselves, and children didn't always welcome a man they hardly knew into their home.

Gina had not been able to wear her engagement ring while she'd been doping planes. It would have ruined it to get that sticky muck on it. Now she took out the three little diamonds in an illusion setting and started to wear it. She hoped she and Jim would be able to work things out. She was envious of what Hannah had – envious of her ring too; her diamonds were three times the size.

Poor Jim had spent the war fighting in the thick of it, risking life and limb for very little money. If they were to get married, she knew she'd have to help with the expense of setting up home.

With that in mind, she rang up Spike, who was still at the American airbase at Burtonwood, and asked him if he could get her some more nylons and chocolate to sell. There were a lot of girls in the Co-op office, she knew she'd soon find plenty of customers. She ought to get her share of the easy money while she could.

'Sure, honey, I'll fix you up,' Spike said. 'Next Saturday OK for you? Usual arrangements – I'll meet you at Reece's dance hall with the whatsits. You got a car yet?'

'No. Can you run me home with the stuff?'

'Have to, won't I? See you, honey.'

Eric wanted to take Hannah out on Saturday night.

'She can come along with us,' Gina said. 'No reason not to. I told her she wasn't going to stop me carrying on with Spike.'

'You'll upset her if she hears you planning things.'

'She needn't,' Gina said. 'You can dance with her and I'll dance with Spike. I'll need you to help unload what Spike brings in the trunk of his car.'

Gina was looking forward to the dance. There was always the possibility she'd meet another man who would sweep her off her feet. She spent Saturday afternoon washing her hair and pressing her best frock, a new red one. She decided not to wear her ring. It might put possible partners off and spoil the fun.

They arrived early in the evening, and Hannah and Eric danced off and left her. It was what Gina expected. She looked round and found Spike hadn't yet arrived, so she stood near the door with the crowd of other girls who were waiting for partners to invite them on the floor. There used to be a shortage of men at dances – too many were away in the Forces – but tonight there seemed to be more.

Gina saw the pimply youth eyeing her as he came up. She didn't fancy him, but any partner was better than staying with the wallflowers. He was quite a good dancer, and twirled her round in the quickstep so her skirt flared out.

The next partner looked better but he had halitosis, and the next couldn't dance. Gina stood the next dance out, tapping her toe to a Glenn Miller tune. Spike was usually here by this time. He fancied himself as a jitterbug champion, and this was one of his favourite tunes.

Then she saw Hannah waving to her, from where she and Eric were sitting down at a small table. She went over to join them.

'Has Spike stood you up?' Eric asked.

'It's early enough yet.' Gina knew he wouldn't; it was a business arrangement. Spike expected to get his cut from this. He'd told her that he was planning on giving his wife and two boys a better life than they'd had before the war.

The interval came and went. When the band returned and started a slow foxtrot, Eric and Hannah took to the floor again.

Gina began to feel concerned that Spike hadn't turned up. Apart from the men who were dancing, others were standing around in groups. She could see several American airmen in their smart uniforms, talking together and smoking.

Another partner came up and asked her to dance. Gina liked the look of this one and as a dancer he wasn't bad. The foxtrot finished before they'd circled the floor. He smiled and asked if he might have the next dance too. He told her his name was Jack and that he'd taken part in the D-Day landings but had now been demobbed and had returned to his old job at Tate and Lyle. He kept her on the floor for another dance.

Gina was beginning to think Spike wasn't going to turn up. He always had before, he was very reliable. She excused herself, escaped from Jack and went to the cloakroom. When she came back on to the dance floor, there was a group of American airmen sizing up the wallflowers, one of whom she'd seen talking to Spike last time he'd come.

Gina went over to him and said, 'You know Spike O'Hanlon, don't you? He said he'd meet me here tonight and he hasn't turned up.'

She saw his expression change to one of concern. 'Is he a pal of yours?'

'Yes.'

'Gee, Spike's not going anywhere right now. He's in the caboose.'

'What?'

'Spike's in big trouble on the base. You won't be seeing him again.'

That took Gina's breath away. 'What sort of trouble?'

The airman shrugged and lowered his voice. 'Caught pilfering from the PX.'

Gina felt her mouth go suddenly dry. Spike was another who had seemed too wily to be caught. 'What will happen to him now?'

'He'll be court-martialled and shipped home to the States.' Dark eyes stared into hers. 'You one of the limeys he's been working with? You'd better lie low for a bit, kid.'

Gina turned away, feeling icy fingers of fear in her stomach. Spike had been caught! It didn't seem possible. She'd liked him, he'd been a good laugh, and he'd provided some of the luxuries for which she craved.

Suddenly, she felt she had to get out of here. It took her another ten minutes to find Eric and Hannah and get them off the floor.

'I've been thinking,' Hannah said, 'if Spike isn't coming we'd better go for the train.'

Gina was more than glad to say, 'Then we ought to leave now. The last train goes at eleven thirty.'

On the train going home, after hearing about Spike, Hannah sat close to Gina and held her hand, trying to provide comfort. She could feel her shaking.

'I didn't think he'd get caught. He's been doing it for years and he was always very careful. I'm scared.'

'It comes as a bit of a shock,' Eric said. He was sitting close beside her on the other side. Gina was weepy enough for him to give her his handkerchief.

Hannah stopped herself saying, 'I told you so. I told you it was dangerous.'

'That Yank I spoke to at the dance – he seemed to think the American police might try to trace us. The ones who sold his goods on.'

'They won't,' Eric said. Hannah thought he looked less confident than he sounded.

'You weren't the only girl involved with him?' Hannah asked.

'Spike said he supplied half a dozen girls, sometimes more. Will the American military police get together with the British...?'

'We live miles from Burtonwood. They'll never find you,' Eric told her.

Hannah could see the stuffing had been knocked out of Gina.

'That Yank told me to lie low for a bit.'

'Don't you worry.'

'What am I going to do? It sends a shiver down my spine to think of what could happen.'

'Forget you ever saw American chocolate and nylons,' Hannah said. 'You must put Spike behind you. Your life is changing, it'll be more interesting. You'll have an office job, and Jim is coming home. Be content with what you have.'

Even Eric was shocked. He'd enjoyed the American luxuries Spike had provided. It had been routine to help Gina make a little on the side from them, and it had seemed as safe as houses.

Peace was proving bleak and comfortless, and the progress Eric was making was slow. He'd decided he must carry on working at the shoe shop for the time being, but now that Hannah and Gina had made arrangements for their future, he felt under pressure to do the same. He was making a big effort to find the right shop for his photography business. He arranged with Hannah to meet him at the Co-op one lunch time and took her to look at some possibilities.

He felt torn in two. He very much wanted to marry Hannah. The problem was that he knew the shop wouldn't earn a living for them yet, and he didn't want Hannah too close until it would.

He wanted to do a few more jobs with Harry to add to his savings. He had money put by, but he never felt he had enough. It wouldn't always be so easy to make money as it was now, and there was the thrill of going out on a job. He didn't want to give that up either. If business in the shop proved slow to build up when it opened, he'd have a cushion to fall back on. But Spike's arrest had shaken him more than he admitted to Gina. It made him more nervous about Leslie and the jobs he himself was still doing with Harry. Eric knew Hannah must not learn about any of this in case she changed her mind about him.

That night, while Hannah was sitting at the kitchen table with them, Gina asked, 'Why are you dragging your feet about starting a business?'

'I'm not! I need time to think,' he said. 'I don't want to rush into things, then find I've made a mistake.'

'Hannah will think you don't want to choose your shop and get married.'

Eric gave Hannah a little smile. 'She knows better than that. We've looked at a lot of shops, haven't we?'

It was Gina who said, 'It's decision time, Eric. Men are coming out of the Forces and, like you, some will be thinking of opening a shop. They'll snap up the best ones if you don't get in first.'

'I know.'

Harry had pointed out that rents asked for long leases were relatively cheap, but they'd go up when demand increased. Eric wanted to get in before that happened.

Gina spread the pile of property brochures across the kitchen table. 'I think you should make up your mind.'

Eric was beginning to think that too, but he was agonising over the good and bad points of each one. He took a gulp of tea.

'I've narrowed it down to two. There's this one in West Kirby with a good flat above it.' He'd taken Hannah to see that one twice. 'We could get married, and live there. Or there's this one in Moorefields in Liverpool. That's a big shop in a good business area, the sort I've imagined having, but it's a lockup and we'd have to live somewhere else.'

Gina said, 'I'd go for that. You'd earn more there.'

'I'm inclined to the other,' Hannah said. 'We'd have somewhere to live, and you wouldn't waste time travelling. You'd be on the spot and so would I. You could call me down if you had several customers in at once.'

'Yes, that could be useful because it takes time to pose a customer for a portrait, and I'd save the expense of travelling in.'

The following day, Eric went round to the agent in his lunch hour and agreed to take a fifteen-year lease on the West Kirby shop. He was simmering with excitement by the time Hannah came up that evening.

'Marvellous!' she said. 'We're nearer being able to get married now.' Her eyes were sparkling. She was really pleased, but that made him feel guilty. He wasn't keeping his promise to her.

But he couldn't, he had to do things the way he'd planned. Once he had the shop up and running and they were married, it would be different. He'd turn over a completely new leaf and go straight.

'Did I tell you it used to be a high-class hat shop but had ceased to trade at the beginning of the war?'

'Yes, there were hat stands there.'

'The owner is an elderly widow. She lived in the flat above it until recently. Now she's moved out to live with her sister in Heswall.' Eric was thrilled. 'I'm going to get it at a very reasonable rent, but I won't be able to earn a living there yet, as there won't be much to sell. I'll keep my job on for the time being. We'll have our home ready for when we get married. The agent has agreed to do a few repairs and repaint it inside and out if we can get the paint.'

He was delighted with the way things were going. He and Hannah were putting together what would be their first home.

Now Hannah wasn't going to work, she had time to look round the second-hand shops and attend auctions to buy furniture. It had to be second-hand; there was some new utility furniture available, but they were not allowed to buy it. A permit to buy furniture would only be issued when they were married.

Hannah bought a table and four chairs from the auction room, and followed it with a three-piece suite from a shop. A week later Eric found a bedroom suite with everything they'd need but the bed. They were both keeping a look-out for that.

He and Hannah now had somewhere to go where they could be alone. Eric got some coal from Harry and they were able to light the fire. It was lovely to pull the sofa up in front of it and sit with their arms round each other. His plans were now taking shape. Best of all, he could see his way to getting married.

'Another twelve months,' he whispered to Hannah, and he knew by the longing in her eyes that she wanted it as much as he did.

'If we say about this time next year, that will give

you time to finish your secretarial course and hopefully enough time for the country to switch over to peacetime production and make cameras and film for me to sell.'

'That means August?'

'Hopefully no later. Perhaps July. Depends how quickly factories can switch back.'

Eric began collecting together all the things he'd need for the shop. He had a large notice printed to put in the window announcing that it would open as a shop selling all photographic needs, and specialise in wedding and portrait photography.

He made enlargements of the portraits he'd taken of Hannah and Gina, and arranged them in the window, together with some views he'd taken of the Liverpool waterfront and of shipping in the Mersey. He was proud of his workmanship and wanted to show the standard he would achieve.

He managed to buy second-hand the lighting he needed and set up a studio for taking portraits in the room behind the shop. There was a cellar where he'd be able to set up his darkroom and eventually bring over the equipment he used at home.

Eric had applied for an allowance of film to use in the business, but he had no idea when delivery might begin.

In September, Gina was glad to start her training at the secretarial college, but she found it hard.

'Especially the shorthand,' she said to Hannah. 'I'll never be able to get any speed up.'

'Yes, you will. It takes practice, that's all. Then

we'll both be able to get good jobs.'

Gina wished she was as confident in the classroom as Hannah was. She'd felt generally unnerved since Spike had been arrested and was missing the luxuries and the money she'd had from him. Now she wasn't working she had less money in her pocket.

One Sunday morning she was moaning about being hard up to Eric. He seemed sympathetic and said, 'Come up to my room.'

She thought he was going to give her a pound or so to tide her over. He'd done that before but she didn't want to take it now because she knew he was saving for his shop and to get married. She was very surprised when he'd put a bank book in her hand, even more so when she saw her own name on it.

'What's this?' When she opened it and saw the balance, it took her breath away. Eric's dark eyes were smiling down at her.

She gulped, stifling a shriek of joy. 'I'm thrilled.' She looked again. 'I can hardly believe my eyes. Where did all this come from?'

'It was Pa's.'

'Never!'

'Not a word about this to anyone else, mind.'

Eric told her the story of how he'd seen Pa bury something under the compost heap and dug it up to see what it was. 'I knew we'd see nothing of it if I left it there, so I took the lot.'

'But what did Pa say?'

'Nothing. He doesn't know I have it. If you steal something and another person takes it from you, what can you do?'

'But he wouldn't steal it, would he? Though if he buried it...?' Gina looked shocked at the thought.

'It was at the height of the Blitz. I think perhaps he looted it.'

Gina sucked in her lips. 'Looted? Pa was always sounding off about people who looted.'

'Well, that's where it came from. I started a savings account for you and another for Leslie.'

'Not for yourself?'

His smile broadened. 'Of course, for myself too.'

Gina laughed. 'Why didn't you tell us?'

'Safer not to. The last thing I wanted was for you and Leslie to go out and spend. Any sudden sign of extra money in the family would have made Pa suspicious. But it's all a long time ago and, with no job, you probably need a bit extra now.'

Gina threw her arms round him in a hug. 'Thank you, thank you, Eric.'

'Never say that I don't look after you,' he told her.

'You always have,' she grinned at him. 'You're the best brother in the world.'

There was little extra to eat over the first peacetime Christmas. The year 1946 came in, and Gina decided peace was proving less than satisfactory. She'd thought, once the war was over, everything would soon be back to normal, but things were in shorter supply than ever before.

In January, there was a world-wide shortage of wheat, which resulted in bread riots in France. The following month the wheat content of the

British loaf was reduced, making it darker. By May, less grain was allowed to be used for brewing, the size of the national loaf was cut and bread was rationed for the first time. Gina heard it called 'victory bread'. It wasn't just bread that was scarcer – the weekly rations of butter, margarine and lard were cut too.

In March, there was a nationwide sweep to pick up black marketeers. Road blocks were set up to stop and search cars and lorries. Shops and restaurants were raided. Gina was worried about Leslie but knew better than to mention his name or Harry's to Hannah, although she spent more time with her than ever before.

She talked it over with Eric, and found he too was less confident that Harry and Leslie could continue to get away with what they were doing.

He said, 'Let's go down on Sunday and see how Leslie's faring.'

'Right. Harry always has lots of lovely food there and he's very hospitable. Let's make a day of it. You could make some excuse to Hannah for once.'

'I'm OK,' Leslie told them when Sunday came. 'I haven't been stopped once – haven't even seen a road block. Everything's fine.'

'Couldn't be better,' Harry laughed. 'The greater the shortages, the stronger the black market. We'll never have another chance to earn money like this. We've got to do it while we can. We can set ourselves up for life.'

'I'm going to buy a car,' Leslie said, 'as soon as I see one I want. I've put my name down for a new one, but they can't give me a delivery date.

It could be years.'

'You should buy yourself a house,' Eric told him.

'I know. I will as soon as I've saved enough. A big house in the suburbs. Heswall, perhaps.'

'Or West Kirby, so you can be near Eric?' Gina suggested.

'Maybe.'

'I'm glad you've come down,' Harry said. 'Can you come and give us a hand tomorrow night?'

Gina knew Eric was doing occasional jobs with Harry and was making good money from them. 'What about me?' she asked.

'You can come too, if you want.'

After church on Sunday morning, Robert Osborne came up to speak to Hannah. She noticed then for the first time that he was walking unaided.

'You no longer need a stick?'

'It's more a matter of not letting myself need a stick. I have to practise walking unaided. Would it be in order for me to ask you to come for a walk?'

'What d'you mean, in order?'

'You have classes to attend and a fiancé who takes up a lot of your time. I don't want to push myself on you if you'd rather not.'

'Of course she'll go with you.' Philomena spoke up impatiently from her chair. 'It's a fine day and it'll do her good to get out.'

Hannah stifled a giggle. Eric had told her that he and Gina were going with Leslie to see some lodgings. 'Yes,' she agreed. 'I'd like to. I'm going out with Eric tonight but I'm free this afternoon.'

'Excellent,' Rob said with a ready smile. 'I'm not

up to the rough ground on Thurstaston Common yet, but I could offer you a drive to New Brighton and a walk along the prom. I'd be glad of your company. Three o'clock, then?'

Hannah knocked on the vicarage door at the appointed time. She noticed Rob was not able to leap into his small car as he used to, and she found he was not able to walk as well as she'd supposed. Several times, he had to sit down on a bench to rest.

'Sorry, you'll have to bear with me,' he said. 'I'm not much good at this yet.'

'You push yourself and I admire that,' she told him.

'I don't want to sit about nursing a gammy leg, or limp around for the rest of my life, so I have to push myself.'

'You're doing well.'

'Not as well as I'd like.'

'You've got to be patient. I can see a big improvement in the way you walk.'

Hannah felt sorry for him. He was missing his RAF friends and being able to get out and about.

'I wish there was something I could do to help,' she said.

'You're more help to me than you realise,' he told her.

June came and brought the final examinations at the college. Hannah and Gina were taking turns to read to each other so that they could practise taking shorthand dictation.

'I'll never pass,' Gina worried, when she stumbled over reading it back.

'Course you will,' Hannah told her. 'You're

better at bookkeeping than most of us.'

They both passed their exams, and were presented with certificates to say they could type and were competent at shorthand and bookkeeping. They had no difficulty finding their first jobs. Gina went as a shorthand typist to the Liverpool Savings Bank's branch at Charing Cross, and Hannah to a solicitor's practice in Hamilton Square.

The weeks were passing but Hannah found it hard to settle in. She wasn't yet confident of her skill as a shorthand typist; she didn't know anybody at work or the routine of the office. Gina said she felt much the same.

When she talked about it to Eric, he said, 'Why worry about settling into that job? Let's get married.'

Hannah thought about it carefully. This is what they had originally planned for this summer, but she knew Eric wasn't yet able to get the stock he needed for his shop, it would not earn enough to keep them. Everything was taking longer than they'd supposed.

'You could get another job in West Kirby for a while,' he suggested. 'So could I. Let's do it.'

Hannah knew Eric was still seeing Harry and was afraid he might be tempted to earn money illegally if he couldn't stock his shop.

'Better if we wait,' she told him. 'Surely by next year factories will be producing peacetime goods.'

Gina received another letter from Jim saying he'd received his demob date, and he'd be home on 8 July. He seemed excited at the prospect. 'Can't wait to see you again.'

He told her his train was due in at two in the afternoon, when Gina would be at work. She decided it would be better to let his family meet him and take him home. Jim's mother hadn't spoken to her since Pa had threatened to charge her for breaking blackout regulations, although he never had. When Gina had demanded to know what he'd actually done, Pa had said stiffly, 'It's still against the law to show a light of any sort, but it's no longer police policy to take minor miscreants to court.' That had been a long time ago, Gina hoped she wouldn't hold it against her. She wrote and told Jim she'd call and see him that evening.

When at last the date came round, she was on edge all day, wondering if she'd find him as attractive now as she had before he went away. Once, she'd thought she'd found the love of her life; now she wasn't so sure. She went home first to eat a sandwich and change into her newest scarlet dress. She took great care with her hair and make-up. She wanted to look her best.

She crossed the road to his house, which was almost opposite. He came immediately to answer her knock and stood staring down at her, his light brown eyes searching hers.

'Hello, Gina.' He bent to kiss her cheek. It was the sort of kiss he'd give his aunt. 'Come in.'

Jim had broadened out and had a sun tan. He was wearing his brown demob suit, which was quite smart. He looked well, more handsome than she remembered. He'd grown a little moustache and the attractive cleft in his chin was more noticeable, but his manner was stiff. He seemed almost a stranger.

'Moira's come over to see me,' he said, and took her into the living room. They were eating their tea at the table. It was Jim's first meal at home and his mother had made a big effort. They were all ill at ease; his mother was treating him like a visitor. Moira's young son was being given most of their attention. Jim hardly seemed comfortable with his own family.

Gina sat down in an easy chair, which meant Jim had his back to her when he went back to the table to finish his plate of boiled ham.

'I haven't come at a very convenient time, I'm sorry,' Gina said, feeling embarrassed. She hadn't been in this house more than twice since Jim went away.

'Jim's friends are always welcome here,' his mother said, offering her a slice of sponge cake. His sister put a cup of tea into her hand.

Gina was very conscious that officially she was his fiancée, not his friend. When the meal finished, she suggested to Jim that they go out for a walk. She had to get out of here, even if it meant taking him away from his family almost as soon as he'd got home.

'I'll show you round the neighbourhood, in case you've forgotten your way round,' she tried to joke.

'I don't suppose it's changed much.'

'After six years of war, it's grown shabbier.'

Gina felt better when they were out on their own.

He took her arm and said, 'I thought about you

a lot while I was away.'

That made Gina feel guilty. She'd looked for other men friends, convinced he'd be killed and she'd never see him again.

'Really? At first you did, I'm sure. Have you thought about me much this last year?'

He looked surprised, a little taken aback.

'Be honest,' she urged. From his letters she'd sensed the distance between them had grown and grown.

'Perhaps not so often,' he admitted.

'We kept writing to each other, but I sensed we were losing touch, growing apart.' Gina was very serious. 'We're different people now. The war's changed us.'

Jim sighed with relief. 'I was wondering how to say that to you. I was afraid you'd be upset. I mean, you've waited all these years for me.'

'I've grown up. I was only a kid when you went.'

'Seventeen. You make me ashamed when I think of what I persuaded you to do.'

'You said it was the first time for you,' Gina said.

'It was.'

She sucked in her lips. He wasn't saying he hadn't done it with any other girl, which was just as well. It was too soon to exchange confidences like that.

He was smiling at her. 'You're still wearing my ring.'

'I couldn't call round to your house to meet you without it, could I?'

'Now I see it again, the diamonds seem a bit puny.'

Gina smiled; she thought so too. 'We're going to have to start again at the beginning. To get to know each other, I mean. It'll either work out or it won't – we'll have to wait and see. No hard feelings, either way.'

'You're right. We'll wipe the slate clean and start afresh.' Jim grinned at her. 'That's a weight off my mind. Everything has changed. It would be impossible to take up where we left off five years ago.'

'The trouble is,' Gina said, 'you haven't been part of my life, and I haven't been part of yours.'

'I'm used to living with a crowd of men. We did what we were ordered to do, ate what they put in front of us. We were told what to do, we didn't have to think. Now I have to start thinking for myself again.'

'You'll have to find a job too.'

'My old one is being kept open for me.'

'Down near London?'

'Yes, but I don't want to go away now. I can get a teaching job anywhere. I think I'll try locally. It isn't going to be easy to settle down again.'

'Did you enjoy the Army that much?'

'Some of it – having comrades all round me all the time, and going for a drink.'

'Let's go for a drink now,' Gina said. 'That seems a good place to start.'

CHAPTER TWENTY-TWO

1947

The winter of 1946/1947 was the coldest on record for many years. For weeks, heavy snow lay in deep drifts all over the country. The big freeze went on and on, and brought frequent power cuts and domestic fuel rationing. Schools, factories and offices closed down because it was impossible to provide heating and power. Britain's economy was brought to its knees.

Betsy and Cicely were spending all day at home, but both Gina and Hannah were still going to their offices. Paraffin heaters that gave off more smell than heat were pressed into service, and they were told to wear their coats if they were still cold.

Hannah found her fingers were almost too stiff to type, but she felt better about her job. She was finding she could take shorthand and type to the required standard and was beginning to enjoy doing it. It didn't surprise Hannah to hear Gina saying the same thing.

'I've got a smashing job, much better than doping planes. And don't we both look smarter when we go to work? I used to feel a real scarecrow.'

Gina was seeing quite a lot of Jim Latimer. Mostly, that meant he was coming round to join them at the kitchen table to drink tea and gossip.

She would much prefer to be taken out but many of the pubs were closed because they couldn't get enough beer and spirits to make it worthwhile opening. The power cuts were scheduled to take place in the daytime, so theatres and cinemas continued to open in the evenings but they weren't heated. Everybody went muffled up in coats, scarves and gloves. They thought it a more depressing time than the war.

Jim had found himself a job at a local school but he wasn't sure whether he liked it. He said teaching children seemed dull after the excitement of fighting in the war. He was restless and unsettled. Gina felt they were not talking to each other as they should. She didn't know if she was included in his plans for the future, and even worse, there were things she was keeping from him – that she'd had other men friends in his absence, for instance.

One January night, Eric was helping Gina make a meal of fried eggs on fried bread, when Hannah knocked on the back door and whirled into their kitchen. He'd suggested earlier that they go to the pictures.

'You're early,' he said. 'We haven't eaten yet.'

'Have you heard the news?' she asked, her face lit up. He knew it must be something important.

'What about?'

'It was on the six o'clock news tonight. The Government is granting a period of leniency for deserters who surrender before the thirty-first of March.'

Eric beamed at her. 'Excellent news if it lets Leslie off the hook. I wonder if there's anything in this morning's paper about it?'

He found what he was looking for on the front page and read it carefully. 'I wonder if Leslie's heard about this? Perhaps we should go down and see him tonight?'

'Why not?' Gina was reading it over his shoulder.

Hannah said, 'If he surrendered, perhaps he could come home again. He wouldn't have to hide himself away from everybody he knows.'

'It only says "a period of leniency",' Gina pointed out, 'not that all will be forgiven.'

Hannah was craning her neck too. 'It says there are over twenty thousand absentees from the Forces, and between eighteen and nineteen thousand have deserted from the American Forces while they've been stationed in England.'

'And that they have to steal from their comrades in order to survive,' Gina added, before turning to dish up.

'I'll come with you to see Leslie,' Hannah said. 'We can go to the pictures another night. I'd better go home and have my tea. I'll see you later then.' The back door clicked shut behind her.

'Oh Lord!' Eric exclaimed.

'I thought you weren't going to take her anywhere near Harry again,' Gina said, cutting into her fried bread.

'I wasn't. How many times have I told Leslie not to let Hannah know what he's doing?'

'He said you were daft having secrets from her, and he's right. She'll find out what you've been up to when you're married. Better if she knows beforehand.'

'No, I'll take her to the pictures as planned. You go down and see Leslie.'

But when Hannah came back, she wouldn't be persuaded to go to the pictures.

'I think we should all go to see Leslie. Don't you see, this is your chance to get him to return to his unit? That will move him away from Harry.'

Gina whispered to Eric, 'She'll not hear much to upset her, if she's set on discussing that.'

When they reached Harry's house, they found Leslie knew all about it.

'It's been on the news all day. I know a couple of other chaps in the same position.'

'Are you going to give yourselves up?' Gina asked.

'Not likely,' Leslie retorted. 'No fear, not us.'

'They're calling it surrender,' Harry said. 'That's enough to put anybody off.'

'We'd still be in trouble,' Leslie explained. 'Perhaps not quite so much trouble as if the war was still on, but "leniency", my eye. We're not risking it. We can't see that they'll go on searching for us much longer. What's the point? They don't want us back in the Forces; they're trying to cut the numbers down.'

Harry said, 'By the way, Eric, I saved you those things you wanted. The job you helped us with went very well.'

'I'll see to them tomorrow,' Eric said quickly, dreading what might come.

'They're out in our wash house, if you want to see them. A brand-new gas cooker and a fridge for your flat, Hannah.'

Eric froze. Oh my God! He should never have

brought Hannah to hear this.

Leslie said to Gina, 'We got a smashing lot of kitchen equipment from that building site on the corner of Daker Street. D'you know the place? Where they're putting up prefabs? You'd be surprised at the stuff they're putting in them – all the very latest. We got a good haul: fifty fridges and a whole lot of other stuff.'

Eric wished he'd been quick enough to stop this. He daren't look at Hannah.

Harry said, 'I'd like them out of here as soon as possible. When can Leslie deliver them? You'll have to be there to help.'

Hannah was on her feet. Eric could see two vivid red spots on her cheeks. 'I can't live with stolen property in my home.'

Her blue eyes flashed with anger. 'It's off, Eric, I can't marry you. You're turning into a real criminal. You all are. After all I've said... I don't know why I try. Even Spike being caught hasn't stopped you.'

'Hannah, listen. I'm sorry...'

'Sorry! What good is that?' Fury was sparking out of her as she twisted his ring off her finger. 'Here, take it back. I can't trust you. You promised to give all this up and you haven't. You're never going to, are you?' She snatched up her coat.

'Don't go,' Eric implored her, but the front door crashed shut behind her.

He was struggling into his own coat. 'Come on, Gina. Let's go.'

'Just like that?' Leslie asked.

'This is all your fault,' Eric rounded on him. 'I

told you to keep your lip buttoned.'

'Well, I never!' Harry said.

Eric rushed up the road after Hannah and caught her up at the bus stop. 'Hannah, please, we can't end things like this. I love you, you love me.'

He could see tears misting her eyes. 'This is what my mother warned me against. It's criminal. It's very wrong. You're stealing things, getting rich at the expense of others.'

'It's Government property, not–'

'Do you think that makes any difference? Your Uncle Tom was just the same. It ruined Mum's life. I won't let you ruin mine.'

'Give me one more chance, Hannah.'

'I've given you lots of chances. Why can't you stop?'

'I will, I promise.'

'What good are your promises? You don't keep them.'

Gina came. 'You left your scarf behind, Hannah.' She wrapped it round her neck for her.

'Here's the bus,' Eric said. He sat down beside her, Gina took the seat behind.

'Let me put your ring back on your finger.' He went to take her hand in his.

'No.' She shook him off. 'This time I mean it.'

'Think it over.'

'Don't you understand? I've thought and thought about this. Ever since I realised you weren't honest, it's been bothering me. I can't marry you. How can we look forward to a happy life when you're doing things like this? Stealing from building sites now!'

She was staring out of the window, her head turned right away from him. She wouldn't let him take her hand in his. Eric felt bereft. All his plans for the future centred on Hannah.

Gina's chin was on the back of their seat. 'Hannah,' she said softly, 'don't end it like this. You're angry with Eric now. Take time to think it over.'

Hannah didn't answer.

When they got off to walk up St Augustine's Road, Eric tried to take her arm, but she wouldn't let him. Gina tried on the other side, but she wouldn't let her either. They were striding up the pavement three abreast. When they came to the gate of Highfield House, Eric indicated that he wanted Gina to go on home and leave them.

'Good night, Hannah,' she said.

In return, she received a very curt, 'Good night.'

Eric followed Hannah up the path to the porch. There were no lights showing in the house, although it wasn't late. At the end of the war, everybody had let their lights blaze out, but now there were Government posters urging people not to waste power. Those and the recent power cuts had had the desired effect.

When Hannah let herself into the porch, Eric followed her before she could shut the door.

'Please,' he said. 'I can't let you go in like this. Let me explain what I've been trying to do.'

She took off her coat and had the key ready to put in the inner door. He could hear the tears in her voice. 'Don't you realise that it's wrong to steal, cheat and defraud?'

Eric flinched. 'Yes, I do.'

'Then why, for heaven's sake?'

'I suppose it's the only way I have of providing security for us.'

'We can work for it like everybody else.'

'I wanted you to have everything. Right from the start, I mean. Once we're married, I'd be as straight as a die. That's always been my intention. I just couldn't resist the chance of getting more things for our flat.'

'Cookers don't matter to me. There's an old one there already. I'd much prefer to cook on that than a stolen one.'

Eric could feel her anger receding. He put his arms round her and pulled her close.

'I'm sorry, love. Gina wants everything new and shiny and I suppose I do too. I should have known you weren't like that.'

Her head was down on his shoulder. He knew she was crying.

'I've upset you. I've upset myself too. I can't think of the future without you.' She was giving no sign of what she was thinking.

'Please don't break everything off,' he pleaded. 'Give me one more chance. I won't let you down again. Let's get married now, as soon as we can. We can live in the flat even if it isn't worth opening the shop. If we get married I'll guarantee to go straight. What d'you say?'

She snuffled and felt for her handkerchief. 'I don't know.'

'Think about it, Hannah.' He kissed her. 'We'll go to the flat tomorrow evening and talk this through. I'll keep your ring until then. I want you to know that I love you very much.'

Hannah knew as she ran upstairs that her mother was in Philomena's flat. She went straight to the bathroom and bathed her eyes in cold water. She didn't want to confide in Mum; she knew what her advice would be. She had to make her own decision about this.

The problem was, she'd been trying to make this decision for a very long time. She had to settle this once and for all. Her head told her to walk away from Eric; her heart that she wanted to marry him.

Everybody thought to be in love was a most wonderful thing. It brought you joy, made you sing, gave you bubbling energy so you could dance all night. Best of all, it gave you triumphant optimism for the future. Just to be with your loved one was perfect heaven.

Hannah was afraid that for her, love was a far more complex emotion. Being in love with Eric made her feel everything with terrible intensity. Yes, there were times when she was in heaven, but others when she'd worried herself sick about what he was doing. How many times had she sweated with fear, imagining the worst? She'd felt more harrowed than he at the thought of him being caught and charged with crime. Love had brought her real fear, but still she couldn't turn her back on Eric. She wanted him whatever the price she had to pay.

She didn't sleep well, but when the time came to get up, she'd made up her mind.

Tomorrow evening, she'd go to the shop with him, and if he'd guarantee never to see Harry Oldshaw again, and do his best to get Leslie away from him, she'd marry him. They'd do it soon; they'd waited too long. Once married she'd be in a better position to see he kept his promises. He needed her. She'd keep him safe, away from the criminals he was mixed up with, if she possibly could.

The next night, Esme was uneasy, and wished Hannah would come home. She was worried about her.

Hannah was happy, making plans for a bright future with Eric, but Esme couldn't be glad for her or share in her happiness. Hannah was looking at Eric through rose-coloured spectacles and could see nothing but good in him. She was proud to wear his handsome engagement ring.

Once, Esme had been like her daughter, trusting and in love, and look how that had turned out. She was so afraid Eric would be like the rest of his family. Philomena was always talking about Hannah.

'She's a lovely girl really, but so headstrong. She told me Eric has taken shop premises in West Kirby with a flat above it, and he takes her there!'

'Yes I know, she told me too.' Hannah had been thrilled about it.

'I told her Eric had no business to take her there without a chaperone. She laughed at me, Esme. You shouldn't allow it. She'll end up like you.'

That was what Esme feared most. She was waiting for Hannah to come home now. She was undressed and ready for bed but knew she'd find it impossible to sleep before she returned.

Hannah had told her at tea time she was going to the flat again, it was quite a journey to West Kirby on the train and she was doing it too often. Goodness knows what they got up to there.

Was that the front door? Yes, Esme relaxed. Hannah came running upstairs, full of joy. There was a new sparkle about her.

'Mum,' she said, happiness bubbling out of her, 'Eric and I have decided to get married.'

Esme said, puzzled, 'Yes dear, you're engaged.'

Hannah's laugh tinkled. 'I mean we've decided to get married straight away. Well, as soon as we can manage it. We're going to see the vicar tomorrow to fix a date.'

Esme felt the bottom drop out of her world. 'What's the hurry? You aren't...?'

'No, Mum, nothing like that.'

Hannah was intoxicated with love. It was putting her in a position where she couldn't look after herself. Esme was fearful Hannah was going to be hurt as she had been, and felt powerless to do anything about it. She could only watch from the side lines. She felt distraught.

Eric was well pleased. He and Hannah had arranged their wedding for 15 March, in six weeks' time. He'd booked a hotel in London for a few days' honeymoon.

Hannah and Gina were busy making plans for their wedding outfits. Because she didn't want to use precious clothing coupons on an outfit she would only wear once, Hannah decided against being married in white. Instead, she bought herself a smart beige wool costume and a little brown hat covered with lots of veiling.

Aunt Philomena said she would hold a reception for not more than twenty guests in her sitting room, and Brenda would do the catering. Brenda decided she could serve cold chicken with salad, but unfortunately, the wedding cake would have to be the wartime cardboard edifice with a sponge cake inside.

A month later, Eric was sitting at the kitchen table catching up with the morning newspaper while he waited for Hannah to come round. He could hear Cicely and Betsy talking in the back kitchen as they washed up after their evening meal. It sounded as though Cicely was getting a little short-tempered. Wednesday would be Betsy's twelfth birthday and she was haggling with her mother to allow her to have a party.

'You know I've got to go to work,' Cicely said. 'How can I arrange a party for you if I'm not here?'

'Gina's taking a few days off, so she can go out with Jim while he's on half-term. She'll help me get everything ready. You won't have to do anything. We'll be on our half-term holiday,' Betsy wheedled. 'Let me have a small party, to cheer us all up. Just a couple of friends from school and Amy from across the road. I'm always being asked to tea at her house. Please, Mam, say yes.'

'Has Gina agreed to this?'

'She will, if you say yes. Can you make me a birthday cake?'

'I'll make a sponge cake, but I can't get icing sugar to make a proper birthday cake.'

'Not even a bit?'

'There's none being made, Betsy.'

'But the war's over.'

'Give over.' Cicely gave up and headed for the living room.

'It's all right if I ask my friends to tea then?'

'I suppose so,' she snapped. 'You'll have to look after them, though.'

Betsy came into the main kitchen and slid into a chair beside Eric, sighing with satisfaction.

'I'm going to have a birthday party. Will you take some photos?'

He laid the newspaper aside. 'I could do a birthday portrait of you, to mark the event. You could put your best frock on.'

'More than one, please,' Betsy wrapped her arm through his. 'Mam says I can ask three friends. Will you take pictures of them too?'

He smiled. 'All right. That can be my present to you.'

'Is that all? You usually buy me something nice.'

'Betsy! I'll be using scarce film on you kids. Anyway, there's nothing in the shops.' Eric decided he'd give her half a crown. She'd have to buy her own present.

She asked, 'Is Gina in?'

'She's up in her room. Off you go and bully her to do things for you.' Eric settled back to read a report in his newspaper.

It was about a man who had owned a small manufacturing company in Manchester making cosmetics, which he'd had to close down in 1940 when he was conscripted into the Navy. In 1941, he'd jumped ship in Portsmouth and returned to his civilian life in Manchester. He'd reopened his factory, staffed it with those too young and too old for conscription and carried on. His past only came to light when he was found to be evading purchase tax on the firm's cosmetics. He was charged with desertion as well as tax evasion and sent to prison.

Eric felt very heartened. If that was the average standard of efficiency used to pursue deserters, Leslie must be reasonably safe.

Gina came down and put the kettle on for tea. He pointed out the piece in the paper and gave it to her to read.

She said, 'Now the war's over, they'll surely forget about deserters. I mean, what's the point in chasing them?'

'Did Betsy find you?'

'She wants me to make her a birthday tea. She's been on about it this last fortnight. I've been hoarding some American frosting that Spike gave me ages ago, but I can't get cake candles anywhere.'

Eric said, 'I think I've seen some in a drawer here.'

'Yes, I had to comb the town for them last year. No, it was the year before that. They've been used, they're half burned down but I couldn't bring myself to throw them away. Have you got a present for her?'

'I'm going to give her half a crown.'

'That's a bit mean. It wouldn't hurt you to give her five bob. I'm taking her out to buy her a dress. She's nagged her mother into providing the coupons. Cicely's also agreed to give her the money to take her friends to a matinée at the Scala. She wants to see Celia Johnson in *Brief Encounter.*'

'Hope that's suitable for twelve-year-olds.'

'That's up to Cicely, isn't it? You'll be here to help with the tea, won't you?'

'From half-five. I've been organised to take photos of the great event.'

On Wednesday, the girls were just about to sit down to the birthday tea when Eric came home from work. Gina had set the meal out in the dining room, which was only rarely used. Betsy whooped with delight when she saw the spread. They were to start with plates of Spam and salad. To follow, Gina had filled little glass bowls with jelly and pink blancmange, and provided evaporated milk to top it.

She'd iced the cake during the afternoon and kept it out of sight until the girls were ready to eat it. Gina had arranged the one unused birthday candle in the middle of the cake with a circle of half burned ones round the edge. She lit them all before taking the cake to the table. The sight provided gasps of surprise and delight.

Eric took a picture of it, with Betsy standing over it ready to blow her candles out, and went on taking pictures of them all.

'Will you develop them tonight?' Betsy asked. 'We're dying to see them.'

'No. When I've had something to eat, I'm taking Hannah to the pictures. I'll do them tomorrow night. You'll have to be patient.'

Eric enjoyed his evening and didn't feel tired when he came home. On impulse he decided he'd go down to his darkroom and develop Betsy's film. Then he'd be able to print it off tomorrow, and Betsy wouldn't have to wait too long for her pictures.

When he came home from work the next day, Betsy was out at a friend's house and Gina was making a meat pie for their tea. Eric had arranged to meet Hannah at seven o'clock and went down to the cellar straight away to print Betsy's film.

Over their meal, he said to Gina, 'I'm pleased with the pictures I took of Betsy's party. She'll love them.'

It was Thursday evening. Arnold had been on the two-till-ten shift all week and was tired and depressed with his lot. By the time he got home and could get to bed, it was late and he liked to sleep on in the mornings. But it wasn't easy in the school holidays when Betsy was at home. It was even worse now Gina was at home too. He could hear them talking and laughing, running up and down the hall and banging doors. Today, he'd had to get up and switch off the wireless in the living room. They'd had one of those swing bands blaring out, and Betsy said Gina was teaching her to dance. They had no thought for anybody else.

Yesterday, Arnold had heard that he'd been passed over for promotion yet again. It stuck in his gullet that Roger Davies had been made sergeant, a lad half his age who had only been in the Force ten minutes. Arnold was afraid he'd have to accept that his age was against him now, and he'd never get any promotion.

It was lunch time when he got up. Cicely was at work and had left him some sausages to fry before he went out. Gina was varnishing her nails at the kitchen table and Betsy was wheedling to have her nails painted too.

'No,' Gina said. 'This stuff's scarce. I'm not wasting it on you.'

Two plates had been pushed to the edge of the table, waiting to be washed-up. Arnold could see they'd had sausages and fried egg for their lunch.

'How about cooking my sausages for me, Betsy?' he asked, knowing Gina never wanted to do anything for him.

'If you'd got up half an hour earlier, I could have cooked for all of us at the same time,' Gina told him. But Betsy came willingly enough to light the gas. The frying pan was still warm; she put in the sausages.

'We left three for you, Pa. D'you want an egg with them?'

'Yes, please.' Arnold sat down at the kitchen table and poured himself a cup of tea from Gina's pot. 'Are the hens still laying well?'

'Yes.' Gina didn't bother looking up from her nails. She rarely made any effort to talk to him.

The tea was stewed and cold. He said, 'Make me some more tea, Betsy, there's a good girl.'

When she pushed the laden plate in front of him, Arnold asked, 'Did your party pictures turn out all right?'

'I don't know. Eric hasn't done them yet.'

'I think he has,' Gina said. 'He was doing something down there last night.'

'Printing or just developing?'

'I think he's done both.'

Betsy squealed with delight. 'Are they good?'

'I haven't seen them, but Eric's pictures are always good.'

'Where's the torch?' Betsy snatched it from the kitchen cabinet and went clattering down the cellar steps, leaving the door open. Arnold could hear her cooing with approval. 'This one of me is smashing. You should see it.'

'Bring them up, Betsy. Let's have a look.'

There was a moment's silence and she came back slowly with her hands full of prints.

'Here's my party pictures, Pa.' She thrust several postcard-size prints in front of him.

'What d'you make of these, Gina?' She was spreading more prints in front of her.

It was Gina's shocked expression that alerted Arnold. He turned one photograph round to see for himself a second before her hand came out to stop him. He couldn't see why she didn't want him to see it. It was a perfectly ordinary picture of his family, the sort Eric had made dozens of times.

It showed Hannah Ashe with Gina and Leslie out in a street he didn't recognise. All were smiling and jolly and showing great exuberance. A piano had been pushed outside and there was lots of bunting and balloons in the background.

'Did you see Leslie on VE night?' Betsy was asking, and Arnold saw the colour drain from Gina's face.

He felt as though an electric current had run through him. He loosened Gina's fingers on the remaining photos. Here was Leslie again, with a face-splitting grin, seated at a table with a complete stranger who was preparing to carve a huge leg of pork.

He leaped to his feet and snatched at Gina's wrist, pulling her off the chair. 'Where is he? Where's Leslie?'

The table in the picture was not in this house, but Arnold was almost certain Leslie had been here.

'I don't know,' Gina groaned.

'Of course you know. Don't give me that. You went out with him on VE night.' He tugged at her again, almost jerking her off her feet. 'You're going to tell me. I'm going to find him.'

Gina was twisting and turning, trying to escape his hold. He jabbed his fist hard against her face. 'Tell me, or you'll get more of that.'

She spluttered, 'Get off me.'

'Leave her alone, Pa,' Betsy screamed. 'Leave Gina alone.'

He hit her again. Gina fell back against the table, upsetting half a cup of tea. It was running all over the oilcloth that covered it and dripping on the floor. She recovered more quickly than he'd expected to kick him really hard in the groin. It made him double up and loosen his grasp on her. She was off, darting up the stairs before he could stop her. He heard the bathroom door slam.

'Hell,' he swore. 'Hell.'

He was shaking with rage that she dared to defy him. Betsy had flattened herself against the wall and looked terrified.

When he'd got his breath back he went upstairs. He guessed she'd have snapped the lock home. The bathroom door wouldn't budge. He swung hard on the knob and shook it.

'Open this door, Gina,' he called. 'I want to talk to you.'

He knew she wouldn't. She'd chosen the bathroom because it was the only internal door that was lockable. She didn't even answer. He looked in her bedroom to make sure it was the bathroom door he'd heard. As he'd expected she wasn't there.

Arnold was shocked to know Gina and Eric were in touch with Leslie – probably had been all the time. It wasn't good enough. They should have told him. How thoughtless his children could be. As a policeman, they must know it would affect him if Leslie were caught. If this came to light, he'd be reprimanded, his honesty and reliability would be questioned, and it wouldn't be Sergeant Woodward who'd deal with it. At the station, they wouldn't believe he couldn't control his own family. They'd all been out enjoying themselves together on VE night. He couldn't get over that.

He marched up to the second floor and flung open the door to Leslie's room. It was neat and tidy, nothing was out of place. He remembered being on nights and trying to get to sleep during the day. He'd thought he had the house to himself, but he'd heard water running in the bathroom and the odd creak above him. He'd come running up, expecting to find Leslie here then, but his room had looked just like this.

Leslie had been as much on his mind then as he was now. No man could be told his son had deserted and not be worried, especially if he was in the police.

Arnold saw the wardrobe door standing open with lots of clothes hanging inside. They were old clothes, not what Leslie wore. He looked at the lock and saw that it had been tampered with. He felt the blood rush into his cheeks as suspicion overwhelmed him.

Leslie had hidden in here! Why had he not searched more thoroughly then? He grabbed at the clothes, throwing them out on the floor. There was a cushion inside, on which Leslie had made himself comfortable!

Had Leslie also hidden in here when the red-caps had come looking for him? He felt his heart jump at the thought. He'd been in a state of panic the day he'd learned Leslie had deserted.

He found a pile of glossy magazines inside too, he took one out, and flicked through it. It was American, the like of which he'd never seen before, advertising all sorts of luxuries they hadn't seen since before the war began. Gina had an American boyfriend, hadn't she?

His gaze rested on something half hidden under the bed. He pulled it out. It was only an old newspaper, but he checked the date: 7 April 1945. Arnold gasped and felt the blood run to his head. Leslie had been called up in December the year before. He felt sick. This was more proof that he'd been here since. He'd need papers and books to read to keep himself sane if he'd been hiding up here all alone. But he'd had Gina and Eric to keep him company, hadn't he? They must have fed him.

He went back to the bathroom door. That it was still locked brought an upsurge of rage. He pounded on the door till the noise reverberated round the landing.

'Gina, don't be silly. Come out this minute. I want to use the bathroom before I go to work.'

That brought no response. Arnold took a deep breath. He felt like breaking the door down to get at her but there was no sense in doing that. Suddenly he remembered he had to be at the station before two o'clock. He had to get going.

'I'll see you tonight when I come home,' he called. 'We'll talk about Leslie then.'

He went down, collected his helmet and jacket from the hall stand and stalked through the empty kitchen. Betsy had disappeared and the greasy plates were still waiting to be washed up. He crashed the back door shut behind him as he went out. His cheeks were burning as he pedalled to Tranmere Police Station.

When the handsome façade of the police station came into view he shivered. He'd have to parade with his colleagues in a few minutes, and he was afraid they might be reminded to keep their eyes open for deserters yet again.

Arnold knew only too well that deserters were driven to break the law in order to live. He was afraid Leslie had and would be branded a criminal with a police record. He could even be close to being caught, and that would bring disgrace not only on Leslie but also on himself. By not dealing with him all that time ago, he could have driven his son into the hands of criminals.

He really needed to know where Leslie was now. Gina knew, and he meant to get it out of her tonight when his shift finished.

CHAPTER TWENTY-THREE

Gina felt shaken up. Her head ached and her face was sore where Pa had punched her. She was bathing it in cold water when she heard him clatter downstairs. She went to her bedroom and from the window, watched him cycle off to work and knew she was safe for the time being. She ran down to the kitchen. Fear had dried her mouth so she put the kettle on for more tea and wondered where Betsy had gone. She'd be upset, poor kid, for causing this. Getting out of Pa's way was the best thing she could have done.

Gina felt her nose. It was sore and there was an angry red mark under one eye, which was sore too. Pa would try again to get Leslie's whereabouts out of her and she'd get another hiding if she wasn't careful. She went back upstairs to her bedroom and looked at the door. It had a robust lock, but she'd never seen a key to it.

She went to Pa's bedroom. All the doors in this house were strongly built and all had locks. Probably at one time they'd all had keys, but now she couldn't find one. She peeped into Pa's bedside drawer and found several. She tried the ones that looked as though they might fit, but none turned her bedroom lock. She went downstairs for the back door key, to see if that would do it. It didn't fit.

She was reinserting the key in the back door

when she heard somebody knock. Only then did she remember Jim was coming round to take her out. She didn't want to go anywhere feeling like this!

She opened the door a crack. 'Is that you, Jim?'

'Yes, are you all right?' She must sound as bad as she felt.

'No, no, I'm not ready. I can't come.'

He'd seen her face. 'Gina! Who's been punching you?' He forced the door wider and put his arms round her, which made the tears spring to her eyes.

'Pa belted me.'

He was angry. 'He did this to you? Why?'

She hadn't told Jim about Leslie. She didn't want to tell him now, couldn't put it into words. 'Not the first time.' She sniffed into her handkerchief. It hurt her nose to blow it.

'Is he in? Let me talk to him.'

'No, he's gone to work. Don't say anything to him. We'll do that – Eric and me. I'm all right, just a bit sore and shaken up. I don't feel like going out. Can we put it off until tomorrow?'

'Of course, if that's what you want. Can I do anything to help?'

'No. I just want to lie down.'

He was hesitating. 'I don't like leaving you by yourself. Will you be all right?'

'Yes. Pa's gone to work.' She wanted to get rid of him. 'Just leave me, Jim. I'll go and rest on the bed.'

He went reluctantly.

Gina went up to her room and lay down. She couldn't rest, couldn't sleep, couldn't settle to anything. She thought of going to see if Leslie was at home, but couldn't get herself going. For most of the afternoon she sat at the kitchen table drinking tea and trying to calm down. She was glad when Eric came home.

'What have you done to your eye?' he asked.

'Oh Lord, does it show that much? Pa hit me. It's sore.'

Now Gina wanted to inspect the damage. It was too dark to see much in the hall mirror so she shot into the living room to look in the glass over the mantelpiece. Eric followed her to the door.

'You're going to get a black eye.' Bruising was beginning to show.

Gina fingered it gingerly and told him, 'Pa went berserk. Betsy found the pictures you took on VE Day and brought them up to show Pa. Leslie was on them, wasn't he? I could see what was going to happen. I held my breath, wondering if Pa was going to put two and two together, but Betsy went on to point out that Leslie shouldn't have been with us then.'

Eric looked grave. 'Damn Betsy!'

Gina turned on him angrily. 'Damn you too. It wasn't Betsy's fault. You shouldn't have left those pictures lying around where she'd find them.'

'No, I'm sorry, Gina. I didn't think. It was a stupid thing to do.'

'He's going to have another go at me when he comes home, isn't he?'

'No, he'll have calmed down by then.'

'He threatened me, Eric. He wants to know where Leslie is now.'

'Don't tell him.'

'For heaven's sake! Why d'you think he hit me? I didn't tell him.'

Eric looked shamefaced. 'Gina, I'm sorry. I didn't think. Such a silly mistake to make.'

'I'm scared Pa will have another go at me when he comes home. I was wondering whether I'd better get out of the way, go to your flat, spend the night there.'

Eric was frowning. 'You'd have to come back here sooner or later, and you'd be worrying all the time about facing him.'

'It would give him time to calm down.'

'He'll have had that at work. Be in bed with the lights out when he comes home. If he doesn't see you, he won't do anything.'

'What if he comes to my room? If I'm half asleep, I won't be able to fight him off.'

'I'll stay up and make sure he doesn't. I'll head him off. Don't worry.'

Gina sighed. 'Had we better warn Leslie? Pa will be watching us like a hawk after this.'

'Let's drop him a note.' Eric found a pad of notepaper on the kitchen cabinet and started to write.

'Tell him not to risk sending any more notes here. Leslie thinks if he writes the envelope in block capitals Pa won't recognise it as his writing, but he'll be like mustard after this.'

They found a book of stamps in a drawer in the hall stand, but it took them a long time to find an envelope, by which time Cicely was home.

'What have you done to your eye?' she asked Gina.

She said savagely, 'Pa hit me.'

'You've got to learn to do as you're told, haven't you?' she snapped.

Eric said, 'Come on, Gina, let's see if we can get fish and chips. I'll take you for a drink after that.'

Gina felt despondent. 'This black eye makes me look a sight.'

'I'll lend you my sunglasses to hide it.'

'It's the middle of winter and there's no sun. I'd feel a fool.'

'We'll go where nobody knows us. It'll probably look worse by tomorrow.'

'Thanks a lot, that's a great comfort. What about Hannah – aren't you going out with her?'

Eric pushed his brown hair back from his face. 'Shall I ask her to come too?'

'If you want, but you'd better tell her I'm in trouble, so she'll understand why I'm playing gooseberry.'

'You're a nut, Gina,' he said. 'What about Jim? Shall I ask him if he wants to come too?'

'No, I've already sent him away.'

Gina didn't feel any less anxious as she got herself ready for bed that night, though she knew Eric was down in the kitchen and would be watching to see if Pa came to her room. Cicely and Betsy had already gone to bed.

Gina had wanted to bring up the poker from the sitting-room hearth. It was rarely used and could be wiped clean.

She'd said to Eric, 'I could keep it beside me in bed. If Pa goes for me I'd have something to protect myself with.'

He was alarmed. 'No, he could wrench it from you, Gina, and use it against you. You'd get a right battering with that. Better if he uses his hands.'

She'd been persuaded not to, but now felt unarmed and vulnerable. She looked round her room for something to hit him with, should she need it. There was nothing, except... She picked up a heavy glass scent bottle from her dressing table and cradled it in her hand. That would be better than nothing. She'd get one crack at him before he even saw that. Eric had told her to go to sleep and forget about Pa, but she couldn't. Her face was sore and swollen round her eye from his last attack. Her alarm clock told her it was twenty past ten. He'd be home any minute now.

Gina put out her light and pulled the sheet up round her ears, but sleep was miles away. She was listening. She got up again and opened her curtains and also her window. She'd hear him come up the garden path now. She was ready, the scent bottle was cold against her palm and the smell of Parma violets was in her nostrils.

Five minutes later, the garden gate squeaked as Pa opened it; then it clanged shut behind him. He was pushing his bike up the path and into the shed. Then the back door slammed and she could hear nothing more. He must be in the kitchen with Eric.

Gina's heart was pounding as she lay listening for any sound that might tell her what he was doing. Yes, she could hear voices now – they must be in the hall below – and Pa sounded angry. He'd be taking off his helmet and tunic. She lifted her head from the pillow. There was an argument going on, the voices were getting louder. That sounded like a scuffle. Was Eric trying to stop him coming up? Pa was shouting.

'Tell me where Leslie is now and we can all go to bed. I mean to find out. If you won't tell me I'll get it out of Gina.' She cringed into her pillow.

'Gina's asleep.'

'I'll soon wake her up.'

Gina sat up slowly, every muscle in her body tensed for a fight.

Her bedroom door burst open and the light went on in the same second. Pa had a savage look on his face, his shoulders were broad and burly. Eric was behind him and seemed slight by comparison. With her heart thudding, Gina tightened her fingers round the scent bottle.

'You know where Leslie is. It's no good telling me you don't.' Pa was spitting out the words at her. 'I know you do, both of you.'

He was coming towards the bed, his arm ready to grab her. Gina leaped from under the covers and out over the bottom rail, to reach Eric's side.

Eric's lip was curling with disgust. 'Pa, you're a bully, you beat up women and children. Can't you face someone of your own size?'

'Shut up,' he growled.

'Look at Gina's eye. You gave her a real going-over this morning. It'll be black and blue by tomorrow. Proud of yourself, are you?'

'I've got a family that would try the patience of a saint.'

'A saint now! You used to knock us about when

we were kids – Mam too. I saw her with bruises many a time. Why can't you keep your fists to yourself?'

Gina shivered. Eric was goading him and Pa was beside himself.

Fury was billowing out of him like steam. 'I'm an honest man, I try to do my duty–'

'You count yourself honest? You count it a duty to loot?' Eric too was losing his temper. 'I saw you burying that cash box in the garden. You'd stolen it.'

'What? You young whelp–'

'You're a thief, Pa, a liar and a hypocrite.'

'I'm taking no more lip from you!'

Gina saw her father's fist come up and catch Eric under the jaw, knocking his head back against the door with a loud crack. He leaped straight on him, and would have kicked him.

That was enough for Gina, she raised her arm and brought the scent bottle down against Pa's skull with all the force she could put behind it. He went down, his body covering Eric's. He was bleeding from the wound to his scalp.

Her moment of triumph turned to horror when she heard Eric cry out in pain, she could see him struggling to breathe and thought it was Pa's weight crushing his chest. She struggled to roll Pa off, but now she could see Eric's face she knew it was more than that. She saw him flinch, every vestige of colour had drained from his cheeks and he was writhing in agony.

'Eric, what is it?' But she knew he was having one of his turns.

'Pain,' he rasped, and let out a shriek like a wild

animal; she knew it must be excruciating. He was clutching at his chest. 'Iron bands round me – can't breathe – it's awful. I can't stand it.'

Pa was still lying alongside him. 'Bloody cry baby,' he muttered. 'Making such a fuss about nothing.'

Gina was gripped with terror. She'd seen Eric have a turn before but this was much worse. She could see sweat standing up in beads on his forehead. He was gasping, his mouth wide open, his breath rasping. She could see the agony on his face, he moaned but the writhing was less. Gina was relieved at first, thinking the pain had gone.

It took her a moment to realise the life was going out of him. He'd fainted? Was he unconscious?

'Eric, Eric, wake up.' He seemed totally lifeless. A wave of panic washed over her. Was he breathing?

'Pa, do something. Help him, for God's sake.'

But Pa was blinking up at her helplessly.

'Cicely,' she screamed. 'Cicely, come quickly.'

It was Betsy who came first. Gina was unfastening Eric's collar and tie, tapping his chin. What could she do to help him? 'Eric, wake up.'

Betsy gasped, 'What's happened? Were they fighting? Pa's bleeding!'

'Betsy, run to Hannah's house. Her auntie has a phone. Ask them to ring for the doctor or ambulance or something. We've got to have help. Tell them there's been an accident.'

'What sort of an accident?' Cicely demanded. 'Put your coat on over your pyjamas, Betsy, and don't forget your shoes. Arnold's bleeding – is he hurt too?'

'Pa's all right, it's Eric,' Gina was screaming. She pushed on Eric's chest: he didn't seem to be breathing. He wasn't! She wished she knew how to help him, how to save him.

'Artificial respiration, how do we do that?'

Cicely stared back at her helplessly.

Gina burst into tears, put both her arms round Eric and held him tight. Stay with me, she implored silently. Stay with me, Eric.

Betsy was hammering on the door of Highfield House with her fists as well as ringing the doorbell. Hannah knew the moment she opened it and saw the child's terrified face that something must be very wrong. 'Is it Eric? His heart?' Betsy nodded. Hannah went straight to the phone.

'Tell the doctor it's urgent,' Betsy panted. 'Very urgent. Tell him he must come straight away.'

Betsy's agitation was drying Hannah's mouth. 'He says he's coming now.'

She put her arm round the child's shaking shoulders, but Betsy shook her off. 'I'm going back.'

'Wait a minute. I'm coming with you.' Hannah was riddled with anxiety. She snatched up her coat and pulled it on over her dressing gown.

Mum called anxiously, 'Hannah, where are you going?'

'Just up to Eric's. I won't be long.'

She had to run after Betsy. She caught her up at their back door. Every light in the house was on.

Cicely was blocking the way to the hall; Gina was behind her. Hannah could see they were both crying.

She said, 'I've rung for the doctor, he says he'll come right away.'

'Thank God for that.' Cicely dabbed at her eyes with her handkerchief and looked coldly at Hannah. 'But we can't do with visitors now. Not at this time. You'll only get in the way.'

Hannah was pulled up short. 'I'm sorry, I just came to ask how Eric was.'

'Hannah,' Gina said, her voice tight with tension, 'I'm sorry. I'll come down to see you when the doctor's been.'

Gina couldn't stop crying. Her black eye throbbed, but both eyes were red and swollen. She went back upstairs and got into bed in her dressing gown, pulling the covers over her, but she couldn't get warm. She was shivering and felt like a block of ice.

It seemed like a nightmare, as though her whole world was coming to an end. She knew Eric was dead, but hadn't been able to say the word to Hannah. The family all knew long before the doctor came. It seemed impossible that he could die like that. It had happened too quickly and too suddenly. Eric had tussled with Pa but not for long and he hadn't received much of a beating. He'd had worse before and shrugged it off.

Pa was sitting on the end of her bed, blaming himself, riddled with guilt, but she was letting him get on with it. If he hadn't gone for her over Leslie, this would never have happened. They'd all be asleep by now.

Only hours before, Eric had been trying to

support her, make her stronger. He'd taken her out to get fish and chips to jolly her along. They'd had to settle for fish cakes rather than fish itself but it hadn't bothered Eric. He'd been hungry and full of life.

The doctor had come, but what could he do? He'd been sympathetic, putting Eric's death down to natural causes.

'I'm so sorry this has happened to such a young man... I warned him to take things easy, not to overdo things. His heart was enlarged. It hasn't been working properly for some time. You knew that?'

Gina shook her head in misery. They all knew some of it. She'd seen him struggling for breath, and occasionally he'd complained of pain, but Eric had always made light of his problem, and had always bounced back. She'd been lulled into thinking he always would.

But it wasn't entirely natural causes. Gina blamed Pa. She rounded on him furiously.

'This is all your fault,' she screamed. 'You killed him!' She couldn't forgive the way he'd called Eric a cry baby, when he'd been dying in agony. 'I wish I'd hit you harder.'

'You were having a family row? Better forget it all now. I'm afraid this would have happened to Eric sooner or later.'

The doctor bathed Pa's head and painted it with yellow antiseptic, before they'd carried Eric out of her room.

The doctor bathed her eye and gave her two tablets 'So you can sleep,' he told her – but she didn't take them then. She knew Hannah would be desperate for news.

When the doctor went, Gina pulled on her coat and ran down to see Hannah. She was waiting for her, sitting near her bedroom window. Hannah waved and came running down to the porch to talk to her.

'Eric died.' Putting it into words made her burst into tears. Gina tried to tell her what had happened, but Hannah was crying too. They clung together for a long time, grieving for him.

Gina went back home and took the pills then, knowing she'd need help to get through the rest of the night.

Hannah was shivering as she said goodbye to Gina and climbed the stairs. She'd been shocked when Cicely had sent her away. It had made everything seem worse.

Betsy had woken all three of them. Her mother had made cups of tea to help them settle down again, but Hannah didn't go back to bed. She had waited for Gina to come and tell her what was happening. She'd kept her dressing gown on, wrapped herself in her eiderdown and sat in a chair by the window sipping her tea.

It was bright silvery moonlight out in the road and looked very peaceful, but her stomach was churning and she felt full of foreboding. She knew Eric must be in a really bad state. After what seemed ages, she saw the doctor go up. She was cold and cramped but still reluctant to get into bed. Gina would know she was anxious. Hannah was watching for an ambulance, thinking they might send Eric to hospital, but at last she saw

Gina coming down the road. She'd expected the news to be bad, but she hadn't expected the finality of death – not like this. She felt numb.

When she reached the landing, she could see the light was on in her mother's room.

Hannah put her head round the door. 'Are you awake, Mum?'

'Yes.' She was reading. 'I can't get to sleep. How is Eric?'

'He's dead.' Hannah felt her lip tremble.

Esme was aghast. 'What! I didn't realise...'

'He died within minutes. Before the doctor got there.'

'Oh God, Hannah! Come here.' Esme lifted her blankets and Hannah got in bed alongside her. She felt her mother's arms go round her in a hug that offered comfort. 'What a terrible shock. I am sorry, love...'

For Hannah, the next day was terrible. It was Saturday and she should have gone to work in the morning, but couldn't face it.

In two more weeks she would have been married to Eric and now her dreams were shattered.

Mum was fussing her with cups of tea and a breakfast cooked before she went to her office. Hannah couldn't eat it. She'd sensed in her mother a feeling of relief that her marriage to Eric could not now go ahead. She got up late and went to see if Aunt Philomena needed anything, but Mum had made her breakfast too.

'I'm sorry this has happened,' Philomena said, looking stern. 'But we all knew he had a bad heart.'

'I didn't realise he might die like that. He was only twenty-seven.'

'Better he do it now, my dear, than later. You could have been left a widow with a young family to bring up on your own. You must look on the bright side.'

As if there could be a bright side to this! They'd never approved of Eric, and thought she'd be better off without him. She thought her aunt heartless.

Hannah went up to see Gina, feeling she at least would understand the grief she was feeling for Eric. Gina and Betsy were sitting at the kitchen table with their arms round each other. Their eyes were as red and puffy as her own. They could speak only of Eric and the savage suddenness of his death. There was an aura of disaster in the house.

When Hannah was leaving, Gina came to the back door to see her out. She sighed. 'I ought to go down and tell Leslie about this. He'll be horribly upset. I'm dreading it.'

Hannah had passed Eric's shoes on the back kitchen floor, his mackintosh was swinging on a peg behind the door, and his hat was on the dresser with a pile of photographs. It seemed as though he'd come running downstairs at any moment to give her a hug, except that she knew he couldn't.

She went home slowly, preferring to be alone, but she needed to stop her tears. She wanted to pull herself together and prepare something for lunch so Mum wouldn't have to do it when she came home from work. She was splashing cold water on her face in the bathroom when she heard the front doorbell ring. Reluctantly she dried her face and went down to see who it was.

She'd left the porch door open when she'd come home and could now see Robert Osborne was on the doorstep.

'Hannah, I've just heard. You must be feeling awful.'

She knew her self-control was in a fragile state and she couldn't hold on to it. Tears were burning her eyes again.

He put out his arms and pulled her against him in a comforting hug. She was crying on his shoulder. Racking sobs were shaking her body. He was patting her shoulder.

'Hannah, I'm so sorry. It's a dreadful thing to happen, just when you were looking forward to your wedding and a rosy future.'

'Not sure about the rosy future,' she gulped. The doubts she'd had crowded back at her.

'Why not?'

Hannah thought about what she'd lost. She'd never mentioned the inner tussle she'd had about marrying Eric to anyone. She didn't know why she had now.

'I can't talk about Eric yet,' she whispered into Rob's pullover.

'No,' he said. 'Perhaps later, I do understand. You aren't ready to talk to anybody yet. I've brought you some flowers.' For the first time Hannah noticed the big bunch of daffodils he'd picked in the vicarage garden. 'But nothing helps when you're hurting like this, does it?'

He kissed her forehead and went striding down

the path.

The days that followed were no easier. Hannah felt devastated by Eric's death. The life she'd envisaged for herself was going to be very different without him.

His funeral was the first she'd ever attended. Her mother took a day off work so she could come with her and Aunt Philomena wanted to come to the church with them. Hannah thought Eric's family seemed like strangers. Betsy was wearing a new navy-blue hat and coat, and the rest of them wore full mourning black. It was a dark overcast day and a sombre and mournful occasion. Gina was very distressed.

Leslie was not with them. In the midst of her own grief, Hannah spared a thought for him. How must he feel, being unable to attend his brother's funeral? Surely if he'd given himself up, he'd have been allowed to come? Perhaps now, he was sorry he hadn't? He'd been close to Eric.

Hannah couldn't keep her eyes away from the coffin standing on its bier. She found it difficult to stop the tears welling up in her eyes, when she thought of Eric lying inside. He'd always been so full of life and mad schemes.

Rob and his mother were there and offered sympathy, which made it harder for Hannah to control her tears. His father took the burial service and said things about Eric that would make his family proud of him. Hannah agreed with all of them but knew there was much left unsaid and possibly unknown. It made the occasion all the more painful.

Aunt Philomena decided she didn't want to

follow the coffin to the graveside and asked to be taken home. Esme took her, leaving Hannah to stand alone, looking down into the deep gaping hole that was Eric's grave. To think of him lying there in the cold earth for evermore numbed her. It began to rain and Hannah had never felt more bleak and empty. When the ceremony was over, she was stumbling back to the gate, half blinded with tears, when Mr Goodwin stopped her.

'Do please come to the funeral tea,' he said stiffly. 'We're going up to the house now.'

Hannah waited for Gina to catch her up. She was keeping a little apart from her family and seemed withdrawn. 'I told Pa he must ask you back,' she said. 'Eric would want you there.'

Hannah was aware that neither her mother nor Aunt Philomena had been invited. She went with Gina, but she was kept busy seeing to the needs of the other guests. Hannah no longer felt at home in the Goodwin house.

Cicely offered her a glass of sherry in the sitting room she'd seen only once before when Eric had taken their engagement photographs. They sat down to a funeral tea, a group of fourteen, in the formal dining room. Gina was busy pouring tea and had little time to talk to her. Hannah made her escape as soon as she was able.

As soon as the guests started to leave, Gina felt she had to get out of the house too. She'd hung on to Jim all through the church service and brought him here with her. She felt she'd been abandoned by both Eric and Leslie, and was very much in need of someone to take their place. She was leaning on Jim for the first time.

'Let's get out of here,' she said.

'Where d'you want to go?'

'Anywhere, a walk.'

'It's raining,' Jim said. He looked pretty miserable too in his brown demob suit, the only suit he had.

'Give me five minutes. I've got to get out of this black dress.'

Gina ran up to her room to change and chose a red dress, the brightest she had. She covered that with her new red mackintosh. Jim was waiting for her in the hall, and she picked up Eric's umbrella as they went through the back kitchen. The rain was sheeting down and looked as though it had set in for the night.

She took Jim's arm as they strolled down towards the river. The rain was drumming down on the umbrella and when they reached the river the tide was out, revealing a wide stretch of dreary mud flecked with broken bricks and other rubbish. It was almost impossible to make out the Liverpool waterfront on the other side because of low cloud and driving rain. Gina had intended a walk along the promenade, but the idea now seemed dire.

Jim began to ask about Eric's death; about the beating she'd received from Pa earlier that same day. Gina told him the whole awful story: how she and her brothers had always been at loggerheads with their father, and how Eric's revelation about the looted cash box had made Pa go wild and thrash him. She found it helped to relate the horror she'd felt.

'I don't think it's safe for you to stay near your father,' Jim said. 'I'll ask Mam if I can make up the bed in our spare room for you.'

'No,' Gina said. 'I'll be fine. This has knocked the stuffing out of Pa.' She couldn't face Mrs Latimer tonight. 'But I won't stay at home for long. Without Eric it's a miserable place.'

'Let's go into the Royal Rock and have a drink,' Jim suggested.

Gina was glad to get indoors. She considered it a special treat to go to the Royal Rock Hotel but tonight even that didn't cheer her. A notice in the foyer regretted that the bar would be unable to open this evening due to shortage of stock, but that drinks would be served as usual with restaurant meals.

'Tea then?' Jim suggested. They sat and drank tea they didn't really want in the almost empty lounge, while Jim talked about the misgivings he was having about his choice of career. Gina could think only of Eric.

'I'm not very good company tonight, I'm afraid,' he said after Gina had been listening to him for the best part of an hour. She felt dejected.

She wanted to see Leslie, and Harry was always good company, but she didn't want to take Jim with her. She'd seen the trouble Eric had had when he'd taken Hannah. Jim was a war hero and would probably share Hannah's views on their activities. She was going to keep them apart.

'Let's call it a day,' she said. 'We're neither of us finding this much fun.'

He said, 'Nothing can be fun when you've just buried your brother, can it?'

She walked back to Grasmere Road with Jim. At her gate he kissed her cheek and then hurried home.

She stood listening until she heard his back door slam, then she went to catch the bus down to Harry's place.

A new Ford Prefect car was parked outside the house. Leslie answered her knock looking pale and woebegone.

'As you can see, I've taken delivery of my new car,' he told her. 'It cost two hundred and seventy-five pounds.'

'I hope it'll take his mind off Eric,' Harry said, but he didn't look happy either.

'We didn't miss his funeral.' Leslie pressed his lips together, showing a tumult of feeling. 'I drove up to the church and parked outside. Harry was with me. I saw you all go in and I could hear the singing. I saw them wheel the coffin out to the churchyard, but I couldn't go close. I didn't want Pa to see me.'

'I found it agonising.' Gina buried her face in her hands. 'You were better off outside by yourself.'

'What's going to happen to his shop?'

'I'm going to move in,' Gina said.

'What about Hannah?' Leslie asked. 'Won't she want it?'

Gina shook her head. 'I asked her. She said it's the last thing she wants now. It would remind her of all she's lost. No, she'd rather stay with her mother.'

'That's all right then.'

'I've got to get away from Pa. I'll pay the rent

and take over the lease, if I can. You can come too, Leslie, if you want.'

'He's all right here with me,' Harry said gruffly. 'He's a bit of company.'

Gina was frowning. 'When I think of how we longed to get a home of our own ... I'm not letting this one slip through my fingers.'

'But what'll you do with the shop part?'

'I don't know. I'll have to think about that.'

She spent the evening with them, then Leslie drove her home as far as the church in his new car.

CHAPTER TWENTY-FOUR

After he'd seen the last guest out after the funeral tea, Arnold shut himself in the living room and threw himself on his armchair to rest. He could stand no more; he wanted to be left in peace.

Since that terrible moment when he'd realised he'd killed Eric, he'd hardly known what he was doing. He'd hardly slept. Over and over, he'd heard Eric's voice, full of contempt, saying, 'I saw you burying that cash box in the garden. I saw you...'

For all these years Arnold had thought nobody knew about his nest egg. He'd imagined it waiting in the ground ready for him to dig up when he wanted it. Eric's voice went on, 'You'd stolen it. You're a thief, Pa, a liar and a hypocrite.'

Arnold's hands itched to shake him. He wanted to find out exactly what Eric had done and when. Yet all afternoon people had been telling him what a fine lad Eric had been.

Arnold felt tormented because he didn't know whether Eric had taken his money or not. He hadn't exactly said, but he seemed to know there was money inside that box. Arnold had been worrying about this for days. They'd been long days of anguish and suffering because he'd killed his son; the money had been an added weight on his mind. He was longing to dig over his compost heap and find out, but the family had been all round him and there'd been people coming to the house. He hadn't dared to in case he betrayed his secret to Gina or Cicely.

The funeral on top of all that left him depressed, weary and aching in every bone. He'd have a little rest, a sleep if he could, then he'd go and dig his cash box up. He had to know whether he still had the money or not.

He was just closing his eyes when Betsy rushed in to swing on the arm of his chair.

'Pa, Amy's asked me to go to her house to play. Can I?'

'Yes,' he said, closing his eyes again. 'You run along.'

A few moments later, the door burst open once more. 'Why did you tell Betsy she could go out?' Cicely was livid, she had her hands on her hips. 'I need her to help clear the table and wash up.'

'She's upset, poor kid. It'll do her good to go out for a bit.'

'I'm upset. It's been a hell of a day. It would do me good to go out too, but no, I'm expected to clear up by myself. You come and give me a hand.'

Arnold was fighting to keep his temper. 'I'm exhausted, I can't.'

'You mean you won't? Don't you think other people get tired? I hate funerals.'

'I don't like them either,' he said, raising his voice. 'Don't provoke me.'

'For God's sake, Arnold, you caused it all.'

Arnold blenched. If Cicely knew he'd killed him, did she know why? He said angrily, 'It was Gina's fault. She was defying me. If she'd told me what I wanted to know in the first place–'

Cicely's face screwed up with disgust. 'If you hadn't started the fight, Eric would be alive now.'

Arnold felt as though he couldn't breathe. 'Are you saying I killed Eric?'

She was staring back at him, defiance in her pale eyes. This wasn't like Cicely. Her voice grated, 'You really believe it had nothing to do with you, don't you? Arnold, if you hadn't been raging at Gina, Eric would have been in his own bed, not trying to keep you away from her.'

Arnold had never felt so low. A vision of Eric lying in his coffin in the cold earth filled his mind. The last few days had been a nightmare. He'd had to nag Gina and Cicely to get mourning clothes to show a bit of respect.

Cicely's face was dark with anger. 'You always think it's somebody else's fault when things go wrong. You never blame yourself, even when you should. What is the matter with you?'

Arnold swallowed hard. 'I shouldn't have hit Gina.' He'd never be able to forgive himself for that. It would be on his conscience for the rest of his life. 'If only she'd told me where Leslie–'

Cicely rounded on him. 'What does it matter where he is? I'm glad he's no longer here with us.'

That roused his ire. 'I suppose you think the same about Eric?' he demanded.

'He was your son, not mine. I'll not miss him either. Your kids have always caused trouble.'

Cicely didn't know about the money, which was a relief, but she was right about one thing: Eric would be alive today if he, Arnold, hadn't been so intent on getting Gina to talk. He'd killed Eric, just as he'd killed Rowena. The two people he'd loved best.

All his life, he'd been provoked by demons driving him to do terrible things. He'd tried to live a good life, but temptation and the devil had driven him to this. He felt total despair. He was sinking. He'd tried to work for the Church and prayed for help and guidance. It hadn't come. He had to make sure the money was still there. If it was, he was going to spend it. He was going to live a little. A car perhaps?

His mind made up, Arnold strode to his shed and selected his favourite spade and garden fork. Down the garden he rushed to the compost heap, to fork the rotting garden rubbish aside with fast, furious movements. The earth was wet and muddy and he noticed for the first time it was raining.

Digging into the earth was heavy work, but he wasn't going to give up. A mound of soggy soil was building up beside him; he expected his spade to scrape against the cash box at any moment. When it didn't, he thought he might have buried it deeper and carried on. When this didn't bring it to light, he thought he must be digging on the wrong spot and made the hole bigger. It was such a long time since he'd buried it, he'd forgotten exactly where.

The moment came when he had to ask himself if Eric had dug it up and stolen it from him. Was Eric going to have the last laugh after all?

Perhaps it had all been a bad dream, brought on by the heavy bombing and the extra hours he'd had to work. Perhaps it was his family preying on his mind. Arnold was exhausted. He looked up and saw Cicely running towards him, holding his best umbrella over her head.

'For God's sake, Arnold, what are you doing? You've ruined your new suit! You've got it soaking wet and covered with mud up to the knees. And look at your best shoes!'

He stood leaning on his fork, breathing hard. He had mud all over himself.

'What's come over you?' Cicely wailed. 'It's raining cats and dogs and you're out here digging. Is it a grave you're digging?'

'No,' Arnold straightened up. 'The money isn't here.'

'What money?'

The money need not concern her. He had no intention of telling Cicely about it.

'There's no money here, Arnold. Come indoors. You'll catch your death of cold out here in the wet.'

She was taking his arm and leading him away. He insisted on putting the fork and spade back in the shed.

'The funeral's playing on your mind, that's the trouble,' she told him. 'Eric's in the churchyard. You don't need to dig a grave for him here.'

'It wasn't a grave.'

'You must feel responsible for his death, if you're still trying to bury him. Come on, get out of those wet clothes.'

Cicely found dry clothes for him. Perhaps he never had stolen the money, never had buried it there. It was all a long time ago and it was the demons and the war and his conscience that had made him believe he had. But now the comfort of having a nest egg tucked away had gone too. He felt bereft.

'Go back to the living room,' Cicely ordered. 'There's a nice fire there now, it'll warm you. I'll bring you a cup of hot tea.'

Arnold felt his way back to his armchair, and collapsed on it in a fever of grief and shame, feeling helpless and hopeless. Like the bursting of a dam, rage and guilt were pouring out of him in scalding tears.

He said aloud, 'I swear it'll be the last time I lift my hand against any of them.'

Feeling deeply despondent, Hannah went home after the funeral tea to find her mother crossing the hall, carrying a tea tray.

'Come and have a cup with me and Philomena, dear,' she said. 'Better than being by yourself.'

Hannah didn't want more tea and would rather have been alone, but couldn't find the energy to say no.

Aunt Philomena wanted to talk about every detail of the funeral service and then asked what the Goodwins had provided for the mourners to eat. Gina would have said she was a nosy old woman. Hannah did her best to respond, but she knew she sounded half-hearted. She wanted to blot the funeral out of her mind.

Aunt Philomena said firmly, 'Hannah, the best thing for you is to go back to work.'

'It'll take your mind off Eric,' her mother added.

Hannah knew nothing could do that, but she'd had enough of sitting about with her mother and aunt, and wanted no more of it.

When she got up to wash the tea cups in the kitchen, she could hear Aunt Philomena saying, 'Probably the best thing that could have happened. Hannah will get over this and she'll be better off without him. I mean, a shoe salesman – she can do better for herself than that.'

'Poor Eric,' her mother said.

'A weak heart too. She could have ended up nursing an invalid for years. No, I think she's had a narrow escape.'

Hannah thought her aunt had meant her to hear that and it made her flood with tears again. It was a long time before she felt sufficiently in control to go back and say good night. She thought her mother, too, was relieved that she wouldn't be marrying Eric, but for different reasons.

For Hannah, Eric's death had come with savage suddenness. When she'd thought about it calmly, she knew she'd had painful reservations about what their future might hold, but she knew he loved her and she'd loved him too much to give him back his engagement ring. Despite everything, she'd chosen to trust him.

Hannah was surprised to see Gina running down to catch the bus to go to work the next morning.

'I couldn't sit around at home any longer,' she said. 'And don't say anything about Eric, or I'll burst into tears again. We've got to put it behind us.'

Hannah knew she wasn't ready to do that yet. She couldn't stop thinking about him, and kept seeing his face everywhere she looked. Gina was stronger than she was about Eric.

The following day, Gina brought her a brown-paper carrier bag. 'Don't look to see what's in it now, wait till you get home. I've brought you a few of Eric's things. I thought you'd like to have them as mementoes.'

'Thank you, I would.'

'He left a fair amount of cash too.' Gina was holding out a roll of banknotes held together with an elastic band.

Hannah drew back. 'Oh no, Gina, I couldn't.'

'He'd have wanted you to have it.'

'I'd rather you and Leslie...'

'We're both getting our share. Eric didn't leave a will, you know.'

Hannah said, 'No, he didn't expect to die, not yet awhile.' She patted the carrier bag. 'I'm more than happy with this, and Aunt Philomena makes sure I have enough for everything I need.'

When she opened the bag's contents out on her bed that evening, she found two framed portraits of herself that had hung in Eric's bedroom. One had been taken the day they'd chosen her engagement ring, and there was also a view of the Liverpool waterfront at sunset, examples of his photographic skills of which he was justly proud. Also in the bag was the watch and signet ring he'd always worn and his Brownie camera and some film, together with several albums of the photographs he'd taken.

Hannah was thrilled to have them, but the sight of them spread out on her bed made her weep again. It took her a long time to regain her composure. Then she went in search of her mother to show her Eric's things. She was downstairs with

Aunt Philomena, who turned his watch over and said disparagingly, 'Not a very good make, dear. Not worth anything.'

Hannah knew he'd recently acquired another watch that he wore when they went out. Eric had thought highly of that, but she preferred to have the one she'd seen him wear almost every day.

When Gina finished work on Friday afternoon, she took a bus up to the north end to see Leslie. She knew that if Eric had still been with them, he'd tell her to snap out of her misery. As all their plans must now change she wanted to get on with it.

Harry opened the door to her. 'Leslie isn't home yet,' he told her. 'He's out on a driving job, but he won't be long. Come in. I've just made a pot of tea. How are you?'

'Cheer me up, Harry.'

'Willingly, if you tell me how. Leslie's down in the dumps too. It'll take time to get over Eric.'

'I know. I'm going to move into his flat this weekend.'

'Won't it give you a longer journey to work?'

'Yes, but I've got to get away from Pa. I might look for a job in West Kirby.' She hesitated. 'I'm sorry Hannah was so cross about the cooker and fridge you saved for Eric. I suppose it's too late to have them now?'

'Yep, sorry it is. If I can help in any other way...'

'Yes, Harry, you can help with my future plans. I'd like to run my own business in the shop below.'

'What sort of a business?' Harry's tone was guarded. 'You need to know something about what you intend to sell. I mean, Eric knew all about photography.'

'I know about clothes. I rather fancy selling women's fashion.'

'I wouldn't rush into it, if I were you. Film and cameras are not on ration, but clothes are. While there's rationing, you won't be able to get enough stock to build a business up. In other words, you won't make much money.'

Gina said irritably, 'It's two years since the war ended, for heaven's sake. Is rationing ever going to end?'

Harry shrugged. 'Sooner or later it will. I thought you wanted to be a secretary?'

'I did, but I think I might like running a dress shop better.'

'There might be more money in it – eventually.'

'I'd like that. It's a shame not to have a go when I'm living on premises which would be just right for it.'

'It's not a bad idea.'

'I remember Leslie telling me last year that you knocked off a lorryload of the latest fashions...'

'Hang on, Gina. If you're thinking we could pick up another load, well, probably we can, but if you suddenly open up a shop full of dresses from us, it can bring down trouble on all of us.'

Gina giggled. 'I wasn't proposing to do that. You know about business – what would I have to do?'

'There'll be permits you'll have to apply for. I think each shop is given an allocation of goods to sell. It'll take some time to set it up.'

'But how should I go about it?'

'OK, you need to do some research. Find out which makes of clothing you want to sell. Whether you want the cheap end of the market or the more expensive.'

'The more expensive.' Gina didn't hesitate.

'You'll need to find out which companies make them, and how they sell them, and the difference between wholesale and retail.'

'I do know that.'

'After you've opened your shop and you have it stocked with clothes from your chosen maker, I could possibly get you more. Then if one of those Government officials gets suspicious and checks your stock, your paperwork will make you look like an honest trader.'

When Leslie came home he looked tired and down in the mouth. 'How are you getting on at home?'

'It's lonely without you and Eric. I've just been telling Harry I'm moving out tomorrow.'

'You ought to look through Eric's things before you do.'

'I already have. I caught Cicely up in his room yesterday, searching through his cupboards and drawers, but fortunately I'd beaten her to it. Eric had a lot of cash stashed away in various places.'

Leslie said, 'A good job Cicely didn't get her hands on that. We wouldn't have seen any of it if she had.'

Gina nodded. 'I found a lot of bank books too. Eric had opened an account for each for us.'

'He always wanted to take care of us.'

'Here's yours.' She opened her handbag and gave it to him.

Leslie whistled through his teeth when he saw how much had been saved in his name. 'He did take care of us.'

She handed over a bundle of pound notes with an elastic band round them. 'This is your share of the cash I found. Eric had over a hundred pounds.'

'Blimey! He was really coining it in.'

Harry asked, 'Did he make a will?'

'No,' Gina sighed. 'I didn't find one but I didn't expect to.'

'He didn't think about dying.'

'No. There are several more savings accounts in his own name.'

Leslie asked, 'Will you be able to get the money out of those?'

'I hope so. I'm a bit worried because Eric has saved too much for it all to have come from his wages at the shoe shop.'

'He'd been working with us,' Harry said. 'He received his share.'

'I know. He earned money from those medical exams he underwent too.'

'I've spoken to Pa and Cicely about it but I only showed them this bank book with forty pounds in it. They said that the only way is to see a solicitor.'

'You don't want to let Pa have the lion's share,' Leslie said. 'You'd better offer to see the solicitor yourself.'

'I already have. I hope Pa won't be poking his nose in. We don't want him to know all the details, do we?'

'Who gets this money then?' Leslie asked. 'I

mean who's legally entitled to it?'

'Pa says it will be divided between him and us.'

Leslie pondered on that for a moment. 'What about Hannah? Eric would have wanted her to have it.'

Gina managed a wry smile. 'Then he should have made a will, shouldn't he? I offered Hannah the cash I found, but she wouldn't take it. I think she thought it hadn't been earned honestly enough, and she said her Aunt Philomena more than looks after her needs.'

'All the more for us, then.'

'Yes, we'll split what I can get between us,' Gina told him.

Leslie drove her home in his new car. It seemed the rest of the family had already gone to bed. Gina crept straight upstairs to the attic and found two small suitcases, took them to her bedroom and packed some of her belongings in them.

Then she opened a drawer in her dressing table, where she'd hidden Eric's belongings. She packed his three bank books and his rent book for the shop. She'd pay the rent when it next fell due. It seemed she had until the beginning of next month. Then she slid the suitcases out of sight under her bed and got undressed.

In the morning, she took the suitcases with her to work, together with the keys to Eric's shop. It was Saturday, and when the office closed for the weekend, she caught the train to West Kirby. She'd been in the flat several times, but Eric had had a lot done to it since she'd last seen it. It was newly painted throughout and looked clean and fresh. The kitchen had a new sink. Eric had brought a few pots and pans and had even made the odd meal here. A few basic foodstuffs remained.

There was one small bedroom which Eric had planned to use as a boxroom. There were also two double bedrooms but one was completely empty, while the other needed only a bed to be fully furnished. The living room had a three-piece suite so she decided she could sleep on the settee until she could get herself a bed. She'd have enough furniture to be able to manage, and was thrilled that she could stay here and get away from Pa at last.

Down in the shop, she removed Eric's photographs and the notice he'd put in the window. There was a cellar, and she found some half-used tins of paint stored there. She brushed a thin coat of whitewash on the window so that nobody could see in.

Then she put her coat on again and went to look at the nearby shops. She had to buy something to eat, and she'd have to register with a grocer to get her rations on a permanent basis. There were many things she needed for the flat. She wanted to make it really comfortable. Maybe Harry could help her get a bed.

April brought floods so severe that two million sheep were drowned. That represented four weeks' meat ration for the population. The floods also ruined five hundred thousand acres of wheat – a month's bread supply. Everybody was forbidden to light a coal or gas fire until October.

'They don't mean me,' Philomena told Esme. 'I'm an invalid. I have to keep warm.'

Brenda continued to light Philomena's fire. She'd had an arrangement with her coal merchant for most of the war. Coal was rationed now, but she had a plentiful stock.

June brought a dollar crisis and the Government announced desperate measures: Britain had to export or die. It was a question of work or want.

To Hannah, life seemed doubly bleak without Eric.

Robert came round one Saturday. 'How about a walk, Hannah?' he asked.

She had no energy and felt more like lying down on her bed. She didn't sleep well and always felt tired.

'Come on,' he urged. 'It's a blustery day – you'll feel better after a good blow.'

He drove her to New Brighton, and stepping out on the promenade against the high wind off the Irish Sea certainly blew Hannah's cobwebs away.

'Let's have five minutes on this next seat,' Rob said. 'My leg's playing up. It isn't quite right yet.'

'I'm sorry, I'm belting along too fast for you. But you are better. We must have come half a mile.'

'I want it to be as good as new,' Rob said, lowering himself on the bench.

Hannah sat in silence, listening to the roar of the incoming sea.

Rob said quietly, 'In this life, Hannah, we all have to take hard knocks of one sort or another. Losing your fiancé so suddenly must have been a terrible shock. It was right to take time to grieve and reflect on your loss, but now...'

Hannah's voice was flat. 'Aunt Philomena says it's time I pulled myself together. I suppose you're going to say the same?'

'I was going to say, look to the future instead of the past.'

Hannah watched a freighter nose its way into the deep water channel in the Mersey estuary. The sun was glinting on a silvery oil storage tank on the Liverpool bank.

'Rob, you're the sort who can push yourself when things get tough.'

He said quietly, 'It's a question of mind over matter. You should push yourself too.'

She shook her head miserably. 'How do I go about that?'

'You're spending too much time looking after your Aunt Philomena. You should get out more. You've got a job – try and make new friends there. Try to get back into the swing of things.'

Hannah covered her face with her hands. Rob didn't understand. 'But I don't really want to.'

'I know the feeling. Everything seems too much trouble, you have no energy, and you wonder why you should bother anyway.'

'Nothing will bring Eric back.'

'No, I'm afraid it won't. I don't know whether it would help you, but I'd feel more normal if you'd come for regular walks with me. I need to strengthen my leg, and it's not much fun on my own.'

'I'll come, of course,' Hannah agreed. She hadn't thought of Rob's needs; she was being self-centred.

'How about coming to the pictures too?'

She nodded. It was a long time since she'd been. 'I'd like that.'

'And dancing would be good for my leg. I'd need a partner who'd be patient with me.'

Hannah smiled. 'I'm very patient. Aunt Philomena gives me plenty of practice in that respect.'

When she returned home, Mum said, 'You feel better after that, don't you?'

Hannah had to agree she did. She felt refreshed. She wasn't sure whether it was Rob who'd been good for her or the buffeting by the strong wind.

'Robert Osborne is a very nice person. You could do worse than him.'

She felt a surge of impatience. She wished Mum and Aunt Philomena wouldn't keep pushing Rob down her throat. 'Rob's a good friend,' she said shortly. 'But he isn't Eric.'

He took her to the cinema that evening. It wasn't a good film and she thought he was as bored with it as she was. If Eric had been with her, that wouldn't have mattered, but Rob didn't hold her hand or kiss her in the darkness as Eric had done. She didn't think either of them enjoyed it much.

But however difficult it was, Hannah found life went on. One evening, she decided to take Rob's advice and make more effort. She took the train out to West Kirby to see Gina.

Gina was all smiles when she opened the door. 'I'm so glad you've come. I didn't like to ask you as this was meant to be your home.'

Hannah didn't begrudge it to Gina. 'Without Eric, I wouldn't want to live here,' she said. 'I'm better off staying with Mum.'

'I was afraid we'd lose contact now we don't see each other every day.' Gina had given in her notice and found herself another job in West Kirby that was only a few minutes' walk away.

'I'm lost without Eric,' Hannah said. 'I wouldn't want to lose you too.'

They talked about Eric all the time. It drew them closer. Hannah took to visiting Gina a couple of times a week. They went to auctions and visited markets, searching for bits and pieces to furnish Gina's home. It took several months before she was satisfied.

'You've got it looking very comfortable,' Hannah told her.

Gina turned her attention to the shop. 'The more I think about it, the keener I become. I think I'm going to go for it. I can't settle to being the office junior.'

She took Hannah round all the big shops on the following Saturday afternoons, to assess the sort of clothes that were on sale, and decided what she wanted to sell in her own shop. Hannah knew Gina had a flair that she didn't possess herself.

Gina spoke of Jim Latimer, who was coming to see her at her shop. One day, she suggested to Hannah, 'Why don't you bring Rob so we can make up a foursome? If you came out one Saturday afternoon, you could help me cook a meal for us all. Then they could take us out somewhere.'

Hannah smiled, 'That would be fun.' The outing became a monthly event, and she began to feel better now she had a social life again.

CHAPTER TWENTY-FIVE

Gina was happy in her new home. One evening, she was at the window of her living room, looking down into the street, when she saw Harry pulling in to the kerb outside. Leslie was teaching him to drive and they often popped in to see her. Gina was being as careful as she could to keep Harry away from Jim.

Harry was helping her with the paperwork she had to complete before she could open her shop. She'd received another whole sheaf of forms to apply for an allocation of clothes for stock. He had also promised to help by bringing her additional clothes to sell once she'd got her business up and running.

Leslie came whooping in. He was in high spirits. 'Remember what I predicted in January? That the Government would do nothing more about deserters? Well, I was right. They've stopped hunting us down. I know somebody who applied to have his old job back in the Co-op. He told them he'd just been demobbed. He's been back working for a week now and desertion hasn't been mentioned.'

Harry was beaming too. 'It seems it's safe for Leslie at last. He's not the first deserter we've heard of who's returned to civilian life with no questions asked. It had to come, didn't it? Stands to reason.'

Harry had brought a cherry cake and some chocolate biscuits with him.

'Lovely,' Gina said, and went to put the kettle on.

Two hours later, when they were about to leave, Gina took them on a tour of the shop. 'Eric was setting this up as a photographer's, and I need to change a few things if I'm going to sell dresses.'

'There's a good counter and a till,' Harry rang it up. 'It works OK. You said this used to be a hat shop?'

There were lots of mirrors, lots of cupboards too, which Eric had had painted grey. The shelves inside were only wide enough to take hats, but that would have suited Eric's purpose.

Gina said, 'I need them wider, at least the width of a coat hanger.'

'Get a carpenter to come in,' Harry advised. 'He could take these lower cupboards right out and fix rails under the upper ones. Do we know anybody who could do that?'

'Yes,' Leslie said. 'There's Bert. He's a carpenter.'

'That's right. He calls himself a cabinet maker – that's even better.'

Leslie smiled at her. 'Shall I ask him?'

'Yes,' Gina said, 'and I thought I'd repaint all this woodwork white. I want it to be lighter.'

The following Saturday afternoon, she'd arranged to meet Jim in Liverpool. He'd agreed to go with her to help pick out some fittings for her shop. Harry had given her the name and address of a dealer.

Jim was waiting for her at the top of the steps in

Liverpool Central Station. She thought he looked attractive in his Harris tweed jacket and grey slacks. He had an honest face, with light brown hair that fell over his forehead.

He was smiling down at her. 'Hello.' He took her hand and wrapped it round his arm. It seemed a warming and friendly gesture. She'd found he still had the ability to tug at her heart.

In the warehouse, surrounded by the detritus of hundreds of shops that had either been bombed or closed down, Gina didn't know where to begin.

'I do miss Eric at times like this,' she said. 'He'd know exactly what I should buy. I used to rely on him for so many things.'

'I've come to stand in for him,' Jim said seriously. 'Let's have a look at that list you made. I don't know much about manikins. What are they?'

'Life-size plaster dolls for displaying clothes. The arms come off so I can dress them. They're jointed ... I want three for the shop window, and possibly another inside to show a really smart dress. These all look a bit shabby and old-fashioned, don't they?'

Gina picked out the four best.

'Just washing would help, Gina. I could do that for you.'

'I could paint their hair, make them look smarter.'

'Paint over these chips in the plaster so they wouldn't be noticed. Once you get them into your shop, you'll see what needs doing.'

That done, he took her for a drink. They sat

close together on the end of a bench. The pub had a supply of beer and was full of customers. Gina had seen a good deal of Jim recently. He said he was settling down to teaching and civilian life. She felt they were no longer the strangers they'd been when he'd first been demobbed, but she hadn't been able to talk to him about serious matters.

As she sipped her drink, Jim moved closer. Against the hubbub of pub noise, he said, 'I've a confession to make, Gina.' He was uneasy and his eyes wouldn't meet hers. 'I owe it to you.'

He was making Gina nervous. She was afraid she'd have far more to confess than he had. Jim was a war hero and thought in the same way Hannah did, that honesty was the best policy. Occasionally, he voiced his opinions on the spivs who'd made money on the black market while he and others like him were away fighting. He thought them the lowest of the low.

Jim knew Leslie had deserted – his family had told him. It seemed the redcaps had been seen visiting number eight, and the rumour had gone up Grasmere Road. Jim knew Gina had been in touch with her brother and that she expected his problem to be forgotten now the war was over. Other than that, she didn't talk about Leslie and she'd kept Jim well away from him and Harry. Now she felt having to keep secrets from him was coming between them.

'I can't imagine what you have to confess,' she told him.

'Well...' Another pause. 'I had a girlfriend, while I was away...'

She wanted to stop this. 'You don't have to tell me.'

'Yes, I do. She was a nurse.'

It was the last thing Gina had expected. 'But you were abroad fighting all the time.' It had never occurred to her that he'd meet any girls. Besides, he was the trustworthy type who wouldn't do anything he shouldn't.

'I had gastroenteritis.' He half smiled. 'Not the most romantic of illnesses. At the time I longed to be suffering from something else.'

Gina nodded. He had written to tell her he'd been in hospital for a few days.

'We were near Monte Cassino for a long time. Italy's a long way away and life there was very different. I thought I could forget all about her, put her behind me for ever.'

'Another country and a long time ago,' Gina murmured.

Jim sighed. 'I find I can't. It's on my conscience and it's coming between us now. I won't feel really close to you until these things are out in the open.'

Gina felt her toes curling with embarrassment. If she didn't take this chance to tell him about Doug Sheffield it would remain a secret between them for ever, something she must never talk about, but she didn't feel ready to make her confession yet. For her there were other things Jim wouldn't like that she ought to tell him.

He went on, 'You were just a kid, seventeen when I went away, and you gave me exactly what I wanted. I've been ashamed of that. I left you and you might have had to face pregnancy and bringing up a child by yourself. Hardly a loving thing to do, was it?'

She said, 'I was worried stiff at the time, until I realised I was in the clear.'

'I know, so was I. I was afraid of being killed and then I'd never be able to help you. Didn't show much responsibility, did I? Whatever was I thinking of?'

Gina was biting her lip. Jim was a loving and tender man – she'd seen that even when she'd been seventeen – but she couldn't resist asking, 'What was she like, this nurse?'

Jim took a big gulp of his beer. 'She came from Birmingham. She was older than you, older than me too but it didn't seem to matter. She reminded me of Blighty and I thought I was in love with her. It lasted three months. She was working in a field hospital. She moved with it and I was sent somewhere else. We lost touch. I'm ashamed of what I did, I have to tell you.'

Gina put her hand on his wrist. 'There's somebody I have to tell you about.'

'Oh!'

'I was never the little innocent, Jim. I've had a few boyfriends while you've been away. Most of them were just friends, someone to go out with. There was only one I really fancied. He worked at the aerodrome too, was one of the managers.'

'He had plenty of money, and could give you a good time?'

'Yes, until I found out he had two little boys and a wife at home.'

It took Jim a long time to ask, 'Did you ... let him go all the way with you?'

'Yes,' she told him. 'And you and the nurse?'
'Yes.'
Gina smiled. 'You're forgiven. Am I?'
'Of course you are. It would be very churlish not to. Five years is a long time to be apart. I felt we had to talk about it, clear the air, so to speak. It was as though we couldn't get back to the way we were until we did.'
'Let's call it moving on,' Gina said. 'I want that too.' She felt they had.
He bent over and kissed her cheek.
She said, 'Let's go home.'

In the autumn of 1947, Christian Dior, the Paris fashion designer, launched his New Look, with full skirts almost to the ankle. Gina loved it when she saw the first pictures in newspapers and magazines.
Throughout the war, women's clothes had been plain and military in style and worn an inch below the knee to be economical with cloth. The Government condemned the new style as frivolous and a wicked waste of scarce cloth. Women were advised to ignore it on social grounds. Instead, they adopted the look *en masse*.
When Hannah came out one evening, Gina showed her the pictures. 'A bit of luxury at last. Aren't they glamorous after all the austerity?'
Hannah agreed. 'I love all the pleats and gathers, the lovely long full skirts and little tight tops.'
'I'm going to stock them. The papers say they're selling like hot cakes.'
'The problem is,' Hannah said, 'there's nothing in our wardrobes that looks remotely like that.

Our clothing coupons will only stretch to one new outfit and the New Look will make everything else look dowdy and out of date.'

'Everybody's going for it all the same,' Gina chortled. 'I couldn't have chosen a better time to open my shop.'

Both Gina and Hannah decided they must unpick the hems on all their skirts, letting them down as far as they'd go.

'I've got some summer dresses I quite like,' Hannah said. 'New only last year.'

'So have I.'

'We could add three or four inches of contrasting material to the skirt and add a collar or some bows or something of the same stuff to the bodice. It'll make it seem like New Look.'

'Can you sew?' Gina asked, thinking of collars.

'Not very well, but Mum can. She'll help me.'

'I don't suppose she'd help me,' Gina said, pulling a face.

When the first allocation of clothes arrived at the shop, Hannah came again to help Gina hang them on the rails and press those that needed it. She picked out the outfits she thought most attractive and they had a good laugh as they fitted them on the refurbished models and stood them in the window.

'Have you noticed?' Gina asked. 'I got a signwriter to come yesterday.' She took Hannah out to the pavement to admire her sign. It read, 'Georgina Goodwin, High-Class Ladies' Fashions' above the plate-glass window.

Gina had had the room behind the shop fitted up with three changing cubicles, and she'd added lots of mirrors and had had a deep red carpet laid throughout.

'It's a beautiful shop,' Hannah said. 'It looks expensive too, though it isn't really.' Gina was placing moderate price tags against the items in the window.

'You were lucky to find a carpet like this.'

Gina said nothing, Hannah would not approve.

'Not Harry?' Her blue eyes were accusing.

'I couldn't get carpet anywhere else. I had to.'

'Gina, I want you to stay away from him. You said you would now Eric was no longer egging you on to join his schemes. Why not be an honest trader? I'm sure you'd feel far less worried.'

'I'm not worried,' Gina said. 'I feel poised ready for action. I'm ready to open now. All I have to do is hand in my notice at the office.'

Harry had suggested she advertise her opening date, and she did so in the local paper. She also had a few posters printed and put them up around West Kirby.

Her big moment came the following Saturday, when she opened her shop to the public. They flocked inside and loved her New Look clothes. Jim was there to help her, though he said he felt awkward amongst so many women. He stood behind the till and took the money and the clothing coupons. Gina knew she'd have soon sold out if she hadn't arranged with Harry to bring her more stock.

When 1948 came in, Gina felt the tide had turned for her. Her shop was doing well and she enjoyed working in it. She was getting over the shock of losing Eric so suddenly and was drawing closer to Jim.

When she said as much to Jim, he told her she must be the only person in Britain who was content with the way things were going. The further cut in beer production bothered many. In addition the milk ration was cut to two and a half pints a week, and the bacon ration to one ounce per week. Potatoes too were rationed: the three pounds each they were allowed helped to fill empty stomachs.

Over the following weeks, several of her wealthier customers asked Gina if she could get fur coats for them. No furs had been available since the beginning of the war and they were now the ultimate luxury and almost unobtainable. She asked Harry if he could get her some fur coats.

He said, 'Did you read in the newspaper that cat burglars had climbed in an upstairs window in some grand house in Chelsea while there was a party going on downstairs?'

Gina shook her head.

'Seemed they got a good haul of fur coats from a bedroom where their owners had left them. I wasn't in on that, though.'

'Well, can you get me some?'

'I'll see. What sort of fur d'you want?'

'Anything. I'd love one myself.'

'Leave them alone, Gina. Safer to have the money than the coat.'

It was several months before Harry told her he thought he might be able to get fur coats for her. 'They'll be musquash and cony, not the most expensive, but New Look length with swing backs, brand-new.'

'Smashing. How many can you get?'

'I've got other customers to supply, but perhaps six or eight for you.'

'That'll suit me fine.' Gina knew she could rely on him to produce what he said he would, and at a price that left a profit in it for her.

It was a year since Eric had died. The first anniversary of it had been last week. Gina had asked Hannah to come over on the following Saturday evening and they'd spent it talking about him.

'It took me a long time to get over the way he died,' Gina said. 'I've been very glad to have his shop. I think it's helped; gave me something else to think about.'

'Poor Eric,' Hannah said. 'I still miss him. I don't think I'm really over him yet.'

Gina said, 'I no longer think of him every minute, but this last week, it all came over me again.'

'Me too. It's sad to think of him dying so young. Eric had such plans for the future.'

'It's no good dwelling on what might have been. Anyway, you've got Rob now.'

'Rob's different. He's just a friend, like he always was.'

'If that's what he says, he's pretending,' Gina told her. 'I see the way he looks at you. If he's holding back, it's to give you time to get over Eric.'

Hannah sighed. 'Perhaps. How's your father?'

'He's never got over Eric. You know he thinks he killed him?'

'He's still very depressed?'

'Yes, he's been on the sick, off and on, ever since. Did I tell you he inherited some money from Eric? Even that didn't cheer him up.'

'It must be hard for Cicely.'

'I don't suppose it's much fun looking after him, but it's Betsy I'm sorry for. She came to stay with me last weekend and she's asked if she can come for the Easter holidays. We found some curtains for the little boxroom so she can use that, and Cicely has promised to send over a bed and a chest of drawers to furnish it.'

'I'm glad. Betsy will be better off here.'

Gina smiled. 'I know. I want to give her a refuge from Pa – that's what I've longed for. She says his temper is no better and he's applied to be retired on the grounds of ill health.'

'I'd heard. He's not been in church recently. The vicar's worried about him.'

'Anyway, I've told Betsy she'll have to help in the shop if she comes here. She said she'd love to, she likes clothes.'

Hannah said, 'I could do with a new dress for the summer. New Look, of course.'

Gina laughed. 'Everything's New Look. I think it'll change women's fashions for the next decade.'

'Can I see what you've got?'

'Of course. Come on downstairs.'

'I need a new coat too. The ones I have are all too short.'

'You must,' Gina agreed. 'It's definitely not the thing to show five or six inches of dress below your coat.' She added wistfully, 'Unless perhaps it's a fur coat.'

Hannah was delighted that the shop was closed and she had Gina's whole attention. She took her advice and bought a dress of sunshine yellow, and a mustard-coloured coat to wear with it.

'I've got just the hat for you too.' Gina brought it out. 'Matches the coat exactly.'

Hannah thought it felt odd to have heavy pleats and gathers flapping round her legs but Gina assured her many of her customers felt the same. 'You look wonderful in that outfit.'

On the first Friday in March, Hannah and Rob were invited to have supper at Gina's flat. Jim was there too and they had an excellent evening. Hannah and Rob left fairly early so that Jim could have a little time alone with Gina.

It was a black night and Hannah was watching Rob's reflection in the train window on the way home when he said, 'What are we going to do to celebrate our joint birthdays? Shall we have a night out?'

'I'd love to,' she smiled.

'How about the Bear's Paw? Just the two of us, not a party. Are you happy with that?'

'Sounds lovely. I'll be twenty-five. I'm getting a bit old for birthday parties, aren't I?'

'Don't say that! I'll be twenty-nine, but my mother's planning to hold one for us. I couldn't persuade her otherwise. It's to be an afternoon tea.'

Hannah laughed.

He went on, 'You and your family are to be invited and she's going to make two small birthday cakes instead of one big one.'

'We'll be celebrating all afternoon and evening then?'

Their birthdays actually fell on the Monday. Rob said, 'That's right. All this is for the Saturday before. We have to work on Mondays, haven't we?'

'I'm due a couple of days' holiday, I've asked if I might have Monday off.'

'Have you?' Rob was interested. 'What a good idea. I've got some days in hand so I could do the same. We could make it a weekend of celebrations.'

Rob was now articled to a firm of solicitors with rooms in Hamilton Square, very close to where Hannah was working. He said he was enjoying it and was sure now he'd chosen the right career. Last summer, they'd started taking sandwiches for lunch once in a while, and eating them in the central garden. When the weather grew cold, they met for a bowl of soup in a small café in nearby Market Street at least once a week.

Rob went on, 'On Saturday, I'm going to book seats for the first house at the Empire too. We'll need something to fill the time between Mum's party and the Bear's Paw. It's old-fashioned music hall. I hope that'll be all right?'

'It sounds smashing.' They were sitting side by side and his hand accidentally brushed hers. It was as though an electric current shot through Hannah. She smiled. 'I'm looking forward to it already.'

They had to walk from Rock Ferry Station. As she took his arm, Hannah knew she was beginning to feel differently about Rob Osborne. Usually, he walked her as far as the porch door, pecked her cheek, wished her good night and turned away.

She used to think of the porch as being Eric's territory. Tonight, on impulse, she pulled Rob inside after her and gave him a hug. He kissed her, really kissed her full on the lips for the first time. It left her tingling all over.

On Saturday afternoon, Hannah dressed herself in her new finery and went down to help her mother, who was struggling to get Aunt Philomena ready.

Rob answered Hannah's knock. 'You look lovely,' he told her, as he helped to get the wheel-chair inside. Hannah had been invited to have afternoon tea at the vicarage several times, and she thought this would be much the same. In the sitting room she saw the tea trolley laid out with two identical home-made cakes.

'Had to be sponge, I'm afraid,' Mrs Osborne said. 'I couldn't get any dried fruit.' There was no icing and no candles either, but jam had been used to stick a coloured printed paper tag on each, which read, 'Happy Birthday'.

Rob handed round cups of tea and cut the cakes. He had her outside again after an hour.

'I'm afraid you must find Mum's tea parties boring,' he said.

'No,' Hannah assured him. 'You always spark the conversation up. Philomena and Mum love them.'

'I'm taking my car tonight.' He still had his MG sports two-seater, but couldn't always use it because of petrol rationing.

'Such luxury,' Hannah said when he opened the door for her to get in.

The show at the Empire was a laugh. Hannah's

sides ached when it was over. She and Rob were in high spirits as they sat down to supper at the Bear's Paw. She was ready for it and the food was delicious. The light was dim and people were getting up between the courses to dance on the tiny floor.

'Shall we?' he suggested. They'd been to lots of dances together. Rob had said he needed the exercise to get his leg back in working order. Having him hold her close felt wonderful. She could feel his body moving against hers.

It was late when he ran his MG up on to the vicarage drive. It was a star-studded, moonlit night. He took her arm to see her next door to Highfield House. Hannah tried to thank him for such a lovely evening.

Rob said, 'Hannah, is it too soon for you?'

'Soon? I'm tired, it's very late.'

'No, no. I meant too soon to think of me. You'd have married Eric if he'd lived another week or two. That must take a bit of getting over.'

'It did. I wept on your shoulder when he died,' she remembered. She felt relieved, safe now, as though she'd come through a bad time. They reached her porch and Rob followed her in.

'That's me, a shoulder to cry on. Would you accept me as second-best?'

Hannah was shaking her head. 'You aren't second-best, Rob. To tell the truth, most people would say you're a cut above Eric.'

She'd never spoken of her feelings about Eric to anyone but now she wanted to. If she could talk through the problems he'd given her, and explain the love that wouldn't let her turn away from him, she thought she'd be able to put her grief behind her now.

She said slowly, 'Eric might not have turned out to be the perfect husband.'

'Oh!'

She knew he was willing her to go on. 'I thought long and hard about marrying him – had quite a tussle with myself.'

'But he loved you?'

'Yes, and I loved him. Loved him too much to say no to him.'

Rob was staring at her. 'You always seemed set on him. I didn't realise you had doubts.'

'Eric wasn't what he seemed.'

'He had another girl?'

'No,' she almost laughed, 'nothing like that. He's dead now, so it won't matter if I tell you.'

She hardly knew where to begin. 'He did things that weren't honest. He hid that side of him from me for a long time.'

She told Rob how he impersonated other men at Forces medical exams. 'There were other things too.'

'Hannah!' Rob put his arms round her.

'He fiddled clothing coupons and stole things. I tried to make him stop. He promised he would more than once, but then I'd find out later that he hadn't.'

Hannah felt tears stinging her eyes. 'I was half afraid to trust him because he'd let me down several times. He was great fun to be with but always up to mischief... No, not mischief – unlawful acts, fraud and theft.'

'Hannah, surely not!'

'I told him he was a criminal and he'd be caught and sent to prison. I almost told him I wanted nothing more to do with him. My head told me to break it off, Mum and Aunt Philomena pleaded with me to have no more to do with him.'

'But you decided to go ahead?'

'I was in love with him, I decided to follow my heart.'

'I can't believe you meant to go ahead and marry him, knowing that.'

'I believed I could help him change, that once we were married things would be different.'

'That's unlikely.'

'I couldn't turn my back on him. I'm glad now I didn't. He'd have been dreadfully hurt. He was too young to die.'

'You could have been heading for a very unhappy life.'

'I know, but I had to risk that. I had to give him another chance.' She shook her head. 'I had my mother's example before me the whole time. She didn't give my father another chance and she had a very unhappy life.'

She told him Esme's sad story. 'I'm afraid there's a lot you don't know about us. Aunt Philomena insisted on keeping it quiet.'

Rob's arms tightened round her. 'Dad says her family was wealthy, that they built his church.'

Hannah smiled. 'Yes, but she thinks of it as her church, not your father's. The rest is true. She tells everybody about her family. It gives her status.'

'Her husband was the last vicar here?'

'Yes, my Uncle Fred. What Philomena doesn't want people to know is that Eric was my cousin. My father was his uncle. He never married my mother.'

'Gosh, I didn't realise. I never picked up the merest hint.'

'You weren't meant to.'

'I can understand why...'

'Mum's put it all behind her now, of course, but there's still Gina. She's my cousin too.'

Hannah wanted to get it all off her mind, how she was worried about Gina breaking the law too, but Gina was still alive and Rob knew her, so perhaps she shouldn't. Then there was Leslie and all his problems.

Rob said, 'I've never been able to think of anybody but you, Hannah. When Eric died, well, I felt sorry for you, but I was not unhappy that you weren't going to be his wife. I felt I could wait. Is there any hope for me?'

Hannah was smiling. She reached up to kiss him. 'You know there is. I've fallen in love with you.'

CHAPTER TWENTY-SIX

That same Saturday night, Gina had gone to bed early. She'd worked hard all day and was tired. It came as something of a shock to be woken up by the prolonged ringing of her doorbell and someone hammering on the shop door.

She felt sleep-sodden as she switched on her bedside lamp. It was getting light, her alarm clock told her it was almost five o'clock. She felt a shiver of fear, but ran through to her living room, which was in the front of the building, and looked down into the street below.

The doorbell rang again, but though from here she couldn't see anybody on the step, Leslie's car was parked at the kerb. She ran down in her nightdress and bare feet to let him in. He slid round the door.

'Whatever's the matter?' Gina was wide awake now and there were icicles of fear in her stomach. Leslie's face was paper white. He had a heavy graze on his forehead that had been bleeding. He looked terrified.

'They've got Harry,' he panted. 'He's been caught.'

Gina shivered, feeling the bottom had dropped out of her world. 'The police have caught him?'

She'd believed they never could. Harry was too careful. He always had his plans cut and dried and he took every precaution. Eric too had thought him as safe as houses.

'We were going for the fur coats.' She realised Leslie was shaking.

'Come on up.' She shot back to her bedroom to pull on a coat and slippers, then into the kitchen to put the kettle on. She took the matches to her living room and lit the gas fire. 'Now,' she said, 'tell me what happened.'

Leslie had to be persuaded to sit down. 'It was my fault. I had a crash. We were being chased and I couldn't shake them off. I think Harry could be hurt.'

Gina's mouth went dry. 'What d'you mean, you *think?* Was he or wasn't he?'

'I don't know. I jumped out and ran for it. I knew if I stayed I'd be caught. The police were not far behind. Harry didn't come.'

'Oh my God! They didn't follow you here?'

'I don't know.' Leslie was shivering. Gina thought he was in shock.

'I'm going to make some tea, then you must start at the beginning.'

They huddled close to the fire. Gina wrapped her hands round the hot mug and began to feel a little warmer. 'You went out to get the fur coats?'

Leslie nodded. 'Yes, from Bunnies. Harry knows one of the girls who works there. He had a skeleton key. The coats were a new delivery up from London yesterday.'

'What did you crash? You weren't in your new car?'

'No, I left that in one of those side streets behind the town hall in Birkenhead, and walked with Harry down to Woodside Station. He broke into a van that had been left outside. We picked up Bill Williams, then I drove it through the tunnel to Bunnies.

'Harry told me to wait outside with the engine running. I was to have the back doors open so they could fling the coats in. Harry and Bill went into the building through a side door. They'd planned to make two trips inside and bring out all the coats they could, but suddenly all the lights went on. I nearly wet myself.

'We didn't know there'd be a security guard. They must have just startled him. Harry and Bill came pelting out with their arms full and I saw this fellow behind shouting after them.' Leslie gulped at his tea. 'They flung their stuff in the back and leaped in after it.'

'"Get going," Harry yelled, so I did, as fast as I could. "It's Plan B now." That was to get back across the river as fast as we could.'

The gas fire hissed and began to give out warmth. 'That's what you did?'

'I tried to. I was about to turn down to the tunnel entrance on the Liverpool side when Harry noticed two police cars waiting there.

'"Go to the bridge at Widnes," he said. "It's too easy to catch us in the tunnel. They can phone through and close the other end."

'I swung away and set off, but the van wouldn't go that fast. When we saw one of the police cars following us, Bill started directing me through the back streets to throw it off – he was brought up round there. We thought we had. It was a race through the night, with nothing much on the roads. We crossed the river and turned for home.'

Leslie paused, his hand still shaking as he reached again for his tea.

'Bill lives in Rock Ferry now and we were going to drop him off. We'd meant to deliver half the furs we'd got to Ethel's shop at the same time. She was expecting us.'

'What about the furs you were getting for me?'

'We'd intended to unload them into the boot of my car and then abandon the van. I'd have brought them over tomorrow – I mean today. I was coming back along the New Chester Road, going at quite a pace. There was nothing behind me and I thought we might be all right, but Harry was dithering.' Leslie seemed to have lost the thread of what he was saying, 'It was a nightmare...' He dried up.

'Harry was dithering about what to do with the furs?' Gina prompted.

'Well, the important thing was not to get caught. I was about to turn up Bedford Road, when Bill said, "I can see a car behind. It's just turned on to our tail."

'Harry said, "I think it's a police car. Yes, it is." Suddenly he shrieked at me, "Don't go near Ethel's shop. Don't go to Bill's either. They're too close. We don't want to lead them in."

'The lights were green but changing as I approached.

'"Don't stop," he yelled. There had been hardly any traffic on the road all the way, but it's sod's law, isn't it? A car was turning out on to the New Chester Road across my path. I swerved to miss it...'

'And you crashed?'

'Mounted the pavement and hit the corner of the building. I jumped out and ran.'

'So Bill Williams was in the van too, when you left it?'

'Yes.'

'Did he get away?'

Leslie shook his head. 'I'm not sure. I was too intent on getting away myself. The good thing about it was that it happened where I know my way about. I shot into Howson Street and through to the back entry, then climbed the wall into the back yard behind the Acme Dry-Cleaning Centre and had a rest. I think I heard the siren of an ambulance, but I couldn't see from there. When I felt better, I legged it down to my car.'

'Then you came here?'

'No, I was afraid they'd make Harry give his address and there's all sorts of incriminating evidence there. I wanted to get there before the police. I burned a lot of stuff – false driving licences and identity cards, that sort of thing. Then I came here.'

Gina was surprised to find Leslie could think on his feet. 'Oh Lord! Are you all right?'

'I feel all shook up. I've grazed my elbow and my knee and my neck hurts.'

'You've twisted it?'

'I'm all right. Can I stay here for a bit?'

Gina was used to taking care of Leslie. 'Yes, of course. There's no bed in the spare room, but you can sleep on the sofa here.' She went to find him a blanket and a pillow. 'What will happen now?'

'I wish I knew.'

'Depends whether the police make them talk,

doesn't it?'

'Harry won't talk, but they've got the stolen van and the fur coats.'

'What about Bill? They've probably got him too.'

Leslie shrugged. 'I don't know. I wish we'd never tried. I wish you'd never asked Harry to get fur coats for you.'

'If you hadn't been getting fur coats, you'd have been doing something else you shouldn't.'

'I know. I feel terrible about what I've been doing – breaking the law left right and centre, taking things that belong to other people. I know how I'd feel if somebody helped themselves to my belongings. I've tried to talk to Harry, but he reckons it's all great fun.'

'Like Eric did.'

'They were a pair, but I can't stand the pace. I'd like to go straight but, living with Harry, it was impossible. I owe him a lot of favours, don't I? He's been good to me, given me a home.'

Gina went back to bed feeling more than worried. She was scared stiff and knew Leslie was too.

It was mid-morning when Gina woke up. She felt heavy with foreboding. What had happened to Leslie last night was a major disaster. The van was without a driver, and so the police would surely question Harry and Bill and get Leslie's name out of them.

She got up to make herself some tea. Leslie was still flat out on the sofa. No point in waking him up yet. She took her tea back to bed and tried to think.

She was implicated too. Some of the furs had been stolen for her, and if Harry was to be closely investigated, other links might come to light. Jim had said he'd have Sunday dinner at home and come out to see her afterwards. She'd asked him to stay for his supper. She didn't want him to know what Leslie had done or that she herself had sold stolen goods through her shop. Jim was like Hannah and would disapprove. Gina felt trouble was coming at her from all directions.

She got up and made a corned-beef pie. It was mostly pastry but if everything was to seem normal, she had to have something to put in front of Jim tonight. Leslie came to the kitchen door as she was taking it out of the oven.

He yawned. 'That smells good.'

'It's not for you, I'm afraid, but I've made some turnovers too. We'll have those for our lunch.' She told him Jim would be coming. 'I want you to move your car, Leslie. Take it now and park it down on South Parade; that way, Jim won't know you're here, and neither will anybody else. We'll eat when you come back.'

Leslie was wide awake by the time he'd walked back, but she could see he was still jittery.

'I want you out of here this afternoon when Jim comes,' Gina said. 'Either out, or in the spare bedroom with the door shut.'

'Just like being holed up back in Grasmere Road.' He pulled a face.

'Worse,' she told him. 'There's no furniture in my spare bedroom. The best I can do is to find you some cushions and a couple of blankets.'

Leslie sighed. 'I'll go out before he gets here, see if I can find out what's happening. Bill's mother might know.'

For once, Gina had to wait for Jim. He was later than she'd expected. She felt on edge and knew she hadn't calmed down. He wrapped his arms round her and kissed her. Gina wasn't in the mood – she had too much on her mind.

When he came up for air, she said, 'How about going to the pictures?' Three hours in a darkened place where she wouldn't have to say much would suit her, but Jim was shaking his head.

'I had a look in the paper. There's nothing much on. Besides, everything's changed for us now. We know what we want and we need to talk. Let's go out for a walk and thrash out our plans.'

Gina put on her coat. It was cold outside. She took him down to South Parade and was glad not to see Leslie's car. She didn't mention him. She insisted on walking round the marine lake, on the wall that retains the water when the tide goes out. There were few others doing it on this chill and blustery afternoon, but the sight of the huge vista of golden sand stretching across the Dee estuary relaxed her.

'Let's find a pub,' Jim said. 'It's too cold to talk out here. We have to walk too fast to keep warm.'

With the drinks in front of them, she could see he was making a big effort to tell her what was on his mind.

He said, 'When I first came home, it was very wise of you to say let's start over again and see how we get on. I was quite relieved at the time. I think we're getting on very well now.'

He smiled at her. He was smiling more these days.

'I've got used to all the cheeky kids at school. I feel established and ready to put down roots, and you've made a marvellous start with your shop.'

Gina pushed her hair out of her eyes. 'Where's all this heading, Jim?' She could guess and she wasn't sure she wanted to hear it now.

'We're settling down, Gina,' he said. 'We do love each other – in fact, I've always loved you. How about getting married? I feel ready for that now, don't you?'

Gina wasn't sure. 'Perhaps not quite.'

She could see Jim was taken aback. 'I thought you'd be all for it. After the other night...'

'I am really,' she said hurriedly. 'I do love you.' He'd be a loving husband. 'I do want to marry you, but...' Her mind was churning with anxiety about Leslie and Harry right now.

'Right, I won't rush you. You must say when you're ready.'

She could see him looking at her engagement ring. 'Would you like a new ring? A better one? We made a new start – why not a new ring?'

She shook her head. 'It's not that,' she said miserably, knowing he was disappointed. Leslie was too much on her mind. On the spur of the moment she started talking about him. She had to tell Jim, she needed his support.

'I'm worried about him.' She told him a little about the theft of fur coats. 'He was driving the getaway van.' She said nothing about the arrangement to sell the fur coats in her shop, or the other stolen property that had already gone through.

She could see Jim was shocked. 'I was afraid for him. Deserters have to live hand to mouth.'

'I'm at my wits' end about this,' Gina told him. 'I don't know how to help Leslie, what to do for the best.'

'You've got to make him go straight,' he said. 'Make him find a proper job and settle down. If you don't, he'll have a terrible life, in and out of prison. I could have a talk to him, if you like.'

'We'll see,' Gina said. Jim didn't understand about having to stand by Harry. First Spike had been caught and now Harry. Leslie was dithering on the edge. It could go either way for him. He might be charged too, so there was no point in talking about going straight until this was resolved.

'Let's go home.' Gina wanted to end this conversation before she said too much. 'I've got a meal prepared.'

When Jim had gone, she peeped into the spare bedroom and found Leslie curled up in a nest of cushions, sleeping like a baby. She woke him up.

'What did you find out? Anything?'

'Yes, I saw Bill Williams. He said he and Harry were taken to hospital by ambulance. Harry's been kept in. He's got a broken leg and other injuries. Bill was discharged and the police took him back to Tranmere Police Station for questioning.'

'Not Tranmere!' Gina was aghast. 'What about Pa?'

'You know he's not on car patrols. He wanted to be but they wouldn't have him.' But Tranmere was Pa's base, which made Gina feel even worse.

'It seems the officers were from there. They towed the van in – and the furs too, of course.'

'What happened to Bill?'

'He was charged with theft of the furs and the van. His case won't come up for a few months. When they asked who was driving the van, he said he was. He reckons Harry will be charged too. I went down to the hospital then and tried to see Harry. They told me he's as comfortable as can be expected, but they wouldn't let me in. The visitors were all streaming out by the time I got there. There's no more visiting until Thursday afternoon, I might try again then.

'I went to Harry's place after that but nobody's been there. I got rid of a few more things that might incriminate me.'

'What are we going to do?' It was a cry from Gina's heart. She went to bed to ponder anew on the problem.

Hannah woke up early on Sunday morning wondering why, after knowing Rob for all this time, she hadn't realised she was in love with him before now. She'd always insisted he was a friend, but he was that too, of course. She was glad she'd told him about Eric last night. He'd understood.

She felt bright and eager to get up, despite her late night, and knew that because she'd been with Rob, neither Mum nor Aunt Philomena would complain about her coming in late. She set about her Sunday morning routine with zest and was looking forward to seeing Rob in church. He'd talked of taking her to Eastham Woods for a long walk this afternoon, but the roofs of the houses opposite were dark and shiny in the rain.

After the service, he said to her as they were filing out, 'Not the best of weather for a walk, but we'll go somewhere. Are you game?'

'Yes. I'll come round about three, shall I?'

It was raining harder in the afternoon as she ran next door to the vicarage. Rob met her at the front door and already had his mac on.

'We're going to Parkgate instead of Eastham. It's the best I can do. I haven't much petrol left.'

Hannah said, 'If it stops we could walk along the front. There's pavement all the way, and the views across the river to Wales are lovely.'

When they reached Parkgate, the rain was drumming down more heavily than ever on the canvas roof of Rob's small car.

'We aren't getting out to walk in this.' He grinned at her self-consciously, and drove all along the windswept front, then turned round and came back. It was impossible to see across the Dee for the driving rain. He ran his MG into the almost empty car park of the Boat House café and switched off the engine.

Rob sighed. 'Not very romantic, is it?'

Hannah chuckled. 'Nothing is in a downpour like this.'

'I was hoping it would be.'

They were sitting very close in the small car. His mood was half teasing. She was very conscious of his presence. She watched a trickle of water run down the inside of the windscreen. 'You've got a leak,' she said, mopping at it.

'Ignore that,' he said. 'Hannah, I want you to imagine we're having a romantic stroll through

Eastham Woods, with a carpet of bluebells spreading as far as the eye can see.'

She laughed. 'It'll be a couple of months before the bluebells are out.'

'Yes, well, I'm not going to let this weather put me off. You know I've fancied you since you came to my twenty-second birthday party?' He sighed again. 'No, not fancied. You bowled me over but I couldn't stay around to tell you so, and I left Eric with a clear field.' He took her hand in his. 'What I'm trying to say, is, I love you very much. Will you marry me?'

Hannah gasped. 'I didn't expect... You've taken my breath away.'

'Well?' His eyes were searching hers.

'Yes,' she smiled. 'Yes, yes.' She put her lips up to his and kissed him. His arms went round her, pulling her closer.

'I've waited a very long time for you – seven years – but it was worth it. Tomorrow afternoon, we're both off. We'll go and choose an engagement ring. I'd like to make it official, stake my claim to you before somebody else does.'

Hannah smiled. 'You know there's nobody else.' She kissed him again. 'I do love you, Rob.'

Rob was raining kisses on her face. Dampness and steam on the inside of the windows meant they could no longer see out, nor could anybody see in.

It was almost an hour later, when he murmured, 'Right, if you're prepared to run for the door, we'll go in and have tea and cakes to celebrate.'

When Rob drew up on the drive that evening, he squeezed Hannah's hand. 'Shall we break the news? Your family first, or mine?'

'Mine,' Hannah said. She led the way into Aunt Philomena's sitting room and found, as she'd expected, that her mother was there too.

Hannah knew that this time they'd both be delighted at the news of her engagement and would share her pleasure in it. She held on to Rob's hand. He beamed at them all as he announced, 'This afternoon, I asked Hannah to marry me.'

Hannah added, 'And I said yes.'

Esme leaped to her feet to hug them both. 'I'm so pleased, absolutely delighted.' There were tears of joy and relief sparkling in her eyes.

'So am I. I hope you'll both be very happy.' Philomena had never smiled more widely. 'Well, Hannah, nobody can say you've rushed into this. I've been singing your praises, young man, for goodness knows how many years. Get out the sherry, Esme. We must drink to their future happiness.'

They had much the same reception from Rob's family. Hannah had never felt happier.

Gina was awake at five again the next morning and by then had a clear idea of what she wanted to do. She slid out of bed and dressed quickly before waking Leslie up.

'I want you to look after the shop for me,' she said. 'Open up at nine prompt. I never have many customers on Monday mornings. I'll be back by lunch time.'

Leslie was still sleepy. 'What are you going to do?'

'I think we might be able to get those furs back.'

Leslie said slowly, 'Is that a good idea?'

'Yes. I'll get my furs and it'll remove the evidence against Harry and Bill. It's got to be a good idea.'

Gina cooked breakfast for them both, then, taking the smaller of the two suitcases she'd brought with her, she caught an early train to Rock Ferry. She knew Betsy and Cicely would be out before nine o'clock, but had no way of knowing if her father would be at home. If she came face to face with Pa, she'd say she'd come to collect more of her clothes. She'd taken everything worth having, but he wouldn't know that.

If he was on the two-till-ten shift, he'd still be in bed. If he was on nights, he'd be on his way to bed. If he was working from six in the morning until two, he wouldn't be at home, and there was no point in going in.

First, she'd see if his bike was in the shed. When she saw that it was, she shivered. It meant she could go ahead with her big plan. Her heart was thumping hard as she went quietly through the kitchen.

When Hannah took Aunt Philomena's breakfast egg into her, she made a great fuss of wishing her a happy birthday. She had a card and a small packet for her to open. Hannah was thrilled to find a gold locket and chain inside.

'It's lovely. Thank you very much.'

'It's eighteen-carat gold,' Philomena informed her, 'and has been in my family for generations.'

'I've never seen you wear it.'

'No, my mother used to. I hope you'll wear it and value it.'

'I certainly shall.' Hannah fastened it round her neck there and then.

'I want you to go to the shops and get a few things for the dinner party tonight.'

Dinner parties used to be Philomena's forte, but she hadn't given one for years. Tonight, she'd invited Rob and his parents to celebrate Rob and Hannah's birthdays.

Hannah was setting off with a shopping bag over her arm, but when she reached the garden gate she saw Gina running down the road with a suitcase. She waited for her.

'What are you doing here? Have you been home? I thought you were never going to set foot over the threshold again.'

'I wasn't.'

Gina was breathing heavily. Hannah could see beads of sweat across the bridge of her nose. 'What about your shop? Aren't you opening this morning?'

'Leslie's there. Why aren't you at work?'

'It's my birthday. I've taken a day's holiday.'

'Of course!' Gina was biting her lip. 'I've got a present for you, but I've left it at home. I should have brought it with me. Sorry, I'm at sixes and sevens this morning.'

She seemed nerve-racked, but at the same time, there was a hint of exultation in her manner, as though she was pleased with what she'd just done.

Hannah said, 'I've so much to tell you. Come

inside for a few minutes. I could make some tea.'

'I'm allowed in your place now?'

'Mum's at work and Philomena can't get upstairs. Come and tell me why you came back home.'

Brenda was polishing the hall floor. Gina followed Hannah past her and up the stairs.

'D'you know,' she said, 'I've never been in your house before. Isn't it clean and tidy?'

Hannah looked back at Brenda, who was smiling up at them.

'Is that your cleaner?' Gina asked when they reached the living room.

'Philomena's cleaner. I told you she had one. You've pleased her, saying the place was clean.'

Gina dumped her suitcase on the floor. It fell over before she'd reached the sofa.

'I should really get back to my shop. Leslie wasn't pleased at being left in charge.'

Hannah righted the suitcase and propped it against the table leg. 'You haven't got much in this.'

'Nothing.' Gina told her why she'd brought it. 'I didn't even go up to my bedroom. I just took Pa's keys from his jacket on the hall stand and ran.'

She jangled them at Hannah now. They were tied together with a piece of string. 'I had Pa's copied, went all the way to New Ferry to do it.'

'You could have had it done nearer. There's a place in Bedford Road.'

'They know us there. It's next door to the dry-cleaner's where Leslie used to work.'

'What d'you want them for?' Hannah's heart

was sinking. She could guess it was some illicit reason.

Gina chortled jubilantly. 'I went in and out twice, and saw nobody. I got what I wanted.' She went on breathlessly, 'Pa always leaves his jacket hanging on the hall stand with his keys in his pocket. I crept in and got them; had them copied, crept in again and put the originals back.'

'Those aren't the house keys?'

'No. I've still got those, though I hardly used them when I lived there. No, these are the keys to the police station.'

'What police station?' Hannah couldn't believe what she was hearing.

'Tranmere, of course. Where Pa's based.'

'What d'you want those for?' Hannah could barely get her breath. Eric had been full of wild ideas and here was his sister, following in his footsteps.

Suddenly Gina was serious and telling her about Harry getting caught while he'd been stealing fur coats for her.

Anxiety made Hannah explode. 'You've got to stop this, Gina. It can only lead to trouble.'

'I know.'

'Look at you, you're a nervous wreck.'

'I feel sick when I think about it. I mean, what's going to happen to Leslie? He was with him.'

'What's going to happen to you? They were stealing fur coats for you.'

'I know and I'm scared. I knew if I could get Pa's keys, Leslie and I could get into the police station and steal those fur coats back.'

Hannah's mouth fell open, 'Are you crazy?'

'No. Leslie thinks it's perfectly feasible too. It'll remove the evidence they have against Harry and I'll get the fur coats. Two birds with one stone, so to speak.'

'You can't just walk in to a police station and take them!'

'There's only two constables on duty at night. Pa says one stays by the phone and the other goes out on patrol. We'd watch and wait until he did. Leslie could distract the one that stays behind, while I pick up the furs.'

'You couldn't just pick them up! They'll be locked away somewhere. It would be like going into the lion's den.'

'It's the sort of idea Eric would come up with.'

'That doesn't make it any better. You're mad,' Hannah lost her patience, 'crazy if you think you'll get away with that. I don't suppose you've any idea whereabouts the coats are being stored?'

'No, but Bill Williams has been inside and he might know. I've copied all Pa's keys.'

'There'll be more than two men there. What about the police cars?'

'There's a yard and a garage round the back. Those running the patrol cars have an office of their own.'

'You'll stay clear if you've any sense.'

'I'd get the coats back...'

'You're never thinking of selling them in your shop? That's asking for trouble.'

'I won't put them on show. I'd be careful. I know several women who want them. I'll show them what I've got quietly in the back room. I'm going to keep one for myself.'

'Gina! Do your customers want to buy stolen goods? Bear in mind they could be traced back to you at any time. It would be enough to ruin your business.'

Gina looked shocked.

'You hadn't thought of that, had you?' Hannah was on her feet, striding up and down the room. 'I never told you how I felt about Eric. I almost broke it off several times because he was doing stupid things like this. I can't believe you're thinking of breaking into a police station! I loved Eric, I wanted to marry him, and I would have done so, but I was scared stiff of what the future would bring. I had Mum's example in front of me. Didn't she have the same trouble with your uncle? And look what happened to him. I knew I'd have the jitters every time Eric was ten minutes late coming home. That I'd feel trouble could overtake me at any moment.

'Spike thought he was too clever to be caught, but he was. Harry thought the same, but sooner or later it happens. Now he's been caught too.'

'Eric wasn't caught.'

'He might have been if he hadn't died. What if he'd been with Harry and Leslie? It's possible he would have been. Do see sense, Gina, please.'

She sighed. 'It might still happen to Leslie.'

'Here you are thinking of marrying Jim, and telling him nothing of all this. He won't be marrying the sort of girl he thinks he is. If he did know, he might not want to marry you. That's what you think, isn't it? He'll know you're storing up trouble for the future, just as I do. Don't you feel guilty, taking things that belong to other people?'

Gina was still dangling the keys from her fingers. Hannah snatched them from her. 'You're just like Eric. I won't let you do this. Stop now, before you're charged with receiving.' Hannah flopped down on the sofa, her anger spent.

'Oh, Gina! What makes you do it? Eric used to tell me it was for fun and kicks, but fun is the last thing I'd get from it.'

Gina was sinking into the sofa cushions.

'Happiness is more important. Money and luxury are not the be-all and end-all of everything. Family affection and love are more important. You should be seeking contentment and happiness. Stop this before it's too late.'

'But what about Harry? I should do something to help...'

'Harry will have to take his chances. He'll be charged with theft and taken to court. If this is the first time, then he's been very lucky. Ask yourself what is more important to you: marrying Jim and having a happy life with him, or sorting out Harry?'

Gina was lying back, looking defeated. She said nothing.

Hannah let her breath gust through her teeth. 'I brought you up here to tell you Rob has proposed.' Her voice was flat. 'I was so happy about it. You drove all that out of my mind, with your ideas of breaking into a police station.'

'I'm sorry.'

'I want to shake you. You should be persuading Leslie to go straight, helping him to do it. You're my family and I'm very fond of you. I want you both to have happy lives. If you carry on like this you risk spending some of your time in prison.' It was a cry from her heart.

After a long pause Gina roused herself. 'You're right, of course. I've got to stop and so has Leslie.'

CHAPTER TWENTY-SEVEN

Gina got up and left without the keys she'd gone to such trouble to obtain. She could see now that Harry's problems had crowded everything else out of her mind. The shop would do all right; she was sure she could make a reasonable living there. Jim had been pleading with her to go straight too. He had a good job and they'd be able to have everything they needed without breaking any laws.

Jim had pleaded with her to talk Leslie into going straight, but he had no idea she was involved too, and here she was, leading Leslie into what could only be more trouble. She had to stop and she had to tell Jim everything now before anything else happened.

She didn't want any more crises like this. Hannah was right: if Eric had been still alive he'd have been caught too. She could think of nothing worse than that, unless it was being caught herself. What she wanted was to marry Jim and have a normal and peaceful life without this sort of threat hanging over her.

The shop was open but without customers when she got back. Leslie was behind the counter.

'Not much doing this morning,' he told her, 'but I've sold a blouse, two belts and a scarf. Did you get Pa's keys?'

Gina nodded. 'I did.' She perched on the counter.

Leslie's face clouded. 'It's on then? When do we snatch the furs back?'

'We're not going to. I've changed my mind and I want you to change yours too.'

'Why? Did Pa catch you at it?'

'No.' Gina told him what Hannah had said. 'Jim's of the same mind. We've got to stop, Leslie. We can't go on like this.'

Leslie sighed with relief. 'Thank goodness for that! I was dreading breaking into Pa's station. I dreamed I'd come face to face with him inside. All this stealing and fraud scares me. I'm sorry I ever got into it.'

'Why didn't you say so?'

Leslie sniffed. 'I didn't want to seem a yellow belly, an out-and-out coward.'

Gina remembered Pa telling Leslie that was exactly what he was.

'Especially when you, Eric and Harry seemed to think it was good fun. I'm so relieved I can put it all behind me.'

'As long,' Gina said, 'as you aren't traced as being the driver of the getaway van.'

'If I am, I'll face whatever punishment comes my way, but I'm going straight from now on.'

When Jim came round that evening, Leslie was in the kitchen with Gina, helping her to cook. Gina ran down to the shop to let him in.

'How are you?' Jim asked. She flung herself at him and gave him a hug. 'Wow, have you had a hard day?'

'I've made some big decisions.'

'About you and me getting married?' He

looked hopeful.

'Yes. We've waited too long already.'

He hugged her more tightly. 'I'm so pleased. When?'

'How about when your school closes for the summer holidays?'

'Excellent. Just gives us enough time to get organised.'

'It means we can have a honeymoon. If I can find somebody to look after my shop.' Gina managed to climb the narrow staircase with Jim's arm round her waist. She drew him into the kitchen and he was about to kiss her.

'Oh, hello, Leslie.' She could see Jim was surprised to see him.

'Leslie's got something to celebrate too,' she told him. 'He's been out looking for a job this afternoon and he's got one.'

Leslie was all smiles. 'It's at the West Kirby branch of the Acme Dry-Cleaning Centre. They've said I can have my old job back. I start next Monday.'

'I'm chuffed,' Gina said. 'We both are.'

'They told me the manager would be retiring in a few months,' Leslie went on, 'and if I've found my feet again by then, they'll consider me for the vacancy.'

'That's really good.'

'I worked in their Bedford Road shop for four years,' he said. 'I was happy there.'

Gina said, 'It's Woolton pie for supper, I'm afraid. I couldn't get any meat or fish. It's all ready. We were just waiting for you.'

Feeling as though her problems could soon be

over, she led the way into the living room where she'd set the table.

Over the meal, Leslie said, 'I'm going home to have a word with Pa tonight. I want to tell him what's been happening to me and see if we can make things up.'

Gina said, 'Ask him if you can bring your bed here. He might let you. There's plenty of beds not being used at home now.'

She smiled at Jim. 'He needs to stay with me until he's back on his feet, but I've told him, when we get married we'll need this place for ourselves.'

'I'll look for lodgings or something,' Leslie added.

'Or we'll see if we can buy a house nearby and you can live in this flat,' Jim said.

'No,' Leslie told him. 'Thank you for thinking of me, but I'm going to stand on my own feet from now on, paddle my own canoe.' He put down his knife and fork. 'I've relied on others far too much and for far too long.'

Later on, when Leslie had gone out, and the gas fire was making comforting hissing and plopping noises, Gina felt the tension leave her as she sat on the sofa with Jim's arms round her.

'Not a white wedding,' she said. 'There's a most beautiful dress on the manikin in the shop. It has big red poppies on a white background. I think I'd like to be married in that.'

Jim was covering her neck with light butterfly kisses. As he moved towards her ear, her hair was covering his face, getting in his way.

'It smells lovely, like spring flowers,' he murmured.

'That's the shampoo.'

Gina pushed him gently back, tossed her hair out of the way and fitted her mouth to his lips. They were warm and moist with passion.

Hannah caught Rob's eye across the wide expanse of immaculate white linen cloth and smiled. She'd been out with him this afternoon and was very conscious of the new sapphire and diamond ring sparkling on her engagement finger.

She felt a flutter of happiness as she looked round Aunt Philomena's dinner table, set with all the elegance her family silver, china and glassware could provide. This was her response to the vicarage tea party held on Saturday.

Philomena was beaming round at them from the head of the table.

'I felt I had to have you all here to celebrate Hannah and Robert's birthdays, and when they came home last night and told me they were engaged ... well, that makes it a treble celebration, doesn't it?'

'Hear, hear,' the vicar agreed.

'Such a lovely meal,' Mrs Osborne told her. 'I've so enjoyed it. You've done wonders, producing a feast like this in these hard times.'

'It wasn't easy,' Philomena smiled. 'But I wanted to make an effort for Hannah's sake.'

'I'd like to thank you, Aunt,' Hannah said sincerely. 'You've always been very generous to me, and I'm grateful.'

She was aware that Brenda had produced the large fat chicken, which Mum had roasted to perfection. Chicken wasn't rationed because not enough was produced to provide a share for everyone.

'I enjoy arranging my little supper parties,' Philomena went on. 'I've so missed giving them since rationing has made it almost impossible.'

Hannah knew her mother had done most of the work for this one, but she was smiling and looked more relaxed than she had done for years.

She had been to the hairdresser this afternoon and had now changed into the pearl-grey New Look dress that Hannah had persuaded her to buy. Tonight, she looked ten years younger than she had.

'Fill the glasses, Esme. I think we should drink a toast to the happy couple.'

Brenda had also provided several bottles of wine, and had made the very fancy gâteau, of which little was left now but the printed paper tags, wishing them 'Happy Birthday'. Originally, they'd been placed between peaks of whipped cream and cherries.

The opulent menu reminded Hannah of Gina and Leslie. She wanted them, as well as her own family, to be happy and lead contented and ordinary lives. She hoped they would.

'I'd like to say,' Philomena went on, 'that this engagement makes me very happy. It's what I've been hoping for for a very long time.'

Hannah met Rob's gaze; his eyes were full of love.

'Not as happy as it makes me,' he said. 'And I'm sure I've been waiting and hoping for it longer than anybody.'

'I'm very pleased.' Esme had a wide smile. 'I'm

sure Hannah will be safe and happy with you, Robert.'

'We Osbornes mustn't be left out,' the vicar said. 'We've been hoping to see Robert happily settled for a few years now.' He raised his glass. 'Let's drink to the happy couple.'

For Hannah it had been a blissful weekend. What she felt for Rob was a very different love to that she'd had for Eric. She thought it could be even stronger and would certainly weather the years more easily. She could rely on Rob, trust him completely. Contentment was what she sought, with peaks of pure happiness like this. She knew she would have that with Rob.

This Large Print Book for the partially sighted, who cannot read normal print, is published under the auspices of

THE ULVERSCROFT FOUNDATION

THE ULVERSCROFT FOUNDATION

... we hope that you have enjoyed this Large Print Book. Please think for a moment about those people who have worse eyesight problems than you ... and are unable to even read or enjoy Large Print, without great difficulty.

You can help them by sending a donation, large or small to:

The Ulverscroft Foundation,
1, The Green, Bradgate Road,
Anstey, Leicestershire, LE7 7FU,
England.
or request a copy of our brochure for more details.

The Foundation will use all your help to assist those people who are handicapped by various sight problems and need special attention.

Thank you very much for your help.